Blood of the Vine

Hunter Spicer

This is a work of fiction. All characters, organizations, and events portrayed in this novel are products or the author's imagination or used fictitiously.

FOR ERIC

PROLOGUE

Carlos Garcia stared nervously out of the window from his spot at the back of the bus, barely recognizing his reflection. The brutal carving in his forehead made him look like a gangster. He ground his jaw and shook his head at the obvious. He looked like a gangster because he was one. The gang carving hadn't won him affection or compassion on the bus trip, not that he expected any. He clenched his hands, watching the dry Northern California landscape zip by. He hadn't been able to sleep for the entire thirty hours since the bus left the filthy detention camp in south central Texas. He unclenched his hands and reached for the crucifix around his neck, holding it tightly. He tried to pray but he was too exhausted. Or maybe he'd forgotten how.

Three years ago, a prayer had been answered. His wife had crossed to safety. Now, he was desperate to find her and warn her that Cadejo was coming. Last he knew, his wife was in Sonoma County. She had a cousin in Santa Rosa, he'd start there. But if he did find her, would she listen? Or would she be repulsed by the gang member he'd become? He hadn't told her—or anyone—he was coming from Guatemala. Maybe that was a mistake.

The door to the lavatory across from him swung open and a man emerged. Carlos choked on the stench. The toilet was overflowing and none of the immigrants had showered in days. The overcrowded bus stank of human sweat,

1

excrement, and rancid pork that one of the West African women had bartered during the bus's infrequent stops for fuel. When the bus first pulled away from the border detention camp, the air crackled with anticipation. They'd been promised jobs in California. Carlos could barely believe his luck. He would have enough to support his wife. Maybe they could start over, this time in safety. But as the trip progressed, moods on the bus grew foul along with the air. Some muttered that it was too good to be true. Maybe. Carlos didn't know. He could barely think with his head pounding from hunger. He'd had nothing to eat since leaving Texas and the last time the water bottles were distributed was hours ago.

He grimaced at how easily he'd been caught at the border. Duped, most likely, by the very coyote he'd entrusted to lead him across. He and a group of a dozen or so had scrambled on hands and knees under razor wire that had torn the back of his shirt to shreds and then through a dank, claustrophobic dirt tunnel from Mexico to Texas right into the hands of ICE— waiting with weapons drawn. He figured the coyote had negocios chuecos with the guards. It stung because he'd given the last of his money to the coyote. That was after paying off two drug lords in Mexico, the border patrol and countless third-rate malandros. His pesos were gone. His cheap watch, cell phone, all bartered away.

At the detention camp, he had seen the guards' eyes narrow as they examined him. The brutal carvings in his forehead meant only one thing. Gang member. They shoved him in a cage with the most hardened detainees where word spread that he was from Zone 3 in Guate City. The detainees in the cage circled but left him alone. No one wanted to fuck with a Barrio 18 torro. If only they knew the truth. Others in the cage weren't so lucky. The guards didn't bother to confiscate blades, knives, or glass from the young men. Why would they, when the brawls provided hours of entertainment? More than one loser, shanked and gutted, was left to rot in the corner of the cage. Carlos's stomach churned as he thought of those corpses, dried out in the Texas heat and covered with flies.

No doctor at the detention camp had tended to the cuts in his back from the razor wire and his shirt—the only one he owned—continued to fray until the back of it was a collection of long strips that fluttered in the hot dry, breezes.

He felt someone sit down next to him and opened his eyes in surprise. The seat next to him was the only one free on the bus. No one sat there because of the stench of the lavatory, or so he told himself. More likely, no one wanted to sit next to a gangster in a shredded shirt. His new seat mate was a woman wearing a multicolored skirt that draped to her ankles. She had a red shawl around her shoulders and her long braids were kept in place by a tête foulard. Her dark skin was smooth, but she didn't seem young.

"Bonjour," she said. "Do you speak English?"

Carlos nodded. He'd learned a little English in his father's store in Guatemala City.

"I wait here for the twalèt," she said and looked at him curiously.

Carlos thought he saw a glimmer of wisdom in her eyes.

"The rest on the bus, they say you are vicious gang member. But I know people." She patted him on the arm. "You are not vicious, are you?" She chuckled as if she'd said something amusing. "You just sad. I see broken heart."

Carlos shrugged. He was too tired and hungry to have a conversation.

"I did not expect to go to San Francisco," the woman continued. "I don't know anyone there. But the offer of a job, I cannot pass, if it is true?"

She held up her palms as if she didn't know whether to believe the promise of employment that had lured most of the immigrants onto the bus at the detention camp. She seemed to study him. "Do you have people in California?"

Carlos shifted uncomfortably. "My wife," he said, wishing the conversation would end.

"Ou gen chans," she smiled. "The saints favor you. My gran timoun yo are in New York. I save money from job in California. Then, I go to New York."

Carlos didn't tell the woman that the saints didn't favor him. Still, he grasped

3

the crucifix tightly. She seemed to study him more. "You don't seem like a happy man to meet with wife," she said. "How long since you see her?"

Carlos cleared his throat. "Three years." He didn't tell the woman that he'd had no contact at all with Maria during that time. They had agreed to it for her safety. No texts. No calls. That was the hardest of all, never hearing her voice.

The woman was silent for a moment. Carlos could feel her eyes scanning his face. "The mark on the head," she said, pointing to the gang carving. "It is less than three years, no?"

Carlos nodded.

"And now you worry that she will not listen to you, a man different from the one she left?" The woman asked the question but seemed to already know the answer. She looked at him with an understanding he didn't want. She pulled a scrap of paper and a nub of a pencil from a wide pocket sewn into her skirt. "Here," she pushed the paper and pencil into his hand. "Write the most important thing to tell your wife. Then, if she do not listen to you, give her note."

The door to the lavatory opened disgorging a man and a foul odor. The woman stood and smiled. "My friend, lanmou se yon mistè." The lavatory door clicked shut.

Carlos held the pencil nub. So much had happened in the three years since he'd helped his wife flee Guatemala. Most significantly, he'd been forced into a gang. That news might have reached Maria. But, even so, he'd kept her secret about the reason she'd had to flee. His father, however, could no longer be trusted. The man suffered from dementia. He didn't know what he was doing when he'd blurted out the truth about Maria in front of the wrong people. Carlos clenched his jaw and scribbled two words on the scrap of paper and slipped it into his wallet. Two words. Even if she refused to acknowledge him. It was all she needed to know.

* * *

Carlos jerked awake, roused by the guards on the bus, now stopped. He opened his eyes, startled that he had managed to doze off, then rubbed his stiff neck and glanced out the window. The bus had parked on a busy city street in front of a large, green glass building. They must have arrived in San Francisco. He looked up and gasped. The green glass building was massive and reached to the heavens. He had never seen anything so tall or ornate.

"You've arrived in sanctuary," one of the guards called out. Carlos could hear the sarcasm, ripe in the guard's voice.

"Listen up," another guard shouted and turned to look at the immigrants in the bus. "Kavali Corporation requires that I read you this notice, so shut your yaps."

He flipped open his phone and read. "Welcome to San Francisco. Per the contractual agreement that you signed at the Intergovernmental Service facility in Dilley, Texas, you are now employees of Kavali Technologies Corporation."

He looked up from his phone. "Congrats fuckers. I would have sent you back to the shitholes you crawled out of. But Kavali is your goddamn savior." He continued reading. "As employees, you have the honor of living and working in Kavali Tower. You'll follow all rules and regulations set forth by Kavali." He flipped his phone shut. "There's more, it's not worth my time. So now you stupid fucks, if you'll follow me, we'll get you into the tower."

Carlos stood and stretched with the rest—undocumented immigrants fleeing from Central America, West Africa, Venezuela, the Caribbean. The bus reeked of body odor and stagnant still air. The chatter grew to a low hum as they moved to the door. He caught sight of the Haitian woman who had sat next to him. She made a fist and held it high. He tried to smile but only clenched his hands.

He was the last to leave the bus and lingered on the sidewalk in front of the green skyscraper. The late afternoon sun warmed his head. He inhaled deeply and almost cried. The air was clean, energetic. He couldn't remember the last time he'd seen a sky so free from dust. And the air had just enough salt to bring back memories, a childhood trip to the beach at Monterrico. He heard the squawk of a seagull overhead and looked up, squinting to see the enormous green glass building rising so high into the sky he could not see the top—somewhere, up there, it seemed to scrape heaven.

"Hey you ugly fuck, get moving." A guard knocked him on the side of the head and Carlos followed the line of immigrants into the massive skyscraper. They moved into a small foyer, then through an open, thick metal door leading to a wide, brightly lit hallway.

"Keep moving," the guards called out, herding them.

The line of immigrants approached a row of cargo elevators. Carlos felt a draft through the back of his shredded shirt. He stopped and looked up and gasped. Stretching above was an enormous cavern inside the building, and hanging in that cavern was something he could barely fathom. Panels, huge, the size of soccer fields, held plants growing from their sides. The plants themselves were gigantic, larger than anything he'd seen. It was impossible, but these were fields—growing vertically. Carlos exhaled in disbelief. He wondered if their new jobs might be working in these gargantuan fields. He stood there, gaping, as the migrants moved forward.

"Move it!" one of the guards shouted, glancing over his shoulder at Carlos. A cargo elevator rumbled open and the migrants surged forward.

Carlos felt a heavy hand thwack his shoulder and another across his mouth.

"Don't get on that elevator if you want to live," a voice hissed in his ear.

He gasped and reached for the cold hand on his mouth.

"No!" the voice spat.

He felt something up against the small of this back. Hard metal directly on his skin between the tattered strips of his shirt. The click of a safety turning off. A gun.

"Step backward quickly and don't make any noise or I'll waste you," the voice said.

Carlos swallowed hard and did as he was told and stepped around a pillar and into a dark hallway. A door slid shut before he could even consider crying out to the guards. Too late. He was alone with the voice.

"Okay," the voice said. "You can turn around."

Carlos turned slowly and gasped, seeing a woman in a security guard uniform, though different from the guards who had transported them from Texas. But it was her face, her skin that struck him most. She was a sickly gray bordering on putrid green. Sweat poured from her forehead. Her hair was matted and her hands shook. She leaned against the wall, her gun trained on Carlos.

"It's all right," she said, seeing the fright in Carlos's eyes. "I was only exposed to the genome for a second." She seemed to shake her head ruefully. "Stupid me after being so careful for years, but I had to see it with my own eyes."

She licked her lips. "It's not contagious, but..." She coughed, deep and raspy and when she sucked in air, her throat gurgled a death rattle. Carlos had heard it many times as he held dying gangsters on the street in Guate City. He looked carefully at her face. Her eyes were empty, almost haunted, as if she'd seen something she wanted to forget but couldn't.

"I'm with WACO," she said through jagged coughs. "We're not really a terrorist group. That's fake news." She clutched her side and seemed to wince from the ragged coughing. "Do you speak English?"

He nodded. His heart thudded and he looked down the dark hallway nervously, wondering if the other guards had noticed his disappearance.

"They won't know you're missing for at least a half hour," she said, her voice thick with mucus. "It's a mob scene down there. Five buses just arrived." She choked and seemed about to collapse from exhaustion, or dehydration, he did not know. He flexed his hands and wondered if he should try to overpower her and take the gun.

"Don't worry," she said as if sensing his thoughts. "I'm not going to shoot you." She bent over and picked up a backpack from the floor. She groaned with the effort and kept the gun trained on him. "But you have to listen carefully if you want to live," she said, her breathing uneven. "Do you understand?"

"Yes," Carlos stammered.

"Good," she swallowed. "You need to move fast. Take this to the Embarcadero, three blocks from here toward the bay."

From the backpack she pulled a small orange card that appeared to be made of metal. Carlos thought it looked like a payment card.

"Do not expose this to natural light," she hissed. "Sunlight, even a flame, will release the genome." She choked. Her eyes widened and Carlos could have sworn they were turning green. "Fuck," she gurgled. "Not much time."

She dropped the card back in the backpack and struggled to stay standing. "Sit on a bench near the bow and arrow sculpture. Wait for a guy named Smiley. He'll be wearing a felt hat. He's with WACO, too. He'll find you. He will give you money, whatever you need."

She coughed uncontrollably and slid down the wall until she was seated. The gun in her hands wobbled. "Tell him that Brie..." she gurgled and gasped for air. She slowly drifted to one side, her eyes wide.

Carlos watched in horror and stepped backward as the woman's face decomposed into long, gooey strands of flesh. He spun around hearing the door behind him lock. He pounded. Yelled. There was nothing from the other side.

"Don't," he heard Brie whisper. He looked back. She was slouched over on the floor. Carlos gulped. It was as if she was melting, becoming a puddle. He pressed himself against the door.

"Don't get on that elevator," Brie whispered. "You'll die down there."

"I...I can't get out," Carlos stammered, his eyes not leaving Brie.

"I will open the doors and turn off the security cameras," Brie choked. "You will have thirty seconds to get out of the building." She reached slowly to her melting face and pressed on a small dot next to her ear. It glowed orange. The door behind Carlos slid open. He peeked into the long white hallway. It was empty. He looked back at Brie. She no longer appeared conscious and was slumped on the floor. Skin oozed from her face in long green tentacles. He stared, barely able to fathom what he was witnessing. For an instant, he wondered if he was in some fever-induced dream on the bus. He scooped up the backpack by her side. As he turned, a glint of metal caught his eye. Her gun. He looked over his shoulder then grabbed the gun and shoved it in his rear waistband. He ran out into the long white hallway.

His heart thudded as he sprinted from the elevators toward the exit. Brie said she'd turned off the cameras. He hoped to god she had. Sweat trickled down his back as rounded a corner and came to the front lobby. The massive metal door clanked and started to slide shut. He had to run. Now. He sucked in his breath, his ragged sneakers pounding on the gleaming white floor. He threw himself through the opening and slid into the lobby as the door boomed shut behind him, the clank of bolts locking into place echoed.

He held his breath and pushed on the glass door to the outside. It opened. He stepped onto the sidewalk and into the roar of late afternoon traffic. He blinked, barely able to believe that he'd been inside the tower only minutes. What was this place?

He turned his face toward the salty breeze. The Embarcadero would be that way, into the breeze. He swallowed hard and wondered if he should bolt, but he needed money. There was no choice. He exhaled and walked toward the Embarcadero to look for the man called Smiley.

* * *

Carlos waited nervously, feeling the cold metal of the gun against his back as he sat on the bench by the sculpture of a massive bow and arrow on the Embarcadero. So far, no man had walked by wearing a felt hat. He saw men in baseball gaps. Runners in visors. Helmet clad cyclists. Each time someone

9

passed, his heart thudded and he tried to breathe normally. He didn't like carrying a gun, especially one stuck in his waistband and barely covered by his shredded shirt. He regretted taking it from the security guard. This wasn't Guate City, after all, it was San Francisco.

People milled about casually in the late afternoon sun. A young girl looked at him curiously and whispered into her mother's ear. The mother's eyes widened as she saw him and she yanked her child away. He could only imagine what he looked like. Torn clothing from the razor wire. Filthy from the detention camp. Foul-smelling from the endless bus ride. The brutal gang carving on his forehead.

He scanned the crowd, searching for Smiley, feeling the stabbing hunger in his stomach. He was starving. It had been two days since he'd eaten anything substantial and, if it weren't for the bottles of water, he doubted he would have had the energy to make it this far. Already, he could feel the gap in his pant waist, his body shrinking by the day. He needed to eat. Anything. He'd already rooted around in the backpack for food. There was none. He eyed a woman with a tamale cart across the pebble path. The smell was intoxicating. He fantasized about biting into a warm tamale. Seasoned pork. Or a tamal de elote. He had to look away. It was too much. As soon as the man from the mysterious organization, WACO, showed up with money, he would eat one.

He unzipped the backpack and rooted around for the orange card. It looked like some kind of payment card. But why wasn't it supposed to be exposed to the light? And what was it that the strange woman had said about a genome? He didn't know what that was. The woman didn't say it *wasn't* a payment card, however. He exhaled, unnerved by the memory of her melting face and left the card in the backpack.

He glanced around the Embarcadero. A couple—a young man and a woman with long reddish hair—approached from the side. The two were bent over her phone and didn't see him. The mother and young girl approached the tamale cart. The breeze carried the tamale scent and his stomach knotted in pain. He couldn't help himself. He needed to eat. He'd use whatever was on the payment card and then find a place to sleep. Find work in the morning when he could think straight. He carefully slid the orange card from the backpack and turned it over in his hands. It was an odd size, bigger than the payment cards he remembered, but it might work at the tamale cart.

Suddenly, he felt something warm in his hand. The card was vibrating and began to glow. A tiny bright orange beam shot up from the card. What the hell was it? He was certain it was no payment card. He slipped the card into his wallet next to the note he'd scribbled to his wife and shoved the wallet into his pocket. The wallet vibrated for several seconds and then was still. He exhaled, feeling unsettled, wondering if he was being set up.

The breeze shifted and again he could smell the roast chicken from the woman's cart. His stomach growled. It was too much. He had to have a tamale. Right now. He waited for the young man and woman to pass him and stood quickly. As he did, he felt the security guard's gun, still stuck in his waistband, rake across the back of the bench. He reached back to grab it and keep it from clattering to the path, but it jerked, caught on something.

He glanced down. A frayed strip of cloth, still attached to his shredded shirt, had become entwined around the gun. He yanked harder trying to rip the cloth free of the gun and then gasped. The frayed cloth had wound its way around the trigger. Was the gun's safety on or off? He didn't know. He stopped yanking and probed delicately at the stuck cloth, trying to untangle it.

A shriek pierced the air. The little girl. She'd run over to pick up her ball and saw him. Gun in hand. Her screams echoed through the late afternoon.

"Oh my god," someone shouted. "He's got a gun." The girl's mother. Staring at him. He stepped backward and as he did, tripped on the park bench. He fumbled. Accidentally yanked hard on the frayed strip of cloth wound around the trigger. It strained. Pulled the trigger.

11

The gun fired.

Carlos inhaled.

Another shriek pierced the Embarcadero.

"He's been shot!" a woman screamed. "Help me!"

The young man who had just passed him—the one walking with the woman with long red hair—grabbed at his chest in disbelief. A crimson stain spread rapidly across the young man's sweatshirt. The man crumpled to the ground and gasped for breath.

Carlos watched, horrified, as the redheaded woman shrieked. She fell to her knees and cradled the man, holding his head as he bled out onto the pebble path. "Help me," she screamed. "He's been shot!" Her screams ricocheted in Carlos's head.

He stood, frozen, as the crowd on the Embarcadero panicked. The mother frantically yanked her tiny daughter behind the bow and arrow sculpture. The two joggers dropped to the ground and covered their heads. Terrified tourists stampeded toward their buses, trampling one another to get away from him.

He stood next to the park bench, eyes wide, his heart thudding. Gun in his hand. He had to think. Fast. No one would believe the word of an undocumented immigrant, especially one with gang symbols carved in his forehead and a stolen backpack. He heard a distant buzzing and looked up. A spherical orange drone hung there, barely visible against the sky, watching. He ignored it.

The two joggers jumped up. They raced away from him, across the green lawn to a police officer and pointed back at him. The officer spoke tersely into a walkie talkie clipped to his shoulder while unholstering his weapon. The officer ran toward Carlos, shouting.

He could hear the officer's boots thudding on the path. Out of the corner of his eye, he saw the officer reach for his weapon. The officer was screaming something in English. Carlos raised his hands. The gun ripped the strip of cloth free from his shirt and it fluttered above him like a flag.

The young man on the ground struggled to breath and his college sweatshirt was now completely drenched in blood. The woman screamed. Pleaded with the dying man. "Please, please stay with me, just look at me," she begged.

Carlos started to tell the officer that the gun was not his, that the shooting was a mistake, but the officer had already dropped to one knee and aimed. Carlos screamed and looked heavenward, begging the saints to save his wife. He heard two pops that sounded like firecrackers and felt a crack in his chest. He looked down. Mouth agape. A crimson stain, like the one soaking the sweatshirt of the young man sprawled on the path, spread across his chest. He convulsed and arced to the ground. The blood from the wound in his chest gushed down the sloping path toward the young dying man. The two men's blood mixed to form a small pool, the blood of each indistinguishable from the other.

Part I

1. MARIA

Maria Garcia gasped when the San Francisco coroner pulled the sheet back from the lifeless body. She hadn't seen Carlos for more than three years and it was impossible to know what had changed her husband more—three years of brutal living or bullet wounds in his chest.

She grabbed one of the metal handles lining the wall of the cold room and looked up at the biting white lights dangling from the ceiling until her breathing calmed, and then looked back at her husband. His face, once plump and almost cherubic, was gaunt and weathered beyond his youthful years. His nose was bent, as if it'd been broken and never tended to, and the number 18 had been cut into his forehead, deeply, creating a shocking crimson scar, unmissable and unmistakable. He'd been shot twice in his left chest and had died instantly, according to the detective standing next to her and the coroner in the cold room.

She smoothed her maid's uniform and nodded, stoic, trying hard not to give away any thoughts.

"The Barrio 18 gang," said the detective, following her gaze.

She nodded slowly. She didn't tell the detective of her familiarity with the Guatemalan gang, how they commanded her former barrio unchecked by Policía Local or padres católicos. She simply nodded at the detective.

"There's more," the detective motioned to the coroner who pulled the sheet back further, exposing the dead man's chest. Maria winced. The scars on Carlos's chest were massive compared to his forehead. The Roman numeral XVIII had been brutally carved into his chest. Her stomach tightened, feeling the cruelty in her gut. She silently crossed herself.

"When did you say you saw your husband last?"

"Almost three years ago, in Guatemala," she replied as calmly as she could.

"Right," the detective said, looking at her slowly until his frown turned to a smile. "You know," he said. "Since you're here to identify the body, I'd like to ask a few questions. Just a few, nothing disturbing. Do you mind coming upstairs with me?"

Maria hesitated. Her heart pounded so loudly she was certain the detective would hear. Her cousin had begged her not to come to San Francisco after she told her she was going to identify her husband's body and claim his belongings. "They'll keep you," her cousin said, "They won't let you go." But Maria had to see Carlos and boarded a Golden Gate Transit bus in her maid's uniform for the two-hour ride from Santa Rosa to San Francisco. How naive she'd been to think that she could march in, identify her husband, and leave with his belongings without answering any questions.

She felt the detective staring at her. "Ready?"

Maria nodded and followed him from the morgue, down a short hallway, and up a metal staircase to the building's lobby. The detective used his badge to open locked doors and waved to a guard as they passed. Maria glanced at the guard's name tag. Franklin. She followed the detective down another hallway, around a corner past the restrooms, and finally into a small room with a door that locked solidly behind them. The detective motioned for her to sit on a cold metal chair next to a plain metal table.

Maria nodded and sat. She trembled. It was freezing in the room. She could hear muffled footsteps outside the thick door. The detective spoke first. "I'm sorry for your loss, Mrs. Garcia. It's never easy to lose a loved one, no matter who he was." He cleared his throat. "It's interesting that you haven't seen your husband for three years and yet he showed up here in San Francisco. Was he on his way to meet you?"

She shrugged. She didn't know. The last time she saw Carlos, he was on the bank of the Suchiate River waving at her as she floated away from Guatemala toward Mexico on a raft made of inner tubes. Fleeing Guatemala was the only way that Maria, and her unborn child, would be safe. They could never be found. That had been thirty-six months ago and Maria had no contact with Carlos since. Her husband's death in San Francisco was a shock, but what had terrified her more was seeing the gang symbols carved into his body. Her husband was a quiet man and had not been a gang member when she left. The detective seemed impatient. "Do you understand me?"

She nodded. "I don't know why he was here."

The detective gave her a curious look. His eyes narrowed and he drummed his fingers on the table. He reached inside his jacket and pulled out a small, bulging plastic baggie. He undid the seal, pulled a latex glove from his pocket, and slid the baggie's meager contents into his gloved hand. He opened a small, cracked man's wallet. She recognized it immediately. She'd given the wallet to Carlos the night of their wedding in the tiny bedroom in his father's house. For our future fortune, she'd said. Carlos kept it in his shirt pocket. You're always next to my heart, he would say, patting the wallet. He was romantic that way.

"There's not much in it," he said, watching Maria's reaction. "Forensics says a worthless, old payment card. And something stuck to it."

The detective held up what appeared to be an orange metal payment card. Stuck to it was a scrap of paper. "He wrote only two words. Must have been in a hurry," the detective said. He paused, as if waiting for Maria to ask a question but she remained quiet and still. He examined the scrap of paper carefully. "*Cadejo sabe*. Does that mean anything to you?"

Maria tensed. She wanted to scream. Her pulse raced and her breathing was shallow but she had to stay calm and not let the detective see her reaction. Yes, it meant something to her. It was the reason she fled Guatemala. She stared vacantly at the detective.

"No," she lied flatly. "I don't know what that means."

The detective nodded slowly. Maria couldn't tell if he was convinced. From the baggie, he grabbed the other item, a chain from which dangled a large crucifix, the bottom of which was fashioned into a sword, yet it was still graceful. The crucifix swayed gently from his fingers, the cold light of the room reflected from the cross and played across Maria's face. She reached out to touch the necklace. The detective pulled it back and turned it over in his hand. "What does this say on the back?"

"Eres único y especial mi amor," Maria said.

"What does it mean?"

"It's something he used to say to me every day,'" Maria said. There was a catch in her throat. "It means, you are unique and special, my love."

Again, the detective shot her a curious look. "Your husband belonged to a brutal gang, but he was…" the detective paused.

She met his gaze but said nothing. The detective didn't finish his sentence and Maria shifted uncomfortably in the cold chair. He put the crucifix and wallet on top of the baggie the table. "That's all there is."

Maria nodded sadly. Carlos had the crucifix engraved for her the day she told him she was pregnant. His adoration was boundless. When she had to flee, she placed the necklace into his palm. "To remember me," she said as the raft jerked from the river bank. They both knew if it stayed around her neck, the crucifix would be stolen as soon as she reached Mexico. And now here it was, tantalizingly close. She bowed her head and said a prayer for Carlos as a wave of grief washed over her.

"Mrs. Garcia," the detective continued. "Carlos was not in the U.S. legally. He crossed the border to Texas through a tunnel, was captured by ICE and transferred to a DIGSA facility in San Francisco that he escaped from. How is it that you're here? Legally, I mean?"

"I have a green card," she responded.

"A green card!" The detective smiled broadly, almost jovially, and slapped his knee. "How could it come to pass that you have a green card but your husband is a gang member who crossed into the U.S. illegally? Why, that's remarkable. Can I see it?"

Maria shook her head. "I don't have it with me."

"No. Of course you don't. Do you have any other U.S. identification with you?"

"No. I didn't realize I would be, um, held."

"I think you mean detained, and you're not being detained. I simply..."

"I know," interrupted the woman. "Mr. Detective, I am very tired and, I don't know the word, sad for losing my husband. I just want to get his things and go home. Can I have them, please?"

The detective leaned forward and scratched the light stubble on his chin. Finally, he said, "Fill out this form, give me your local address and contact info. If everything checks out, I'll see what I can give you—the necklace maybe— when we are done with our investigation."

Maria managed a thin smile. She'd hoped there would be more. But she'd already discovered in Carlos's belongings the reason why he'd been on his way to find her. The words on the scrap of paper told her everything she needed to know.

* * *

Maria sipped apprehensively from a water glass as the detective scanned the form. She hadn't been entirely truthful when answering the questions. How could she be?

The locked door to the small room buzzed open and a man poked his head in. He wore a white coat that went almost to his knees. He looked at Maria and then at the detective.

"Detective Thorn, we have a problem," the man in the white coat said flatly and flicked his chin. The detective sighed and walked to the door. The two men conferred in hushed tones.

The detective glanced away and Maria quietly put her hand on top of Carlos's wallet and slid it toward her. She dropped the wallet onto her lap and pulled out the piece of paper stuck to the orange metal card. She gasped. The paper was stuck to the metal card with large smears of blood. Carlos's blood. He must have bled into his wallet as he died. Her eyes teared as she read the last thing he'd written. *Cadejo sabe.*

She looked up. The detective had his back to her. She gulped and slipped the bloodstained note and orange metal card into her pocket then shoved Carlos's wallet back to the center of the table as the detective turned.

"Goddamn billionaire," she heard the detective exhale. He swiped the wallet from the table, dropped it in the baggie and looked at her. "Another fuck up in Forensics," the detective spat, as if she would understand. His brow furrowed and moved toward the door. "Stay here, we'll finish in a minute," he commanded and flicked his badge against the door lock and it buzzed open. "I'll be right back." He marched away.

Maria bolted to the door, catching it before it swung shut and holding it barely ajar. She held her breath, expecting the detective to notice that the door hadn't clicked shut, but his footsteps continued down the hallway. She slipped a trash can in between the frame and door and reached back to the table for the crucifix. Her eyes watered but she didn't have time for sorrow. She had to get out of the building.

She exhaled, pushed the door fully open and peered into the hallway. It was empty. The detective disappeared around the corner. A janitor's cart sat outside the restroom. A small yellow pylon stood in the entrance to the women's restroom with a sign reading *Closed for Cleaning.* She glanced in both directions, then slid into the hallway, letting the door click and lock behind her.

She padded quickly down the hallway toward the lobby and peeked around the corner. The guard to the lobby stood at his post, chatting with two uniformed officers. The lobby door buzzed open and another officer walked in, nodded to the guard and began moving toward Maria. She sucked in her breath and stepped backward into the hall, looking for a place to hide, knowing that she couldn't stay in the building. She sprinted back to the janitor's cart and stuffed her coat into a trash bag hanging from the side of the cart, then smoothed her maid's uniform praying the ruse would work. She yanked the pylon from the doorway to the women's restroom and jammed it on top of the cart as the officer rounded the corner. She grabbed the handles to the cart and pushed it toward him. The officer glanced up from his phone and pursed his lips in a half frown, half smile.

"Hey," he said. "You're not Diego! Where is he today?"

"No, Officer, Diego is sick today. I clean instead." Maria smiled broadly and pushed the cart around the corner toward the lobby door. The officer smiled and nodded and continued walking away from her.

"Officer Franklin, hola!" Maria called out as she approached the guard at the door. "Officer, can you open the door, por favor? My hands are…I'm not sure of the words…busy?"

"Ma'am, I'll need to see your badge," said Officer Franklin. The man frowned and Maria held her breath. Her escape was so close.

"Really?" said the older of the officers standing with Officer Franklin. "You born in a barn, Franklin?" he said, needling the younger man. The officer pulled open the door for her and Maria pushed the janitor's cart through the door and toward the lobby.

"Gracias," she said, offering her most friendly smile as the officer tipped his hat.

Maria abandoned the janitor's cart in a dark corner of the SFPD headquarters, donned her threadbare coat, and slipped from the police station into the streets. She didn't remember walking to the Transbay Terminal, or even taking a breath, but once she climbed onto the bus, she let out her first full gasp.

* * *

She sat in the back of the bus where she could be alone with her thoughts and watch the sun drop below the horizon on the ride back to Sonoma County. She needed to feel its warmth on her face. The man on the cold slab was her husband, but what had he become? He wasn't the man she'd fallen in love with. Her eyes welled up as she pulled the orange payment card from her pocket and looked at the scrap of paper stuck to it with Carlos's blood. Her heart pounded as she read the words. *Cadejo sabe.* The words echoed in her brain.

She wiped a tear and turned the card over curiously. Almost no one used these old cards anymore. This one was thicker than a standard payment card, bigger and a strange orange color. One side was rough—almost pitted and encrusted with tiny gems and a button-like circle, the other side had strange markings—a company logo maybe. Maria held the card up to the window in the sunlight. The card grew warmer in the sunlight and began to vibrate. Suddenly, the button on the card glowed and an orange beam of light shot out. The card hummed and the strange orange beam swept across the ceiling of the bus, as if it were searching for something. The light turned into tiny strands that seemed to weave with one another. Maria had seen the shape before, but she couldn't remember where.

The back of Maria's neck prickled and she looked around at the bus to see if anyone had noticed the odd display of light. She poked desperately at the card but the beam continued its movement. She pulled the card out of the sun and shoved it back in her pocket. After a moment, the card stopped vibrating. Maria exhaled and left the card in her pocket.

She gazed out of the window at the setting sun. She took the sword-like crucifix from her pocket and slipped it over her head, trying not to weep at its familiar weight. She bowed her head and offered a prayer to the saints, the same one she'd said for three years.

2. BEL

Bel McMaster dropped to one knee and wiped his brow. The late afternoon sun blazed unrelentingly and baked the vineyards around him. He plucked a shriveled grape from a cluster and plopped it in his mouth. His nose wrinkled at the fruit's bitterness. "Too soon," he muttered to JC, the winemaker crouched next to him. "We need at least two more weeks."

He shaded his eyes and looked up at the sun, burning sharp in the cloudless sky. Sonoma County's warm summer days balanced with cool nights used to make for a perfect wine-growing climate, but now the summers were brutal, filled with searing heat that threatened the very crop that made the region famous. And nothing Bel and JC tried had worked this season, not the shade nets, misters, or reflective sprays.

JC plucked a grape and chewed glumly. "The sugar isn't right for October." He let the juice dribble from his mouth and spat the grape on the ground. "Look at this rot," he said and kicked at the base of a vine. "We could lose fifty tons in this field alone."

"That's four years in a row," Bel muttered.

"Five," JD corrected.

A gust whistled across the parched slopes, kicking up a cloud of dust that blew into Bel's eyes. "Fucking Diablo winds," he coughed and tried in vain to wipe the dry dirt away before it caked onto his sweaty face. He hated the Diablo winds—unpredictable gusts that blew from the Sierra Nevada mountains in the east, blasting Sonoma County with bone-dry, blistering-hot air instead of the cooler, wetter winds that came from the ocean to the west. Diablo winds were wicked, causing temperatures to spike and dry out the vines. Locals claimed Diablo wind supercharged the ions in the air and put people on edge—emergency room visits increased, tempers flared, and passions ran wild. It wasn't just local lore, it was fact. His life was proof of the power of Diablo wind.

"Shit," he said, seeing a champagne-colored sedan bumping toward them, moving carefully between the tidy rows of pinot vines that whipped in the parched gusts. He rubbed his hands on his pants and stood. The car stopped next to Bel's tattered pickup truck. The door opened and a spike of a heel emerged, just thin enough to be out of place in a vineyard. A woman stood, straightened her linen jacket and walked toward the men, her scent blasting through the air. He coughed. He didn't know if it was the cloying perfume or her timing, but he had an allergic reaction to Kelly Garret. Or maybe it was the bank she represented.

"Beautiful day, Bel," Kelly hollered to be heard above the wind. "I've always loved this part of your estate." She gestured to the expansive fields that commanded a full view of Sonoma County's two most famous valleys—the Russian River valley to the south and the Dry Creek valley to the north. Bel grimaced as he watched her survey his hillside vineyard.

"I've often wondered why you didn't build your hospitality center here," she continued and tucked a stray blond hair behind her ear. "The view is amazing, it's close to the highway and you're right in the middle of one of the most famous fields in the county."

"That's exactly why I didn't build here," Bel snorted. "Kelly, you know how perfect this microclimate is. We've won more awards than I can remember from this plot of land."

JC shook his head emphatically. "The pinot that won the Paris Wine Competition came from right here."

"You don't think I know that, gentleman?" Kelly said with a condescending smile that infuriated Bel.

He crossed his arms and glared. "What do you want?"

"I'm not here to give you advice on real estate or wine-making," Kelly said sharply. "You missed our appointment this morning. And that was rescheduled from last week, which—if memory serves—was rescheduled from three weeks before that. You need to stop avoiding me. You have to stop avoiding the bank." She paused. "Bel," she softened. "I know how tough things are right now, and I'm really sorry. My timing is awful…"

"Awful?" Bel interrupted.

"I've known you and your family my whole life," Kelly shook her head. "That's what makes this so difficult. The note is past due. We talked about this in the spring, the bank was clear about the terms, the collateral, and the timing." Kelly glanced around the vineyard. The vines were heavy with late harvest clumps of grapes that rocked back and forth in the winds. "I need to hand you this in person," she said softly, her voice almost lost in the Diablo winds. She produced a manila envelope from her Hermès bag and handed it to Bel.

He accepted it vacantly. He knew it was coming. "Please open it, Bel," Kelly said, gently.

He slid the documents out of the envelope and started to read.

"You've got to be fucking kidding," he muttered, staring at Kelly. "The house wasn't included in the deal, how can the bank be claiming that?"

"Bel," she said patiently. "We told you. If you didn't respond to the first foreclosure proceeding the bank had the right to claim additional property, including all fields, warehouses, and the family home. It's all there. You signed the documents."

"And the Baxter family?" Bel spat, looking up from the documents. "I suppose they have something to do with this?"

Kelly Garret shifted uncomfortably and looked away from Bel. "They are the main backers of the loan, Bel. You knew that when you signed…"

"Does my wife know?" Bel interrupted. "Have you told Maureen?"

"It's not up to me to tell your wife, Bel," she said evenly. "I told the sheriff not to come out with me. We're not taking anything today, there are no eviction proceedings. But Bel, we're close to that. I can wait for another 30 days, but that's about it."

"So you're not here to take my bank payment card?" Bel said with as much snark as he could and folded his arms in defiance.

She shook her head sadly. "Bel, no one uses payment cards anymore."

He felt suddenly foolish, as if she'd accused him of living in the past, just like his wife did.

Kelly sighed, perhaps aware of the contrast between the warmth of the autumn sun and the chill of her mission. "Please don't ignore this, Bel." She looked away and then continued. "Yours is the only winery in the valley not taking out loans for genetic research or planting new clones. Bel, you're holding onto an era that no longer exists."

Bel looked at her. "No longer exists?" he exclaimed indignantly. "Of course it does! The only thing that's changed is Mother Nature. She's an absolute bitch. A monster."

Kelly snorted. "She's not a monster, Bel, she's a mirror. She reflects our choices. And maybe you should do what every other vintner in the valley has already done and give up on the pinot. Too finicky. It rots in the heat. Or stop farming on southern slopes. You can't fight the climate, Bel. You'll destroy McMaster Vineyards if you can't change."

Kelly paused at her car. Her hair whipped in her face and she tried unsuccessfully to keep it from her eyes. "I wasn't going to mention this Bel, but the

French Wine Ministers are in town."

Bel raised his eyebrows and tried not to convey his curiosity. Why were the French Wine Ministers in Sonoma County? And more importantly, why didn't he know about it? "What are they doing here," he shouted above the wind.

"They're restarting the Paris Wine Competition," she said. "First time in fifty years." She slammed her car door and leaned out of the window.

"Why am I only hearing about it now?" he said, indignant.

"The competition is invitation-only this time." She offered a conciliatory smile.

He hated Kelly Garret. He felt his heart clench as he watched her champagne-colored sedan bump away through the vineyard. Not even the decimated grape he'd just chewed or impending foreclosure was as bitter as being overlooked by the very competition that put McMaster Vineyards on the map.

"Fuck me," he said and squeezed his eyes shut. He'd been avoiding this moment for years, and now it was here. He was standing in the place his father often referred to as paradise on earth and on the verge of failure. Failure meant losing everything his family had built, the world's most famous California winery, McMaster Vineyards.

* * *

Bel's pickup truck bounced between the pinot vines that whipped and bowed in the gusts of wind. He followed a dirt road that climbed a steep hillside, its tight curves snaking around clumps of pines and eucalyptus. On the hill's ridge, he stepped out of his truck and gazed over the sprawling valley.

He breathed in the dry air, taking in the view which never ceased to stun him. He loved this spot more than any on the estate. From here he could see his dreams stitched into the undulating acres of California's most beautiful—and valuable—vineyards. The tidy rows of vines drifted into the horizon where they met Sonoma County's grass-covered hillsides. This time of year, before the winter rains, the distant hillside grass was golden brown and brushed against the vivid blue sky—a blue so intense that Bel used to wonder if the sky had been painted by God.

His father brought him to this spot when Bel was a child. Sometimes in the winter, the fog from the Pacific drifted over the fields, its tendrils snaking low in between the hills while the sky above remained clear. His father said that low-hanging winter mist was part of the county's secret. Then, Michael McMaster would bend to examine the dormant vines and feel the soil. The elder McMaster had a way with vines, people used to say. It was as if he could hear them whisper.

Bel opened the truck and reached for a bottle of wine under the driver's seat and lifted it to his lips. He closed his eyes and drank heavily, barely slowing to savor the McMaster vintage. Its contents warmed his belly. He gazed across the estate below again, focusing on the family home in the distance, a grand, twenty-seven-room, three-story Queen Anne with a mansard roof punctuated by sharply peaked dormers. A large porch circled the home with ornate posts supporting its roof. The image of the house, gracing each label of McMaster Vineyards wine, was almost as recognizable as the McMaster family name itself.

From up here, the estate was beautiful. Peaceful. That's why he loved this spot so much—it hovered above the stomach-churning reality of running the winery. Years ago, he'd brought Maureen here and proposed. Later, he spirited their twins here and taught them to ride motorcycles away from their mother's disapproving stare. As the children grew and left, the spot had become just his except for periodic intrusions by his son. Bel sighed. Ned had found him up here on a day like today. Told him he was dropping out of UC Davis. Bel took another swig from the bottle and snorted at the irony. His golden boy, favorite child. *You're supposed to help me modernize*, Bel had screamed. And now this—a possible foreclosure because he couldn't modernize fast enough. But it wasn't Kelly Garret's warning of the impending foreclosure that consumed him. It was what she'd said about the resurrection of the Paris Wine Competition. He could hardly believe it. The Paris Wine Competition surpassed all wine competitions. It was the reason that McMaster Vineyards rocketed to fame. Bel's father had swept the competition fifty years before—a stunning upset that vaulted Sonoma County to the top of wine-making with McMaster Vineyards at the very pinnacle. It was too much to dream, but if he entered and won, he might be able to turn the vineyard around. He closed his eyes and let the gusts whip around him, listening for them to whisper. *You could win.*

* * *

Bel paused at the stairs leading up to the estate's Queen Anne house. His stomach clenched. This was the only home he'd ever known and it had rarely been a peaceful one, certainly not during the height of his father's drinking and definitely not now with his marriage. As he stood there, a gigantic redwood tree murmured in the wind. It was one of the few old growth redwoods on private property in Sonoma County, it towered above the house. He liked to think that the tree gave him words of encouragement, and right now he could use some wisdom.

He sighed and wobbled up the stoop, feeling the effect of the bottle of wine he'd finished on the ridge. When he entered the foyer, he told himself not to look up but his bloodshot eyes ignored his wishes. Suspended three stories above was a mammoth, crystal-laden chandelier that his wife Maureen had recently custom made, replacing a simpler chandelier that had hung in the grand entry his entire life. This fixture was enormous and clumsy—so heavy that the building contractor had to install special beams in the attic ceiling to support it. Bel hated it. More than that, he hated his wife's neurotic need to impress.

He belched and moved toward the kitchen but stopped abruptly at the sound of glass breaking from Ned's bedroom. Bel hurried up the stairs and stared into his son's bedroom in disbelief. The room was in shambles with clothes strewn about the floor. Dresser drawers gaped open and the closet door hung ajar. In the middle of the room, crouched on the floor, was his wife,

Maureen. Shards of broken glass surrounded her. She didn't look at Bel but stood and marched into her son's bathroom. She returned with a broom and dustpan and began furiously sweeping up shards of glass from the bedroom floor.

"What the hell are you doing?" Bel asked his wife. "What did you break?"

Maureen didn't look at Bel. "I'm throwing things away," she replied. "It's my therapy. This room needs to be repainted. It still reeks of pot in here, if you can believe that. And yes, I broke one of Ned's bongs."

"But what about..." Bel started to protest and then stopped.

Maureen stopped sweeping glared at her husband. "What about what?" she asked. She walked over to Bel, put her face close to his and sniffed. "That's what I thought," she said. "You're drunk already and it's barely past noon." Maureen resumed sweeping. "Jesus, Bel," she muttered. "I don't know how you function."

Bel walked over to the bedroom window and looked across the field of vines. There in the distance, a small plume of dust rose from one of the dirt roads on the far side of the vineyards. Bel's heart skipped a beat. When Ned lived at home, that was one of his favorite motorcycle routes.

"You've had visitors today," Maureen said. "I can hardly keep up." She set the broom aside and brushed dust from her hands and her slacks. She was tall and slender and looked brittle and completely out of place in Ned's room with its neon posters and guitars. "What did the banker want?" she asked acidly.

Bel gritted his teeth. How did she already know about the banker? "What is this?" he avoided the question and picked up a phone case from Ned's bedside.

Maureen stopped sweeping and looked at him incredulously. "What the hell does it look like? It's a phone case."

"Why is it orange?" he asked.

"Sonoma Orange Bud," Maureen said. She looked at him with disbelief. "The cannabis strain he created in his high school biology class!"

"Oh, right." Bel nodded sheepishly. Ned had been suspended for a week but got an A in the class anyway. He set the case back by the bedside. "Why did he leave it at home?"

"Who knows?" Maureen spat. "I want to know why the banker was here today. JC told me that Kelly Garret was in the fields today."

Goddamn JC. "She, um, just stopped by," Bel stammered.

Maureen crossed her arms and shook her head. "Stopped by?" she said incredulously. "Because she was in the neighborhood?"

"Something like that."

Maureen snorted and moved back to Ned's collection of bongs. She put a cardboard box on a dresser and began carelessly tossing the bongs into the box.

"Why are you doing this?" Bel asked. He turned to his wife, stumbled and reached for the side of Ned's bed to steady himself. He tried to pull a bong from Maureen's hands. "Stop it!" he said but he lost his balance, teetered forward and crashed onto his son's bed.

"Bel, wake up!" Maureen yelled. She took a step back and stared at Bel. Her dark eyes ablaze. She ran a hand through her ash blonde bob in frustration. "Jesus, Bel, you...you," she dropped her voice to a whisper tinged with anger. "Oh Bel," she said. "You really need to follow your therapist's advice and deal with this."

Her face turned to stone. Bel hated that look. Maureen had a regal beauty when she was young which had calcified as she'd aged. She was tall and commanding, but she'd hardened into someone who scared Bel, especially when she had that look on her face, a mixture of disgust and pity, as if she couldn't believe the man he'd become. Bel sat up on his son's bed and scratched his thinning hair.

"Deal with what?" he muttered.

"Are you kidding me?" Maureen snapped.

"It's just, that, well, when I came in, you had broken his favorite bong."

"Favorite bong?" Maureen's voice rose again. "How the hell would you know that?"

Bel started to protest but he was afraid that Maureen might be right. He had no clue which bong was his son's favorite. Or even why Ned had a bong collection. The kid had vaped for years.

"Follow your therapist's advice," she said. "Go to San Francisco and see your daughter. And, when you're there, ask her about the case. She says she's on the verge of a big break."

Bel rubbed his head and pushed himself to the edge of Ned's bed. "I'm not ready to see her yet," he mumbled, gazing at the wall where several large pictures hung of the twins, Ned and Nadine. They shared a love of motorcycles and in one of the pictures they stood proudly next to their new dirt bikes— their favorite birthday present ever, they'd said. Ned and Nadine were inseparable and loved celebrating their birthday together; it was a tradition they'd continued even after leaving home. Nadine always planned their birthday celebrations. She was the elder by mere minutes and relished the role of bossy older sister. Bel's gaze returned to his son and he shook his head. His therapist told him it was normal for a parent to have a favorite child, but just don't show favoritism, she cautioned—a warning that Bel had repeatedly failed to heed.

"I don't give a shit if you're ready. Go to San Francisco. She has new information from her investigation," Maureen said. "She's planning an important live interview." Maureen turned to face her husband. "You need to see her. You don't get to stop being a parent because you're angry at your child."

"I said I wasn't..."

"Get your ass to San Francisco or I'll call your mother." She was clearly serious; she couldn't stand Bel's mother and feeling was mutual. Maureen paused and her voice rose higher. "And for god's sake, you're already a drunk, don't become a cruel one like your father."

His wife's words smacked Bel across the face. She was right, again, but he told himself that it was his daughter who hated him, not the other way around. His daughter hated him because she didn't really know him. But his wife? He sighed. She hated him because she knew him too well.

* * *

Bel gripped the steering wheel and grimaced as the Diablo winds, fierce for this time of day, battered his pickup truck and blew clouds of gritty dust across the highway. Despite the gusts, the sun continued to shine brilliantly, occasionally blinding Bel with its intensity. The wind whipped harder as Bel's truck emerged from a stand of redwoods near Monte Rio on his way west toward Jenner, the tiny coastal town that clung to crumbling cliffs just below his newest vineyards.

He tipped a bottle to his lips but it was dry. He tossed it to the back of the cab. He was still woozy from the wine he'd had on the ridge but the conversation with his wife caused him to root around under the seat for another bottle. He felt none.

He reached the Pacific coast and turned north on Highway 1. His beat-up truck shuddered in the sporadic gusts that raised blinding clouds of dirt. He squinted to see through the windshield and jerked the truck to the right as an approaching car emerged from a dust cloud, its horn blaring. He rubbed his temples. If he couldn't have wine, he needed coffee.

Bel turned into the parking lot of a Quick Mart. A cyclone-like gust of wind spiraled and whipped up a funnel of dirt that encircled Bel's truck. He squinted and flicked on the truck's headlights. He gasped. Before he could think or brake, there was a loud crunch and the truck banged to a sudden stop.

The dust devil cleared. The front of his truck was wedged firmly into the front quarter panel of an old tan Toyota sedan. The driver of the Toyota leapt from his car, shouted something indistinguishable at Bel and bent to examine the damage to his car. Bel swore under his breath and kicked open the truck door.

"The hell, man!" The driver approached Bel. He was shorter than Bel, young with a square jaw and a mane of jet-black hair that was neatly combed back. He wore a workman's jacket with a name stitched on it. Juan, it read. His face was red with anger. "Couldn't you see me?" he asked incredulously and pointed at his car. "Are you blind?"

"Sorry," Bel mumbled and held up his hands.

"Sorry?" The man stepped threateningly close to Bel. "Sorry?" he repeated and jabbed Bel in the chest. "That's my car!" He pointed at the vehicles which sat jammed together. The wind which had briefly abated, now sprung up again and dust devils spun in the parking lot. "You hit my car!" the young man spluttered again, his voice teetering on disbelief.

Bel scratched his head and struggled to remember what to do in a situation like this. "I'll get my insurance card," he muttered.

"How about if you back up your truck so we can see the damage?" A woman's voice spoke. Bel hadn't seen a passenger in the car, he'd assumed the man was alone. He spun around as a figure emerged from a dust devil.

She was wearing a hotel maid's uniform and approached him with calm confidence. He tried not to stare but the woman's beauty was ethereal. Her face was heart-shaped with luminescent beige skin and full cheeks that were flushed. She had plump lips, slightly parted, and a delicate nose. Her dark tresses were pulled back into a loose bun and wisps of hair dangled down freely and fluttered in the breeze. But it was her eyes—Bel couldn't stop looking at her eyes. They were a shade of amber that he'd never seen before; amber and flecked with gold. The color was almost jewel-like. Bel was speechless and heard a roaring in his ears which might have been the wind, he wasn't sure. His face and skin felt suddenly warm. The woman was intoxicating.

"I asked if you could back up your truck," she repeated calmly with a soft accent.

Bel nodded silently and obeyed. The couple's Toyota creaked as he backed

36

his truck. He got out and walked over to the man and woman who surveyed the damage to their car. The front quarter panel of the Toyota was painfully crushed and pressing against the front tire of the car. The man had crouched down and stared at the tire, muttering under his breath. He stood as Bel approached.

"Hell man," he said, his voice still tense. "It's not drivable. We have to get to Santa Rosa!" The man glared at Bel as he spoke, his dark eyes flashed with anger. He balled his fists and took a step toward Bel.

Bel tried to assess the situation but was strangely lightheaded in the presence of the woman. He would provide his insurance, naturally, and call for a tow truck. The idea of waiting for a tow truck with the young woman caused blood to rush to his face again, but the woman's husband was hot-tempered and most likely wouldn't take kindly to a middle-aged man leering at his wife. Bel could offer to drive them to Santa Rosa. He seemed to recall that he was supposed to be in that direction later anyway. Was he having lunch with his mother today in Healdsburg? Or was that tomorrow? His mind was muddled.

"Give me your gloves," the woman's voice interrupted his thoughts. She spoke to the young man who dutifully complied, pulling a pair of worn work gloves from his rear pocket. She slipped them onto her delicate hands, hitched up her maid's skirt and crouched next to the car's front tire. Bel tried not to stare at her exposed legs but found it almost impossible to look away. The woman planted one tennis shoe-clad foot on the car's tire, grasped the cracked plastic quarter panel and yanked. The plastic groaned and wobbled. The woman took a breath and then pulled harder, her back and leg muscles tensing as she leaned from the vehicle to wrench away the broken panel. Suddenly, there was a loud crack and the plastic panel shuddered and snapped, freeing the car's tire.

Bel watched, slack jawed, as the young maid marched to the rear of the car, opened its trunk and tossed in the damaged plastic panel. She dusted off her gloved hands, slammed the car trunk and returned to the men.

"Try to turn the wheel now," she commanded the handyman. The young man slid into the front seat. The car spluttered to life and the man yanked the steering wheel back and forth. The tires moved unencumbered, grinding on the gravel parking lot as the young man tested the steering. Juan looked at the maid, shrugged his shoulders and gave a weak smile.

"It's drivable," the woman said to Bel. "But we still need your insurance, Mister...?" Her voice trailed off and she waited expectantly.

"McMaster," Bel stumbled over his words and extended his hand. "Bel McMaster."

"McMaster?"

The woman arched her eyebrows and was silent for a moment. She looked at Bel and then at his battered pickup truck. Bel tried to read her expression. She seemed to know his name, many people in the county knew of him, of course, but she might not have expected wine royalty to drive a decrepit vehicle. Or, it might just be wishful thinking on his part, that such a lovely creature would already know his reputation. Bel pulled an insurance card from his wallet and extended it to the woman, but the man approached and grabbed it.

"Do you work across the street?" Bel asked the woman, motioning to the Jenner Inn clinging to the cliff across the highway and praying that he wasn't being obvious. "I could swing by and make sure you're okay, maybe pay your deductible?"

"That's not necessary," Juan replied, stepping in between Bel and the maid. He flicked the insurance card back to Bel and nodded for the maid to get back in the car. Bel stood transfixed as the young woman moved to the side of the car. A gust of wind caused her upswept bun to come undone and her hair fluttered behind her, shimmering in the late afternoon sun. The maid's uniform, already fitted, pressed against her body even more. Bel's heart leapt at the sight of the woman's figure in the golden light of the sun, dust swirling around her feet like a heavenly veil. She paused at the side of the car and returned his gaze.

For a moment he forgot to breathe as she looked at him with her piercing amber eyes.

Then, the car door slammed and the Toyota peeled from the parking lot, showering gravel behind it. Bel leaned against his battered truck and gazed in the direction of the departed car. Something warmed his belly and he sighed with contentment. He couldn't remember the last time he'd felt this way. He smiled as he examined the dent in the front of the truck. It wasn't that bad, really. He stopped smiling when he looked at a text from his mother reminding him of their lunch tomorrow.

3. MARIA

The old Toyota rattled in the gusts of wind which howled inside the drafty car. Maria exhaled shakily and checked the passenger window to make sure it was rolled up. Her hands trembled but she managed to pull her hair back in a bun and brush the dust from her shoes. She closed her eyes and tried to calm her thoughts. She should have been filled with anticipation—tomorrow was her day off and Juan was taking her to Santa Rosa for her weekly visit with her son who stayed with her cousin Gabby. She'd have twenty-four hours to fuss over her three-year-old, take him to the playground, maybe spoil him with a treat if the lady with the empanadas cart was on her usual street corner. But not even thoughts of rambunctious Alarico and his mop of dark curls could bring a smile. She was unnerved. There was the biting pain of seeing her husband's body, of course. And now, Bel McMaster. The chances of meeting the winemaker weren't exactly zero—he had vineyards directly across from the inn where she and Juan worked after all—but it was an unsettling coincidence.

"Bel McMaster," Juan said as if reading her thoughts.

She nodded but said nothing, still incredulous and shaken.

"He can't find out who you are," Juan continued. "Who knows what he'd do?"

She stared out of the window and watched the golden coastal hills zip by.

She was well aware of the danger if the famous winemaker discovered her identity. She'd be turned over to ICE, or worse.

"But man, he couldn't stop looking at you!" Juan glanced across the seat at her.

"Juan, please stop," she said sharply. She held up her hand and silenced him. She was used to it, the reaction of men and even women to her beauty—sensuality actually. She had been renowned in the barrio and all of the tempestuous jóvenes had vied for her attention. Now by chance, she'd attracted the attention of the one man she never wanted to encounter.

"He thought we were married," Juan continued, oblivious to Maria's protest. "And I'm pretty sure he was trying to figure out how to get around that."

Maria frowned. Bel McMaster was more handsome than she'd expected. His face was worn, but his jaw was firm, his sandy hair was rumpled in an adorable way, and his emerald eyes were sharp. He was the first man she'd looked twice at since leaving Guatemala.

"Maybe someday you'll get married," she said quietly, changing the subject. "That's why you came to this country, after all."

"You haven't told me about the trip to the morgue in San Francisco," Juan said, ignoring Maria's comment. "Did you get Carlos's belongings?"

"His crucifix and an old metal card." Maria shuddered, still shaken by the sight of her dead husband on the cold tray in the basement morgue of the San Francisco police headquarters. She intentionally didn't mention the scrawled note from Carlos that she'd managed to carefully peel from the metal orange card. The mere mention of Cadejo would send Juan to a dark place. She wasn't ready for that conversation. Not yet

"And the police? Did they have clues?"

She shook her head. "They wanted to know why Carlos was coming to San Francisco. I told them I didn't know."

"What kind of card?"

"This," she said and held the orange metal card, taking care to keep it from the sun's rays.

Juan furrowed his brow. "An old payment card?"

"Maybe," Maria shrugged. "It does something odd when I hold it in the sunlight."

"Odd?"

"It glows, sends out light."

"Why?" Juan asked.

Maria shook her head and tucked the card back in her pocket. "I don't know."

"It's strange that the police didn't tell you anything else about Carlos. Where he found the gun? Why he was on the Embarcadero?" Juan let the questions hang.

Maria exhaled. She didn't know. But it wasn't Carlos who dominated her thoughts. She touched the crucifix around her neck and said a prayer, begging the saints to keep the gangster Cadejo from finding her.

* * *

Maria and her cousin Gabby threaded their way through the grocery aisle while Alarico and Gabby's daughter Ana danced up ahead. Maria couldn't help but smile as the two three-year olds darted around the stacks of fresh produce, their laughter blending in with the murmur of busy shoppers. Maria and Juan had picked up Gabby and her daughter from their bungalow for the weekly grocery shopping excursion to Lola's Market in Santa Rosa. The store was filled with late-afternoon shoppers like her and her cousin. Parents, hotel maids, food-truck cooks—worn at the end of the day and ready to be home with family.

Maria picked up a sweet pepper and rolled it absently in her hand. Gabby was going to make a stew of chicken and zucchini tonight and normally the thought would have warmed Maria. But instead, she couldn't shake a chill. She exhaled and put the pepper into the basket hanging from her arm.

"Juan told me you didn't get many of Carlos's belongings," Gabby said, reaching in front of Maria to place a jar of cumin into the basket. "I told you there wouldn't be much." Of course, Juan had already told Gabby, probably when Maria was getting Alarico's coat from the bedroom. Maria, Gabby and Juan told each other everything. No secrets. Maria sighed. Until now.

"You know I had to see Carlos's body," Maria said softly. She'd had no contact with her husband for three years since fleeing Guatemala. There were rumors, of course, but she had to see what he'd become.

She brushed her hand over a display of avocados. She'd met Carlos in a store like this in her barrio. They both worked there, the store in Guatemala City belonged to Carlos's father, Eduardo. Carlos worked at the meat counter and Maria in the checkout lanes. She would find excuses to talk to Carlos during her breaks, ask his opinion about a cut of beef for pepián or how to season pork shoulder. His smile was infectious and she loved the way his white shirt clung to his finely muscled back. How young they'd been. How in love.

"It was foolish to go to San Francisco," Gabby continued, her voice quavered. "You could have been detained by ICE." She grimaced and grabbed Maria's forearm. "Is it true what they said? Had Carlos been carved? Símbolos de pandillas?" She spat the words softly and then kissed the back of her thumb.

Maria gripped the handle of the grocery basket. Her eyes welled. "Yes," she nodded. "He was carved. His forehead and his chest. Barrio 18."

Gabby shook her head slowly. "Cadejo marks his torros. That can only mean one thing." She looked directly at Maria. "Carlos became one of them."

Maria reached for the crucifix around her neck. "He must have been forced into the gang," she whispered. She didn't say what was really on her mind. Yes, Carlos had been conscripted by the gangster Cadejo. That much seemed obvious. But Carlos would have gone to his grave protecting Maria's secret. The question ricocheted, eating away at her. How did Cadejo discover her secret?

Her heart thudded. She didn't know the answer and the uncertainty gnawed at her. Even worse, she couldn't tell Gabby and Juan. If she told Gabby the words that Carlos scrawled on the wrapper just before he died on San Francisco's Embarcadero, her cousin would explode. Tell Maria she had to run. It was the last thing Maria wanted. She would do anything to keep the life she'd made for her and Alarico.

"No one knows why Carlos was in San Francisco?" Gabby asked, her brow creasing.

Maria shook her head and cringed at her lie of omission. The words continued to echo. *Cadejo sabe.*

Gabby tucked a strand of hair behind Maria's ear. "It's not your fault," she said quietly. "No one blames you for leaving Guatemala the way you did." Maria nodded and looked at her son playing with his cousin Ana near the bright piles of oranges and zapote. "And praise the saints, Juan is only alive because of you," Gabby continued and pulled her into a hug.

Maria's eyes watered. Juan had been like her little brother as long as she could remember. He had been sent down to Guatemala City from his farm family in the highlands after he was caught dressing up in his sister's clothes. He was barely eight years old and to protect him from his father's vicious beatings, Juan's mother begged an old aunt to take him in. The aunt lived just upstairs from Maria and her mother's tiny apartment. Juan's country mother prayed the city would be a safer place for her son. And for a while, thank the saints, it was.

Maria wiped her eyes and said nothing. She adjusted the grocery basket and sighed. Alarico and Ana were out of sight, they'd zipped ahead and into the next grocery aisle. She turned the corner and froze. A man was bent over talking to Alarico and Ana. Her voice caught in her throat. The man was dressed completely in black. His dark curly hair was oiled back and he had a sharply defined nose. He looked up at Maria. His eyes were the color of coal and he might have been handsome but his mouth was frozen in a sneer.

Maria screamed. She dropped her grocery basket. The cheese, beef, and vegetables scattered across the floor. Her heart raced and she gasped for air. It was impossible that Cadejo had found Alarico and her. Her throat closed. She couldn't call out. She tried to ball up her fists but was paralyzed with fear.

"Maria, what is it?" Gabby was at her side and reached to pick up the spilled groceries.

Maria's heart pounded. The man stood. He wasn't Cadejo. He smiled at Maria curiously and walked away.

"What was that about?" Gabby said and looked at her, eyes full of concern.

"Nothing, I...I couldn't see the children," Maria stammered.

"Okay," Gabby said slowly and guided them to the checkout. "You are staying over tonight, right? We have a full day tomorrow." She smiled as she helped the grocery bagger. "The playground. Ice cream with the kids."

Maria tried to shake the chill from her bones. She couldn't wait to hold her little boy all through the night and wake up with him in her arms.

"And that self-defense class that I've been telling you about," Gabby continued and loaded the grocery bags into Maria's arms. "You're going with me. Tomorrow afternoon."

Maria started to protest. "I don't have the money..."

Gabby held up her hand. "I'm paying. Not up for discussion. Half the class are hotel maids like you."

Maria exhaled and consented. It was easier than arguing with her cousin, and somehow, it lessened the guilt she felt about keeping her secret. And maybe Gabby was right. Maybe it would help her feel safer, more secure. Still, her heart continued to thud as she slid in between the kids in the back seat of Juan's battered Toyota where he'd waited for them to finish their shopping.

"So many sexy men in Sonoma County," Juan said, flashing Maria and Gabby a view of a Spanish language hookup app. He smiled and started the car.

Maria's heart slowed as she looked from Gabby and Juan in the front seat to Alarico and Ana nestled beside her. It should have been perfect. Her chosen family. The safety of Sonoma County thousands of miles from Guatemala. She ran her fingers through Alarico's unruly mop of hair and he looked up at her with a silly grin and crinkled eyes—eyes the color of coal. She reached for the crucifix around her neck and silently whispered a prayer, but even as she prayed, the words rocketed through her brain. *Cadejo sabe.*

4. BEL

The Healdsburg Hotel was known for three things: a temperamental Michelin-rated chef, geothermal saunas in its world class spa, and a wine-royalty owner, Odette McMaster, Bel's mother. He watched her glide regally between tables on the hotel's outdoor terrace, silver hair pulled tightly into a bun and her long neck adorned with a muted silk scarf that fluttered in the hot, dry breeze. She stopped to greet a table of admiring diners. Bel's stomach clenched as she stared with reproach at the table's server. He knew that look well. Deep disappointment at some minor infraction.

Bel signaled his waiter and pointed to an empty wine glass. "Don't be shy," he said, his stomach tightening as his mother floated toward him.

"Belmond darling, you look well," she said, sitting down across from him and adjusting a pearl earring. "Considering everything you've been through."

He seldom wanted much from his mother, especially her pity. She slid the knife of her place setting a fraction of an inch to the left, gently patted the thick white tablecloth and smiled thinly. She narrowed her eyes as Bel raised his glass in a mock toast and then drained it. His mother pursed her lips but Bel ignored her and signaled again to the waiter.

"I'm glad you could join me here today," Odette said with a regal ring. She had grown up on a cattle farm south of Sacramento but her intonation sounded

47

as if she'd gone to an old-world finishing school in New England. "I have something I want to discuss with you."

"That's great," Bel said hastily. "I have something I want to talk with you about, too."

"I'll go first."

Bel gritted his teeth.

"I got a call from Kelly Garret," she said.

"My banker is calling you?" Bel muttered. "Unbelievable. What did she say?"

"She's my banker, too," his mother said evenly. "She told me about the loans coming due on the property and about the possible foreclosure."

Bel straightened, feeling his face flush. God help him if his wife found out. "She shouldn't have. You gave me full control of the estate years ago, and that includes financial decisions."

Odette's eyes narrowed. "The financial well-being of McMaster Vineyards is my business so consider me involved. It's dependent on one thing and one thing only, Belmond. Our reputation. It's the most important thing we have as wine-makers but it's suffering. And you must do something about it now."

Bel cleared his throat. "I'm actually glad you brought that up, Mother. That's exactly what I wanted to talk about." He took a long sip from his wine glass and set it softly on the table. His stomach clenched again as he looked across the table at her. "The French Wine Ministers are in town," Bel said.

"Yes, I know." His mother tapped her bony finger on the table. Of course she knew. Nothing happened in Healdsburg without the knowledge of Odette McMaster. She'd known Cedric Tari, who led the French Wine Ministers, since before he was born.

"Then I assume you know that they're resurrecting the Paris Wine Competition."

"Yes, there hasn't been a true competition since your father won a half century ago," Odette said slowly. Bel sensed apprehension.

48

"Exactly," Bel said and took another swig of wine. He motioned again to the waiter to fill his glass. "And this time, there will be a new McMaster in the competition."

Odette shook her head. "And who might that be?"

Bel drew in a breath before he spoke. "Me. I want to enter. But I don't just want to enter, I want to win."

Bel watched his mother again tap her long index finger on the white table-cloth. She was quiet for a moment and then exhaled. "Oh, my dear," she said finally.

"What? McMasters win."

"Not now, my darling."

"Not now?" Bel said, unable to quiet his voice. His mother's eyes narrowed and she leaned forward.

"You will not raise your voice to me," she said. "Certainly not here."

Bel's stomach wouldn't stop. It clenched even tighter. He didn't know why his wine glass was perpetually empty. He motioned to the waiter and leaned forward toward his mother. "Yes. Here. I need your help. The competition is by invitation only. I need to get an invitation, and I thought you could, you know…" Bel paused, trying not to look desperate.

Odette tightened her jaw. "No, I don't know."

"Ask the French Wine Ministers to get me an invitation. To get McMaster Vineyards an invitation."

Odette shook her head. "Belmond Michael McMaster." She sat back in her chair with crossed arms and gazed absently toward the modern hotel, its folding lobby doors retracted wide open on the hot, October afternoon. "Winning that competition was the best thing that ever happened to us," she said, her voice faraway. "Overnight McMaster Vineyards was a sensation. We couldn't bottle the wine fast enough. Even the White House, for heaven's sake, put in an order."

"Mother, please stop," Bel held up his hand. The stories of his father's success after winning the competition were anything but uplifting for Bel. The anecdotes had been told again and again until they were etched on his brain. He ran his finger around the rim of his wine glass and avoided his mother's gaze.

"Your father delivered those cases personally to Washington."

"I know, Mother." He continued to run his finger on the rim of the glass until it emanated a low tone.

Odette reached across the table and batted her son's hand away from the glass. "You're deluding yourself," she snapped. "You haven't produced a decent pinot in five years, and," she held up her hand to silence his protestation. "You can't blame it on the climate."

Bel looked away from her icy gaze. He knew what she was thinking. What she thought of him. He could tell by the look on her face—a mixture of pity and disgust. Just like the look on his wife's face. And the look on the banker's face. Odette pushed her chair back and stood. "When I said you need to fix the reputation of McMaster Vineyards, I didn't mean make a fool of yourself in the process," she said.

Bel watched vacantly as she floated away, breezily greeting guests on the afternoon terrace. He tapped his wine glass with desperation as the waiter approached. "Just leave the bottle this time," he glowered.

5. MARIA

Maria inhaled nervously as the woman in front of her somersaulted and flopped to the ground, landing on her back with a thud. The group of women around her gasped.

"Okay ladies, did you see what I did?" The self-defense instructor stepped forward on the gym mat, lit by a shaft of weak late afternoon light that streamed in through the dirty storefront window. Maria nodded unsurely. The instructor, Lila, was tiny and moved with the agility of a gymnast. "If your attacker comes at you from behind, you have to use all parts of your body. Elbow, hip, and shoulder," Lila continued. "And the element of surprise. Keep your attacker uncertain."

Maria glanced at the faces of the other women in the class. Some, like her cousin, nodded confidently as if they, too, were ready to throw a would-be attacker to the ground. Others, like her, seemed apprehensive and mentally rehearsed Lila's lightning moves.

"She's fast," Maria whispered to her cousin. "I don't know if I can keep up."

"Of course you can," Gabby said and frowned. "I saw you on the playground with Alarico."

Maria grimaced. The playground this morning had been a hive of energy and for a few hours she'd managed to forget the dire warning of her dead husband

and dive headfirst into the joy of being with her son. But running from a playful three-year-old was a world away from fighting off an attacker.

"Get into pairs to practice," Lila called out. "And remember, you're not trying to win a martial arts competition, only to inflict enough damage on your attacker so that you can run and save yourself. There's no shame in fleeing!"

Maria positioned herself behind her cousin and threw her arm around Gabby's neck in a chokehold. Gabby tucked her chin, grabbed Maria's forearm and twisted it aside.

"You've got this," Maria exclaimed.

Gabby shrugged. "I've been coming here for a while. Lila is a good teacher." Gabby sighed and looked at her. Maria could feel her cousin's mood darkening. "I've been waiting all day for you to tell me," Gabby said. Maria could hear a note of reproach in her cousin's voice.

"Tell you what?" Maria's heart thudded. Gabby couldn't have found out about the note that Carlos had left.

"About your chance meeting with Bel McMaster." Gabby's eyes narrowed. "Why is it I have to learn these things from Juan? I feel like you're keeping secrets from me these days." Gabby moved behind Maria and squeezed her arm around Maria's neck.

Maria gulped and tucked her chin, as Lila had instructed. But she couldn't get out of Gabby's grip.

"There's nothing to tell," Maria gurgled, struggling to get free. She felt Gabby tighten her hold from behind.

"Does he know anything? You didn't tell him your real name?" Gabby asked worriedly.

Maria choked and tapped Gabby on the elbow. Her cousin released her grip and Maria gasped for air. "No, of course not," she said incredulously, massaging her neck as she turned to face her cousin. "And Mr. McMaster gave his insurance information to Juan. I won't see him again." Maria tried to keep the exasperation from her voice. Her cousin worried, but she had a right to. Gabby had loaned Maria her green card, the one Gabby received when she'd married an American, so that Maria could get the cleaning job at Jenner Inn. Everyone Maria worked with knew her as Gabby Flores. Maria and her cousin understood that anything more than a cursory ICE inquiry at the inn could unmask Maria. That would be disastrous for them both.

They were interrupted by the sound of Lila clapping her hands. "Our last exercise for the day is defending against a chokehold while you're pinned on the ground," Lila said above the din of the women practicing their releases. She pointed to Gabby. "You're my victim," she smiled and motioned for Gabby to lay on her back on the gym mat. Lila straddled Gabby and put her hands to Gabby's throat. "When your attacker is on top of you and choking you, your first move is to open your airway. How do we do that?"

"Tuck your chin," called out several of the students.

"That's right," Lila nodded. "Your next move is the two-hand release on the inside of his forearms." She motioned to Gabby who yanked unsuccessfully at Lila's arms.

"But," Lila said looking up. "I have the advantage. So Gabby's next move is to get me off of her. She will lift her hips with her legs and roll to the side."

Gabby obediently lifted her hips and tilted. Maria watched with trepidation as Lila fell in slow motion off of Gabby and to the gym mat. The instructor and Gabby made it look so easy, but Maria knew from experience it was anything but.

"One final demonstration," Lila said as she bounced to her feet. She pointed to Maria. "Gabby's cousin," Lila said and motioned her to the floor. "Your name is?"

"Um, also Gabby," Maria stammered and laid on her back on the gym mat.

"Two Gabbys in one family!" Lila smiled and straddled Maria. "Sometimes when you're pinned," Lila said loudly to the group of women who clustered around, "one of your arms might be immobile. An injury. A second attacker." Lila pointed at Gabby who knelt and put her knee on Maria's forearm, immobilizing it. "For all you maids, pay attention," Lila said. "Any time you have a group of bros at your hotel...a bachelor party, tech retreat...you could get pinned by multiple attackers. You will need these moves."

From the mat where she lay, Maria smiled weakly up at Lila. She could feel the instructor's hands closing around her throat. Her heart started to beat faster. Her vision blurred. She tried to focus on what Lila was saying and control her breathing.

"Now Gabby here can only use one arm," she heard Lila say. She tried to exhale. Lila's weight was pressing down on her. Maria fidgeted but couldn't move. She was trapped.

"Gabby, I want you to use your free hand to strike me in the throat," Lila said. Or at least, Maria thought it was Lila. She couldn't think. Her breathing was rapid, shallow. It wasn't Lila on top of her. It was him.

"No, please," she whispered. "Please, stop."

But he wouldn't. She gasped for air.

"Gabby?" she heard a woman's voice. Distant.

He was thrusting faster. Harder. His hands tightened around her neck. It was Cadejo. She panicked. Couldn't breathe. She could hear his voice in her ear. Guttural. Low. "I knew you could come to me someday, Maria," he said.

She was choking. Her arm was pinned. She couldn't move.

"I'll make you mine, Maria." His voice filled her brain. "You'll never leave me."

She was losing consciousness. Had to make this stop. She screamed. "GET OFF ME!" She cried out to the saints. "MAKE HIM STOP!" She was sobbing.

She could feel someone raising her into a sitting position. It was quiet. Still. She gulped and looked around at the circle of women staring down at her.

Gabby pulled her to her feet and smothered her in a bear hug.

"It's okay, honey," she heard Lila say from behind her. "He can't hurt you anymore. He's not here."

Maria exhaled shakily, stepped back from Gabby and looked around the room at the wide-eyed women. Some stared at her with shock. Others nodded with quiet understanding. Maria reached for the crucifix around her neck and wiped a tear from her cheek. She prayed that Lila was right. That he couldn't hurt her any more. But still, her husband's words echoed. *Cadejo sabe.*

6. BEL

Bel followed a young woman down a narrow, almost claustrophobic hallway. He'd expected his daughter to answer the front door of her San Francisco apartment and was surprised when she didn't. A different young woman wearing a headset and holding an e-tablet and makeup brush yanked open the door instead.

"We need to move," the young woman said breathlessly, urging Bel. "Your daughter's live vodcast starts in two minutes." She flicked a button on her headset. "It's Nadine's dad," the woman said, "I'm bringing him back now." She glanced back at him with curious eyes. "I don't know, he didn't say," she whispered into her mic.

The narrow hallway from his daughter's apartment opened into a large brightly-lit broadcast studio. Bel stopped in his tracks. His jaw dropped. Cameras and lights hung from the ceiling. Massive video screens lined one wall in front of which were stools comprising the broadcast set. He knew that his daughter had a studio, but he hadn't expected something so professional. So grownup.

"This is all for Nadine's show?" he asked the woman who moved hurriedly into the studio.

The woman turned, her face puzzled. "Yes, this is Nadine's studio."

A male voice boomed through the studio. "Places people. One minute to stream."

"She live-streams daily to her followers," the woman continued, still looking at Bel curiously. "*Uncoding Technology.* You must have heard of it?"

Of course, he'd heard of it, from his wife. But he'd never seen his daughter's show. He reddened.

"Over there," the woman pointed to a tiny control booth in the corner of the studio. "You can sit behind Nigel and watch."

The woman darted over to the broadcast set where his daughter paced, and dusted powder on Nadine's cheekbones and chin. His daughter looked different than the last time he'd seen her, her hair was shorter and dyed green. She had more piercings up the sides of her ears than he remembered, if that were possible, and a colorful tattoo peaked above the collar of her shirt. Maybe it was new. Bel smiled weakly and waved. She rolled her eyes and turned from him.

"I need everyone off the floor now," the male voice boomed through the studio again. "Corissa, get on the social feeds." The woman dusting powder on his daughter's face held up her palm. The voice continued. "Nadine's dad, get in the control booth."

Bel glanced again at Nadine who was now engrossed in her e-tablet. She didn't look up as he walked to the control booth. "You must be Nigel," he said, sliding into a swivel chair.

Nigel, even more heavily pierced than his daughter, didn't look at him but flicked a series of sliders and hologram screens. "Uh huh," Nigel grunted.

Bel looked curiously through the soundproof glass and into the studio. Except for his daughter and Corissa, the studio was empty. "Who is Nadine interviewing?"

Nigel glanced over his shoulder and frowned. "Mohan Mallick."

Bel rubbed his forehead. The name was familiar but he couldn't place it.

"Who is he?"

Nigel spun, incredulous. "The founder of Kavali Technology!"

Bel's stomach dropped as the pieces slowly clicked together. Nadine's interview was related to the investigation his wife mentioned. His daughter's break in the case. He reached inside his jacket where he'd stowed a flask of wine but he didn't pull it out.

"Where is Mr. Mallick?" Bel said uncomfortably and sat forward in his chair. His daughter and Corissa were the only two people in the studio.

"'Hologram. Disk on the stool, courtesy of Kavali Technology," Nigel said curtly. "You'll see him in a few seconds." Nigel moved a slider and the broadcast cameras hanging from the ceiling winked on.

Corissa took one last look at Nadine's face and dashed toward the control booth. As she did, Bel saw a beam of light burst from the puck on the stool next to Nadine. The light fluttered and then formed the shape of a man. Mohan Mallick. The tech titan's hologram was full-sized, seated on the stool next to Nadine. Mohan was slim and fit, almost ridiculously so. His hair was full—bordering on bushy—and the color of the midnight sky. He was movie-star handsome with eyes the color of dark chocolate and stubble on his square jaw that was expertly trimmed. Bel disliked him instantly.

"My guest today needs no introduction," Nadine's voice echoed through the control room. "He is the founder and CEO of Kavali Technology, the world's largest biotech company. He holds thousands of patents in plant genetics and is no stranger to controversy, having raised the ire of bioethicists around the globe for his secretive work on genetically-modified organisms. Organizations such as the World Anti-Cloning Organization and Greenpeace have vehemently protested the mysterious cloning and threatened legal action. The World Anti-Cloning Organization has even reportedly infiltrated Kavali in an effort to force greater transparency."

She paused and swiveled toward the holographic image of Mohan Mallick.

"And, he's about to host a grand opening for his latest project, the world's tallest building, Kavali Tower, right here in San Francisco." She smiled at Mohan, but Bel noticed her eyes stayed narrow. "Welcome to *Uncoding Technology,*" she said.

Mohan smiled back, but there was something about Mohan's presence, even though he was a hologram, that Bel found unnerving. His appearance was almost too perfect, his skin too smooth, his teeth too white. Bel shuddered wondering if the man was even real.

"This is quite a moment in time for you," Nadine continued. "Kavali now is one of the world's most valuable technology companies..."

"The most valuable," Mohan interrupted with a tight smile.

Nadine nodded and didn't miss a beat. "The most valuable, and you're just about to unveil the world's tallest tower, one that has been steeped in secrecy."

"Our grand opening is in three days," Mohan said. He spread his arms wide. Bel watched carefully. Despite his wife's criticisms, he had an eye for detail. Mohan behaved like a preacher, messiah-like. Bel shuddered. Mohan's confidence reminded him of his father. "You'll be there, of course?" Mohan's question of his daughter sounded more like a command.

"I wouldn't miss it for the world," Nadine responded. She cocked her head to the side. Bel recognized the move. Nadine tilted her head when she was annoyed. "Mr. Mallick. You've been secretive about what's inside the tower. Some would say obsessively so. There have been no media releases, no pictures, it's been top secret..."

"Nadine, what is not a secret is the economic impact of Kavali Tower," Mohan interrupted. "I've single-handedly brought the San Francisco economy back from the brink of disaster." Mohan spread his arms wide. The man caused Bel's stomach to churn. He fingered the flask of wine inside his jacket. "Pumped billions into the city," Mohan continued. "Kavali Tower is a beacon of hope."

"That wasn't my question," Nadine accented each word. Bel could sense

Nadine's annoyance from inside the control booth. His daughter was a bossy older twin who wanted control of every situation. He could hear the exasperation in her voice. "Engineering plans submitted to the city years ago show an enormous space, almost a cavern, in the center of the building." Nadine leaned forward and her voice dropped. "What's in that cavern, Mr. Mallick?"

"Nadine, nearly every major technology of the past five decades has been birthed here in the Bay Area. The semiconductor, the internet, artificial intelligence. I am following the traditions of the geniuses before me and creating world-changing technology, right here!"

"You're not answering my questions," Nadine said sharply. "The cavern inside Kavali Tower...there are rumors of course. Plant matter and soils have been shipped in from across the world. Some of the leaked reports from inside the tower are of great indoor gardens that rival those from ancient Babylon. Others have said you've perfected the art of vertical farming. But if that were true, the scale of agriculture inside the tower would be unheard of, and again the secrecy has been..."

Mohan interrupted again. "Whatever is inside the cavern—Kavali Cavern is what you in the media have dubbed it." He smiled and Bel thought the tech titan looked pleased with himself. "What I've created inside Kavali Tower is something that will change the course of human existence."

Bel looked at the massive video screens behind his daughter and Mohan. Reactions from vodcast viewers scrolled across them. Social comments, engagement logograms, emoticons from Nadine's engagers.

"He's trending positive, unbelievable," Nigel muttered.

"Isn't that good?" Bel's brow creased.

"Nadine's sentiment is always great," Nigel said and swiped a hologram and pointed. "It's Mohan, he's controlling the conversation. Nadine needs to take it back."

Nadine smiled thinly at Mohan and leaned closer to him. "You're a genetic engineer," she said. "And when I hear a genetic engineer talking about changing the course of human existence, I have to wonder if you mean changing our genetic composition. Or the genetics of plants, animals. The world around us. Maybe even without our knowledge or permission." Nadine's smile turned to a frown. "I've heard rumors of genetic research called Project Synthetica. Top secret. What, exactly, is Project Synthetica?"

Bel thought Mohan looked uncomfortable and seemed to shift on his stool. But it could have been the hologram flickering. He briefly thought about his own genetics background. He'd been a promising student at UC Davis in his day, and he had to admit, tense as the interview was, he was intrigued by Mohan. New farming techniques. Plant genetics. It's what he should have pioneered himself. But his father Michael McMaster didn't want a scientist for a son. He wanted a real vintner. Bel sighed and again fingered the flask of wine in his coat.

"You're a bright young lady," Mohan replied. "You know that the genetics of plants and animals is constantly changing. All I do is speed up the desired changes, those that give us an advantage. Project Synthetica, as you already noted, is confidential."

"Mr. Mallick," Nadine said to Mohan, her jaw tight. "You do seem to have trouble answering my questions." Bel could tell his daughter was perturbed. "But let me ask a different one," she said and leaned back. "Even with all the secrecy. Even with all of the security. Something was stolen." Nadine said those three words slowly with a pause between each. She reach up and twisted a piercing. She did that when she was emotional.

"Here we go," Nigel said. He turned and grimaced at Bel. "The little prick thinks he controls all the media, but he doesn't control Nadine McMaster! He's going to be surprised!"

Bel flinched, but it wasn't with pride. It was with dread. He reached inside his coat and this time quietly pulled out the wine flask and took a healthy swig.

"A theft from Kavali that you've covered up." Nadine continued.

"No chance," Mohan responded.

Bel watched his daughter. She was clearly agitated now.

"Something was stolen," Nadine said. Her voice quivered.

"There has been no breach. Kavali has the world's tightest cybersecurity."

Nadine pointed a finger at Mohan. "I said stolen, not breached." She shook her finger like she was scolding the tech titan. Her voice increased in pitch. Bel drank again from the flask but the liquid did little to calm his convulsing stomach. "It wasn't a digital theft." Nadine exhaled and continued pointing at the tech titan. "A gun. A gun was stolen from Kavali by an undocumented immigrant named Carlos Garcia. I have proof, an eyewitness account. And that makes you responsible for my brother's…"

Her voice caught and she tried to catch her breath. The massive screens behind her flickered. The scrolling comments and logograms disappeared and then reappeared as if nothing had happened.

"Shit," Nigel said under his breath. The young man desperately flicked at a holographic slider. Bel looked at Nigel but said nothing.

In the broadcast studio, Mohan shook his head. "Oh Nadine," he said. "Guilt is such a troubling thing. It obscures the truth. But do you know what the truth is?" The massive video screens behind the broadcast set again flickered and this time went completely dark. Nadine didn't seem to notice and kept her attention on Mohan Mallick.

"Son of a bitch," Nigel exclaimed. He punched at the control panel and swiped at sliders in mid-air, muttering obscenities to himself.

"What's going on?" Bel asked.

"We're getting jacked."

"What?"

"Someone is taking control of my video feed. I don't have control of the broadcast!" Nigel pounded on the control panel and then he looked up slowly. Out in the studio, the massive video screens had just flickered back to life.

"Bloody 'ell," Nigel stood slowly. A video started to play behind Nadine and Mohan.

"That's Nadine," Bel said, his jaw slack. "That video, it's Nadine, from…" He let the words hang and didn't finish the sentence.

"Hey my chum chums," Nadine said in what appeared to be a selfie video that now broadcast on the massive screen at the back of the set. She seemed happy. In the video, the sky was blue above and her hair was longer and reddish, the way Bel remembered it. There was something familiar about the setting. "It's my birthday and you all know what I do on my special day!"

Bel's stomach turned. It couldn't be. His daughter must have been selfie casting on her most recent birthday—the twins birthday. Ned's birthday. Bel looked desperately out to the studio where Nadine's face drained and she spun to the screens behind her. "Is this really broadcasting right now?" Bel asked, turning to Nigel.

"Fuck," Nigel grunted. "Yes, this is fucking live-streaming to the world."

In the studio, Nadine snapped from her daze. She pivoted to face the control booth. "Turn it off," she screamed at Nigel.

Nigel swiped frantically at holographic sliders. "I can't," he said desperately into his headset. "Someone has control of the broadcast."

The video on the huge screens continued. "I celebrate my birthday with my twin! My brother, Neddy." Nadine was giddy in the video. She jumped up and down like a child and then pulled her twin brother into the frame.

Bel's heart plummeted as he watched, unable to tear his eyes from his daughter's selfie video. The sunlight played off of his son's hair which floated lightly in the breeze. Ned smiled shyly and punched his sister in the arm.

In the studio, Nadine shrieked. "Stop!" She screamed at Mohan who sat silently on his stool. "You son of a bitch! I know it's you." Then she ran frantically toward the control booth and pounded on the sound proof glass. "Shut it down!"

The rogue live stream to Nadine's viewing audience continued. In the old selfie video, Nadine and Ned walked, chatting with each other and mugging for Nadine's live selfie-cast viewers. The light was golden as the sun started to set. The twins strolled on the Embarcadero, laughing and carefree. They passed a man seated on a bench. The man had dark hair that partially covered a vicious gang carving on his forehead and he rummaged in a bag.

"Please god, no." Bel whispered to himself. He drained the rest of the flask and let it clatter to the floor. Nigel was too preoccupied with the control panel to notice. In the studio Nadine had started to wail. "Turn it OFF!" she begged.

On the video screens, Ned and Nadine stopped and stared into Nadine's camera. Nadine said something indistinguishable and the twins laughed. Then suddenly, Ned jerked and stumbled into his sister. They both looked in shock at a crimson stain that seeped across his UC Davis sweatshirt. Ned reached out to his sister, grabbed for her shoulder and then crumpled to the ground. Nadine must have dropped her phone but it kept broadcasting from a frantic angle on the gravel path.

Nadine's screams filled the studio. Bel couldn't tell if the screams came from the video or from his daughter now curled in a ball on the floor outside of the control booth. "Help me," she shrieked in the video. "He's been shot. My brother. Oh god, Ned."

Bel stood and stumbled to the control room door. He jerked it open. Nadine sobbed uncontrollably. Mohan Mallick's hologram mysteriously disappeared. Bel turned his eyes from the massive video screens, desperately searching for the hallway back to his daughter's apartment. If there was one thing he didn't need to see again, it was his son's dead body.

* * *

Bel stared out of the two-story windows in Nadine's living room. As the mid-autumn sun drifted down toward the horizon, its rays bounced off the mirrored downtown buildings and illuminated the room with a golden glow that didn't match Bel's dark mood. One building dwarfed them all, a green glass and steel structure so tall that it seemed to pierce the sky. Kavali Tower. The building stood out not just for its size, but also for its gothic ornate glass work that shimmered against the dusky sky. The lights in Kavali Tower fluttered on and the building glimmered ominously. Bel shook his head at the sight. The lair of Mohan Mallick. He shrugged and looked away.

He moved around Nadine's living room, opening cabinets and drawers in search of a bottle of wine—or any alcohol to drink. But he found none. He wanted something to dull the hard ache in his gut.

He closed his eyes and tried not to think about his son. Ned's last carefree minutes on the Embarcadero with his sister. Bel needed something distracting, pleasant. The maid. He sighed at the thought. He didn't even know her name but he kept his eyes closed and smiled as he remembered her emerging from the dust cloud in the parking lot. She'd been ethereal. He sighed and opened his eyes. It was crazy, but he wanted to see her again. He would have to track her down, but that wouldn't be hard. There was a good chance she worked across the street from the Quick Mart at the Jenner Inn. Angry footsteps interrupted his thoughts.

"I got played." Nadine marched into the room. Her face was puffy and lined with faint tracks of mascara. There was a catch in her voice and she paced. "Mohan Mallick fucking played me."

Bel cleared his throat. "What happened?" he asked hollowly.

Nadine twisted a piercing in her ear. "The hologram disk from Kavali," she said angrily. "We brought it inside the firewall like idiots and it sniffed our network. Nigel destroyed that disk with a baseball bat." She managed a half smile but it disappeared from her face in an instant. She shrugged her shoulders and stared at him. "I'd ask why you're here but Mom called yesterday," Bel could sense Nadine's anger shifting from Mohan to him. "Mom said that you were finally ready to apologize. To make amends." Nadine put air quotes around the words as if she didn't believe it. "But I'm pretty sure she gave you an ultimatum. There's no way you'd come here on your own." She snorted and tugged at a piercing in her ear.

His daughter was right, of course. Maureen had forced him to come and apologize for the way he'd screamed at Nadine that night in the emergency room. *It's gone on long enough,* Maureen had shouted. But if he'd been close to apologizing when he arrived, he wasn't after seeing the video of his son's death. "I didn't know you were selfie casting," he said softly. His eyes were lifeless as he looked at his daughter.

"What? Why are you even bringing that up?"

"Because I didn't realize my son's murder had been broadcast to the world, in real time," Bel said louder, his stomach clenched. He hadn't known and suddenly he felt like he'd been intentionally left out of an entire chapter of something essential and brutal. "You didn't tell me."

Nadine looked at her father incredulously. "There was a lot going on that night, Dad. I mean, I had just held my brother as he died."

"He was my son!"

Nadine exhaled slowly and was silent. "I thought I'd scrubbed it from my social," she said quietly. "I didn't think it was important to tell you, and now Mohan found it somehow. He wanted to send me a warning. But this is just a minor setback. I have to keep going."

Bel's stomach clenched tighter. This was one of the reasons he didn't want to visit his daughter. She was on a mission to never forget the very thing he was trying to never remember. Except, it was all he could think about. The late-night call from the detective. The panicked drive from McMaster Vineyards to San Francisco General. He and his wife, alone in the car together. Nadine inconsolable and covered in Ned's blood. His son, lifeless on a cold table. He tried time and time again to shake the pictures from his head.

"Please, just let this go." Bel tried to keep the anger from his voice. The idea of apologizing to his daughter now slipped further away. "We know who did it."

Nadine's eyes widened and she stopped pacing long enough to stare at her father. "No," she whispered. "No, I absolutely cannot just let this go." She pounded a fist in her palm to accentuate the words. "We aren't being told the truth. Carlos Garcia didn't intend to shoot Ned. He didn't even pull the trigger."

"You don't know that." Bel shook his head. He could hear the argument coming and he wanted to stop it but Nadine continued.

"His shirt was caught on the gun. The detective said it was a freak accident."

"The killer was Carlos Garcia!" Bel's voice rose.

"It was an accidental discharge of a gun that belonged to Kavali and should have been secured. They're responsible. I just have to find out what else was stolen. Mohan Mallick is desperate to get it back. Then I can get the truth!"

Bel shook his head angrily. His daughter was being eaten by guilt, but even so, he couldn't bring himself to comfort her. He looked away from her and out of the window at the San Francisco skyline, now fully lit in the early evening. Every day his daughter lived and worked here in the shadow of Kavali Tower, continually blaming herself for the death of her brother. And the brutal truth was that Bel blamed her, too. But it was worse. The words that he'd screamed at her in the emergency room. Words a parent should never even think. In front of Maureen and the emergency room doctors, he'd pointed at his son's dead body and shouted in grief-stricken rage at his daughter. "I wish that was you."

7. MARIA

Maria grunted as she scrubbed the toilet of the guest room and then she leaned back on her heels. It was impossible to remove the calcified rings left in sinks and toilets by Jenner's well water, but the inn's manager, Belinda, insisted the maids scour until they broke out in a sweat. Maria stood and looked in the bathroom mirror. The dark circles under her eyes were a reflection of the broken sleep she'd had for the past few nights. She tossed and turned, the feel of hands wrapping around her throat. She shivered at the thought. A loud thump split the silence and she jumped and darted into the bedroom of the guest suite and hurried to the billowing curtains. The wind blew mightily along the craggy Pacific coast, but it was especially powerful right now and had pushed the window open and knocked over a lamp. She righted the lamp, closed the window and sighed. Diablo is what Belinda called the wind. It was a fitting word. Devil indeed.

She paced the guest suite and thought about her resolve to stay in Sonoma County. She looked again at herself in a mirror, this one large and gilt-framed hanging above a small desk. She ran her hand along the desk and thought about all of the belongings guests put here, items that she dusted slowly, wondering what it would be like to own such things. Sleek laptops, cases of wine collected from tasting trips up and down the Sonoma coast, or if the suite was occupied

68

by a bachelorette party, mounds of jewelry, most of it cheap but still unafford-able for her. She looked up into the mirror and her reflection gazed back. She wanted so much for her son, the things the hotel guests had. Not their belong-ings, but their lives of plenty, free from want and fear. That meant getting Al-arico an education, and for now, that meant no more running. She closed her eyes and wondered if she was incredibly brave or incredibly stupid. Sometimes the line between the two was nonexistent.

The door to the guest suite flew open and Maria spun, her heart racing. It was just Rosa, one of the maids. "There's someone in the lobby for you," Rosa said breathlessly. "A man." The curiosity in Rosa's eyes was evident.

Maria clutched her crucifix. "A man? Do you know who?" She tried to keep her voice steady but her heart raced. She'd been so careful for three years to cover her tracks. Everyone at the inn knew her as Gabby, except for Juan, and her secret was safe with him. There was simply no way that Cadejo could have tracked her to the inn. Still, her husband Carlos died trying to warn her about Cadejo. The Guatemalan gangster must know something about her wherea-bouts.

"No idea," Rosa shrugged. "Belinda told me to find you. The man says he has business with you."

Maria stared blankly at Rosa and her mind raced. She couldn't just walk to the lobby like a lamb to the slaughter, she had to get away from the inn. Her heart pounded and her breathing was shallow. The guest room was on the sec-ond floor but she could dart down the back stairs and out of the rear of the building before anyone noticed. Then what? Jenner Inn was on a cliff. And the highway ran in front of it. She had no car, Juan picked her up most days. And even if she hid in the storeroom Belinda would come looking.

"Gabby? He's waiting."

"What does he want?"

Rosa stared at her. "I have no idea."

Maria reached for her crucifix. She couldn't go to the lobby without knowing who was there. "Tell me what he looks like."

"He's white," Rosa said and looked at Maria curiously.

Maria exhaled shakily. Then the man wasn't Cadejo. She pulled off her cleaning gloves and followed Rosa down the hallway to the balcony that overlooked the lobby.

Light poured in from a row of salt-stained windows that overlooked a small grassy courtyard. Worn wicker furniture was scattered about the space and a chandelier shaped like a ship's wheel hung from a timbered ceiling that peaked two stories above.

Voices wafted up from the lobby. Maria gripped the railing of the balcony tightly and forced herself to look down. Bel McMaster stood there talking with Belinda at the reception counter. He must have heard her enter because he turned to look up. She reached for the crucifix around her neck, wondering why the famous winemaker was there to see her? If there was a problem with the car insurance, he should have asked for Juan. As she walked down the circular staircase she could feel three sets of eyes on her. Rosa's curious stare. Belinda's protective look. And Bel McMaster's gaze seemed to be, could it be, desire? She knew the look—she'd seen it in hundreds of men—but it was almost impossible to believe that he'd come back to the inn just to see her. She took the stairs slowly as she wound down to the lobby, her mind racing.

"Mr. McMaster," she said when she reached the lobby floor. "We already have your insurance."

He reddened. "Call me Bel, please," he stammered. "Belinda here tells me your name is Gabby."

Maria sucked in her breath wondering how he'd described her to the inn manager.

"I just wanted to make sure you were okay after the accident," he continued.

Maria's suspicion was confirmed, the look in Bel's eyes was indeed desire.

Just over Bel's shoulder she could see Belinda's eyes narrow. The manager also understood the reason for Bel's visit and she crossed her arms. Maria glanced up where Rosa still stood on the balcony. Rosa had no discretion and all of the maids would hear about this little scene as soon as the winemaker left the lobby.

"We are fine," Maria said. "You didn't have to come." She said the words loudly, as much for Belinda and Rosa's benefit as for Bel's.

"Well," Bel said slowly. "I could text you money, for the inconvenience. It's the least I can do."

Behind Bel, Belinda now drummed her fingers on the receptionist counter.

"That's kind," Maria said, uncertain of how to respond. She shifted uncomfortably and wished to god that Rosa and Belinda would leave the lobby. She could hear the needling of the other maids now. Gabby the celebrity, a famous white man giving you money. If only they knew the truth.

"That requires a phone number," Bel prodded. "Of either you or your husband."

"Oh," Maria gasped and for one horrible second she thought that Bel meant Carlos. But she exhaled as she realized he mistakenly thought Juan was her husband. Before she could stop herself she said, "He's not my husband." As if on cue, Bel's face lit up and she could have kicked herself. She should have lied, said that Juan was her husband. She shuddered at the thought of telling him the truth: her husband was Carlos Garcia, the man who had shot and killed his son. She struggled to slow her heart.

"He's your boyfriend?" Bel pressed.

She heard Belinda harrumph and saw the manager shake her head.

"He is just a friend, Mister..."

"Bel, please."

"Bel, but we are fine. You do not need to worry about us. Juan can probably fix the car himself. He is the handyman here."

They were both silent. The sunlight streaming into the lobby was painfully bright and she could see tiny particles floating through the air and settling on the furniture. Belinda would probably summon her to dust the lobby later in the day and possibly mop the floor to clean the mud left by the winemaker's boots. Her heart continued to thud, but she realized that it wasn't just her fear of being unmasked by Bel. Worse, he was drawn to him. She wanted to reach out and touch his craggy face and more. The saints would surely condemn her for thinking this way.

"That's great, Bel said. "Well, then, I guess..." His voice trailed off, and then suddenly he blurted. "Do you like wine? I own the vineyards across the highway. Maybe you'd like to see them? We could go for a walk on the hillside. The view of the ocean is amazing from up there."

Maria's heart stopped. So, there it was, Bel McMaster had just put his cards on the table. Offering money for the collision had been a pretense to see her again and now everyone in the lobby knew for certain.

Over Bel's shoulder, Belinda cleared her throat and shook her head vehemently.

"I don't think that's a good idea," Maria stammered.

Bel's face seemed frozen but he smiled sadly. "Of course," he said simply and then turned and walked from the lobby.

Maria heard Rosa scamper away through the second-floor hallway. She was certain that the maid would waste no time getting to the break room. Even though Maria had rebuffed the winemaker, speculation would fly. Maria grimaced thinking of the gossip if the maids knew the awfulness of the actual connection between her and Bel McMaster.

"Gabby, come here," Belinda's voice was sharp and she crossed her arms. The manager's frazzled hair bobbed as she shook her head. Belinda watched out for the maids, treating them as if they were her brood. She hadn't asked too many questions when Maria applied at the inn, barely raising an eyebrow at the clear discrepancy between Maria's appearance and Gabby's picture on the green card. "Honey," Belinda's voice was firm. "You're a smart girl. You know what he wants. Make sure you stay away from him."

A bang sounded behind her and she jumped. The screen door to the lobby thumped, unlatched, against the doorframe in the gusting wind.

"Fucking Diablo wind," Belinda muttered and hurried to fasten the screen door. "You be careful, Gabby," she called over her shoulder. "If you see that man again, you're playing with fire."

8. BEL

Bel stood in the wainscotted hallway of the Queen Anne, gazing absently at the gallery of decades old family photos that adorned the walls. In one photo, Bel's parents, Michael and Odette, stood proudly in a field of red and orange pinot vines in early autumn. Michael held a small first place medallion from the Paris Wine Competition, the award that rocked the industry. Bel stared at the picture. His father exhibited a grand passion, certainly, but more than that, he exuded confidence. Bel desperately wanted that for himself. He knew if he could truly believe in his own abilities he might have a peace that had eluded him his entire life.

"You're back."

Bel jumped at the sound of his wife's voice. Maureen had materialized in the hallway. "Come here," she said sharply and nodded to the library.

Bel felt like a student summoned to the principal's office as he followed her into the formal library where Maureen leaned against a large dark-stained desk that absorbed the soft afternoon light spilling in through the open French doors. Sheer linen curtains fluttered in the pale breeze, creating an ethereal aura.

"Your visit with Nadine was eventful," Maureen said, the disgust evident in her voice as she drew out the last word. "I wouldn't exactly say you addressed your issues." She crossed her arms. "But the fact that you've regressed to a boy-man isn't what I want to talk about," she said with an irritating clip to her voice. "I've made a decision about the future of McMaster Vineyards."

"*You've* made a decision?" he asked incredulously. Did she know about the foreclosure? The banker said she wasn't going to tell Maureen, and god knows his mother wouldn't. Odette and Maureen disliked each other intensely. It must have been someone else. Healdsburg was a tiny town. People talked.

Maureen's eyes narrowed. "Have you been drinking?" she accused. She wore a narrow skirt and light sweater that clung to her thin figure. Maureen had strong features—a prominent nose and high cheekbones. Her features had been attractive to Bel when they were younger, but now he barely noticed what she looked like.

"You've been drinking, Bel. Again."

Bel didn't bother to correct her. He couldn't stand it when she assumed he was drunk before noon, especially when she was right.

"The estate is faltering," she said, uncrossing her arms and walking around the desk. "So I'm introducing a new crop. We're going to start growing cannabis. McMaster Vineyards new business will be making and selling cannabis products."

Bel's jaw went slack. He couldn't have heard her correctly. "Are you out of your mind?" he spluttered. "You can't make a decent living as a pot grower. You grew up in Sonoma County. You know what the growers are like. Worn down people with beaten up trucks. Grimy hair, walking around with big wads of cash. What kind of life is that?"

"It's different now, and you know it," Maureen said firmly. "First of all, it's legal. Second, the Healdsburg Bank does business with cannabis growers. No one is walking around with big wads of cash."

"But, but…" Bel stammered as he thought of his objections. The very idea of growing cannabis at McMaster Vineyards was outrageous, but at least she hadn't mentioned the foreclosure. A small miracle.

"And there's more," Maureen continued. "Since you can't be bothered to use your genetics training, I've hired a genetic researcher. One who works with cannabis. He's created cannabis plants that are sturdy and can withstand the heat. He's going to apply his research to our vineyards and splice cannabis DNA into the grape vines to make them less susceptible to the drought and rot."

Maureen stood stiffly. Her jaw was as rigid as Bel's was slack. The half-bottle of wine that Bel had just downed dulled his senses, but deep down, he could feel a boil. The irony of growing cannabis so soon after Ned's death was cruel and heartless. Then there was the reputation of McMaster Vineyards. His wife meant to sell cannabis products from McMaster Vineyards. The thought was unimaginable. Screw it, maybe it would be better if the bank foreclosed.

"No," Bel said and slapped his hand down on the desk next to Maureen. "We are not growing pot, we are not selling pot, and we definitely are NOT mixing plant genes. Those vines were planted by my father. He created the world's most unique pinot clones. We aren't fucking with that!"

Maureen shook her head. "For god's sake, Bel," she exclaimed. "Your devotion to your father's outdated ways is pathetic. We're the only vineyard in the valley not experimenting or replanting. The fields are wilting and you—you're a trained geneticist arguing about the purity of a gene? You haven't been in your lab in months!"

"Enough!" Bel shouted and pounded his fist on the desk and then turned to leave. "I've had enough of this. No crazy genes, no replanting, and absolutely no pot."

"Bel, stop," his wife commanded.

It drove Bel crazy when she used that tone of voice. Transactional. Their relationship had become a series of transactions that Maureen dictated. "It's because you can't be trusted to make a sober decision after noon," she'd say, giving him that look. God, he hated her judgment. If only it weren't so accurate. And everything from her appearance to the way she modulated her voice was in order to patronize him. And it worked. He felt like a scolded boy.

Bel stopped at the library door. "What?" he hissed.

Maureen's heels clicked on the stone floor as she moved from the desk to one of the overstuffed library chairs. "I hear you've been trying to get an invitation from the French Wine Ministers to enter the Paris wine competition," her voice was thin.

Goddamn this town. He had told almost no one. He cleared his throat. "I don't know what you're talking about," he said, trying to keep his voice steady.

"Ahh," Maureen sighed.

"Ahh," Bel shot back, wondering at what point in a relationship the unsaid becomes more meaningful than the said. The sighs and the pauses grow even more searing than the words themselves.

"So, you're not thinking of entering the competition?" his wife continued. She didn't wait for an answer. "I want to make something very clear," she said, walking to the side of another of the library chairs. Bel shifted so he could keep his back to her and stared into the wainscoted hallway. "The days of McMaster Vineyards as a premium label are done, you know that. Bel, you're going to have to accept my plan. We can grow cannabis and at the same time still make decent wine, and there's no shame in selling it at a lower price point, reaching new audiences..."

"Never!" Bel shouted and smacked his hand on the doorframe. "I will not let you turn McMaster Vineyards into a, a low-cost joke like, like..." Bel paused and glanced down the hallway. God, he hated this argument with Maureen. It was the same every time.

"Like what?" Maureen said, her voice turning steely. "Like what, Bel?"

Bel hung his head and sighed.

"Like my family vineyard, right?" she continued. "Again, with my family. Good god Bel, here we go again. Let me remind you that when your father was out winning awards, my father was building a business that brought wine to the masses and made millions."

This argument was unwinnable for either of them. Maureen would accuse Bel of snobbery and Bel would demean Maureen's family's box-wine business as common. Theirs could have been a marriage that united two ends of the wine spectrum in a fairytale union, the Baxter family wealth reigniting the McMaster fine tradition, but instead it had devolved into a series of raging disputes. Bel wondered if their marriage ever had a chance.

"You haven't produced a decent pinot in years," Maureen snapped. "You'd never win. You will embarrass yourself if you enter that competition."

He could feel her eyes boring into his back. First his mother, now his wife. Carbon copies. Thank god they hated each other. United they'd be intolerable. A burning flush crept up Bel's neck.

"You don't know what you're talking about," Bel said with all the backbone he could muster before he lurched from the library.

"For once, I hope you're right," she called after him.

* * *

Bel leaned on the railing of the porch that wrapped around the Queen Anne and looked up at the enormous redwood that stood steadfastly to the south of the house. It murmured in the afternoon breeze, something unintelligible. He shook his head as he thought about the madness with Maureen. Cannabis? That was insane. He exhaled and looked toward the top of the massive redwood. He loved the tree, it was almost sage-like. It's a wonder you like wine at all, the tree seemed to murmur in the breeze. The tree, of course, witnessed it. The first time Bel was viciously beaten by his father in front of a crowd.

It had been a gusty evening in early October decades ago. The Diablo wind had sprung up as Bel's father, Michael, beckoned his field crew and wine makers to the porch for a celebration of mid harvest. It was the month after the Paris competition upset and Michael was riding high. He was intense, insisting everyone have a good time. He'd popped the cork on bottles of McMaster Vine-yards first try at champagne and then opened bottle after bottle of the award-winning pinot.

Bel was seven years old and stood to the side of the porch, a goofy grin on his boyish face, taking in the excitement. His parents were on the verge of something enormous, and even as a young boy he could sense it. The evening crackled with excitement and anticipation. McMaster Vineyards was going to be big. His father was going to be famous.

He felt the clap of a hand on his shoulder. "Son," his father had slurred. "It's time you learned to love wine. You're a McMaster!" A bottle was shoved in his hand and he drank as mightily as a young boy could. Before he could stop himself, he'd curled his lip and spit the wine out. It was sour and burned his throat. The puddle of wine quivered on the porch floor and Bel looked up slowly at his father, towering above him.

"Not exactly like the old man!" someone called out and the field hands tit-tered nervously. The first crack across his face had been a shock. He was too stunned to cry out. The second and third blows hurt, but the real pain came later in the beating when his brain understood what was happening. His mother, Odette, slipped noiselessly from the porch and the field crew and wine makers slinked away in drunken embarrassment or denial.

Bel closed his eyes and tried to push the memory of that horrid night from his mind. It had been just the start. The routine beatings were bad enough, but what made Bel sick were his desperate attempts to win his father's favor. It's why he continued to try to farm in the same way his father had. His banker was right to tell him to modernize. On some level, he knew it. He'd ignored his genetics training and instead desperately tried to reproduce his father's success, exactly as his father had done it so effortlessly decades before.

He opened his eyes and kicked at a post on the porch. Bel looked up at the redwood tree as if expecting some grand insight but he heard nothing.

Bel left the porch and slipped past the carriage house, converted years ago into the McMaster Vineyards business office, on his way to the winery building. The last place he wanted to be was in the office with his manager, Virna, reviewing slumping sales. But she saw him and called out.

"Bel, Bel, come here. It's urgent!" Virna waved her arms. It was always urgent with Virna. He sighed and turned to follow Virna into the office. "You might want to sit down, Bel."

Virna put her hand to her chest and took a deep breath. "Fontaine Rouge in Vegas just called."

"God this can't be good," Bel said, ignoring Virna's theatrics.

"They canceled their order," she said dramatically.

Bel stared at Virna blankly. For once, her drama might be warranted. "What do you mean, they canceled their order? They're our single biggest customer. They serve McMaster Vineyards wines in over a dozen restaurants in the hotel and casino. What are you saying?"

He had a gnawing in the pit of his stomach as he struggled to recall his last conversation with the Las Vegas resort. It hadn't gone well.

Virna spoke slowly. "The lead sommelier called, he canceled for all of the restaurants, all of them, effective immediately."

Bel lowered himself slowly into an office chair, not taking his eyes off Virna. Each restaurant in the sprawling casino complex had its own sommelier, Bel knew some of them by name. Or at least, he used to, when he paid attention to that sort of thing. "Tell me exactly what they said, Virna," Bel said carefully. "Who did you talk to? What did he say?"

"Herve, the lead sommelier. He said that McMaster Vineyards quality has changed. He doesn't think we're a luxury brand anymore. And wine isn't popular. The younger crowd orders craft cocktails or beer from local microbreweries. Or if you can believe this, the casino has even started to sell cannabis in some of the bars."

"Fuck me," whispered Bel. He pointed his finger at Virna. "Do not tell that little tidbit to my wife."

Virna nodded slowly, her eyebrows knit.

"I have to call Herve," Bel said, pulling out his phone. The phone rang and immediately rolled into the sommelier's voicemail. Goddamn, thought Bel, the little prick won't even take my call. Bel pounded his fist softly on Virna's desk, recalling his last conversation with Herve. The most recent vintages didn't live up to the McMaster Vineyards reputation. The casino's French sommeliers now recommended French wines to the more discerning customers. Then stop hiring fucking French sommeliers, Bel had shouted.

"Goddam," Bel said to no one in particular. "A slowdown maybe, but to cancel the entire order?" Bel stood and banged his way toward the office door, scowling at nothing and everything. Sure, the last years had been tough, they'd been tough for everyone in the county. To take it out on McMaster Vineyards made no sense. He looked back at Virna. "I should have given that little idiot a bigger kickback," he spat and let the door slam shut.

* * *

Bel clenched his fists as he looked out over the vineyards. The wind had calmed and the leaves of the vines fluttered gently, almost peacefully in the baking sun. The day was not shaping up as he'd planned. But then, few days did anymore. His phone buzzed. At least Herve had the balls to call him back.

"What the fuck are you doing?" he hissed. "Not even a courtesy call before you drop us from the wine list!"

"Mr. McMaster?" A French-accented voice spoke but it was not Herve. "Hello, Mr. McMaster, this is Cedric Tari of the French Wine Ministers. You have, er, left many messages for me."

Bel slapped his forehead. "Yes, yes, Mr. Tari, thank you so much for returning my call." How many voicemails had he left for the wine minister? He only remembered two which meant he had drunk dialed. God, he hoped he'd been coherent. "Mr. Tari, I'll get right to the point. The Paris Wine Competition is incredibly important to McMaster Vineyards. It's how we made our name, as you know." Bel thought he heard a heavy sigh on the other end of the phone but he kept going. "I, we, would very much like an invitation to compete again this year. It would mean a lot." It would mean everything, actually, but Bel tried not to beg.

"Mr. McMaster," Cedric Tari exhaled. "As you know, the rules of the competition are clear. There are ratings your wine must achieve. And of course, any bottle of wine entered into the Paris competition must be single-vineyard and estate-bottled. Do you understand?"

"Yes, absolutely. Lots of respect for the rules," Bel said, clearing his throat. "But Monsieur…"

"I am so glad to understand that. I am curious because I believe that McMaster Vineyards has not had a suitable harvest of the pinot for at least five years, according to our climate reports. Nor have you achieved the minimum ratings from the Paris Wine Spectator, so, as you can see, this is the source of my confusion."

Bel clenched his jaw and stared across the field of fluttering vines. Did they have spies everywhere, in every appellation? A suitable harvest? Bel was holding the winery together by sheer force.

"Mr. McMaster, hello, are you there?"

"Yes, yes, I'm here," Bel fumbled. "I can assure you, Monsieur Tari, McMaster Vineyards is doing fine and we continue to produce single-vineyard wines. It's true, our ratings, well, they…"

"Mr. McMaster, I am so very sorry, but the rules are clear."

"Please!" Bel exclaimed. This competition was his one chance, his only chance at redemption. He couldn't let it slip away because of silly ratings. "Mr. Tari, surely you of all people respect tradition. Tradition is the very foundation of French wine. It's what gives the industry its authority. McMaster Vineyards is a part of that tradition. We are the first California wine to ever win the Paris Wine Competition and it is inconceivable to the world of wine and the traditions they hold dear that McMaster Vineyards would not be invited to the competition." Bel held his breath. Had he overplayed? The French Wine Ministers were sticklers for rules, rigid to a fault. There was silence on the other end of the phone.

"Mr. McMaster," Cedric said finally. "I knew your father well. We became close after his win and I was one of his biggest, er, how do you say, fanatique?

"Fans."

"Yes, of course." Cedric cleared his throat and Bel could almost hear the Frenchman considering. "Perhaps, for the memory of your father, I will make a visit to McMaster Vineyards. I will look at your operation, taste some recent vintage and we take it from there. But Mr. McMaster, I must warn you, there is to be no funny business."

"Me?" Bel tried to inject indignation into his voice.

"Your tanks, barrels, labels must all be your own, Mr. McMaster. No tricks."

Bel's heart leapt as he flicked his phone off. He had a chance. He sighed. The vines in the vineyard bowed mightily in the afternoon gusts. The Diablo wind had returned.

9. MARIA

Maria squinted against the setting sun and looked nervously around the parking lot of the Quick Mart. Usually, Juan drove her home after her shift, but today she'd worked a double—she was still behind on rent and hadn't had the stomach to view her other bills. Working the extra shift meant waiting in the dusty parking lot across the highway from the Jenner Inn for the infrequent bus that ran from Jenner to Guerneville. She pulled her coat tightly. Often, she found waiting for the bus peaceful, she could watch the sun slide behind the inn on its way to the horizon, taking her cares with it. But today, she was on edge.

A group of teen boys approached, most likely finishing after-school sports at Jenner High School. She'd waited with them at the bus stop before. Their jostling and swaggering didn't generally upset her, but today she cringed. They reminded her of the torros in her barrio. Cadejo's army of boys. Young and brutal. She exhaled, reached for her crucifix, and turned away. Something slammed into her back. She gasped. A ball rolled away from her feet.

"Sorry ma'am," one of the boys called out. They giggled and shoved.

Maria shifted uncomfortably. She looked at her watch. Still ten minutes until the bus. She couldn't stomach being here with the boys. It was silly, but her heart raced. *There's no shame in fleeing,* her self-defense teacher said repeatedly. Maria tucked her head, held her crucifix tightly and walked across the parking lot. She'd wait inside, away from the boys and the brutal memories they awakened. She jerked open the door, heart still pounding, and bumped into someone. A man.

She exhaled. "I'm so sorry," she muttered and looked up. "Mr. McMaster," she stammered.

Bel stepped back and held the door open. "We have to stop running into each other at the Quick Mart," he smiled. She noticed for the second time how green his eyes were. Kind, yet sad. "At least you already have my insurance," he said.

She managed a weak smile. "I was just waiting for the bus," she blurted out, wondering why she felt the need to tell the winemaker. She saw him look toward the highway. The whoops of the boys crescendoed.

"When you're done shopping, perhaps I can wait with you at the bus stop?" he asked, flicking his chin at the boys. She squirmed uncomfortably. She didn't want his help or even his understanding. Still, walking with him to the bus stop was harmless.

"Of course," she shrugged. Now she'd have to find something to buy in the Quick Mart. She barely had any money in her wallet so she wandered the short aisles, pretending to examine the cans of soup and took the cheapest one she could find to the check-out register.

He'd waited by the exit and together they meandered slowly back toward the bus stop by the highway. After a moment, he spoke. "I should apologize," he said. "I was too forward in asking you to visit my vineyard." He cleared his throat and didn't look at her.

She walked silently at his side. She didn't tell him that she was used to men being forward. Few of them, however, apologized for their behavior. She clutched her crucifix tightly.

"But when I..." he turned to face her. His eyes fell to her hand wound tightly around her crucifix. He glanced again at the boys jostling by the bus stop. He nodded slowly as if a realization hit. "I see." his voice trailed off.

Maria swallowed uncomfortably. She was tempted to ask Bel was it was he saw, but she was afraid she knew. He'd seen inside of her for a split second and understood one of her fears. Maybe in that split second, he'd pieced something together about her past. She hadn't expected this level of observation by Bel, nor did she want it. All men noticed her beauty. Some saw her resolve. Almost none saw her vulnerabilities.

Bel looked at her thoughtfully. "My father was famous for many things," he said slowly. "Including his drinking. And he was a mean drunk." He paused.

Maria's heart twinged and she tried to stop it. She didn't want him to share stories about himself that might form some sort of common bond and melt her defenses. And she was certainly not going to open her heart for a man just because he was damaged. Still, he wouldn't stop.

"And my mother was only concerned with my father and his reputation. When he was alive, she would never question him. When he died, she worked to protect his legacy. I've always been a sort of...afterthought." He fell silent and gazed at her.

His eyes were clear and despite her determination not to, she saw inside of him, too. A battered child. Ignored and forced to raise himself. Replicating those cold, anxious childhood relationships as an adult. And yet something tender.

The sound of a motor whining broke their stare. The bus rumbled to a stop. She knew that she should get on board and not look back. Not encourage him. Nothing good would come of mixing with Bel McMaster. Still, her heart had melted a bit. Bel wasn't the privileged, clueless man she'd expected. He'd been beaten by his father. Raised by a cold mother. Most likely caught in a loveless marriage. And now, he'd cleverly seen a part of her that she'd kept hidden from nearly everyone. Her heart was a mix of contradictions.

"Thank you for walking with me," she said. She entered the bus, looked back and saw him standing there. Alone. Mourning a dead son. Her heart broke.

She stopped. "Mr. McMaster, how about you show me your vineyard to-morrow?" she called out.

His face broke into a wide grin. The bus pulled away. She found a seat, held her crucifix and hoped to god she hadn't just made the biggest mistake of her life.

10. BEL

Bel paced in his office in the winery, still savoring the glow of seeing Gabby. Meeting her hadn't been quite the coincidence she might have thought. In the past few days, he'd made it a habit to stop in the Quick Mart before and after checking the vineyards on the ridge above the convenience store. The clerk now knew him by name and smiled when he walked in. And JC must have noticed how frequently Bel visited the coastal vineyards, but hadn't said anything.

Bel ran his hand through his hair. Despite the warm thoughts of Gabby, he needed to confront a bitter truth. The phone call with Cedric Tari provided an opening, but his wife and mother were right. He hadn't produced decent wine in five years. Certainly nothing that could win the Paris Wine competition. In fact, he had only ever made one vintage that came close to the award-winning wine of his father. The year was 2009. One of Bel's first years at helm of McMaster Vineyards and everything came together as if by magic. The weather, JC's talents, Bel's enthusiasm. That 2009 vintage kept McMaster Vineyards on the map. He'd sold practically all of it. Today, there was just one single bottle of the 2009 pinot locked in the office safe. Wildly valuable as a collector's item, but far too old to win a competition.

He exhaled and wandered into the winery itself and gazed up at the enormous stainless steel fermentation tanks, as if they would provide inspiration. A

handful of JC's staff hustled about, repairing the destemmer and checking temperatures of the barrel racks. The winery itself was cool—the building was built
into a hillside behind the tasting center and was the oldest on the estate. He
gazed past the fermentation tanks to the tiny wine lab he'd added to the winery
years ago after he'd graduated from UC Davis. He snorted and shook his head.
Back then, he was going to revolutionize the winery. How naive he'd been. His
father had no interest in modernizing. Bel hadn't challenged his father nor used
the lab in years. Imagine if he had. He shook his head and walked back into his
office, still pacing.

He swiped at his e-table to activate the estate AI bot. Despite Cedric Tari's
admonition for no funny business, Bel was going to have to get inventive if he
wanted an invitation to the competition.

"HALLIE," he said when the AI bot flickered to life. "I need you to check
the Sonoma Vintner e-Mart." He cleared his throat. "Are Ramon Navarro or
Sonoma Ridge selling bulk wine on the open market?" He squirmed as he asked.
A Ramon Navarro pinot noir had once been mistaken for McMaster Vineyards
at a blind tasting. As for Sonoma Ridge, well, he was desperate.

HALLIE answered immediately. "Ramon Navarro has a small amount of
two-year bulk pinot listed. I would remind you that McMaster Vineyards is not
registered to participate in bulk auctions because of our commitment to estate-
produced..."

"Thank you, HALLIE, I'm aware of that," Bel interrupted. He rubbed his
temples. Ramon had hired his own onsite geneticist years ago, if memory
served. Bel had shrugged it off at the time. After all, Bel's own son was going
to be his savior. He gritted his teeth and ignored the pang in his chest.

"Has Ramon Navarro deposited any new DNA sequences to the Global
Vintner DNA Repository recently?" Bel shook his head as he asked the question. The competition was just a couple months away so planting new clones
was out of the question. Still, it was worth knowing what valley vintners were

up to.

"The Ramon Navarro Family Vineyards have made six recent submissions to the Vintner DNA repository," HALLIE said. "Primarily for disease and heat resistance."

Bel continued to pace. No, Ramon Navarro wasn't worth pursuing. Bel would never be able to buy bulk wine anonymously anyway.

"However," HALLIE continued, "there is one entity that has made over seven hundred requests for sequences of Sonoma County vines in the online DNA repository, over half of those for McMaster Vineyards pinot clones."

Bel's head snapped up and he felt a chill in his spine. He stopped pacing. "A local winery?" he asked incredulously. No vintner in the valley had a lab that could initiate that volume of requests.

"It's not a Sonoma County entity," HALLIE responded. "It is a research and multinational corporation called Kavali Technologies."

Bel sucked in his breath. Mohan Mallick. Examining the DNA sequences of McMaster Vineyards vines—the publicly-available ones, anyway. What was it that Mohan had said during the interview with his daughter, change the course of the world through better genetics? Bel couldn't remember exactly. He'd been a little preoccupied. His gut clenched at the memory.

Bel frowned and walked to the window. The wind had picked up again and the vines whipped madly. What was Mohan Mallick doing with the genetic information of McMaster Vineyards vines, and more importantly, could it help him in the wine competition? He had to know. The Kavali Tower grand opening was two days away. It was his chance. But his stomach clenched at the thought of who he'd have to ask for an invitation. His daughter.

11. MARIA

Maria shifted nervously as she pushed her son on the playground swing. His squeals of delight made her heart leap for joy, but they also drew the attention of the afternoon crowd.

"Higher, mama! Higher!" Alarico demanded, pumping his tiny legs. Maria pushed him harder and he soared above the other children and nannies in the playground, shrieking with joy. She found it impossible not to smile. But there were so many people here today and she couldn't stop scanning faces. Santa Rosa's Guatemalan population wasn't large but it would only take one person from her old barrio to recognize her. She shivered despite the warm sun.

Maria left Alarico and Ana to play and sat next to her cousin on a park bench. She exhaled nervously, her eyes darting around the park. Gabby had been surprised when Maria showed up unannounced on her porch wanting to take the kids to the playground. The second visit to Santa Rosa this week. Maria gave no reason, and Gabby only smiled curiously and got coats for Ana and Alarico.

"Have you thought more about moving here to Santa Rosa?" Gabby asked. Her cousin had wanted Maria to move closer for months, and since Maria froze in self-defense class, Gabby brought up the topic with renewed urgency.

"I'm not ready to leave Duncans Mills," Maria said slowly. Every time tires crunched in the Jenner Inn parking lot or the bell on the inn door chimed, her heart stopped, wondering if Cadejo had finally found her. It's why she lived in the tiny hamlet of Duncans Mills and worked on the coast. More remote and fewer people to recognize her. She could see her cousin stiffen.

"We talked about this after Lila's class," Gabby said sharply. "You should be closer to your people. You could sleep on the old couch on our back porch. Alarico would love it. You could see him every day."

Maria felt her jaw tighten as she watched the children swing from a metal helix in the middle of the playground. She stared at the metal climbing apparatus. It looked so familiar, and then she exhaled. Of course, the interlocking strands that projected from the orange card. Alarico tried in vain to pull his legs up on the helix but his grip gave out. Maria nearly laughed out loud as her son he fell on top of his cousin, but instead she sighed and glanced at the people seated close by.

"Look at the children, Maria. Don't you want to be with your son?"

Maria grimaced. "You know I don't want to live in Santa Rosa," she said, irritated. "It's just not safe."

Gabby started to respond but was distracted by the buzz of her phone. She flicked it on and read, her brow creasing. She looked up at Maria, her jaw slack.

"That was from Juan," she said angrily, her eyes flashing.

Maria's heart sank. A text from Juan could be about only one thing. Gabby was about to be furious.

"He says that Bel McMaster, of all people, came to the inn to see you," Gabby said, incredulity written across her face. "You want to know what isn't safe, Maria? Talking with Bel McMaster!" Gabby crossed her arms and stiffened her back. "And once again, I have to hear from Juan and not you!"

Maria could see the hurt and anger in Gabby's eyes, and she knew her cousin was right, of course. It was beyond dangerous to spend time with Bel McMaster.

"What did he want?" Gabby asked, her jaw clenched.

"To take a walk," Maria said. "He asked if I would taste wine with him."

Gabby sat back on the bench. "Oh, Maria," she said, her voice thick with disbelief. "You're not stupid. Men like Bel McMaster only want one thing from pretty maids. You said no, of course."

Maria said nothing. She looked at Alarico and Ana. They'd tired of the helix and had returned to the whirl. Ana's hair flew behind her and Alarico's laughter rose above the din of the playground.

"Maria?"

"I said no, and then I changed my mind," Maria said and made a small sign of the cross over her heart. She couldn't bring herself to look at Gabby.

"¡No lo puedo creer!" Gabby exclaimed incredulously and glared at Maria. "That is absolute insanity."

Maria was silent. She knew it was crazy. Of course, she knew, and for so many reasons. First, Bel thought her name was Gabby. Second, her husband killed his son, which Bel didn't know. And third, the memory of her husband still clutched her heart. But she couldn't deny that something stirred inside.

"Maria," Gabby said sternly. "You of all people should know how dangerous it is to see people you should not. When Juan started sneaking about with the torro of Cadejo..."

"No, please no!" Maria shook her head vehemently. The vicious ending of Juan's lover in Guatemala City was burned in all of their brains.

"You have to listen to me," Gabby said and grabbed Maria's hands. "Juan tried to be careful. Only met his amante in back alleys. Secret sex in the sacristy. They thought they could fool Cadejo, but you know exactly what happened!" Her cousin's voice teetered on disbelief.

Maria looked at the ground. "Of course, I know," she whispered and fingered her crucifix.

"Then stay away from Bel McMaster!" Gabby pounded her fist on the park bench. "And that cross around your neck isn't going to protect you or Juan."

Maria exhaled and stood. "It's time for me to go, I've been here too long."

She had started taking precautions when she came to visit in Santa Rosa, like hiding her hair under a hat and wearing baggy clothes. She adjusted her cap and looked across the playground where she saw a man by the metal helix. Her heart stopped. He wore all black and had dark wavy hair that was combed back. She inhaled sharply. His features were sharp and even from this distance she could tell that his eyes were the color of coal. Gabby followed her gaze.

"Who is that?"

The man put a baseball cap on his head. The sun reflected off of his bare neck. He had no tattoo. "Nobody," Maria said and exhaled. She started to wonder what was crazier. That she had started to see Cadejo around every corner. Or that, despite her cousin's fierce admonition, she was going to see Bel McMaster.

12. BEL

Bel still couldn't believe Gabby had agreed to meet him in his coastal vineyards and sip wine. When he'd parked his truck in front of the Jenner Inn, he half expected the frizzy haired manager to run out, call him a pervert and shoo him away. But Gabby had been waiting in a plain dress and sweater. Her hair was pulled up into a graceful bun, not the tight braid from days before. His heart pounded as she followed him up the long snaking path to the top of the ridge across the highway from the inn, nimbly clamoring over rocks and weathered stumps. For the first time in days, he could exhale and think of something other than McMaster Vineyards, the wine competition, and his wife and mother.

They reached the top of the ridge where the Pacific Ocean churned far below, its expanse broadening for miles until the silver-gray waters met the cobalt blue sky far at the horizon in the distance. Behind them, the coastal vineyards of McMaster Vineyards unfolded across the gentle hills and directly below, the concrete ribbon of Highway 1 clung to the cliff and separated the Quick Mart from the Jenner Inn. From up here, the inn was tiny and seemed on the verge of tumbling into the sea below.

Bel took Gabby by the hand and led her through a row of pinot vines. Her hand was firm, maybe a little calloused from cleaning, but soft all the same. He realized he hadn't touched or held a woman since, well, he couldn't remember.

It felt so good to be touched. She squeezed his hand and smiled shyly. He smiled back and then stopped to pluck a grape from a cluster and handed it to her.

"The grape came off the stem easily," he said. "That means it is ready to harvest. Now taste it."

Gabby wiped the grape on her sleeve and put it in her mouth. Bel watched as she chewed. Her lips were unbearably ripe and full, the opposite of the shriveled grape. He had to look away and toward the ocean. He was trying not to be obvious. His actions in bringing Gabby to the ridge might not have been completely calculated, but the feeling that welled inside him was one hundred percent sexual. He told himself he wasn't that kind of man. The kind that stops looking at his wife when she reaches a certain age and instead chases young women with ripe lips like Gabby's. Except, it appeared he was that kind of man.

"What do you taste?" he asked, turning back to the maid.

"It's sweet," she said with uncertainty. "Not like a grape I'm used to."

Bel nodded encouragingly, like a teacher coaxing a student. "And...?"

"Maybe it tastes like a different fruit," she said slowly.

Bel smiled. "Yes!" he exclaimed. "What kind of fruit?"

"I don't remember what it's called," Gabby said. "It's small and red, it comes from a tree."

"A cherry," Bel cried with satisfaction. "You taste cherry and that's exactly right. Grapes grown for wine often taste like other kinds of fruit, it's what gives the wine its unique flavor." He couldn't tell whether Gabby was satisfied with herself or relieved that she'd passed a test. He might be over enthusiastic.

"Sorry," he said. "I get a little carried away, sometimes."

"It's OK," she smiled. "I know so little about wine. There is much to learn."

A drop of grape juice lingered on her lips and before he could stop himself, he'd reached out and brushed it away. His heart thudded, her lips were as warm as they were ripe. He held his breath wondering if he'd been too forward but Gabby only smiled. He exhaled. "There is a lot to learn," he stammered, unable to pull his gaze from her amber eyes. "I guess I've had a lifetime of education. And, six years at UC Davis," he said.

Gabby looked up at him. "McMaster Vineyards, it was started by your father?"

So many people were curious about the elder McMaster. Bel lost track of the number of times he'd been asked to recount his family history. Inevitably, the questions would come around to his father's win, leaving Bel feeling like the unworthy bearer of a famous name. But with Gabby, it was different.

"Yes," he said. "My father, Michael McMaster, came to America from Ireland. He fell in love with Sonoma County and got a job at a winery until he saved enough to start his own, McMaster Vineyards."

They arrived at a small three-sided shed that sat atop a rise. The open side of the shed faced west toward the ocean and inside were assorted field tools and a small table on which stood two bottles of wine. Bel led her into the shade of the shed and they gazed westward over the ocean. The wind died down and the ocean turned a brilliant blue, like the sky. The surface of the water was dappled with dots of light from the setting sun that looked like shimmering diamonds.

"Hermosa," he heard Gabby whisper.

Bel reached in his pocket for a corkscrew. He wondered again if he was being obvious. A walk on the ridge. Tasting wine in a rustic shed. The rumble of the ocean. "This wine came from these fields," he said, pointing to the two bottles on the table. Of course it was obvious. He was seducing her, no matter what he told himself his intentions were.

He poured wine into two glasses and held one to Gabby, showing her how to swirl wine in the glass and hold it to the light. She seemed amused by the pageantry and giggled as Bel pushed her nose into the glass and told her to breathe deeply. He watched her sip and took his own, closing his eyes and chewing the wine, letting it drench his tongue and warm his throat.

When he opened his eyes, Gabby was watching him. Her amber eyes were wide and unblinking. Her expression had changed from amusement to something else. He reddened as if he'd been caught misbehaving. For a brief moment he stared at Gabby, unable to pull his gaze away.

"You have such a passion," she said as if in a trance. "You love the wines."

Bel cleared his throat. "I do," he said. At that moment, he wanted to pull her close, tip her head up and taste her ripe lips as they melted into his. Then, he would run his hands slowly down her sides to her full hips. He felt a firmness grow between his legs and his breathing deepened.

"Tell me about your family," Gabby said, interrupting Bel's thoughts. Her expression had changed again, still curious but there was something about the way she asked him that suggested she already knew the answer.

Bel frowned at the thought of his family. "I married the daughter of my father's rival," he said. "My wife's father is Eamonn Baxter who has the county's largest vineyards, bigger than McMaster Vineyards. His wine isn't ultra-premium, it's wine for the masses, as they say. You can buy it in jugs or boxes."

Gabby looked puzzled. "And that is not a good thing?" she asked. "What is different with wine in a box?"

Bel looked at the vines fluttering on the ridge. "You know," he replied finally. "That is a really good question. Maybe the difference isn't as big as we think. But to winemakers, it matters, I suppose." He cleared his throat. "We have two children. Or, I should say, had two children," Bel continued. His eyes clouded and he looked away from Gabby and out over the ocean. He would never get used to talking about Ned in the past tense. "Nadine is our daughter," he said with a distant smile. "Driven, smart. Graduated from Stanford with honors and started her own business. She has a media company that investigates technology leaders."

"She sounds very intelligent. You must be proud of her," Gabby said.

Bel frowned. "I am," he said hesitantly. "I feel like…" Bel stammered for a moment and stopped. He reached across the table and grabbed the open bottle of wine and splashed some into the maid's glass and then into his. He tipped the glass back and drank deeply, forgoing any pretense of sipping. The wine was warm and comforting. Gabby lifted her glass, too, drained it and then set it firmly on the table.

Bel shook his head and smiled. He paused and his eyes teared. "I had a son," he finally blurted out. "My son Ned. He was everything I wanted to be," Bel couldn't believe he'd admitted that to a total stranger. "He was talented, care-free. Brilliant in the fields with the vines. He was going to be a plant geneticist and work with me at the estate. But he…"

Gabby put her hand on Bel's forearm. "I'm so sorry."

It sounded as if she knew already. Of course, Ned's death had been all over the media for days, and now he'd discovered that Nadine had inadvertently selfie-casted his son's death in real time. The look he'd seen on Gabby's face when he'd first introduced himself—it wasn't awe or desire. It was pity. She pitied him, and that was the emotion Bel hated more than any other.

Suddenly he wanted to be off of the ridge and away from the vineyard. He didn't want to be here in a rustic shed overlooking the Pacific Ocean with a beautiful young woman who was by his side because she pitied him. He felt his stomach tighten with grief and shame and even betrayal.

But then she spoke and Bel thought he heard compassion in her voice, not pity. "I cannot imagine what you have been through, Mr. McMaster," she said. "I am so sorry for your loss."

Bel looked into her eyes and his heart pounded. He couldn't remember the last time a woman treated him with anything other than sarcasm and contempt. A tear slid down his cheek and she reached out to wipe it away. He felt her arm around his waist. And then her petite, warm body against his. As they stood, Gabby embraced him with silent consolation. They watched as the sun pulled its last rays down below the horizon and the Diablo winds returned.

Part II

13. BEL

Bel paused at the entrance to Kavali Tower, unable to believe that he'd come to San Francisco twice in one week. *You hate the city,* his daughter had spat when he asked to be her plus-one to the tower's grand opening. She was right. But she'd grudgingly agreed to invite him when he admitted his sudden fascination with Mohan's secretive genetic work.

He inhaled and entered the cathedral-like lobby and caught a whiff of something familiar. Gabby's scent still clung to his shirt. He hadn't changed it this morning intentionally. He snorted at his boyish ridiculousness, but god she was gorgeous. Her smell brought back thoughts of last night on the ridge and he felt an erotic charge. That feeling dissipated quickly as he caught sight of his daughter at an endless reception counter. He pushed his way through the crush of people and ignored the din of excited chatter.

Nadine stood close to a receptionist who wore a light-colored shirt emblazoned with a Kavali logo and together the two women flipped through holographic images floating above the counter. Nadine all but ignored him as he approached.

"Dad," his daughter said coldly, barely turning to look at him. "This is Daisy Jain." Nadine's voice turned warm as she leaned in to the receptionist. "She was just telling me about the theater on the top of the building."

Was it his imagination or did the receptionist blush?

"It's called the Lotus because the auditorium roof unlocks and opens to the sky, unfolding like the petals of the lotus flower," Daisy said. There was something seductive about the young woman. Her voice had a lilt, Northern India, perhaps. A golden nose ring pierced one nostril and her right forearm was covered by a sleeve tattoo.

Nadine leaned even closer to the receptionist. "Are you sure you can't come up to the theater with us for the grand opening?" Nadine asked. "Maybe you could be our personal guide?"

The receptionist hesitated and Bel noticed a tiny dot near the tragus of her ear. It could have been jewelry, but before he could ask, the dot glowed a pale orange. The woman's smile faded. "The event is about to begin," she said. "Come," she beckoned Bel and Nadine. "I've got a shortcut." Daisy led them around the mass of people waiting for elevators up to the theater and stopped next to a sheer white wall that stretched to the high reaches of the vast lobby ceiling. She pressed the orange dot next to her ear. A section of the wall quivered, retracted and then slid aside noiselessly. Bel looked curiously at his daughter who shrugged and they followed Daisy into a short, empty hallway and toward a private elevator. Daisy touched her eardot again and the elevator door slid open.

"Here," Daisy smiled. "You can have an elevator to yourselves. The view on the ride up to the auditorium will be amazing."

"That was so very sweet of you," Nadine said. She made no move to get on the elevator. "I was thinking, maybe we could tap?" She held out her phone. Daisy nodded and tapped her phone on top of his daughter's.

Bel cleared his throat. "Um, Nadine?"

"Sure, Dad." She followed him on the elevator, still gazing at Daisy.

"What was that about?" Bel said as the doors hissed shut. "You don't even know her." The elevator rocketed upward through Kavali Tower.

"I was trying to get information from her," Nadine's demeanor darkened and she turned away from him to look out of the glass elevator's windows. "Everything about this place has been so secretive. I figured that the staff had to know something."

"Flirting for intelligence?" Bel asked incredulously.

"Well," Nadine shrugged. "I got facts about the tower that I didn't have before." Her phone buzzed and she looked down. A smile spread slowly across his daughter's face. "And we're having lunch tomorrow."

"You might have learned facts about the auditorium," he said, unable to keep a note of disapproval out of his voice. "But you're never going to find what Carlos Garcia stole from Kavali by poking around this tower."

"And you're never going to learn the secrets of Kavali's genetic research at Mohan Mallick's presentation," she shot back and twisted a piercing in her ear. "So I guess we're both fucking wasting our time." She kept her back to him and stared out of the elevator window. Floors zipped by at breakneck speed. Bel couldn't tell what they held—offices, labs, living spaces based on the descriptions he'd read.

He exhaled. It was always so difficult with Nadine. With Ned it had been uncomplicated. His son was the idealized version of who he'd wanted to be. With his daughter, he was confused, and that made it easy to be angry with her. "Listen Deeny," he said. Suddenly, his jaw dropped. He forgot about Nadine. He forgot about Gabby. The scene outside the elevator was too unbelievable. It was as if they had smashed up through the floors of the building and into a mammoth green cave that stretched toward the heavens. There were no interior walls or floors in this part of Kavali Tower—just the building's outer glass skin.

The enormous cavern was filled with gigantic fields that hung from their sides vertically, like enormous strips of wallpaper, and were planted with vegetables, fruits, trees, and crops—more varieties of plants and trees than he could count. Bel stared, barely able to believe his eyes. Some plants were familiar—potatoes, carrots, lettuces, squashes, beans—but their size was alien.

He blinked. Even from this distance in a speeding elevator, the plants were clearly enormous. No, they were beyond enormous, and comically so. Their scale was mind blowing. As if a giant had planted them—mangos as big as a human head, melons the size of a small vehicle, ears of corn as large as an elephant's trunk. And the plants grew sideways, sticking out horizontally from the gargantuan vertical panels.

As they raced by, the plants seemed to ripple, almost as if it were responding to the elevator. Wide eyed, Bel moved closer to the window and looked up. Above him stretched acres and acres of the most perfectly-groomed fields he'd ever seen filled with ludicrously oversized fruits and vegetables, stretching into infinity above into the yawning cavern.

"This is what that son of a bitch is doing," he muttered.

"So they're true," Nadine said and stared out of the elevator. "The rumors on the darknet....." Her voice trailed off and she aimed her phone out of the elevator, snapping images.

"What rumors?" Bel asked sharply.

"They're just rumors," Nadine responded testily. "That Mohan Mallick has obtained the genetic sequences of all the world's plants and recreated their genomes artificially."

"Of course they're artificially-created," Bel snapped under his breath. He wasn't sure if he was annoyed that his daughter was the better investigator or that she didn't see fit to share information with him. "That's the only way you could get them this large."

Nadine fell silent and stared out of the windows, her back to him. Bel continued to gaze in disbelief. His stomach started to clench as he thought about HALLIE's findings–that Kavali had downloaded genetic data on McMaster Vineyards vines. As if on cue, up above, he saw plants that looked all too familiar.

"It can't be," he muttered. The elevator continued to rocket up, rapidly approaching massive field panels planted with row after row of grape vines, perfectly trimmed with clumps of plum-colored grapes dangling down like jewels. But these weren't normal sized-grapes. They were the size of melons. Perfectly shaped.

Bel's heart nearly stopped. He might not have had his father's innate skill with the vines, but he had an eye for detail. Even from the elevator, he recognized the dark green leaves and the rich dark purple grapes. They were pinot. But not just any pinot.

"Those rumors," he asked Nadine, unable to tear his eyes from the vines that came closer and closer. "When they said every plant in the world. Did they mean every wine grape clone?"

Nadine cleared her throat. "It's darknet stuff Dad. Hard to separate conspiracy from..."

"Did they mean even grape clones from McMaster Vineyards?" The elevator raced higher. The vines slipped from sight, now below them. He spun to face his daughter, not believing what just raced by the window. Except he'd seen it. With his own eyes.

"Yes," Nadine said cautiously.

God, he'd been naive. To come to Kavali Tower with some misguided notion that the world's richest man was creating biotechnology that might benefit him, a winemaker from Sonoma County. Bel's stomach was so tight he could barely breathe.

"But, even if those vines are based on McMaster Vineyards pinot," he stammered, as much to himself as his daughter, "You couldn't possibly make wine from them." He pointed at his daughter. "Even *you* know that good wine depends as much on the exact combination of soil, sun, water as the grape variety." No one would ever be able to make McMaster Vineyards wine, even if they copied his grapes. It was impossible without the mineral-rich dirt of

Sonoma County and its dry summers.

"I know, Dad." Nadine sighed and rolled her eyes. "It's called terrior."

Bel nodded vacantly. Nadine had learned the bare minimum of vineyards and wine-making. But even she knew that terrior couldn't possibly be reproduced inside a building. A skyscraper of all places. There was nothing to worry about. These vertical vineyards were simply a science experiment. But if that were the case, why was his stomach so tightly clenched?

* * *

They entered the auditorium at the top of Kavali Tower on the mezzanine level, stories above a massive circular stage surrounded by steeply pitched seats rising almost to the sky.

"This way," Nadine shouted over the roar of the crowd. "We're sitting with the media."

His daughter led him up to seats that seemed to be perched on a cliff. The crowd was crazy with anticipation and the din was overwhelming. Bel felt dizzy as he sank down into his chair. The auditorium darkened. In the distance, a soft mechanical clank sounded and the domed ceiling lifted and split into a dozen finger-shaped segments—the petals of the Lotus. The early afternoon sun streamed into the auditorium and blinded Bel. He shaded his eyes, squinting to see. Nadine pushed a button on his armrest and a pair of holographic sunglasses materialized and perched on his nose.

From above, a tiny figure appeared against the white light, a spec of a figure that grew as it descended. The audience went insane, whistling and chanting Mohan's name. The figure, Mohan Mallick, grew larger, gently lowered by dozens of buzzing orange drones. The moment Mohan's feet touched the stage, the tech titan flicked his head up and extended his arms into the shape of a V. The roar of the crowd was deafening.

"Holy fuck," Bel muttered, his stomach churning. "This guy thinks he's god."

His daughter shook her head. "Those drones, I feel like…."

Her voice was swallowed by the roar of the crowd as huge holograms of Mohan popped up throughout the auditorium, towering above them. He was even more handsome than he'd appeared in Nadine's studio. His features were slim, his eyes dark, and he had a trace of dark stubble on his square jaw, just enough to give him the appearance of a celebrity. From the stage below, Mohan looked up at the audience.

"For thousands of years, human food production has been at the mercy of the climate." Mohan's powerful voice echoed through the auditorium. Bel squirmed. There was something so overly confident about the tech titan. A confidence that reminded him of his father. "Over time, farming became industrialized and food production efficient," Mohan continued. "But ironically, the very industrialization that brought efficiency also brought destruction."

As the tech titan spoke, holographic images flashed throughout the auditorium—melting glaciers, wildfires, wilting fields. Now, Mohan paced the stage purposefully. "Famines have ravaged the world. Sub-Saharan Africa. Central America. The food wars of the Middle East. These regional battles for sustenance will only grow. And if we don't do something now, we are facing war on a global scale."

A murmur rippled through the audience. Bel snorted. Mohan was so clearly setting himself up as a messiah. Typical tech bro. *I and I alone can solve this intractable problem.*

"But I have a solution!" Mohan proclaimed. Bel rolled his eyes. "A solution that will prevent food wars. A solution to end world hunger!" White light flooded the stage from above, illuminating Mohan and making him appear godlike. "The gardens that you saw on the way up to the Lotus Theater are teeming with life. Weren't they something?" Mohan called out to the crowd and someone in the audience responded with a cheer and in seconds, the crowd was on its feet, chanting, "Mohan, Mohan!"

Mohan held up his arms in a V to quiet the crowd. "Every one of those *beautiful* plants that you saw on your way up here to the Lotus," Mohan paused. Bel felt as if the tech titan were looking directly at him, talking to him like his father used to. "Every one of these vines," Michael McMaster used to say and sweep his arm across the horizon. "Every one of them holds the secret to McMaster Vineyards."

"Every one of those plants," Mohan continued, "holds the secret to our survival." He held up his finger. A bright light appeared at his fingertip—a holographic image that grew into a spinning DNA helix. "Those huge, gorgeous plants that you saw, each one is based on incredible advances in genomics. Advances that will change our very approach to food production." The DNA helix replicated itself and suddenly there were dozens of holograms of helixes spinning throughout the auditorium.

"Every plant in Kavali Tower is synthetically created." He paused and gazed at the spinning helixes. "Using an entirely new DNA modification. Our proprietary, synthetic strands are the basis of plant life. This DNA is so incredible, that our plants can grow in any climate. And," he paused for a beat, "at up to fifty times normal size."

The crowd shifted and started to cheer again. Bel glanced at Nadine. "Am I the only one that thinks gigantic vegetables are bizarre?" Bel whispered.

"We call the genome for these synthetic plants," Mohan was practically beaming, "Synthetica."

Segments of the giant holographic images of spinning DNA helices stretched. Pieces of the DNA strand lighted and then disappeared and were replaced by new strands. Dots labeled A, T, G and C glowed brightly and reorganized, inserting themselves into the genome.

Mohan smiled beatifically, Bel thought, as if the tech titan were teaching a lesson in spirituality. Bel snorted and looked around. The crowd was hanging on the tech titan's every word.

"Climate change is not a death sentence," Mohan thundered from the stage. "With Synthetica, I can grow plants in any climate and any part of the world. I can grow them in buildings or even caves. A single potato," Mohan paused, "a single potato can feed a village for a month!"

"Yeah, but it tastes like garbage, I bet," Bel muttered to his daughter.

Mohan wasn't finished. He raised his hands to quiet the crowd. "I went even further," Mohan said, pointing at the holograms of DNA and plants that now seemed to float everywhere in the auditorium. "For years, scientists have been able to genetically modify the taste of food. The sweetness. Aroma. Acidity and texture. But there's always been something missing. That special flavor that comes from the intensity of the sunlight. Exact air temperature. The minerals in the soil."

Bel sucked in his breath. Mohan was talking about his very occupation.

"Winemakers have something they call terrior." Mohan said. Bel's heart dropped. It wasn't possible. "It's the combination of all of the elements that affect the authentic taste of the wine—sun, soil, water, air." Mohan continued. "What if you could build terrior into the genome of the grape." Mohan gazed upward, godlike. "So that grapes, no matter where you grew them, no matter the climate, produced the same amazing wine." Bel felt like he was going to vomit. "I can and I did!" Mohan shouted.

The crowd was on its feet, wildly cheering. This was madness.

"And not just grapevines," Mohan continued. But Bel had heard enough. He stood and lumbered past his daughter. "I'm out," he shouted at Nadine and stumbled toward the exit without looking to see if she was following.

Outside the auditorium Bel gasped and tried to catch his breath. He wasn't sure if he'd just seen the future of McMaster Vineyards. Or its finale.

* * *

The Sky Bar was long and narrow, snaking along the top edge of Kavali Tower just beneath the Lotus Theater. The bar's ceiling sloped upward to meet a glass wall which curved along the entire length of the room. Bel moved uneasily toward the teak-covered bar. The view out of the windows would have been jaw-dropping if he'd been in the right mood. The financial district of San Francisco was almost three quarters of a mile below and its buildings were tiny from this height. But he saw none of it. His stomach was in knots as he tried to figure out the truth of Mohan's boasts.

"It's an awesome view, isn't it?" The bartender materialized seemingly from nowhere. "What can I get you?"

"I'd like a whiskey with..." Bel stopped as a thought popped into his head. It was crazy, but he had to know. He leaned toward the bartender. "The vineyards hanging in the tower," he said, trying to keep his voice from quivering. "Have you produced...?" He couldn't bring himself to finish the question.

The bartender smiled slowly. "I know who you are," she said. "You're Belmond McMaster from McMaster Vineyards."

Bel's eyes narrowed and he shifted uncomfortably. "You know me?" he asked with resignation.

The bartender smiled brightly now. "Who in the wine business doesn't know Belmond McMaster? And Daisy from reception told us you were in the building." She dropped her voice. "Did you want to know if we make our own wine?"

Bel nodded. "The pinot vines that I saw," he stammered. "With the huge grapes."

The bartender exhaled and glanced around as if she were being watched. "Stay here for just a second," she said quietly. She disappeared around the corner of the bar and was back in seconds holding a bottle. She uncorked it and poured a glass for Bel. "We aren't supposed to serve this yet," she said conspiratorially, sliding the glass toward him. "But I'll make an exception for Belmond McMaster!"

Bel swirled the glass, looked at the wine's color in the light, and resisting the urge to gulp it, sipped and let the liquid run over his tongue. Then he swallowed and stopped. He looked at the bartender suspiciously and took another sip, this time pulling air in through his teeth. The wine had an unmistakable flavor, a combination of cherry and nutmeg. He would know it anywhere.

"It can't be," he said, reaching for the bottle and staring at its label. "Kavali Vineyards," he read and then looked up dazed at the bartender. "I know this wine better than I know myself. I could swear I'm drinking a 2009 estate-bottled pinot noir from McMaster Vineyards. I sold cases of this, it was our biggest seller, it was…" Bel lost himself in his words. The harvest was epic. "It can't be from here." He shook his head.

"It's from here," the bartender said simply. She seemed to be carefully watching Bel's reaction.

He took another swig, holding the wine in his mouth longer. It was even better than the first sip. Bel's eyes teared in despair. "How, how old are those vines in the tower," he stammered, trying not to lose his composure.

"Let's see," she said, "I started here about three months ago and the vines were just being planted. First harvest was about six weeks ago."

Bel set the glass down in disbelief. It took years—decades—for the vines at McMaster Vineyards to reach their full potential. And Mohan Mallick had figured out how to do it in weeks in a tower in San Francisco with something he called Synthetica. *You haven't produced a decent pinot in years*, both his mother and wife had said. True. But it appeared Mohan Mallick had. And the Kavali wine wasn't just decent. This pinot could win awards. Bel lowered his head in stunned silence.

14. MARIA

Maria sat alone atop the massive cliff behind the Jenner Inn, her head bowed against the strong ocean gusts as she whispered to the saint, her prayer all but drowned by the roar of the Pacific pounding mercilessly on the narrow beach below.

"Saint Peter, my protector," she whispered. "I beg, watch over my little Alarico. I deserve nothing, but hear my humble plea. For, the love of my son I entrust to thee."

She shuddered and squeezed the crucifix around her neck. The specter of Cadejo was always with her now. She exhaled. Her cousin was right. The necklace wouldn't protect her, and maybe the saints wouldn't either since she had walked the ridge with Bel McMaster. Something warmed inside of her when she thought of the winemaker and she tried desperately to stop it. She screwed her eyes closed tightly and prayed even harder, begging the saint to stifle her desire. Her feelings for Bel weren't right, and she knew it. She pleaded with the saint to take the longing away, but it seemed the saint was not listening to her prayers.

"I thought I'd find you out here."

Maria opened her eyes to see the outline of Juan against the rising sun. He had come down from the inn and stopped at her side.

"Belinda hates when you start your shift late."

"It's a beautiful morning," Maria said softly. She'd avoided Juan for the past twenty-four hours. She feared he knew her well enough to know something was up.

Juan nodded. "You didn't come to work yesterday," he said evenly.

Maria shrugged. She'd never called in sick before. But, yesterday, she had spent the day alone for the first time since she could remember. She needed to think about what had just happened on the ridge with Bel McMaster. It wasn't that she didn't know how she felt, she was sure of it—and that was the problem.

Juan cleared his throat. "Two nights ago, I saw a truck in the parking lot. A familiar truck. I thought to myself, it can't be. But I looked and there was a dent in the front fender. What a coincidence." He grimaced. "You need to be very careful before you do this."

"Do what?"

"Maria! Don't be stupid. Belinda saw you leave with a man who looked just like Bel McMaster. What were you thinking? Running across the highway and ducking into the bushes like some teenagers? Have you lost your mind?"

"Juan, it's not like that. All we did was have wine."

Juan shook his head slowly. "When I said that Bel McMaster was trying to figure out how to get around me to get to you, I didn't think you'd actually encourage him. And just wine? It's never just wine. I'm a man, I know. And now, you've given the maids something new to gossip about. They know you went somewhere with that white man at sunset."

That white man. Just hearing the words caused her to flinch. She looked over the churning ocean out to where the water met the horizon. That white man, Bel, had held her tightly. Confessed emptiness at the loss of his son. She tried to tell herself that his color didn't matter. Everyone grieves, after all. Two nights ago, the wind on the ridge had calmed as the sun disappeared, dipping beneath the sea, and Bel had asked about her. He'd wanted to know where she grew up, did she have siblings, what had she been like as a child. She'd been guarded at first, but the wine, the warm autumn evening, the roar of the ocean. Despite everything, she'd been romanced. She smiled then frowned, and quietly offered a prayer to the Señor. It wasn't right to be happy.

"Did you think I wouldn't find out?" Juan asked. Maria thought he sounded hurt. She could only imagine how he'd feel if she knew the other secret she was keeping, the one about Cadejo.

"I was going to tell you," Maria said quickly. She now felt doubly guilty, not telling Juan about Bel or Cadejo.

Juan sighed and lowered himself next to Maria. The silence was punctuated by the crashing waves. Finally, he spoke.

"I know what it's like to want someone you're not supposed to want. To be afraid every day that you might be beaten or something worse, just because of who you want to be with." He turned to Maria and tipped her chin up. "It rips out your gut when you love the wrong person. Your heart will be broken. Maybe worse. And for what?"

Maria didn't answer. She stared out at the ocean. "People do stupid things," she said distantly.

"They do. Just promise me you won't do anything you regret." Juan stood and extended his hand. "Come with me," he said and smiled sadly. "I want to make sure you have somewhere safe to go."

Maria took his hand and they walked to the edge of the crumbling cliff. The roar of the ocean intensified and the salty air whipped her hair.

"This way," Juan said. "Trust me."

Maria followed him through a thicket of coyote bushes and sagebrush. He climbed onto a gnarled Monterey cypress that was balanced on the lip of the cliff. The tree hung precipitously over the cliff, barely clinging to the cliff's rim. Juan shimmied out onto a massive branch that extended out into nothingness then swung from the branch and dropped. Maria gasped as Juan disappeared from sight. She climbed out on the tree branch and carefully slid forward, her eyes tearing from the whipping wind.

"Down here!" Juan waved from below on a hidden narrow path cut into the side of the cliff just under the tree. "Come," he said, stretching out his arm.

Maria shimmied further onto a massive branch and then closed her eyes and dropped toward Juan on the tiny path. She lost her balance but he caught her. She exhaled and leaned against the cliff wall, feeling unsteady on the treacherous edge that plunged sixty feet to the ocean.

"This way," Juan said, grabbing her hand and moving quickly. Maria made the sign of the cross and followed him, her eyes never leaving the narrow, sandy path. They stopped in front of a tiny cave chiseled into the rock face by winter rains and winds.

"We're here," Juan said and ducked into the cave.

Maria followed him inside the small cave where the whoosh of wind and the roar of the ocean echoed. It was damp but peaceful and she felt safe inside the earth like this. Fingers of light stretched in through the opening, illuminating it with a hazy glow.

"No one knows this cave is here," he said. "I don't even think Belinda knows and she's been managing the inn for decades."

"How did you find it?" Maria asked, gazing around the tiny chamber, noticing a few rocks the size of small chairs, as if they'd been placed by someone.

Juan was silent for a moment. Finally, he said, "Antonio showed me."

"The dishwasher?" Maria asked, recalling the immigrant taken by ICE.

Juan nodded, his face pinched in pain.

"I'm sorry," she said slowly. "I didn't know you were dating."

"It doesn't matter," he said, but his jaw was clenched and she knew it mattered—a lot.

His face grew grave. "If you ever need a place to hide, run here as fast as you can. Don't let anyone see you climb onto the tree branch. They won't see the path from the cliff. Do you understand?"

Maria nodded and slowly dropped to her knees. She lowered her head. "I beg of you, Señor de Esquipulas," she whispered. "Do not make me have to hide in this cave. Ever." She opened her eyes and looked up. This time, she hoped the saint would listen to her prayers.

15. BEL

Bel moaned and opened his eyes. He lay still and rubbed his pounding temples, struggling to recall where he was. He licked his parched lips and grimaced. He was on his daughter's couch. It all came flooding back. The gigantic vertical fields. Mohan Mallick's smug savior-complex. The countless bottles of wine he'd downed in Kavali Tower. He was barely able to walk by the time Nadine found him in the Sky Bar. The humiliation. A middle-aged man, too drunk to drive home, passed out at his estranged daughter's apartment.

He shifted on the couch and his leg brushed against something cool and hard. He reached down. A bottle of Kavali Vineyards wine, unopened. He'd snatched it when the bartender turned her back and taken it with him. He shook his head at his desperation and stowed the bottle in his coat.

He sat slowly and stared out of his daughter's living room window, rubbing his unshaven jaw. Kavali Tower dominated the San Francisco skyline. He snorted. The arrogant building didn't just threaten to scrape the sky, it threatened to rip it apart, along with his very way of life. Bel had to know if it was true, the claim made by the bartender at the Sky Bar. It was a preposterous notion, but could immature grape vines produce award-winning wine in six weeks?

His estate AI bot, HALLIE, wouldn't be much help. The secrets in Kavali

Tower were locked up tight. That left his daughter. Fuck. He wasn't sure he could deal with her now, but there wasn't much choice. She was already investigating Mohan Mallick, and besides, he might need the hacking skills she'd honed in college. He stood, winced at the pounding in his head and gathered his coat and the bottle of Kavali wine.

Voices drifted down the narrow hallway from the broadcast studio. He checked his breath and cringed. Swallowing his pride, he walked unsteadily down the claustrophobic hallway. The studio was empty and dark, the voices came from the far side where light spilled from a small room that he hadn't seen the other day. He walked over and poked his head in. The room was filled with computers and monitors, and holograms floated about. Sure enough, his daughter had built a hacker lab. Nadine, her engineer Nigel, and the intern Corissa were hunched over a rotating image and didn't seem to hear him enter. He cleared his throat. Three sets of eyes looked at him.

"Someone is alive, sort of," Nadine crossed her arms. God she was starting to remind him of his wife. "It took a little effort to pry you out of Kavali Tower last night," she continued sharply. "That was quite the show you put on."

Bel reddened. The memories from the Sky Bar weren't coming back yet. Maybe that was a blessing. "Well," he stammered. "I wasn't expecting to taste something so, so…"

"Yeah, I know," Nadine interrupted. "The best pinot ever. You told me, and everyone in the bar, multiple times. This wine could win awards," she said in a voice that sounded like a slurring middle-aged man. "The bartender finally…" She uncrossed her arms and stopped, possibly realizing she was punching down. "It doesn't matter, Dad. I suppose you're out of here." She turned back to a spinning hologram which Nigel and Corissa studied intently.

Bel's gut clenched. He couldn't leave, not without knowing what Nadine was researching. But that would mean watching as she continually examined Ned's death. God he hated this. He gritted his teeth. "What are you working on?" he asked.

His daughter kept her back turned and Nigel answered. "We've spent the morning reviewing the video that Nadine shot at Kavali Tower," the young man said. "And we're focused on this." He waved to the hologram. Several orange drones spun in the hologram. Bel squinted. Even in his current state, he recognized them. Mohan Mallick had made quite an entrance, after all. "Those are the drones that lowered Mohan Mallick to the stage."

"Exactly," Nadine nodded, her jaw tight. "When I saw these drones in Kavali Tower, I knew I'd seen them—or one of them before. Here." She pointed to a screen with a blurry image. It was a frame from her selfie cast, the one she'd been making on the Embarcadero with Ned the day he was shot.

"I can't look at that again," Bel said and turned. He heard Nadine sigh.

"Just this image, Dad, look," Nadine said firmly and pointed. "See, hovering above Ned and me, and just above Carlos Garcia. It's a drone. An orange drone." She turned and looked at her father. "It's a Kavali drone. Now why would a drone from Kavali be hovering above Carlos Garcia?"

Bel's stomach turned somersaults but he forced himself to stare at the image. The picture of the man who killed his son. He'd never really looked at Carlos Garcia before, but there Carlos sat, alone on a bench mere feet from his daughter and his son. Except for the horrible carving in Carlos's forehead, he seemed like a normal, slightly sad man sitting on a bench rummaging through a bag and holding a small metal card to the light. But Bel couldn't help himself and his eyes moved to his son. Ned. Just seconds before his death. That smile, so goofy. The green eyes that sparkled. So alive. Bel felt like he was going to vomit.

"I can't," Bel said. He moved to the door.

Nadine grabbed his arm. "Dad, don't you see how important this is? That drone had to be recording video. If Nigel and I can hack into the Kavali network and find the video from this drone, there's a chance we can figure out what Carlos Garcia stole!"

"And then what?" Bel stopped at the door.

"What do you mean?"

Bel turned. "You know what I mean. You're so desperate to prove that the shooting was a preventable accident. That some big corporation is responsible for Ned's death, not this...this immigrant on a bench." Bel's stomach clenched and he could feel his eyes swelling. "But it just doesn't matter. Because whatever you learn, it will never...never bring back my son. He is gone, Nadine." Bel punched at the air and looked up, daring the tears to come to his eyes.

"Dad, I..." Nadine was silent. He could feel her eyes on him. He was so tired of the ache of Ned's absence, and holding his daughter responsible was so god-damn exhausting. But he just couldn't stop. He exhaled and turned to face her. "And you're so focused on that fucking gun, that you missed the most obvious thing in that picture." Thank god his eyes were just misty and not running with tears.

"Obvious?"

"Carlos Garcia is holding the very thing you're looking for." Even hung over with his head thudding, his ability to see details took over. He could hear his wife's refrain. *You have an eye for details, but you're still an alcoholic even if you're high-functioning.* He sighed. "Look at that card in his hands. Fifty bucks says that's what this whole drama is about."

"No, Dad," Nadine grimaced. "That's just an old payment card. We zoomed in on it a hundred times."

Bel snorted. "Then zoom one hundred and one times. Have you ever even used a payment card?"

Nadine shook her head and looked at Nigel. "Um, no. I just use my watch."

"Same," Nigel shrugged. "Never had a card."

"Well, children, if you had," Bel stretched out the last word and quietly wiped away a tear, "you'd know that card in Carlos Garcia's hand is too big and thick for a payment card. It's something else."

Nigel's eyes widened and he spun to the video screen. He magnified the image of Carlos Garcia. "Fuuuck me," Nigel hissed. He looked up. "I think yer old man's on to something."

Nadine bent forward to stare at the image. "Larger," she commanded Nigel. "Removable media," she said finally.

"No one would ever allow removable media in Kavali," Nigel breathed. "You'd be stopped at security."

"Unless the thief was security," Bel replied, his voice still shaking.

"That's what the detective said," Nadine nodded. "That a security guard was most likely the thief."

"Whatever was stolen from Kavali is probably on that media card," Bel said. "And if Mohan is searching for it, that means it wasn't just stolen from Kavali. It was stolen from the police after Carlos Garcia was killed."

"Damn, or they lost it," Nigel straightened up. "We have to find that bloody card. Then we'll have our leverage."

Bel reached inside his coat pocket. The bottle from Kavali. An exact copy of his pinot. He so needed a drink right now. Suddenly, it clicked. "You don't need to find the real card to have your leverage," he said quietly.

"Of course, we do," Nadine said. "We need have that card. We'll trade it for Mohan's admission of blame in Ned's death."

"No, you'll never find the real card. If Kavali can't find it with all of their resources, you have no hope." Bel shook his head and looked around the tiny room. "You only need to have a copy of the card."

"A copy?" Nadine scrunched her forehead.

"You have a 3D printer in here, right?" Bel asked, certain that she did. Nadine's hacker lab seemed nothing if not well equipped.

"Well, sure..."

"Then make an exact copy of the card with your printer," Bel commanded.

"It would be a fake," Nigel shrugged. "We'd never fool Mohan Mallick."

"It's not Mohan you need to fool," Bel said and rubbed his chin. "You only have to fool someone around him. Make someone who knows Mohan think that you have the card."

"The detective," Nadine exhaled.

Bel nodded. "The detective must have fucked up. It's the only way the card could have been stolen from the police. You try to fake out the detective. He tells Mohan he thinks you have the card. Then you're someone who needs to be bargained with. That's what you need in this game...leverage."

"And it gives us time to hack the Kavali video feed," Nigel said. He spun and darted across the tiny room, then pushed hardware aside and opened a gray metal cabinet. "'aven't used this since eternity," he exclaimed and rolled a small table with a 3D printer.

"Not sure that you'll really be able to hack into the world's biggest biotech company," Bel muttered.

"We might," Nadine said. She looked at him suspiciously. "You're helping us," she said tentatively, "and that's...nice." She managed a half smile. Her eyes, however, stayed narrow.

Bel's stomach clenched as Nigel started the printer, its high-pitched whine filling the room and fabricating the card. Bel looked at his daughter. Despite her thin smile, he could tell she was puzzled by his help. Nadine was the one, after all, who wanted the leverage against Mohan Mallick. But, as he fingered the bottle of Kavali wine in his coat pocket, the one that could win awards, he knew he wanted leverage, too.

A crazy thought bounced through his brain as he watched his daughter work with Nigel to create the fake memory card. It turned out he and his daughter shared a commonality after all. They both needed something from Mohan Mallick.

16. MARIA

Maria walked quickly across the parking lot and toward the rear of the Holiday Inn in Windsor. The late morning sun was already strong and tiny waves of heat shimmered on top of the vehicles parked behind the hotel. She lowered her head and scurried toward the entrance and nearly ran into an SUV parked directly in front of the door. She sighed and stepped back and then frowned. On the side of a small SUV was a logo—interconnected lines that intertwined. She stared. It looked so familiar.

She shook her head, pushed hard on the metal door and it swung open, scraping along the worn carpet to reveal the employee waiting room of the hotel. It wasn't a room, actually, more like a dim hallway with a row of padded chairs along one wall and several closed doors along the other. The hotel manager was interviewing applicants for the maid position, and the front desk clerk said he thought Maria was the only one to show up, so Maria was surprised to see two other women waiting in the padded chairs. Odder still was that both women were wearing identical maid uniforms.

Maria smoothed her pants. She'd finally given into her cousin's insistence that she interview for jobs closer to Santa Rosa and had chosen her outfit carefully. A navy tunic and sensible knit slacks. She wanted the appearance of someone ready for work. She'd pulled her hair back into a thick braid, Guatemalan style. Her cousin would be happy, Maria wasn't trying to appear too American today. Gabby would also be thrilled if Maria got the job at the Holiday Inn. Windsor was barely ten miles from Gabby's house and the buses were far more frequent to Windsor than to Jenner. But Maria's stomach was jumpy. The town of Windsor wasn't as crowded as Santa Rosa, but it was a far cry from Jenner and its "off the beaten path" appeal.

Maria smiled at the two women waiting in front of her. The woman closest to her, the older of the two, smiled back, but the younger maid seemed agitated and didn't meet Maria's gaze. Instead, she restlessly fingered the collar of her uniform, raised it to her mouth and chewed nervously. Maria smiled sadly— when she was younger and frightened, she'd chewed on her clothing, too. She glanced at the young woman's name tag. *Maria* it read. She leaned toward the young woman. "That's my name, too!" she said with her biggest smile, then frowned as she realized what she'd done. Here, her name was Gabby. She could not afford slip ups. She walked past the two women and down the short hall to an alcove with a water cooler. Clearly, she had time if there were two interviewees before her. She grabbed a paper cup, filled it and sipped. As she stepped back to the hallway, one of the doors flew open. Maria looked up, expecting to see the hotel manager. Instead, she nearly gasped out loud. A gigantic man emerged, his ICE uniform straining at the seams. His arms were as big as tree trunks and he towered above the women seated in the hallway. Maria stepped back into the tiny alcove with the water cooler. The ICE agent hadn't seen her.

"OK," the ICE agent grunted. "We're ready for the first Maria Garcia. You!"

Maria's blood ran cold and she froze, unable to move. Had the ICE agent said *the first Maria Garcia?* The words ricocheted in her brain and she felt numb. She held her breath and thought of the two women sitting on the padded chairs. She tried to control her breathing as her mind raced. The women were dressed identically. The thought dawned on her that the two women weren't interviewing. They already worked here. One was named Maria, she knew that for certain.

And the other? Was she named Maria, too? Her mind raced. What was ICE doing questioning women named Maria Garcia? Her heart thumped as she considered the possibility. Whatever it was, she couldn't stay here. She had to leave. Now. She peeked around the corner her heart pounding. The ICE agent glanced in her direction. *NO*, she screamed silently, begging him to look away.

"What's taking so long," another voice called out. A second man emerged from the office. He had brown skin and eyes the color of chocolate. Even as her breathing grew shallow, Maria couldn't help but notice the stubble on his face was meticulously groomed. On his shirt was a logo just like the logo on the side of the SUV.

"They don't look like the pictures from the police station," the ICE agent shrugged.

The smaller man wearing the logo shirt grimaced. "Those photos are blurry," he said. "That's why we need to swab the subjects."

Maria's stomach convulsed. Suddenly it clicked. The logo on the man's shirt was the same logo on the card from Carlos's wallet. The orange card that vibrated in the sunshine. She went numb as the realization dawned. These men knew the name *Maria Garcia*. They were from the company that Carlos had stolen from. Her mind reeled. Was it possible they knew she had the card that her husband had taken and they were trying to get it back?

Maria felt like she was going to hyperventilate. She was dizzy and couldn't catch her breath. She stepped backward and banged into the water cooler, cursing herself. Her throat started to close and she reached for the crucifix around her neck. But it couldn't be. How did they know her name? The only place she'd given her real name was….the police report. She smacked her head. Oh, what an idiot she'd been. The police had given the report to ICE and now ICE was searching for her. And, somehow, they had her picture. Her heart pounded.

She heard footsteps approaching. There was nowhere to go, the only exit was the way she'd entered, right by the ICE agent. Maria closed her eyes and tried to breathe.

"Hey there sweetheart," said a voice. "What are you doing back here?"

Maria opened her eyes. A petite young woman stood in front of her.

"Are you," the woman consulted her e-tablet, "Gabby Flores?"

Maria stared at the woman blankly, still panting.

"Oh, it's OK," the woman said, looking at Maria with concern. "ICE is seldom here." She beckoned Maria. The short hallway was now empty. The two maids and the two men were behind a closed door. Maria's heart thudded as she followed the hotel manager into her office. "Brittney," the hotel manager introduced herself and held out her hand. "Sorry about that," she said as she sat behind a chipped metal desk. "Fucking tech billionaires." Brittney shook her head. "Do you know who that is?"

Maria shook her head numbly, her heart still racing, unable to speak. She lowered herself onto the edge of the chair, ready to bolt if the ICE agent entered the office.

"That's Mohan Mallick," Brittney said with an irritated shake of the head. "One of the richest men in the world. Made his fortune in biotechnology of some kind."

Maria inhaled and nearly choked. "One of the richest men in the world?" Maria stammered, still barely able to talk. She didn't dare finish saying the sentence out loud. One of the richest men in the world *who was looking for her.* Or specifically, the card that had been in her dead husband's wallet. That was the only answer that made sense.

"Fucking asshole," Brittney continued. "Shows up here with ICE like he owns the world. You know, I dated a tech bro and they're all the same." She sighed as if she were weary beyond her years. "They learn about life and women from their VR headsets and when they're confronted by the real thing, they're total douches."

Maria was still trembling, but she had to ask the question. "Are both of those women really named Maria Garcia?" she stammered and grabbed her crucifix.

The manager looked at Maria and her gaze softened. "Oh honey, I'm sorry. You're shaking!" She leaned forward toward Maria. "It isn't like this around her normally, I swear. These people. ICE. The CEO of Kavali. We don't get raided, really."

"But those women…"

Brittney nodded. "The younger one goes by Maria. I think her name is…" Brittney flipped through her e-tablet and then said slowly, "Maria Felipa Morales de Garcia. But the older maid, she's only been here a couple months. We call her Lupa. Totally forgot her name was Maria until ICE showed up."

Maria took a deep breath and tried to slow her heart. "Why is ICE searching for a woman named Maria Garcia?"

"I don't know," Brittney shook her head. It was clear she was annoyed by the intrusion. "They just showed up, ICE and the billionaire." She rolled her eyes. "Wanting to see everyone named Maria Garcia. Some lame story about genetics testing. So I called Mel at Best Western. My BFF from high school. Who knew we'd both manage housekeeping. Mel said same thing happened there. ICE swoops in yesterday wanting to see employment records. Anyone with a name close to Maria Garcia gets a swab in the mouth."

Maria's heart started pounding again. She could barely hear over the rush of blood to her ears. They were searching for her. She should stand right now and run out of the door. But then what? The bus wasn't due for another twenty minutes. She'd stand at the bus stop, alone, exposed.

"Gabby, honey," Brittney reached forward with a tissue. "You don't have anything to worry about. Your name isn't Maria Garcia."

But it was. Her name was Maria Garcia and a very rich and powerful man was looking for her. One who could get ICE to do his dirty work. Maria swallowed hard. First Cadejo and now a billionaire named Mohan Mallick. She resisted the urge to say a prayer right there in front of Brittney. One thing was clear. She needed to get the card that Carlos had in his wallet back to Mohan Mallick. But she couldn't just march up to him and return it. Mohan was working with ICE. They'd figure out who she was in a second and she'd be jailed, maybe deported or worse—separated from her son. No, she needed the tech billionaire to think she'd never had the card in the first place. It was the only way that he'd stop searching for her. But how?

While Brittney talked about the Holiday Inn's cleanliness practices, Maria said a silent prayer. *Help me Señor de Esquipulas to return the card, I beg of you.* She prayed that this time the saint would answer her prayer.

17. BEL

Bel pulled his coat tight and dipped his head as he stepped out of SFPD Head-quarters next to his daughter. The gusts from the bay were strong, whipping through San Francisco's China Basin neighborhood and propelling him and Nadine off the ground. They turned onto Fourth Street and the gusts abated, blocked by nearby squat buildings. The person they were looking for was there in front of them, just as they'd been told.

"Detective Thorn," Nadine called out.

Bel hurried after his daughter. Since deciding that she was his best shot at uncovering the secrets of the Kavali synthetic genome, he'd inserted himself into her investigation at every turn. She was cautious, but he'd seen a flicker of a smile when he arrived at her apartment this morning.

The detective stood next to a Halal food truck. He looked up, surprised. He bit into his chicken shawarma and his eyes narrowed. "How did you know I was here?" he asked and wiped a dribble of hot sauce from his chin with a thin paper napkin.

"Madeline at the front desk told us," Nadine answered. Bel had tried to contain his surprise at SFPD Headquarters. His daughter seemed to know her way about the San Francisco police department. She'd easily chatted with the supervisor just inside the building and greeted several of the officers by name.

She'd even whispered to him that she'd helped get Detective Thorn's daughter into Stanford.

The detective grimaced. "She really shouldn't do that," he said. "I've told you everything I have in the case." He balled up the napkin and tossed it into a nearby trash can. "That was our deal, and there's been nothing..." The detective stopped in mid-sentence. Bel looked at his daughter. She held up the replica of the orange card that Carlos Garcia had in his hands on the Embarcadero, the one that she and Nigel had fabricated with their 3D printer. Bel had to admit it looked authentic—as authentic as could be created from a grainy photo. The detective seemed spellbound.

"Where did you get that?" The detective whispered. He reached for the card.

"Not so fast!" Nadine exclaimed. She dropped the card in her pocket and crossed her arms. "Clearly, you have not told me everything. Now, suppose we start over and maybe I'll tell you how I got it."

"How do I know that's the stolen card?" The detective asked. Bel couldn't help but smile. The detective had just confirmed their suspicions.

"Tell me yours, I'll tell you mine," Nadine smiled. "This Kavali media card, we know that Carlos Garcia had it on the Embarcadero just before he was shot. What happened after that?"

The detective's eyes narrowed and he looked around. Bel thought the man looked nervous and seemed to fidget in the midday sun.

"I was an idiot," the detective grimaced, his eyes continuing to dart around the street. "But this is just between us, right?" The detective pointed at Bel and Nadine. Bel nodded. "The kid in Forensics says it's just an old payment card in Garcia's wallet. I take his word. Then, just as Kavali tells us about the fuck up, she comes to identify the body and..."

"She?" Nadine interrupted.

"Yeah, Garcia's widow, Maria. I assume that's where you got the card?" He paused and stepped back, his eyes narrow with suspicion.

"Of course," Nadine said hurriedly. "Mm...Maria Garcia. Where else would I have gotten it?"

"Uh huh" the detective nodded slowly. "How'd you find her anyway?" He crossed his arms. "Mohan Mallick is personally overseeing the manhunt. He's got half the ICE force in Sonoma County looking for her. Fucking tech asshole." The detective jutted out his jaw. "And yet, somehow, you find her and convince her to give you the card?"

"I'm not ICE," Nadine said smoothly. "The Sonoma County Guatemalan population doesn't scatter when I walk into their neighborhood."

"Right," the detective said, arms still crossed. Bel could tell the detective wasn't convinced. "What's on it?"

"The card?" Nadine raised an eyebrow.

"Come on, Nadine. You say you're a journalist but we both know you still hack. What's on the card?"

Nadine shrugged and started to speak but Bel interrupted.

"It's the genome," he said with a confidence he wasn't sure he felt. "The DNA modifications that Mohan introduced to the world. The Synthetica genome is on the media card." Bel's heart thumped and he swallowed hard watching the detective's reaction.

Out of the corner of his eye he saw Nadine's brow raise but she said nothing. The detective's eyes widened. The man looked slowly from Bel to his daughter. "Sure," the detective said and nodded slowly without commitment. "But if you'd really hacked it, you wouldn't be talking to me, you'd be negotiating with Mohan Mallick for whatever it is you want."

The detective uncrossed his arms and jammed his hands in his pockets. The wind whistled around the corner of a nearby building causing Bel to shudder. The detective started to walk away and then turned. "Nadine, Mr. McMaster," his voice had lost its edge. "Be careful. Whatever is on that card, it's dangerous. And Mohan Mallick is not to be fucked with. ICE not only outsources their

DNA tracking of immigrants to Kavali." The detective glanced over his shoulder. "But now Kavali is the largest private contractor managing immigrant resettlement and deportation." The detective paused as if expecting a question on the incongruent combination. "Mohan has contacts in high places," the detective warned and hurried away leaving Bel alone on the street with his daughter.

Nadine shook her head slowly. "Why would a biotech company deport undocumented immigrants?" She stared after the detective, seemingly lost in thought.

Bel shrugged. The combination made no sense, but he didn't understand complex businesses.

"And you're turning into quite the investigator," Nadine said, looking at him curiously. "Though in hindsight, it's obvious that the Synthetica genome was stolen." She tugged at one of the piercings in her ear. "But what would a security guard want with that?"

"Mind if I see it?" Bel asked. He turned the card over slowly in his hands. "Sell it to the highest bidder?" he suggested.

Nadine shrugged. "It's a map of patented genetic material. That makes it difficult to find a buyer." Nadine looked at him thoughtfully. "No, the guard would have wanted something besides a buyer, and besides, it doesn't matter. The detective said Garcia's widow has the card."

"Maria Garcia," Bel said slowly. Despite the lie they'd told the detective, there was no way he and his daughter could find Maria Garcia. She was probably undocumented, like her husband. She could be anywhere. "So, what do we do now?" He slipped the orange card quietly into his pocket.

"The detective will tell Mohan," Nadine mused. "And then, we see if Mohan takes the bait and comes after us." She twisted a piercing as she looked at him. "I can't believe you're helping me, Dad." He thought he saw a glimmer of respect in her eyes. "It's like we're a team." She smiled, almost shyly.

Bel looked away. They weren't really a team. His daughter thought he was helping her with her mission to extract an admission of guilt from Mohan. She would be disgusted if she knew what he really wanted. He turned and smiled as best he could. "Yes," he said. "We're a team."

18. MARIA

Maria shielded her eyes against the setting sun as she clamored up the dirt path to the ridge of Bel McMaster's coastal vineyard. The ocean behind her was calm but the early evening air was breezy, almost blustery. The gusts came from the east and were warm and dry, not like the chill that came off the ocean. She stopped halfway to the top, looked across the Pacific and fingered the sword-like crucifix around her neck. She'd told no one about the chance encounter with ICE and the billionaire Mohan Mallick at the Windsor Holiday Inn. The entire incident happened so quickly it almost could have been a dream, except when she'd returned home and opened her dresser drawer, the strange orange card was still there. Its very presence caused her to lose her breath and fall into a chair. First Cadejo and now Mohan Mallick. It was too much.

When Bel McMaster texted wanting to see her again, it was a welcome distraction, but she'd paused before answering. Juan was right, the maids had gossiped about the white man who had come calling and she didn't want to give them any more fuel. After walking in circles with her heart racing, she texted back, but now she felt like a Catholic school girl who'd just snuck out behind the gymnasium to see a forbidden boy. She almost expected to see a nun, arms crossed, as she crested the ridge. But her heart leapt when she saw him instead.

Bel McMaster stood at the other end of the path, up a gentle slope, bathed in the setting sun, staring at her. He'd probably watched her dart from the inn and across the road, and he just stood there, waiting with a goofy, wistful grin. He waved and she waved back, her heart thumping. She felt his eyes on her as she walked up the remainder of the path.

"I wasn't sure you'd come," he said.

"I wasn't sure I would either," she said, which wasn't the least bit true. The wind gusted and blew her hair in her face. She'd undone her thick braid tonight and wore her hair loose, the way the American girls did. Gabby would tease her about it if she knew.

"You said you wanted to see me tonight," Maria said to the winemaker.

He smiled, sadly. "Thanks," he cleared his throat. "Things have been bumpy." He paused as if he were about to say something else, but then pointed to the tiny shed. "I thought maybe you might like to try something new?"

She followed him into the shed where he'd placed two bottles of wine and glasses on the rustic wooden table.

"Sonoma County chardonnay," he said. "Not every wine drinker is a fan. Some say it's too buttery, too rich. But I think there's something, well, almost carnal about it."

Maria wasn't sure whether to smile or frown. *Carnal.* The nuns in school used that word for things that were of the body and shameful. Maybe they were right and she should be ashamed to be here with the winemaker. But the sun-dappled ridge and the roar of the ocean felt as if they'd been blessed by the saints. And standing next to Bel, she felt a constant tingle. It couldn't be wrong.

Bel smiled at her and rummaged through his pockets. "It's in here some-where," he said and emptied the contents of his coat pockets on the table into a small pile. "Ah," he exclaimed and reached for a wine opener.

His smile was almost too much and Maria glanced away, looking at the pile of his belongings on the table. She gasped and squinted, not fully believing her eyes. Peeking out from beneath his wallet on the table was the corner of a card. She wouldn't have looked twice except the color was unmistakable. An orange that she'd seen only once before—the same orange of the card that she'd found in her husband's wallet. With the stuck note from Carlos that she'd eventually peeled off. Slightly larger than a payment card. The card with the logo. The card that Mohan Mallick wanted back. A chill ran down her spine and she glanced up at Bel, busily opening the bottle of wine and then looked back at the table.

Maybe she'd been wrong at the Windsor Holiday Inn, maybe there were many of these orange cards that vibrated in the sun. Her heart raced. She was nervous and confused. Maybe Mohan Mallick wasn't looking for the card her husband stole after all, but then, why was he interrogating the women both named Maria Garcia at the hotel? With Bel intent on the wine bottle, she spun as if to look outside and made herself trip and fall into the table. The table tipped and Bel's pocket belongings scattered to the ground.

"Oh, I'm so clumsy," she exclaimed and dropped to her knees, rapidly gathering up his belongings. She reached for the orange card and glanced up. Bel looked down at her. She couldn't decipher his look, amusement? She stood and placed his items on the table except for the orange card. Her heart was beating so loud she thought he'd be able to hear it. She held the card up into the sun's rays.

"Such an unusual color," she said, trying to keep her voice calm. She turned it over in the sunlight. It seemed identical to the one in her drawer back home— orange on one side with a logo, pitted and metallic on the other. The card remained still, however. It didn't vibrate. She kept holding it in the sunlight. But nothing.

Bel looked at her curiously. He reached out and took the card, then turned it over in his hands thoughtfully. "Yes, it is," he agreed slowly.

"My payment card is just gray," Maria said. "A boring color." She tried to sound casual.

"Oh, it's not a payment card," Bel responded. He seemed distant. "It's a…" he seemed like he didn't want to finish his thought. He looked up at her, his eyes far away. "It's a replica of something," he said quickly and slipped the card into his pocket.

Maria drew in her breath. A replica. The word was the same in Spanish. A copy. A chill went down her spine as it struck her. What if she replaced the replica in Bel's pocket with the real card from Carlos's wallet? After that, maybe she could tell someone that Bel had the real card. It would divert ICE from looking for her and send them to Bel. Ned McMaster had been on the Embarcadero that night, after all. It wasn't impossible that the card could have ended up in his pocket instead of her husband's.

She exhaled. It was ridiculous. The plan was flimsy at best, and how could she pull it off? Bel just said he had a replica, he knew his card wasn't real. And besides, who could she alert that Bel had the real card without giving herself away? She had no connections to the billionaire and she certainly didn't want to contact ICE. Then there was the fact that Bel was starting to enter her daydreams. She couldn't put him in jeopardy.

Bel looked at her with those emerald eyes and her heart melted. No, she couldn't. She smiled at his infectious enthusiasm. He popped the cork on the bottle and splashed wine into a glass.

"The process for making this wine is an old family secret," he said. "We don't actually use French oak, but that's all I can tell you!"

She caught her breath as he pressed the wine glass into her hand. He was from an old family. An old white and famous family. No harm would come to him if he had the real card. ICE would never arrest him. Cadejo would never threaten him. She stood straighter and took the glass from him. She would go through with her plan.

"Smell," he said softly.

She stuck her nose into the glass and inhaled. She smelled vanilla and some sort of fruit. Peach, maybe.

"Now taste," he commanded.

She sipped. He was right. The wine was buttery, smooth in her mouth. It trickled sensually down the back of her throat and warmed her insides. She closed her eyes and tried not to think about Mohan Mallick or Bel McMaster or what she was about to do. "That," he said proudly, "is a true McMaster Vineyards Chardonnay. As wholesome as apple pie."

"It's beautiful," Maria said. "It makes me think of my grandmother, baking in the kitchen."

"Chardonnay can do that to you," Bel said softly. "It can make you think of baked goods." He was watching her closely. When she raised her eyes and met his gaze he looked away.

She exhaled and tried to steady her thoughts. Her first step was to take his replica card. She'd replace it later with the real thing. Right now, she would have to stay focused and not get carried away with her desire for the winemaker.

"Come," she said and grabbed his hand. "The sun is just about below the ocean. Let's watch." She pulled him from the shed and as she did, dipped her hand into his coat pocket. Then, together they walked to the edge of the ridge. The wind had quieted and the ocean was placid, like liquid sapphire. The golden rays of the setting sun splayed across the horizon and surrounded them with a warm, amber light. She shivered and put her hands in her pockets. One hand touched an object in her pocket, rigid and flat, the size of a payment card and pitted on one side. It had been easy to lift from Bel's pocket. He hadn't even noticed.

She felt Bel put his arm around her shoulders as the sun's yellow light turned into dusk. Maria leaned toward him, trembling in the cooling air. The sun slowly slid below the horizon and with it went the evening's final light.

19. BEL

Bel walked into the McMaster Vineyards tasting room and couldn't help but smile even though the space was devoid of paying customers. Normally the lack of wine-tasters and tourists would have depressed him, but thoughts of Gabby last night on the ridge ricocheted through his brain. He sighed and sat on one of the high stools near the room's large retractable walls, pushed open this afternoon to let the warm vineyard breezes waft through the space. He couldn't stop thinking about a drop of chardonnay that had lingered on Gabby's perfectly-shaped lips. He spun on the stool like a boy, wondering what that drop would have tasted like if he'd slowly licked it off. He felt a hardening between his legs. As he spun, a bottle inside his coat jostled. The bottle of Kavali wine that he'd surreptitiously taken from the tower.

He reached inside his coat and pulled out the bottle of wine and set it on the counter. It had been in his truck for days and he'd grabbed it on the way into the tasting room curious if it would still impress him the way it had in Kavali Tower. He motioned to the wine pourer on duty, Keisha, and asked her to open and decant it.

"Ah, Mr. McMaster, your wife said I could find you here," called a voice. Bel spun to see a dapper man wearing a coat and pleated slacks walk brusquely across the McMaster Vineyards tasting room. Though Bel hadn't seen the man

in years, he recognized him immediately. The head of the French Wine Ministers cut an imposing figure, despite his diminutive size.

"Monsieur Tari," Bel spluttered. "You're here!"

"A great observation," Cedric Tari replied. "I told you that I would visit,
and so I am." The Frenchman paused for a moment as he smoothed the front
of his lapel. Cedric Tari was the most senior of the Paris Wine Ministers, the
man who decided the fate of winemakers around the world. Bel tried to hide
his shock at the fact that Cedric Tari was standing in his tasting room.

"I didn't expect you so soon," Bel continued. He looked around the tasting
room frantically, as if he should be putting things in order.

The Frenchman held up his hand. "There is no need for anything special,"
he said. "I stopped at the estate house but your wife said you were not there.
Your wife said I could find you here, drinking, which I find funny."

"Funny," Bel cleared his throat. "Well, that's not really…"

"But perhaps more funny," Monsieur Tari continued, "was a young man
your wife introduced me to. A cannabis researcher." Cedric Tari spat the word
cannabis quickly, as if merely saying the word polluted his palate. "You must
tell me that I am wrong." Cedric Tari stood silently in front of Bel. "Surely you
know our rules."

Bel's mind raced. With so few bylaws about the wine competition, there
couldn't possibly be a rule prohibiting growing cannabis alongside grape vines,
could there? But god damn Maureen anyway. His blood started to boil. His wife
knew what she was doing. She had told Cedric Tari of her cannabis plans for
one reason—to jeopardize his chances at getting an invitation to the competition. Bel clenched his fists.

"We have a… researcher on the estate," Bel fumed, his face reddening.
"From the university, creating cannabis clones. University-sponsored. All legal." The words tumbled out of Bel's mouth before he could stop them. The
mix of half-truths and lies sounded almost believable.

"Our new rules are clear, Mr. McMaster," Cedric Tari responded. "No crops, especially cannabis, can be grown alongside your vines. I am afraid you will be disqualified."

The Frenchman smoothed his coat and turned to leave the tasting room. Bel's heart was in his throat. What new rules? He couldn't lose before he'd even been invited to enter the competition. Winning in Paris was his only hope at redemption. Everything hinged on it. Behind him, Keisha placed the decanted wine from Kavali Tower on the bar.

"Wait, please," he called out. Bel jumped after the Wine Minister. "Monsieur Tari, please, just a moment." Bel exhaled, trying to dispel his anger at his wife, and looked around the tasting room desperately. There, on the counter, was his answer. He cleared his throat. "I have something I want you to taste, Monsieur Tari."

The Frenchman stopped. He returned to the counter; his expression amused. "Mr. McMaster, you have had a difficult time. And the past years, they have not been kind, have they not? Perhaps now is not..."

"No," interrupted Bel. "Please."

Bel set a red wine glass in front of Cedric Tari. He reached for the decanter, poured a careful measure of the Kavali pinot and slid the glass toward Monsieur Tari. The French Wine Minister's expression had changed from amusement to sorrow.

"A recent vintage?" he asked with an arched eyebrow. He shook his head sadly and reached gingerly for the glass. The Wine Minister swirled its contents and waved his hand above the rim to coax the fragrance to his nose. He looked at Bel with surprise and then put his nose far inside the glass, inhaling deeply.

"What is this?" he asked. Then Cedric Tari put the glass to his lips and drew the wine across his tongue. His eyes closed to half-mast and he seemed to chew the wine, rolling it across his tongue and not breathing for seconds on end. Bel watched as the Frenchman moved his cheeks slowly, as if he wanted the wine in his mouth to encounter every single one of his taste buds.

"Well," Bel asked. He held his breath and prayed that the bottle of Kavali wine was as good as he remembered and would fool the Wine Minister. "What do you think?"

Cedric Tari snapped open his eyes, as if returning from a trace. "It is magnifique," he said softly. He held the glass aloft and examined the wine's color in the sunlight that streamed in through the open walls. "I never thought I would taste this again," he said. "The reports of the climate change, the drought, the destruction of the terroir of your pinot fields. I feared the worst. But this…." The Wine Minister tipped the glass and watched the red wine with awe. Then he brought it to his lips and sipped reverently. Again, he savored the wine. Then, quite suddenly, his expression changed and he set the glass down on the counter with a smack.

"This isn't some sort of trick," he said to Bel, his eyes narrowing.

"Trick?" Bel asked as innocently as he could. "I am as proud of that pinot as any I've ever made." He flushed as he told the lie, praying to god the ploy would work.

Cedric Tari stared at Bel for a moment, his cheeks red with both excitement and indignation. "I must see for myself," Monsieur Tari said at last. "I must examine your facility and ensure that this wine is coming from your vats. There is to be no funny business."

"Absolutely," Bel said, nodding.

"I will come back with the delegation. We shall inspect the entire winery," said the Frenchman as he started to leave the tasting room. As he reached the door he stopped and turned toward Bel. "And Mr. McMaster, your cannabis experiments are over. You must not proceed with planting or else you will be disqualified."

"But," Bel started to protest but the French Wine Minister held up his hands.

"These are the rules, I do not make them. Do not plant that hideous crop."

* * *

Bel stumbled on the porch stairs to the Queen Anne. He cursed under his breath and tried to focus his bloodshot eyes through the glass front door and down the long hallway beyond the grand foyer. Light spilled from the dining room into the hall and he could hear the clink of dishes and silver. He gripped the railing hard and gritted his teeth. How dare she. How dare Maureen tell Cedric Tari of her ridiculous plans to plant cannabis at McMaster Vineyards. He squeezed the railing so hard he thought it might crack. She wanted him to fail. His own wife.

After Monsieur Tari left the tasting room, Bel finished off the decanted wine from Kavali. Then, he'd motioned to Keishi to open a bottle from McMaster Vineyards which he also finished. Keisha pursed her lips when he asked her to open a third bottle but he ignored her and downed it anyway. His fury increased with each glass, with each bottle. And to think that tonight Maureen invited their daughter to dinner. He knew exactly what she was planning. To tell Nadine about her plans to plant cannabis and then get their daughter on her side, just like she always did. All of Maureen's protests about his need to repair his relationship with his daughter were a ruse. She was an expert at playing the kids against him.

He pushed open the front door and lumbered down the hallway, his anger escalating at the sound of laughter echoing from the dining room. Maureen and Nadine were already there.

Maureen looked up with surprise when he entered. Maybe she thought he wouldn't come. "Bel, how nice of you to join us," she said. He could hear the ice in her voice. The lights in the dining room were too bright and he squinted. It was just the three of them in the spacious room. His gaze lingered on a fourth chair, Ned's place. Bel's heart contracted as he remembered how his son would have bounded into the dining room followed by a cloud of pot smoke, mumbling apologies after his mother had shouted up the stairs.

"How dare you," Bel hissed. He gripped the door frame to steady himself. "How dare you tell Cedric Tari about your stupid plans."

Maureen looked at him, disdain dripping. God, he wanted to wipe away that look of disgust from her face.

"Nadine," Maureen said, ignoring him and turning to face their daughter. "For years your father has been mismanaging McMaster Vineyards. He overpaid for vineyards by the coast, incurred overruns on the visitor center that isn't even up to new fire codes, and bought oak barrels of questionable origin. But, even worse, we are woefully unprepared for changes in the weather, for climate change. We've lost the pinot crop for five years in a row. Frankly we're in worse shape than ever. And because of his bad decisions, your father has borrowed money and defaulted on the mortgages from the bank."

Goddamn Kelly Garret must have told everyone in town about the loans. "I am getting us on track," Bel stammered. "I have a plan to restore our reputation. And this winery carries my family name, not yours!"

Maureen laughed, a bitter laugh that Bel recognized from nearly every argument they'd had over the past years. "You think entering that silly wine contest will help you restore our reputation?" Maureen put air quotes around her final three words and her lip curled. "Pathetic, Bel. Absolutely pathetic."

"And your plan to grow pot is better?" Bel looked at her with as much incredulity as he could muster. "A cannabis farm!" he screamed. He turned to his daughter. "This is why your mother invited you here tonight. To tell you, and this is too unbelievable to make up, that she wants to turn McMaster Vineyards into a pot farm!" Bel spat out the words and laughed derisively, staring at his wife with fury and disbelief.

"That is not why I invited my daughter to dinner." Maureen smacked her hand down on the table and stood. "My family trust, the Baxter Trust, is buying the bank note against the land and the winery and I will be the sole operator of McMaster Vineyards."

Bel's jaw dropped as he struggled to comprehend what his wife had just said. That she was buying McMaster Vineyards? He stood in shock and silence. Her words circled in the air around him until Nadine finally spoke. "What do you mean, you'll be the operator? You and Dad already own it."

"Correction. I'll be the sole operator," Maureen repeated.

"You can't do that," Bel said, feeling his chest tighten. Deep down his blood started to boil. He couldn't even look at his wife.

"I did and I am. As of this morning, my trust is now the owner of the properties, the business, and this house."

"What the fuck does that mean?" Bel teetered from the door to the table and slammed his fist down. "You can't buy the mortgages without my signature. This stinks of your father. Did he put you up to this?"

"The property was in foreclosure, Bel," Maureen's voice shook with fury. "Which you neglected to tell me. I had to find out for myself. Buyers were circling like vultures and the bank was preparing an auction, so I took steps to protect the property."

Bel's face darkened and he moved toward his wife, kicking a chair out of the way. It crashed backward onto the oak floor. "Protect the property?" he shouted, jabbing his finger at his wife. "Protect it from what? I have the situation under control!"

"Under control?" Maureen laughed. "You must be joking! Five years of total crop losses. Secret mortgages that none of us knew about. Not to mention your near constant inebriation. And Virna tells me we didn't make payroll last month. Were you going to tell me about that?"

Bel picked up a plate from the table. "McMaster Vineyards is my family vineyard," he screamed. "Not yours. You cannot and you will not take it!"

"Bel," Maureen shook her head and said forcefully. "It's done. The trust owns McMaster Vineyards. I am saving our asses and saving our reputation. McMaster Vineyards is mine to manage."

Bel smashed the plate against the table. It splintered into shards that scattered across the floor. He kicked another chair and lumbered to the sideboard, picked up a large, weathered stone ring sculpture and hefted it in his hand. "No you will not!" he shouted. He banged the sculpture on the sideboard and cursed, spittle flying from his mouth. Then he spun, raised the stone sculpture and flung it at the wall. It hurtled past his daughter and crashed into a bronze-framed mirror which exploded.

"Jesus, Dad!" Nadine gasped.

Bel looked around the room—at Nadine's look of disbelief and his wife's scorn. He looked at the wild and beast-like reflection in the shattered mirror and saw his father, Michael McMaster. A broken, haggard drunk who beat his son senseless.

He stumbled to the doorway, banged his fists on the door frame and lumbered from the dining room, his footsteps uneven as he left the house.

* * *

Bel unlocked the metal door of his winery lab and pushed it open. The overhead lights automatically flickered as he stumbled in, blood still coursing with rage. The lab was dusty from disuse and neglect and he hadn't been here since Ned's death. He dropped onto a stool and wiped a layer of grime from a refractometer. The equipment was out of date but it still worked. He looked around and his eyes watered. This was the McMaster Vineyards wine lab that his son would have modernized, ushering in a new type of genetic research to the winery. Hell, Ned might have even created synthetic genetic material like Mohan had. Never mind that Ned had just dropped out of college, the kid was brilliant. A lump caught in Bel's throat. Losing his only son, his heir. And now his wife accusing him of mismanaging the estate and trying to prevent him from entering the Paris Wine Competition. Jesus, that woman. He was doing everything he could to keep McMaster Vineyards afloat.

The windows shuddered and Bel glanced outside. The Diablo winds, strong again tonight. The vines next to the winery whipped in the gusts. They were some of the oldest on the estate planted by his father over fifty years before. Michael McMaster knew how to put the vines in the right soil, and then, he let the vines do the work. His father was insistent that the vines fight to survive—not over-irrigating them but stepping back as the vines were forced to push their roots deeper and deeper into the soil to find water. The harder the vine worked to stay alive, the smaller and more intense the fruit would be, Michael used to say. Bel put his head in his hands as he realized that it wasn't just the vines—everything around his father had to fight for survival. Fuck it. He pounded his fist on the lab table. That's what he needed to do. He just didn't know how.

He looked up at a soft knock on the door. Nadine. His gut tightened at the thought of his drunken tirade in front of his daughter.

"I haven't been in here in a while," she said and sat quietly next to him. She was silent for a moment and looked around the room. Faint light shone in the office windows that looked out into the cavernous winery with its rows of large, stainless fermenting tanks, each of which reached high to the ceiling. "I remember you and grampy here in the lab when I was a kid. I never knew what he did, but it always seemed so..." she paused and brushed at the grime on the lab table as if searching for a word. "Scientific."

Bel snorted. "Your grandfather was hardly scientific. He was intuitive." He sighed. "But your brother, he was the scientific one." Bel tried to keep the pride from his voice.

"I worry about you, Dad." Nadine twirled one of her short ponytails. The wind continued to blow steadily and the outside window rattled. "Mom told me that you had some idea about entering a contest..."

"A competition," he said quickly.

"Right, a competition." His daughter turned to look at him. "The one that grampy won. But Dad, how? How would you ever win a competition with, well, the way things are at McMaster Vineyards?"

Bel looked away and through the lab's interior windows to the winery. He blinked slowly as he considered the rows and rows of tanks filled with fermenting wine. Wine that these days was virtually worthless—certainly not up to the McMaster reputation. He sighed. His daughter, at least, was being diplomatic. Not like his mother. His wife. Cedric Tari. All of them said there was no way he'd win. He'd be a fool to enter. They were right, of course.

He didn't bother to tell his daughter that there was a wine that could win the competition. Because even if he managed to steal another bottle of Kavali and enter it in the competition as his own, he'd never pass the winery inspection. He'd been able to fool Cedric Tari once with the bottle of wine from Kavali, but next the Wine Ministers would examine everything. Tanks. Barrels. Hell, they would probably even taste the grapes on the vines.

"I thought…" Bel stared vacantly at the fermenting tanks. He cleared his throat. "I thought that if I entered and won," he said quietly, "that I could restore the reputation of McMaster Vineyards. Turn things around." And finally have a reputation equal to my father, he thought.

Nadine looked at him with a sad smile. "Dad," she said quietly, "There's no wine left that you could enter into that competition. You've sold all the decent stuff and Mom tells me that we barely have anything left." Even his daughter who wanted nothing to do with the wine business knew he was delusional, he could tell.

"It's true, I'd need a miracle," Bel said reluctantly. That miracle might have come from the Kavali genome, but any hopes he'd had about discovering its secret by tagging along with Nadine were going nowhere. He was right back to where he'd started.

Nadine's watch buzzed. "I'm sorry," she said. "I have to go."

Bel stifled a belch. "Sure," he responded. And then without thinking he said, "The receptionist?"

Nadine looked up quickly, her eyes curious. "Yes" she said.

His daughter was right to be surprised. He'd hardly paid attention to her girlfriends over the years. But he certainly remembered the receptionist with the odd orange dot next to her ear and the power to open doors at Kavali Tower.

"She has a name, Dad," Nadine continued. "It's Daisy and I like her." Nadine smiled at him. Was she looking for his approval?

The outside windows rattled against the Diablo wind. "Right. She's Daisy."

"I'm having dinner with her at my place tomorrow night," Nadine said carefully, as if she were uncertain. "Maybe you'd like to join us?"

A thought crossed his mind. Daisy's eardot. That eardot made it possible to enter Kavali Tower. The eardot that could lead him to the hanging vineyards. He sucked in his breath.

"Dad?" Nadine looked at him curiously.

"I'd love to," Bel stammered. His mind raced. Suddenly, there was a next step in his fight for survival.

20. MARIA

Maria glanced around the bakery section of Lola's Market furtively. Any time she was in Santa Rosa now, she was alert, edgy. Always on the lookout, never certain who might be nearby. The self-defense classes with her cousin helped. She was now able to overcome her panic when the instructor pinned her on the floor. Still, she couldn't relax.

Her hands shook as she dropped shortbread cookies into her shopping basket. The cookies were a treat for her son and his cousin Ana, a treat that she could afford after picking up an extra shift earlier in the week. Gabby said she would cook tonight, something from her freezer. The children wouldn't care but Maria wanted to give them something to look forward to after dinner. She touched the crucifix around her neck and tried to smile. Despite her anxiety, she loved the satisfaction of being able to buy a treat for her son.

She wove through the supermarket aisle toward the checkout lanes, passed a row of bank teller machines and glanced up at the security monitors mounted above them, pausing. In the grainy black and white images, she noticed a man looking at her from the next aisle. It took barely a second for her to realize they were watching each other. Her heart raced and she felt a catch in her breath as she realized that the man with the slicked back hair, dark slacks and black fitted shirt was not a local. He might have been handsome with his lean jaw and heavy-lidded eyes, but his features were hardened and his mouth held a perpetual sneer. It was the tattoo on his neck, the number eighteen in Roman numerals, that gave him away. Maria sucked in her breath. There was no mistaking the man this time. He was Cadejo.

She stepped backward. Chills ran down her spine, her heart thumped and her breathing was shallow. Of all the times that her cousin couldn't shop with her. She had to get to Juan. He was waiting for her in his car in the parking lot. She couldn't tell from the monitor where in the store Cadejo was. By the front doors, maybe. She grabbed her phone and punched a frantic text to the handyman.

ICE AGENT IN STORE. BRING CAR BEHIND STORE NOW!!

She dropped her basket to the floor, spun around and darted down the aisle of the store. She kept her head low. When she reached the back of the store, she looked frantically for a door to the store's rear section. There it was. *Employees Only.*

She slipped into the cold darkness of the store's loading dock. The room was large and dim. The smell of overly ripe vegetables and cardboard hung in the air and rows of crates ran from one end of the room to the other. Maria paused as her eyes adjusted. She scanned the loading dock for an exit. At the far end was a row of closed garage doors and next to them a green exit sign winked. Maria moved silently toward the door.

Behind her, she heard footsteps. The hair on her forearms stood up and she stopped, frozen and listened. She took another step and heard a voice, a man's voice. Guttural and smug.

"Maria, I know you're here."

She wanted to scream. She knew the voice better than any other. That voice had looped in her head for years. She flattened herself against a palette of crates. Her heart was in her throat, pounding so loud it deafened her. She struggled to listen. This time, the sound was unmistakable. Polished boots on concrete. The footsteps echoed through the dim loading dock. She held her breath and moved to the end of the row of crates. The boots on concrete stopped. He was listening for her. Waiting.

She took off her shoes and padded toward the green exit light. Then, she stopped and listened. The loading dock was silent except for her panting. Her heart pounded. The exit was so close. Juan would be waiting on the other side.

She walked on the balls of her feet toward the doors quietly as she could. Something buzzed loudly. Maria gasped. The buzzing continued in her pocket. She wanted to scream as she pulled out her phone, frantically trying to silence Juan's texts. The light from her buzzing phone lit up the dark warehouse, illuminating Cadejo's face when she looked up. He leered at her in the pale, white light of her phone.

She shrieked as he reached for her. She shoved him hard and ran toward the exit. Cadejo's boots thundered on the concrete behind her. Maria's hand brushed an open crate of fruit. She grabbed frantically, wrapping her hand around a zapote, spun around, and heaved it. The fruit flew through the air and splattered on the concrete. Cadejo's boot slipped and he fell to one knee. He growled and scrambled to his feet.

Maria sprinted to the exit. She bashed against the door and burst into the sunlight. Juan was there, waiting in his car. She leapt down the concrete stairs and bolted toward the car. Juan stuck his head out of the window and his eyes opened wide as he saw her screaming from the loading dock. Cadejo exploded through the door, jumped down the stairs and was right behind her. She could hear his boots pounding on the gravel.

"Drive, drive!" Maria screamed at the handyman. Juan looked at her wild eyes, ducked into the car and threw the old Toyota into gear. The car trembled forward. Maria sprinted hysterically after the moving vehicle. She could feel Cadejo's breath on her neck.

She jerked the passenger door open, screaming at Juan.

"Go, go, go!" she shouted. The car veered forward and Maria clung to the frame of the open door. She glanced over her shoulder and shrieked. Cadejo was right there. He reached toward her. She had one leg in the car and, still holding onto the door, she kicked backward with all of her might. Her heel thudded into Cadejo's chest and she heard him curse. She tumbled into the moving car and slammed the door.

Cadejo pounded on the trunk as the Toyota lurched from his grasp. The car veered into the street. Maria peered through the rear window and gasped. Cadejo had jumped into a black sedan. The tires on his car squealed. He was right behind them.

"Move, move," Maria screamed. "Drive faster!"

"That isn't ICE," Juan screamed at Maria. "Is that who I think it is?"

"Not now, please," Maria shouted.

Juan shook his head nervously and accelerated. The Toyota jumped forward on the busy city street. Traffic was heavy and the lanes were clogged. Juan swerved to the left against oncoming traffic. Horns blared. Drivers cursed. Maria could see sweat starting to run down Juan's face. She turned and looked behind them. Cadejo's black sedan pounded through an intersection and squealed to avoid a truck.

The stoplight in front of them turned red. "Don't stop," Maria shouted frantically. Juan raced around waiting cars. Traffic entering the intersection from the left and right screeched to a stop. Brake lights flared. One car slammed to a halt. The Toyota raced ahead. Juan barreled through the intersection.

She turned and squinted through the rear window. The black sedan blew through the red light and smashed two cars aside. The cars spun and careened into each other, stopping helplessly by the side of the road.

Juan gripped the wheel while sirens sounded all around them and emergency vehicles raced through the approaching intersection. Traffic had stopped in both directions. There was no way through.

"There," Maria screamed, pointing to a freeway entrance. Juan yanked the steering wheel hard to enter it. The Toyota launched over a curb and for a moment they were airborne, weightless. They banged down hard on the freeway entrance, tires squealing.

Juan stomped on the accelerator. The car whined and roared onto Highway 12 and into mid-afternoon traffic flowing westward from downtown Santa Rosa. The car rattled mightily as Juan wove madly through the highway traffic.

Maria rolled down the passenger window and stuck her head out. The black sedan was just four cars behind them and rapidly accelerating as it caught up to the Toyota.

"He's catching us," Maria screamed above the roar of the wind.

"We can't outrun him," Juan shook his head. The dashboard of the Toyota quivered.

Maria looked desperately behind them. Cadejo's sedan would catch them in mere seconds. The beat-up Toyota was already shuddering.

They sped from the city limits and into the surrounding vineyards. Cadejo was only two car lengths behind them. Maria trembled. She saw the vineyards next to the freeway and picking crews taking to the fields for the evening shift. An idea popped into her head.

"Take this exit, Occidental Road!" she commanded. "NOW."

Juan nodded. The Toyota screamed across three lanes of traffic. Smoke poured from the tires. The putrid smell of burning rubber filled the air. Maria clung to the door handle as the car screeched onto the exit ramp and barreled through the intersection. She said a silent prayer to the saint and crossed herself.

"Don't stop," Maria screamed. "Go to the fields. Park there!" She pointed to the field workers' cars, a long row of beat-up cars and pickups—Toyotas, Hondas, and Dodges.

"Are you kidding!" Juan yelled incredulously. And then he looked at Maria. "Shit, it just might work."

Maria glanced back at the freeway. The black sedan had slammed on its brakes and squealed past the Occidental Road exit. The car now barreled backward on Highway 12, threading its way to the missed exit. Cars and trucks blared around Cadejo's car.

"Hurry!" Maria screamed.

The Toyota bumped onto a dirt road next to the vineyard and flew past the row of vineyard workers' cars until they came to a space. Juan parked the Toyota in between a battered Corolla and a faded Civic.

"Now!" Maria commanded. She and Juan leapt from the car and sprinted toward the vineyard. They each grabbed a hat and a plastic bucket from a stack near a folding table with picking supplies and darted down a row of vines, blending in with the evening work crew. Maria tried to slow her breathing, but she still gulped for air. She tucked her hair under the cap and slouched her shoulders.

She kept her back to parked cars, but glanced surreptitiously as Cadejo's sedan lumbered from Occidental Road and onto the dirt road of the vineyard. The black sedan moved slowly past the row of vineyard workers' cars. It stopped near Juan's car and Cadejo got out. Maria held her breath.

Steam rose from the front of Juan's old Toyota. There was no disguising the fact that the car had just been driven. She gripped the edge of the picking bucket tightly as she watched Cadejo feel the hood of the car. The gangster walked to the edge of the vineyard and stood there, scanning the field. Maria's heart stopped. He was going to walk down the very row of vines where she stood.

"Hey," a male voice called out. A man, his blond hair whipping from under his cap in the evening breeze, walked toward them. He had the look of a foreman and scowled at Maria and Juan as he approached. "I don't pay you to talk. Why aren't you picking?"

"We, we…" Maria stammered and tried to keep her back to the edge of the field and Cadejo. "That man behind me," Maria finally breathed, "he's impersonating ICE. Harassing the field workers. Demanding money."

The blond man looked suspiciously from Juan to Maria and then shook his head. "Fucking asshole," he muttered under his breath. "Keep working," he said. "I'll take care of this." The man strode away and waved his hands at Cadejo.

Maria pulled the brim of her hat low and peeked toward the edge of the field. The blond foreman was animated in his interaction with Cadejo. The gangster pointed and seemed to shout, but the two men were too far away for Maria to hear. Finally, she saw Cadejo spin and walk angrily back to the black sedan. He banged his fist on the roof of his car and squealed from the vineyard in a cloud of dust and gravel. Only then did Maria realize she'd been holding her breath. She exhaled slowly and turned to Juan. He had his arms crossed.

"That was Cadejo," Juan said, his voice tight.

Maria nodded.

Juan dropped his head and his shoulders sagged. "I thought I left that man behind," he said.

"I'm so sorry," Maria whispered. She pulled Juan into an embrace. The evening wind whipped up, warm and dry and from the east again. But the breezes weren't calming, they only seemed to agitate Maria.

"You have to tell me everything," Juan said, his voice felt so far away.

"I will," Maria replied and pulled him closer. "I will."

21. BEL

"I brought something special tonight." Bel pulled a bottle from behind his back where he'd been hiding it and handed it to his daughter as he entered her San Francisco loft.

Nadine examined the label. Her brow knit curiously and then she looked up at him, eyes wide. "Is this what I think it is?" she breathed.

Bel's heart swelled for a split second. She actually recognized it. His daughter had seemed both eager and reluctant when she'd invited him to dinner with Daisy so he wanted to bring something impressive. But he shifted uncomfortably at his real motivation in bringing the rare wine. To assuage the guilt for what he was about to do.

He followed her as she practically bounded to the living room and once there, he turned his nervous glance to the San Francisco skyline, framed by his daughter's loft windows. Kavali Tower dominated the other buildings, grasping at the heavens. His heart raced as he looked at the building. If things went according to plan, he'd be entering Kavail Tower in mere hours and then racing back to his lab with a cutting from Mohan Mallick's genetically engineered pinot vine. After that was anyone's guess. The bartender in Kavali Tower claimed that the vines grew in under six weeks. Preposterous. Still, it was his only chance. He exhaled to calm himself as his head swam.

"Daisy, do you know what this is?" Nadine exclaimed to the woman in the living room. Daisy moved to Nadine's side and slipped her arm around his daughter's waist.

Daisy was taller than Bel remembered and dressed differently, which made sense. Last time he'd seen her, she'd been wearing a company-branded outfit and her hair pulled from her face. Tonight, she was total SOMA chic, wearing a fitted kutura over wide slacks.

"This is one of the most famous bottles of wine in the world," Nadine continued. "It's a McMaster Vineyards pinot from 2009."

"Single vineyard," Bel said and cleared his throat, suddenly feeling even more guilty because of his daughter's excitement at the gift. "One of the last bottles in the world." His daughter was right. It was one of the world's most famous bottles of wine. Collectors would have paid a huge sum just for the privilege of putting the bottle in their rack even though the wine inside was past its prime. But he couldn't believe Nadine knew. Maybe she had been paying attention all those years when he waxed on about wine at the dinner table.

"How very kind of you, Mr. McMaster," Daisy looked up from the bottle, her arm still around his daughter's waist. She had a formal way about her, and a sort of classic style as if she were from a generation not her own. "I can't wait to taste it."

"Well," Bel held up his hands casually, he hoped, trying not to betray his anxiety. "It should have been opened more than a decade ago. California pinots are meant to be enjoyed young."

"That is a wonderfully American concept," Daisy said. Her voice had a lovely lilt. "Such emphasis on the young, the youth. Even the wine you prefer young instead of old."

Bel smiled as best he could. Out of the corner of his eye, he saw his daughter searching in the tiny cabinet that served as a bar in her living room. He reached into his pocket. "Need this?" He flipped her a wine opener. She might have been listening to him pontificate about wine all those years at the dinner table, but she certainly hadn't adopted the wine lifestyle.

As Nadine tackled the cork in the pinot, Bel swallowed nervously. Here he was, pretending to have a civilized conversation with his daughter and her new girlfriend, while at the same time plotting to steal from said girlfriend to break into her place of employment. He closed his eyes and exhaled. Maybe that was the positive aspect of being beaten as a child. He knew how to disassociate. He kept smiling and opened his eyes. Daisy had stopped talking and was watching him.

He cleared his throat. "Americans do seem to prefer young wines," he said. "But of course, it's always been hard to compare an American pinot noir with a French red Burgundy. Americans have a preference for big bold flavors. Those aren't always a function of age."

"Yet, your father's pinot won a contest in France? Nadine told me."

"It was a competition not a contest," Bel said. "And yes. My father figured out how to make an American pinot noir that charmed the French, and the entire world for that matter."

"Hadn't your father already died in 2009?" Daisy looked puzzled as Nadine handed her a wine glass and made a show of holding the bottle for inspection, as a sommelier might. Nadine poured the wine into their glasses. Bel swirled it and held his glass up to the light. It was still clear.

"He had," Bel said, still gazing at the glass of wine in the light. "But I kept his chief winemaker on staff, a Frenchman named Jean Claude, and together we continued to make some of the world's best wines. The harvest of 2009, however, was something every winemaker dreams of. The weather was perfect, the winds calm, the summer days warm. It was a once in a lifetime event." Bel brought the glass down to his nose and sniffed. The bouquet was still surprisingly bold. The cherry and vanilla were there, mixed with the smell of Sonoma earthiness. Bel closed his eyes and for a moment was transported back in time

160

to the old McMaster Vineyards tasting room when he'd first opened a bottle of the 2009 pinot. JC had been there, Maureen still loved him. The twins were tiny and playing in a corner. He knew the moment he tasted it that the pinot would be a phenomenon. And it almost was. But his mother Odette, she'd stepped in. Stopped the shipment to the French Wine Ministers. Bel's eyes fluttered open. He exhaled and sipped the wine. It tasted beautiful, still, after all these years. A bit of sourness on the finish, but any wine aficionado would know that this wine could have won awards.

He looked at his daughter and Daisy. They sipped the wine and looked at him expectantly.

"It's still amazing," Bel murmured, thankful to have something to take his mind off his upcoming actions, if only for a moment.

"I remember this," Nadine said and held up her glass. "We drank a lot of this when I was a kid."

"You did?" Daisy laughed and looked at Bel. "You let your children drink wine?"

"Well," Bel flushed, his stomach now fully in knots of guilt at Daisy and Nadine's gentle teasing. "They weren't children, they were..."

"Kids, Dad," Nadine interrupted. "We were kids. But it seemed normal, somehow, because Dad was a winemaker."

"You know," Daisy said thoughtfully as she sipped her glass of wine. "Wouldn't it be amazing if your wine kept its flavor forever?" She looked at Bel and tucked her hair behind her ear. Bel sucked in his breath. There was no orange dot next to her ear. It must be in her purse by the front door.

He exhaled slowly. "You remind me of your boss," he said almost without thinking.

"My boss?" Daisy looked at him curiously.

"Mohan Mallick." Bel tried not to grimace. "His presentation at the top of Kavali Tower. He said nearly the same thing." Mohan's big show at the top of the tower seemed years ago, but it had only been days. The dying October sunlight slipped around his daughter's living room as Bel sipped the wine again, slowly. He was determined not to get drunk tonight. He had to keep his wits about him. If he was able to find that orange eardot, he needed to be clear headed and use it to break into Kavali Tower.

"Oh, yes," Daisy's smile was far away. "Mohan Mallick."

"Why did you decide to work at Kavali?" Bel asked. His heart continued to race. Surely his daughter must notice that he was agitated. If she did, she said nothing.

"Oh," Daisy seemed surprised, almost as if she'd never been asked that question before. She rubbed her hand on the side of the wine glass. "Well, I suppose because my father works there. He's an engineer. And it just seemed like a good place to start my career."

"An engineer? Does he work with the plants?" Bel tried to hide his curiosity.

"Sort of," Daisy said. Bel couldn't tell if she was avoiding the question. "He's more of a manager."

"Ah." Bel sipped the wine again. It had aged surprisingly well. The primary flavors were still there and each sip seemed to resurrect a new set of memories. This sip brought back memory of a tasting with a wine master's club in London. The looks of amazement and respect. And Odette, glowering in the background. Her husband's reputation was not to be fucked with.

He turned from Nadine and Daisy and again looked at the San Francisco skyline. The sun had sunk below the horizon and the buildings were lighted and bright, except for Kavali Tower which seemed like a dark needle threading the sky with its own inkiness. Bel swallowed hard. Suddenly, he wasn't sure he could go through with it. And yet, he had no choice. He closed his eyes again. His stomach churned. It was now or never.

"I need the restroom," he opened his eyes and turned to Nadine. She waved him away and he slipped from the living room, leaving the two women deep in conversation.

The hallway was dark. He didn't turn on overhead lights but flipped on his phone flashlight and pointed it at the small table by the front door. Daisy's purse. God, he felt like a hood for hire as he picked it up and quietly unzipped it. His stomach contracted and glanced back at the light spilling from the living room. His daughter and Daisy continued their chatter. He rifled through the contents of her purse as carefully as he could. His heart thumped. A pair of headphones. Hand sanitizer. The voices stopped and he looked up, standing completely still. He could feel beads of sweat on his brow. A shadow flashed across the hallway and then the voices resumed.

Daisy's purse contained a wallet which he opened and flipped through. A few cards, nothing of note. And no orange dot. His heart was thumping loudly now. He tried not to think about the creepiness of searching through his daughter's girlfriend's purse. God he was desperate. He couldn't catch his breath. The orange eardot wasn't in the purse. There was nothing that would get him into Kavali Tower. Fuck.

"Dad," Nadine called out. "Is everything OK?" There was silence from the living room. Bel set Daisy's purse back on the hallway table as quietly as he could.

"Dad?" He heard a chair squeak. His daughter was standing. His hand brushed against a coat handing from a peg. Daisy's coat.

Footsteps sounded across the living room floor. "Dad?"

Bel grabbed the coat and frantically pawed through a pocket. Nothing, it was empty. The outside breast pocket. Empty. He patted the coat. There, a bump. The inside breast pocket. He pulled at it. Daisy's phone. The screen activated from the motion and illuminated the hallway. He looked up madly. No Nadine yet. The phone's home screen picture was of Daisy with her arm around another young woman. A recent ex-girlfriend maybe, judging from the happy look on Daisy's face. The other young woman was wearing a uniform. Bel frowned. The logo on the arm of the uniform was familiar. It was a helix under which was the word "SECURITY". He didn't have time to consider who Daisy might have dated before Nadine and as he stuffed the phone back into the coat pocket, it clinked against something hard.

"Are you alright?" Nadine was nearly to the hallway.

There it was, stuck deep in the breast pocket. A tiny orange dot. That had to be it. He yanked the tiny crystalline eardot out of Daisy's coat pocket and stuffed it into his pants pocket.

The overhead lights flickered on. Nadine stood at the end of the hallway, her face narrow with concern. "Are you OK?"

"I'm not feeling well," Bel said and swallowed hard. "I should leave." He hoped the eardot, deep in his pocket, would not glow.

Nadine frowned and walked toward him shaking her head. "Not with that," she said. She took the coat gently from his hands and looked at him with concern. "This is Daisy's."

Bel's heart raced. He could swear Nadine must be able to hear it thumping. Or that an orange glow would shine from the eardot inside his pocket. "God, I'm an idiot. I just need to go." He grabbed his coat from a peg and moved to the door. "Sorry," he mumbled over his shoulder and let the door slam behind him.

On the sidewalk, he tried to slow his racing heart as he stared up at Kavali Tower in the distance. He felt like a shit, but as he pulled the orange dot from his pocket and held it in his hands, he knew he had a way in. He exhaled and started walking toward the tower. Now, he just had to get the clipping from the vine. God this had better work.

22. MARIA

Maria paced back and forth in the hallway on the second floor of the Jenner Inn. Her shift was over and it was late, but the last place she wanted to be was in the break room with the other maids. She couldn't stand their prying eyes, the gossip about the white man, the speculation over missed shifts. Yes, she'd snuck up to the top of the ridge to see Bel McMaster again—but if only they knew about Cadejo and Mohan Mallick. It had been just two days since Cadejo had chased her and Juan from Lola's Marketing in Santa Rosa. Nearly two weeks since Mohan Mallick almost discovered her at Windsor Holiday Inn. Her heart had barely stopped thudding. Her mind racing. She exhaled and looked down at the patterned carpet in the hallway. She tried to shake it off but she'd woken in a cold sweat from a recurring nightmare that night. Cadejo's hands reached toward her from a bank of gray fog. She'd bolted up in bed and clutched the crucifix that never left her neck, whispering to the saints to deliver her from this misery.

She'd called in sick after the encounter with Cadejo. It was only the second time since she'd worked at Jenner Inn. For other maids, calling in twice would have been a trifle, but it raised red flags for Maria, the most dependable maid at the inn. Belinda called, concerned, disbelieving Maria's story of stomach virus. Maria couldn't stand lying. But more than anything, she couldn't afford to lose her job.

Juan had barely left her side, the two of them craving the security of their shared past. She'd told him everything. The note stuck with Carlos's blood to the mysterious orange metal card that glowed in the sun. The billionaire, Mohan Mallick, who knew her name and was scouring Sonoma County for her with ICE. The replica of the card that she'd lifted from Bel McMaster. She'd unloaded her burden and felt relieved but Juan had tensed at the memory of Cadejo's brutality.

Their initial terror gradually gave way to jagged relief as the uneventful night passed. They'd debated whether they should return to Jenner Inn. In the end, they had no option. Juan was already in debt. His asylum lawyers weren't cheap even with help from the local LGBTQ chapter. And Maria was behind on rent after taking off time to go to the morgue to identify Carlos's body. Missing more days would put her even further behind. Her cousin could help with her bills only to a point.

She looked up from the patterned carpet and tried to catch her breath and grabbed a feather duster to be closer to Juan in the lobby where he was fixing a light. Just being in the same room with him would calm her.

She heard the lobby door squeak and voices. Guests checking in, most likely San Francisco weekenders. They were picky but not rude. She sighed. They'd inspect the suite and call down the lobby with some concern—a smudged mirror, a room that didn't warm fast enough. She had stayed late so Belinda would dispatch her or Juan. Extra towels or an adjustment to the thermostat. *They just want to be heard,* Belinda would say. Maria shook her head. Someday, she dreamed that she would be heard.

She rounded the corner and stepped onto the tiny balcony that overlooked the lobby. Shafts of light from the dying October sun cut through the lobby from the skylights in the ceiling. Below, two men stood at the reception desk, their heads bent toward Belinda. Out of the corner of her eye, Maria saw a movement. Juan flagged his arms furiously from the corner. Maria squinted. Juan seemed alarmed. His motions were jerky and pointed at the two men with Belinda.

Maria looked at them and slowly sucked in her breath. They had their backs to her, but she recognized them instantly. She froze. The giant man in the ICE uniform from the Holiday Inn. The billionaire, Mohan Mallick was here. Talking to Belinda.

She felt weak and let go of the duster. It fell over the edge of the balcony and drifted down. Maria put her hand over her mouth and silently screamed. The duster clattered on a lampshade below. The two men turned slowly and looked up at her. Mohan Mallick was holding his phone in front of Belinda as if showing her an image. Even without seeing the image, Maria knew it was a picture of her. The two men stared. Maria couldn't breathe.

"Maria Garcia." Mohan exhaled the words slowly, as if he were seeing an apparition.

Maria took a step backward, her heart thudding. "No," she whispered, her eyes wide.

Juan found his voice first. "Run, Maria!" he screamed. He threw his tools to the floor and flew toward the staircase. The gigantic man in the ICE uniform was the next to snap from his daze. He hollered something unintelligible and lumbered after Juan, sprinting up the stairs behind the handyman with surprising dexterity.

"Run!" Juan screamed again, now at the top of the staircase. Maria trembled and then spun. She raced down the hallway, her white sneakers thudding on the spongy carpet. She could hear Juan sprinting behind her. She shoved the maid's cart out of the way and swiped her key card on a guest door. The lock flickered but didn't open. The hallway started to shake and she looked up. The gigantic man in the ICE uniform had entered the hallway and hurtled toward her, the floor shuddered violently under his weight.

"Please, please," Maria whispered to the saints and swiped her card again. The door clicked open. Juan was at her side. She shoved the door, pulled Juan in after her and slammed the door shut. The locked door quaked as the giant man bashed it from the other side. The door handle rattled.

"They found us," Maria cried and pulled Juan close. The door thudded again and vibrated against its frame. Other voices sounded in the hallway. Mohan Mallick. A woman's voice shouting—Belinda, refusing to unlock the door.

"You have to hide," Juan hissed. "The cave. You must go there now!"

"We're on the second floor, there's no way," Maria was frantic. They were trapped in the guest room. Her heart raced.

"You'll jump," Juan said. He moved quickly to the glass door to the room's outside balcony and slid it open. "Come!" he beckoned from outside.

Maria darted to the outside balcony and looked over the edge. They were at the rear of the building facing the ocean. Directly below was a brick terrace, but just beyond that the ground was dry and grassy.

"Climb over, I'll hold you," Juan commanded.

The door to the room cracked and the frame started to splinter. The locked door wouldn't keep the giant out. They had only seconds. From the hall, Maria could hear Belinda still yelling with little effect. The giant pounded on.

Maria hitched her skirt and put her sneaker up on the railing. Juan grabbed her wrists. She swung out over the railing and hung from Juan.

"Ready?" he asked, and before she could nod, he released her. She dropped to the ground and grunted. Pain flashed and she winced. Her ankle. She stood and cried in pain but there was no time. She could hear the thumping of boots on the ground coming from the front of the inn. ICE agents. They would have the building surrounded in seconds.

She tilted her head up. "Jump," she hissed at Juan.

He shook his head and smiled sadly at her. "I'm going to buy you time."

Maria shook her head in disbelief. "No!" she nearly screamed. "Juan, no, please!"

She heard the echo of the door splintering in the guest room above. The sound was horrifying. The door was almost beaten down.

"You need to run, now Maria."

She looked up at Juan, his square jaw, his soft brown eyes and for a moment she saw Carlos, waving to her as she drifted away on a raft of inner tubes.

Juan turned from her and slid the glass door closed. The click of the door reverberated in her brain. She couldn't move and her best friend was gone. She stared up, gaping, but the thudding of boots coming from the front of the inn yanked her from her daze. She had to run. She ignored the pain shooting through her ankle and sprinted across the lawn behind the inn toward the cliff. The sound of pounding boots from the front of the inn grew. She was almost to the cliff. She could hear the shouts of the ICE agents, unintelligible. The clicks of their weapons being loaded. She couldn't let them see her.

Maria dove into the thicket of coyote bushes and grabbed the branch of the Monterey Cyprus. She edged out over the cliff and dropped. She landed on the path and stifled a cry. She flattened herself against the rock face. Above her, she heard voices, angry and shouting. Footsteps thrashed through the grasses.

She held her breath and inched down the path silently. The violent sounds of footsteps and hollering faded until she reached the cave. She darted in the entrance and fell to the floor. The weak rays of the evening sun barely lit the damp space.

She brought the sword-like crucifix to her lips and whispered, "Why?" She nearly screamed and looked up at the rocky ceiling, terrified of what the ICE agents would do to Juan. He didn't deserve this. Why had the saints forsaken him? Why had they forsaken her?

But even as she shouted out the question, she knew the answer. Deep down, she knew why. The saints were punishing her because of the bargain she'd made that had saved Juan's life.

23. BEL

Bel stood at the base of Kavali Tower and gazed up. The sun had long since sunk below the horizon and the building's lights now glowed brightly, but even so, the tower was ominous. In the daylight, he'd been able to see to the very top, but in the darkness, the building seemed to stretch beyond the heavens and out of sight. His heart pounded and he looked around the plaza in front of the building at the people scurrying to and from the main entrance, most of them with heads bowed over glowing screens. No one seemed to recognize him.

The tower's facial-recognition cameras inside would be a different story, however. Bel had powered down his phone blocks ago on the walk from his daughter's loft to the tower to avoid electronic detection, but it wasn't until he passed a street vendor hawking facial recognition-thwarting glasses that he stopped to consider how many times he would be photographed and scanned in the tower. The street vendor was sketchy but swore that the glasses, when paired with a baseball cap, would foil Kavali's facial-recognition system. Bel didn't have a choice.

He donned the glasses from the street vendor, pulled his cap low and walked around the Kavali Tower plaza and to the building's corner. The main entrance was too heavily guarded. He needed to find an entrance that was smaller where he could slip in, unnoticed. He pulled his jacket tight, lowered his head and walked quickly. The winds from the bay whistled down Mission Street and tugged at him. His heart thudded as he scoured the side of the building. No entrances as far as he could see. He rounded another corner and his gaze caught a queue of people entering the building wearing uniforms. The nighttime cleaners. It was a service entrance.

As he drew closer, a bus rumbled to a stop next to the service entrance, threw open its door and an armed guard jumped out. Bel sucked in his breath and flattened against the building. Another guard joined the first followed by a line of men and women who shuffled into the service entrance. Bel frowned. Why were workers being escorted into the building by armed guards? He looked closer at the guard's uniform. ICE. He shivered. These weren't nighttime workers. Maybe they were undocumented immigrants? He inhaled and remembered what the detective had said. Kavali was in the deportation business. It made no sense. Regardless, he had no choice but to wait, sweating as the line of immigrants entered the tower. Then the bus, emptied of its human cargo, lumbered away.

Bel glanced over his shoulder and tried to calm his thudding heart. There was no sign of the immigrants as he joined the queue of nighttime workers. The line moved quickly to a revolving door that led to a tiny, barren lobby. As he entered, he saw that the cleaners didn't have orange dots next to their ears. Instead, each looked into a camera that silently scanned their face. A thick security door then clicked open. Fuck, he'd hoped there would be no facial scanning yet, but that was naive. Still, this entrance was his only option. He shuffled forward in the queue and when it was his turn, walked up the camera. Sweat ran down his back and he exhaled slowly and adjusted the glasses on his face. As the camera's beam scanned his face, he pulled the small orange dot from his pocket and held it next to his ear. The dot seemed to leap from his fingers and he felt it adhere to the side of his face, next to his tragus. He touched the eardot gingerly and it buzzed. The camera in front of him flickered off and the security door clicked open.

Bel stood still, hardly able to believe it had been that easy. The glasses had worked. And the eardot had opened the service door to Kavali Tower with barely any fuss. Sweat was now pouring down his back. He didn't know what to do.

"Hey amigo, think you can move them legs?" A man in coveralls standing in line behind Bel gave him a shove. Bel stumbled through the security door and into an endless, brightly-lit white hallway. The security door clanged shut behind him. He shuddered and took in his surroundings. There seemed to be only one direction to go. Forward. He started moving as quickly as his shaking legs could carry him.

The hallway twisted and turned and Bel kept walking quickly, keeping his head low to avoid what he assumed were cameras everywhere. He tried to keep his pace moderate, but his heart was thumping and it was all he could do not to break into a sprint. Eventually, he came to an intersection. The hallway to the left and the one that continued in front of him were marked with dozens of arrows and names of destinations. But he didn't have to read them. It was the arrow that pointed to the right. *Kavali Fields: Restricted.* That hallway was barred by a massive steel door that looked like it belonged in an underground nuclear bunker. Thick. Impenetrable.

Sweat poured down his back as he approached the door. It was time to see what this eardot could do. He looked up and touched his eardot. At first nothing, but then a deep clank. The door quivered and slowly rumbled open.

As Bel walked through, he looked up and gasped. Above stretched the gargantuan vertical canyon filled with acres of enormous hanging fields. Somewhere up there his coveted pinot vines were growing, in a city skyscraper.

To his side was a large bank of glass elevators. Even at this late hour, dozens of them rocketed up and down their transparent tubes carrying people to god knows where. He sucked in his breath and walked as casually as he could. He touched the eardot and an elevator door hissed open. Damn, that receptionist had access to everything.

Inside the elevator, he flipped through a series of hologram screens trying to find his destination. But it was impossible. The coding system for the fields was complex. He exhaled and looked around the elevator. God, what was he going to do? The eardot next to his tragus buzzed but he ignored it and ran his hand through his thinning hair. The eardot buzzed again and he heard a female voice that seemed to come from inside his own head. *Where do you want to go?*

Bel jumped. It was the eardot. It was speaking to him. It knew he was in the elevator.

"Um," his voice shook. "The pinot vineyard, the pinot that comes from McMaster Vineyards."

The reply was instantaneous. *The Pommard or Volnay clones?*

Bel gasped. No one knew the origins of the McMaster Vineyards pinot vines. His father, Michael, had been elusive about his award-winning vines. But once, when he was close to death and drunk, he'd confided in Bel, told him how he'd slipped into two award-winning Côte de Beaune vineyards after dark and sliced off vines then smuggled them from France to Sonoma County. No one knew Michael McMaster's secret except for Bel. And now apparently, Mohan Mallick.

"The Pommard," he stammered.

The elevator rocketed up and Bel grabbed at a handrail. The elevator raced skyward through the gargantuan hanging fields, He leaned back against the elevator wall, his stomach in knots. The crazy billionaire geneticist, Mohan Mallick, had decoded the McMaster family secret. The irony stuck and he hung his head. Mohan, his father, himself. They weren't that different.

The elevator chimed and slowed to a stop. The doors hissed open and Bel stepped onto a tiny catwalk. He looked down through the mesh floor of the catwalk and his knees buckled. He was thousands of feet above the base of Kavali cavern standing on a flimsy metal catwalk. The cavern's bottom wasn't even visible from this height. He grabbed for the handrail and slammed his eyes shut. *Breathe, just breathe.* But he couldn't just stand here with his eyes closed. *You're ridiculous, Bel.* He slowly opened his eyes and looked up instead of down. Gigantic panels hung everywhere, dwarfing him, each teaming with perfectly-groomed and ridiculously-oversized plants and trees.

He took a tentative step. The tiny catwalk trembled but seemed sturdy. He gulped and tried to walk steadily. He kept his gaze straight ahead, not able to look down.

The catwalk meandered among the gigantic vertical fields bursting with plants—practically every recognizable or exotic plant from around the world, but Bel was interested in only one. The McMaster Vineyards pinot vine. The elevator had deposited him in an area of red wine vineyards, but the oversized vines around him weren't pinot. Shiraz maybe. And syrah. He kept moving, grabbing onto the railing of the tiny catwalk periodically to steady himself. His heart pounded as he rounded another bend and wove between two huge vertical panels. He ducked around rows of cabernet vines that stretched vertically, He thought he heard a rustle and stopped, his heart pounding. He looked up at the enormous black grapes that almost faded into the darkness of the nighttime tower. The vines above him fluttered. Odd. There was no breeze, the air was completely still. A shudder ran down his spine. It seemed as if something was watching him. The vines? He shook his head and kept moving. He wanted the pinots.

He rounded another huge hanging field and stopped dead in his tracks. His heart thumped. There in front of him, a cloud of orange drones hung, tending to a vertical vineyard. They sprayed a mist of some kind and buzzed around the plants. Bel gulped. They didn't seem to see him, surprisingly. He held his breath and stepped backward. The catwalk trembled but didn't squeak.

He took another step backward and eased around the corner and out of sight of the drones. He exhaled and turned. And there they were. An enormous panel with grapevines planted in perfect rows that ran vertically to the heavens, and from the vines swung clusters of perfectly-shaped, huge grapes the size of melons, their light ruby-red color glistening in the muted light of the tower. He inhaled and held his breath as he walked toward the vertical field. The grapes were grotesquely large but beautiful nonetheless. And they were unmistakably pinot. As he approached, his heart thumped. He stopped at the edge of the catwalk and lifted his eyes, gazing at the vertical rows. He reached out and reverently touched the vine closest to him. It felt exactly like a grape vine should. He laughed at himself. Of course, this is how it should feel. It's a fucking grape vine. He snapped off a length of vine and stowed it in his coat. As he did, the vine seemed to recoil. Bel stared. It wasn't possible. He reached out to snap off another piece and the vine pulled away from his grasp. What the hell. Impossible. He grabbed at the vine and snapped off another section and stuck it in his pants.

"You certainly don't look like my receptionist."

Bel spun. His heart jumped into his throat. It was Mohan Mallick. Standing on the catwalk behind him. He was impeccably groomed just like he'd been on stage in front of thousands. Behind the tech titan, dozens of spherical orange drones hovered ominously, tiny lights flashing and small limb-like protrusions dotting their surfaces. Their buzzing made his skin crawl.

"*Your* receptionist?" Bel stammered. He stepped backward against the railing and tried not to look down. Sweat trickled down his neck.

Mohan Mallick grimaced. "Daisy Jain," he said through gritted teeth. "The young woman who is dating your daughter, Mr. McMaster. Somehow," Mohan continued with a wry frown, "you have her UAD." Mohan reached forward and flicked the eardot from Bel's cheekbone and into the palm on his hand. Mohan narrowed his eyes and the cloud of drones moved closer. Their incessant buzzing rose in pitch to a fevered whine. Mohan flicked his wrist and the drones rose up above them and circled.

"I would ask you why you're here," Mohan hissed and leaned forward, his face directly in front of Bel's. Bel could feel the tech titan's red-hot spittle on his face. "But I know." Mohan reached inside Bel's coat and extracted the length of Kavali vine. "Pathetic that you have to steal from me because your own vineyards are decimated," Mohan sneered. "Decimated by climate change that you helped usher into this world. And yet, as the climate changed, you were too fucking stupid to change with it." Mohan snorted and grabbed Bel's chin. "But you have no problem deceiving a bunch of decrepit judges to win a goddamn meaningless award, do you, Mr. McMaster?"

Bel's heart sank. Mohan knew about the competition. He knew why Bel was here. Bel's heart thudded.

Mohan released Bel's chin and stepped back. "What's to stop me from commanding my drones to pump you full of holes and throw you over the railing?" Mohan's voice lost its lilt. "No one will know. Your phone is turned off. Your truck is still parked at your daughter's." Mohan spun and walked away, back toward the elevators. The cloud of orange drones descended in the tech titan's place, their buzzing drilling into Bel's skull.

Fuck. The tech titan knew how he'd gotten the eardot. Bel couldn't move any further backward. The thin railing cut into his lower back. His mind raced. "I can get something you want," he stammered, shouting to be heard above the drones' buzzing. He tried to think and speak at the same time. "The card."

Mohan stopped moving away. He cocked his head. "What card?"

"The card." God what did Nadine call it. He couldn't think with those goddamn drones buzzing in his face. "Removable memory card. Orange. Metal."

Mohan turned. He seemed to consider Bel. He flicked his wrist again and the drones backed off but their buzzing continued.

"It was stolen by a Kavali security guard," Bel licked his dry lips as he struggled to recall everything the detective had said. "And then by Carlos Garcia."

Mohan's expression gave away nothing. "Go on," Mohan rumbled.

Bel's mind raced. "We found her," he continued. "The wife of Carlos Garcia. In Sonoma County."

Mohan's eyes narrowed and he said nothing. But he wasn't moving away and the drones stayed put. "How odd," Mohan growled. "Because I just saw her." He stared at Bel for what seemed like an hour and then grimaced. Bel gulped. If Mohan had really just found her, he had no leverage. Bel held his breath. Maybe Mohan was bluffing, because if he knew where Carlos's wife was, he would have ended the conversation already. "She is...resourceful," the tech titan said finally. Then he crossed his arms. "What is her name?"

Bel exhaled. "Maria," he breathed. Thank god, he'd remembered her name. "Maria Garcia."

Mohan stared at him, eyes narrow, piercing. "You expect me to believe that you found the widow of Carlos Garcia in Sonoma County and convinced her to give you something that might have been stolen from me?"

"Yes," Bel lied. "I know her. I know Maria Garcia." He was now drenched in sweat.

Mohan snorted but not as derisively as before. "And you have it, this orange metal card?"

He wiped the sweat from his brow. "I'll trade you," Bel said before he could stop himself. It was crazy but he kept going. "I'll trade the card for fermenting pinot wine." He couldn't believe he'd said it, or that he was here, suspended on a catwalk in Kavali Tower bargaining with one of the world's richest men.

Apparently neither could Mohan Mallick. "Absolutely not," he spat, then flicked his wrist and the drones descended. Their buzzing ate into Bel's ears. As they approached, dozens of them, he saw that the protrusions poking from their spherical sides were tiny needles, comically small, like the twig arms on a snowman.

Mohan walked away, striding down the catwalk. A drone buzzed directly in front of Bel's face. A needle. Inches from his eye. A drop of fluid hung from the needle. His heart raced. He pushed himself back against the railing. The drone advanced. Bel felt himself tipping backward.

Bel had one more card to play. "Synthetica." He yelled as loud as he could over the mind-numbing buzzing of the drones. "It's on the media card. The orange card I got from Maria Garcia. I have your genome, Mohan."

Mohan spun. His face was purple. The tech titan's eyes turned pitch black and lost all signs of life as he strode back toward Bel. "Where is it? I want it right now," Mohan screamed.

"It's in Sonoma County...it's complicated," Bel stammered. "It will take me a few days." Bel could barely breathe. His arms were out to his sides and he struggled to keep his grip on the thin wire railing.

Mohan stopped and stared. Bel could practically feel the man looking right through him. "Forty-eight hours," Mohan barked. He waved his wrist and the drones dissipated, flying off into the inky reaches of the cavern. The sudden quiet was almost as unnerving as the buzzing.

Bel swallowed hard and slowly stood up straight, willing himself not to look into the abyss of the cavern he'd almost plummeted into. His heart thudded as he tried to catch his breath.

Mohan pointed at him, eyes full of rage. "Get me that goddamn card, Mr. McMaster, and you'll get your wine. But you better not be fucking with me." The tech titan spun and marched toward the elevator. "Follow that drone and get the hell out of my tower," he called over his shoulder and pointed at one of the orange spherical drones buzzing in the distance.

Bel doubled over and fought to catch his breath. His heart was racing so fast he feared it might explode. He gulped and righted himself and nearly jumped backward. A single orange drone hovered in front of him. On the drone was a badge with the symbol of a helix and the word SECURITY. He frowned. The logo was familiar.

"This way," the drone said in a flat, mechanical voice and flew toward the elevator bank.

Bel wiped the sweat from his brow. As he followed the drone, he tried not to limp, but the second length of vine he'd stuck in his pants—the one Mohan didn't find—jabbed him in the leg. If his heart hadn't been thudding so fast, he might have smiled at the thought that he had gotten what he'd come for.

24. MARIA

Maria couldn't sleep. She'd paced in the tiny cave for hours, jumping at any sound that wasn't drowned out by the constant roar of the ocean below. She'd almost driven herself crazy wondering what had happened to Juan. She exhaled and wiped her eyes. She couldn't stay hidden anymore. She needed to leave while it was still dark or she'd risk being seen by the light of dawn. She slipped from the damp cave and onto the path that led up to the inn. Her heart pounded and she stood completely still. No sound of footsteps over the pounding of the waves at the bottom of the dark cliff. She exhaled, kissed the crucifix that hung from her neck, and kept close to the rock wall feeling its rough surface with her hands. The moon was bright, but one slip would send her tumbling into the ocean far below.

She crept around a corner and stopped. Faint light from the inn spilled over the cliff above. The outside floodlights stayed on all night, illuminating the sidewalks around the building. She listened intently. Still no sound of footsteps. She used the handholds carved into the side of the cliff, hoisted herself up to the edge and scanned the lawn behind the inn. It appeared empty.

Keeping low, she darted to the building's edge and peeked around to the parking lot. Sedans, SUVs, a small van, but no ICE vehicle. She exhaled and moved quickly to the employee parking lot. There it was. Juan's beat up Toyota.

He hadn't answered her texts all night and Maria feared the worst. That he'd been taken by ICE. Maria choked back a sob and reached under the dented fender where Juan kept the hide-a-key. *For emergencies,* he'd said. As if he knew something like this would happen.

Maria unlocked the door, slipped the key in the ignition and held her breath. The old combustion engine chugged and then roared to life. She exhaled. She eased the car into gear and glanced to her right and left. Her heart stopped and she screamed. There was a face outside the driver window. A person, reaching toward her. Maria jammed her foot on the accelerator when a voice called out.

"Gabby, wait!"

It was Belinda, her frazzled hair bobbing in the nighttime gusts. Maria screeched to a halt and ran toward the manager. "Where is Juan?" she cried, her voice shaking. "Did they take him?"

Belinda reddened and she nodded. "Some nonsense about interfering with an investigation," Belinda spat. Maria could hear the disbelief in the manager's voice. "ICE wouldn't tell me where they were taking him. In all my years..." She left the sentence unfinished and dropped her voice. "Gabby, or Maria if that's your name. You need to go now. They'll be back." Belinda pushed a folded piece of paper into Maria's hand. "Meet me here. It's a safe place."

Maria looked at the inn manager with surprise. Belinda had always been kind and motherly but not someone Maria thought to turn to in an emergency.

"I can't stand what ICE is doing to people like you," Belinda said, as if reading her thoughts.

"I, I have to get someone, first," Maria stammered. "My son."

"I'm a mother, too," Belinda smiled. "Now go. I'll meet you soon."

Maria nodded and jumped in Juan's car. The headlights cut through the inky darkness as she headed east toward Santa Rosa. Toward Alarico.

* * *

Maria parked Juan's car a block from Gabby's house and turned off the engine. She sat there, trying to catch her breath. Dawn was still a couple hours away and the neighborhood was dark. She was shaking. ICE knew where she worked; it was only a matter of time before they traced her back to her cousin. They might already be in front of Gabby's house, waiting. She was taking a chance just being here.

She pulled on a cap and pushed up her hair and slipped from the car, nervously looking up and down the quiet street. Despite the early hour, lights flickered in the tiny bungalows. Maids like her, nannies, handymen preparing for jobs at hotels or large homes on the west side of town, hurrying to arrive before their wealthy employers woke. She pulled the brim of the hat low, her heart nearly in her throat, and scurried down the sidewalk to the house directly behind Gabby's. It was owned by an old widow who sat on the porch in the mid-afternoon, but in the wee hours of the morning would be asleep. Maria held her breath and darted down the old woman's driveway and to a break in the ficus. Parting the bushes, she slipped into Gabby's empty backyard. She moved silently up the back stairs. Her hands shook as she pulled a key from her pocket and unlocked the back door. The kitchen was still, only the ticking of a wall clock broke the silence.

"Maria!" a voice exclaimed. Maria jumped and nearly screamed. She brought her hand to her mouth. It was Gabby, standing with a cup of coffee in the darkness. Her cousin set down the cup and threw her arms around Maria.

"They took Juan," Maria burst out, letting her cousin pull her into a tight hug. The terror that she'd held inside during the frantic drive from Jenner exploded and she sobbed in her cousin's arms. "They took him and no one knows where." Maria wiped tears from her face and tried to stop shaking. "ICE knows who I am," she said. "They know where I work." Maria bowed her head.

Gabby squeezed her and for a moment they stood there. Then Gabby said slowly, "That means ICE knows you are using my green card." Maria could see the realization dawn on Gabby's face.

"I'm so sorry," Maria stammered. Her nose started to run and she unceremoniously wiped the back of her hand across her face. "I must take Alarico now. I have a safe place to go." She tried to say that convincingly, but she realized she didn't know if that was completely true. She was entrusting her safety—and her son's—to the manager of Jenner Inn. "And you should go, too. Take Ana to your in-laws. Go to Turlock."

Gabby scrunched up her face. "But I'm not..."

"What, illegal?" Maria spat out the word. "It does not matter, Gabby." She said the words with more force than she'd intended, but she continued. "I told you before, ICE is working with Mohan Mallick, the billionaire. He was at the inn yesterday."

"But Maria," Gabby protested, her face creased with fear and exasperation. "I can't leave. Toby will be home in two days."

"Please, Gabby," Maria pleaded. "I am begging you. Go. Do not stay here. They will take you." A loud bang sounded in front of the house. Maria grabbed the crucifix around her neck, her eyes wide. It was just an old truck, backfiring. She moved quickly to the tiny bedroom off the kitchen. Alarico looked so small and defenseless curled up in a ball in his Acrata super hero pajamas. She scooped him up and the little boy looked at her groggily.

At the back door she turned to her cousin. Besides Alarico, Gabby and Juan were the only family she had and she'd put them both in grave danger. "I'm so sorry," she said, her voice choked with sorrow. "I just wanted something better. Somewhere safe...for my son." Just looking at Gabby made her heart contract with grief. She couldn't stand it anymore. She darted out the back door and across the yard, tears flowing down her cheeks.

* * *

Maria pulled Juan's car to the side of the highway and tried to slow her breathing. She hadn't been able to stop looking in the rear-view mirror since leaving Santa Rosa. Every set of headlights that came up behind the battered car set her heart racing. ICE, Mohan Mallick, Cadejo. All of them searching for her. It was too much. She could barely catch her breath. Mercifully, the road was deserted now.

She consulted the crumpled paper in her lap and glanced outside, her brow furrowed. She was at the right spot according to the crudely-drawn map, but there was no turnoff. She edged the car forward. Alarico shifted in his car seat. He would be hungry. As if on cue he let out a cry and kicked the back of her seat.

Maria turned and tried to shush the boy. "Quiet," she hissed. "We'll be there soon."

"I want Ana!" Alarico screamed and kicked harder.

A set of headlights appeared on the road behind them and illuminated the inside of the car, blinding Maria. Her breathing grew shallow. She desperately tried to calm her son. The headlights grew larger and seemed to slow. Maria grabbed the crucifix around her neck and whispered a silent prayer. Alarico's cries subsided and the boy played with the straps on his car seat. Maria held her breath as the vehicle behind them approached. A delivery truck. It rumbled by without stopping. Maria exhaled.

The headlights from the passing truck reflected off a tree ahead. Maria frowned. She drove forward slowly and there it was. A faded wooden sign pointing to a barely-visible dirt road. She eased the car off the highway and onto a rutted road that cut through the deep wood and rose up a steeply pitched hillside. The car bumped and shook as Maria drove around deep potholes. The road appeared traveled but not well maintained, as if the people who used the road didn't want to call attention to it.

She drove the rutted dirt road until she came to a fork. The main road continued up the wooded hillside, and to her right, two tracks meandered through an even more thickly-wooded section of the hillside. She inhaled and looked right and then left. Then she consulted the crumpled map and looked again at the two rutted roads. She said a silent prayer and turned the car to the right. It scraped and thumped, grinding its way up the steep hillside.

The hill eventually crested and she drove into a tiny clearing just as the sun rose above the horizon. In front of them sat a home, blue clapboard with a gently pitched roof and a small porch. The paint was faded but the windows were clean and the yard tidy. Giant redwoods surrounded the clearing. The trees towered above the small home and brushed the glowing early morning sky.

Maria sat for a moment in the car, dazed and unsure. Still shaking, she unbuckled Alarico. She held the boy in her arms and examined the home nervously. It was quiet here. For a moment she let herself think that they might be safe. Then, the door to the home flew open and a dog bounded toward them. Maria froze. The dog approached, growling. It sniffed her legs. Alarico's eyes grew wide.

"She's friendly," a voice called out. A woman stood on the porch, her frazzled hair bending in the light breeze. It was Belinda. She smiled at Maria and Alarico and called to the dog. "I made tea," she said.

Alarico scrambled from Maria's arms and darted after the dog. Maria tried to exhale as she followed Belinda into the house but her heart still raced. Inside the house was dim. The walls were paneled with knotted redwood that was stained a caramel color. Worn furniture was scattered about a large open room.

"Here you are," Belinda said. She motioned to a sofa and placed a teapot on a side table. "One of the things I love about living up here in Cazadero is how private it is. Just a bunch of us old bohemians in the woods. No one knows we're here and we like it that way."

"Belinda, I don't know how to thank you," Maria said. Her hands continued to tremble as she lowered herself to the sofa. She scrunched her eyes shut. The past few weeks had been a bad dream—a nightmare really. Even here in the cozy living room, Maria couldn't relax. When she opened her eyes, Belinda was staring at her intently. The inn's manager leaned forward and took Maria's hand.

"First things first," Belinda said. She held out a small cloth bag to Maria. "Turn off your phone and put it in here."

Maria scrunched up her forehead as she reached for her phone.

"Us old bohemians like our privacy, including digital privacy. The bag is lined. ICE won't be able to track your phone. But," she paused and shook her head, "that wasn't just ICE looking for you," Belinda said quietly. "Do you want to tell me about it?"

Maria nodded reluctantly. Something about Belinda was trustworthy. Her world weariness. Her frustration with ICE. But even more importantly, the manager might have connections who could help free Juan. She exhaled and tried to figure out where to start.

"Your name," Belinda coaxed. "Is it Maria Garcia?"

"Yes," Maria said quietly, looking down at her hands. "And Juan was like my brother in Guatemala City from almost my earliest memory. We were raised together. Our barrio was a dangerous one, though we didn't know it as children." She smiled sadly, thinking about the carefree days—too few of them—when she and Juan played in the dusty streets between the cinder block homes.

"When we were teenagers, a mobster took over the barrio. He was brutal. The killings increased, they were horrible. Mangled bodies in public, meant to teach us our place." Maria shivered at the vivid memories that still burned in her brain. People she knew, cut to pieces for almost nothing. Not just for paying a bribe too late, but for simply daring to criticize the mobster.

"His name was Cadejo." Saying the name caused her to retch. She told Belinda how Cadejo had extracted dues, ruthlessly murdered his competition, and used brutality to exert control over the barrio. She'd gotten married during that time, and somehow she and her husband Carlos had miraculously managed to avoid run-ins with the mobster for years. And then, haltingly, she told Belinda how their world crumbled. Cadejo's visit to the store to see her beauty for himself. And soon after, how Juan was caught having sex with one of

Cadejo's soldiers in an alley.

After he was caught, Juan had languished in the hidden, fetid basement prison for days guarded by young torros who took turns beating his naked body. They heated a metal poker and held it to Juan's buttocks, cackling as Juan howled while his flesh seared. They took a leather strap and flogged his groin until it was cut into swollen strips of flesh, ignoring his pleas as rivers of blood cascaded down his legs. The torros gave him no food or water. The stories of the torture circulated through the barrio, further cementing Cadejo's reputation for inhumanity.

Maria had searched frantically, begging every torro that she found to tell her where Juan was being held. She had known some of the torros since childhood, but they told her nothing. No one dared cross Cadejo.

She went to the police. That was futile. Her priest was no help and even suggested that Juan was receiving retribution for his homosexual sins. Her husband joined the search as did her father-in-law, but they couldn't find Juan. Time was running out.

Maria was increasingly desperate. Juan had been imprisoned for a week and he would die if she couldn't free him. His body would be thrown into the street as a dire warning. No one was to deviate from the law of Cadejo.

Then, late one night, a sympathetic toro slipped quietly into the store. He'd known Juan and Maria since they were children. He whispered something into Maria's ear and fled. Finally, she had a location for Cadejo. The next day she put on her best dress and braided her hair tightly. Carlos begged her not to go but there was no choice. Juan was family.

She tried to stop herself from trembling as she walked through the dusty streets. Eventually, down a hidden alley, there it was. A two-story cinder block building caked in grime. No different from most buildings in the barrio except for the barred windows and razor wire around the entrances. Maria thought she saw torros on the roof. Probably with rifles as big as they were. She rapped nervously on the metal door. Bolts slid aside and Cadejo himself answered. Maria was shocked. But of course he knew she was coming. He knew almost everything that happened in the barrio.

"Maria Garcia." His voice was guttural and his eyes were dead. She could barely stand to look at him. "The most beautiful woman in Zone 3." He reached out and stroked her cheek. She was repulsed but stood her ground.

"I've come for Juan," she said as forcefully as she could. "I'm here to take him home."

Cadejo leered and opened the door more broadly, beckoning Maria in. She flinched. No sooner had she walked into a dark hallway than Cadejo clamped his hands on her shoulders from behind. He spun her around, forced his lips on hers and thrust his hand up her skirt.

Belinda drew in her breath and leaned toward Maria. "He raped you!" Belinda exclaimed.

"No," Maria shook her head and exhaled slowly. Her eyes filled with tears and she looked down. "No," she repeated.

It was a bargain. One that they both understood. She would spend one night with Cadejo in exchange for the life of Juan. Maria couldn't bring herself to look at Belinda as she described those horrible hours with Cadejo. Her torn dress. His callous thrusting. The smell of his marijuana-tinged breath. She almost vomited at the memory. And then when it was over, his leering gaze on her sweat-stained naked body. She could still hear his menacing whisper. "Maria Garcia, I will make you mine."

She shivered uncontrollably.

Belinda put her arms around Maria and held her before asking quietly. "And then Juan was free?"

Maria wiped the tears from her face and nodded. "Yes, and before his wounds even healed, he fled from Guatemala. He had to if he wanted to stay alive. Carlos and I promised to follow him a year or two later when we saved money. But then, I…I found out I was," Maria faltered and held her crucifix tightly. She looked out of the living room window where her son romped on the forest clearing with Belinda's dog.

"You were pregnant," Belinda said softly.

"The baby was Cadejo's," Maria breathed.

"But surely it could have been your husband?"

Maria shook her head and looked down at her hands. "Carlos was injured when he was young. He could never father children. But I could not let Cadejo know. I didn't want my baby to be born in Guate and become a gang member or worse. When I told Carlos, he was furious. He wanted to kill Cadejo but I said no. I told him we had to flee immediately. We told no one we were leaving, not even Carlos's father. We took a bus north to the border, but we only had enough money for one of us to cross the river to Mexico. Carlos said I had to go alone and raise my baby here in California." Maria raised her head and tried not to weep. How could the saints have been so cruel as to tear her tiny family apart? "And now Cadejo is here. Trying to find me."

Belinda leaned back on the couch and sucked in her breath. "Does he know that he has a son?"

Maria looked toward the heavens. "I don't know, but if he does, that might be why he is here. To take his son away to Guatemala." Maria made the sign of the cross and tried to ignore the dread in the pit of her stomach. It was a fear that had eaten at her for more than three years. "Carlos was coming to warn me. But he was shot and killed."

Belinda shook her head slowly and brought her hand to her mouth. Maria couldn't bring herself to reveal the connection to Bel McMaster. Her heart beat faster when she thought about him but her face flushed with shame. She pushed her feelings for Bel aside and leaned forward, gripping Belinda's hands tightly. "I went to see Carlos's body in the morgue. They gave me his crucifix and showed me his wallet. In Carlos's wallet there was this." She pulled out the pitted card and held it up, taking care not to let it near the sun's rays that flick-ered into the living room. She didn't mention the replica that she'd lifted from Bel McMaster, still tucked away in her pocket.

Belinda took the card and turned it over in her hands. "Kavali," she read slowly and then looked up at Maria. "What is it?"

"I don't know, but a very powerful man wants it back. He was the one who came to the inn with ICE yesterday."

Belinda sat back, her eyes wide. "Oh, my sweet one," she said quietly. "You've been dealing with too much. A mobster. The man from Kavali. And ICE. We have to keep you safe."

Maria exhaled nervously but before she could speak there was a shriek from the front of the house. Maria jumped from the chair and bolted to the front porch. It was just Alarico and the dog, romping on a bed of pine needles. Maria tried to slow her pounding heart and said a silent prayer to the saints. As she prayed, she wondered, even in a peaceful place like this—the brilliant sky, ma-jestic trees, the air with just enough ocean salt—what would it take for her to feel safe again?

She looked back into the living room at the pitted card lying on the side table next to the teapot. She had to get the real card to Bel without him know-ing. Then, somehow, she had to get word to Mohan Mallick so that he'd think she'd never had it in the first place. She exhaled. It was time to see Bel McMaster again. Her heart fluttered but she tried to ignore it. No, she couldn't let feelings for Bel McMaster get in the way of what she had to do next.

25. BEL

Bel looked anxiously from the plumber at his side to the rows of tidy fermentation tanks in the McMaster Vineyards winery building. The early-morning sun drifted in lazily from the skylights above and dappled the floor with unfocused dots of light. The scene should have been blissful, but it was anything but. Bel looked at his watch. Thirty-six hours until he promised to be back at Kavali Tower. Not only did he need to find the orange card his daughter had fabricated—it was irritatingly missing from his coat pocket—but he needed to move things along with the plumber just in case he was able to close the deal with Mohan. The man, not the usual McMaster Vineyards plumber, was incredulous.

"You want to do what?" the plumber asked for the second time. Bel had sketched out his needs, but the plumber, Toby was his name, clearly didn't understand. "You got a clean shop here already," Toby said. "These tanks look solid. Good couplings. New fittings. Why ya want me to mess with it?" He looked at Bel quizzically and hitched his pants.

Bel wiped his brow. After returning from Kavali Tower last night, he'd spent the wee hours of the morning going through the winery building and storage sheds, making a list of each item that the French Wine Ministers would examine during their visit. Most of it—barrels, machinery, even the vines—wouldn't raise alarm. But the Wine Ministers would ask to taste the wine in the fermentation vats. Bel had sampled nearly a dozen of his fermentation tanks and spit out the liquid. The spice was flat and the fruitiness was overwhelming, almost cloying. There was zero chance that the wine in the fermentation tanks would pass the finely-tuned taste buds of the Wine Ministers. They wouldn't believe in a million years that his wine was worthy of entering the competition. It would have to be replaced. Fast.

"I need to replumb the fermentation tanks so I can fill them with liquid from the top after I've drained them from the bottom," Bel said slowly to Toby.

The plumber rubbed his chin. "I hear what you're saying, but why, Mr. McMaster? That don't make sense."

Bel sighed. He didn't want to explain details to the plumber. "I'm going to empty these tanks," Bel said again firmly. "And I need to refill them, quickly in a matter of moments, from the top."

"What's wrong with them pipes from your presses," Toby said. "Your system should work the way it's supposed to."

"Stop!" Bel banged his fist on the side of a tank that reverberated. He looked desperately around the winery. The squat fermentation tanks were huge, reaching almost to the ceiling high above. They couldn't be quickly emptied and re-filled without new piping.

"Listen," he whispered to Toby. "I want to fill the vats however I need to. From a tanker truck maybe. Can you run new pipes to the top of each vat."

"Oh." Toby's eyes widened. Bel could see the gears clicking in the plumber's head. Toby turned, hitched up his pants and ambled toward the door. "Can't be done," he called over his shoulder. "Take days to do."

There had to be a way. Bel had come so far, he couldn't stop now. He tipped his head back and looked at the winery ceiling. Of course. Half the work was already completed. "Wait!" he called after Toby. "Come back, it can be done." He pointed up.

The plumber stopped and followed Bel's gaze. He rubbed his chin and then looked at Bel curiously. "All I see up there is them pipes from your presses and the…" He stopped and stared at Bel. "You can't possibly mean…"

"Yes," Bel nodded vigorously. "The fire suppression system."

The plumber shook his head and stared. "You want me to replumb your fire suppression system and run pipe from it to your fermentation tanks?" he asked incredulously. "Dude, that is messed up."

"But wait," Bel grabbed the man's arm. "It could work, right? The pipes are already there. We just flush the water from the fire suppression and connect them to the fermentation tanks. Simple."

Toby looked at Bel as if the winemaker were crazy. But he narrowed his eyes and scanned the pipes along the ceiling. After a moment he spoke. "Yeah, it's possible, Mr. McMaster. But this don't meet building code…"

"Fuck code," Bel said. "You said on the phone you'd plumb what I need for a price."

Toby scratched his jaw. "So I did," he sighed.

"Then, name your price."

The plumber hesitated. He scratched out a number on a pad and stuck it in front of Bel. Bel nodded. He walked from the winery floor and trembled thinking about what he was doing. He turned and watched the plumber start to work on the tanks, praying this would be worth it.

* * *

Bel stood and smacked the old DNA sequencer in frustration. He wiped his brow. It had been years since he'd extracted and analyzed DNA in this dusty lab. While the plumber banged at the pipes in the winery, Bel had fumbled his way through crushing the leaves of the Kavali vine, adding fluid to create a slurry and operating the ancient centrifuge. He could barely remember the last time he'd turned that old thing on. The DNA sequencer still worked, thank god, but the results were confusing and HALLIE wasn't that helpful. Bel poked his e-tablet to see if HALLIE had analyzed the sample he'd uploaded.

"Your samples are still cloudy," HALLIE said. Bel thought he could hear a note of reproach in the bot's voice. Imagine if she knew what he'd done to get the grapevine. "But this time, I was able to get a partial reading of the new vine to compare against the McMaster Vineyards clonal database."

Bel held his breath. Finally. "And...?"

"A portion of the nucleotide sequence of the new vine meets the threshold match for similarity to the McMaster Vineyards pinot."

Bel exhaled slowly. "So the son of a bitch copied our vines," he muttered. But that still didn't explain how the Kavali vines could grow so big and without sunlight.

"What about the rest of the genome. Are any of the hormone genes..." Bel cleared his throat. "Are they unusual in any way?"

"They are unusual," HALLIE said. "But I am compelled to mention that some segments within the plant genome are puzzling and I cannot identify them."

Bel frowned. "Puzzling?"

"Plant DNA of this type is, by its very nature, inert." HALLIE continued. "Yet, the segments that I cannot identify are replicating and mutating at the very same time. Plant DNA does not self-mutate. A parent cell always produces identical child cells."

Bel frowned more deeply. "I don't understand. What's causing the mutation?" He shuddered. Plant DNA should be stable.

"I am unable to decipher," HALLIE responded.

Bel banged the lab table, exasperated, and walked to the windows looking out into the winery. He'd never figure out the secret of Mohan's synthetic material at this rate. And he still had to find that fucking fake card that Nadine fabricated.

At least the plumber was out there getting the fermenting tanks ready. He gazed absently at Toby who had scaled one of the large, stainless tanks. The plumber clanked away at the fire suppression pipes that ran across the ceiling. As Bel watched, his attention drifted to a tiny blinking light in the corner of the ceiling. A camera. Shit. His blood ran cold. He'd completely forgotten the estate security system. It was recording the plumber. Bel darted back to the table and grabbed his e-tablet. He punched at the screen.

"HALLIE," he said, his voice breaking. "I need something else."

"Yes, Mr. McMaster?"

"HALLIE, I need you to shut down all the security cameras in and around the winery, and erase the recordings from this morning." There could be no evidence of the plumber. God knows what the French Wine Ministers would want to review. "And the fire suppression system, take that offline, too." Might as well give Toby a break and not drench him if he accidentally activated the system.

"The fire suppression system is interconnected with the full security system across the entire estate," HALLIE responded. "If I take it offline, the estate will be defenseless against fires, accidental..."

"Yes, I know," Bel interrupted. "I said to take it all offline."

"As you wish." A sharp light emanated from the e-tablet and scanned Bel's retinas. A moment passed before HALLIE spoke. "Bio-ID complete and command executed. I've disabled the entire estate security system," said HALLIE. "Only you, Mr. McMaster, will be able to restart the system."

Bel watched as the surveillance monitors on his e-tablet flickered and died. His phone buzzed and he glanced at the screen. Nadine. He'd been avoiding his daughter all morning. His stomach clenched as he flicked off his phone.

He turned back to his lab table and surveyed the mess that he'd made of the Kavali vine. He was a worthless geneticist, always had been. Not like his son. An ache spread across his chest as he considered that this was the very work he would have loved doing with Ned. He exhaled and closed his eyes. If only he had another geneticist here on the estate. He lifted his head as it struck him. Of course, Maureen had hired that kid just out of college, the one who specialized in cannabis.

Bel darted from the lab, out of the winery and jogged up the path toward the parking lot. Even the morning sky above was cloudless and blue, wind whipped the vines. The gusts had been endless this autumn, but he barely noticed. He needed that kid who seemed to be lurking around the house or trailing Maureen. Over the howl of the wind, he heard something else. The rumble of trucks. He frowned. Trucks shouldn't be entering the upper parking lot. There was no way Mohan would have sent tankers full of fermenting wine from Kavali. That wasn't possible. After all, Bel hadn't yet upheld his part of the deal. He rounded the corner of the carriage house and came to a complete stop. His jaw dropped. A line of panel trucks extended down the driveway to the estate entrance. Workers in coveralls jumped to the ground and darted about, throwing open truck doors and starting to unload.

"Hey," he yelled at one of the workers. "What is this?" He pointed to the long rolls of Mylar being unloaded from the back of a truck.

The worker just shrugged and dragged another roll from the truck bed. Bel looked around frantically. There had to be someone in charge. This delivery must be a mistake. "Hey you," he jogged toward a woman holding a clipboard. "What's going on?"

"Mr. McMaster?" she asked curiously. "These are your grow houses. And that," she pointed to the rear of the long line of trucks, "that's your cannabis."

"My what!" Bel spluttered and raised his hands to the sky. He'd been so focused on the panel trucks that he hadn't noticed the row of flatbed trucks closer to the estate entrance. The beds of the trucks were packed with plants. And even from the parking lot, there was no mistaking the smell. They were, indeed, cannabis.

"I think you mean, my cannabis," said a woman's voice.

Bel spun. "Maureen, you, you," he could barely speak. "You didn't!" He spun again, staring with disbelief at the hubbub of activity. A team of workers had unloaded a bevy of compact loaders which buzzed toward the pinot fields next to the driveway. The compact loaders ran on treads and had large steel buckets attached to their fronts which gave the little machines a lopsided look, as if they would tip forward. Bel watched in horror as the first of the compact loaders bumped into the vineyard. The operator lowered the machine's bucket and tore at a row of vines which snapped like twigs.

"What are they doing?" Bel breathed, barely able to believe his eyes. These vines, these prized vines were the very backbone of McMaster Vineyards.

"Don't be so shocked," Maureen crossed her arms and surveyed the work crew. "We need space to put up the grow houses. And those vines haven't produced anything decent in years. They're practically dead."

"They're not dead!" Bel spluttered. He had to make them stop. "Stop, please!" he screamed. He ran frantically to the woman with the clipboard. "Make them stop," he shouted. "This is a mistake."

The woman with the clipboard looked curiously from Bel to Maureen. Maureen shook her head imperceptibly and the woman walked away.

Bel spun, his face red with fury. He pointed and marched toward his wife. "You cannot destroy my vineyards."

"As of tomorrow," Maureen said, arching an eyebrow. "These will be my vineyards. The lawyers are coming to complete the transaction." She paused and stared at him. "Your mother got wind of it and is showing up with her lawyers." Her voice turned oily. "I say bring it. I love a good fight. But right now, what I say goes. And those dead vines, they go."

"They're not dead!" Bel screamed. His legacy was being destroyed before his very eyes. The French Wine Ministers would turn on their heels and walk the second they saw these grow houses. It was lunacy. And he felt so very powerless. Bel balled up his fists and faced his wife. "Stop this madness now!" The

197

veins in his neck bulged. He was livid. But Maureen just stood there, her arms crossed and her blond bob fluttering in the breeze. He wanted to smack that smug grin from her face. He raised a clenched fist.

"So now you're going to hit me?" Maureen asked. Bel could see the disgust in her eyes. "You've turned into your father in every way except one." Her lip curled as she spoke. "He was a talented winemaker." She turned on her heel and walked back to the Queen Anne.

Bel spluttered. Once again, Maureen was right. He tilted his head back and screamed at the blue sky. Then, he saw what he'd come for. The young geneticist over by the flatbed truck examining the cannabis plants.

"Hey you!" Bel yelled angrily as he strode toward the truck. The young man's eyes widened. "Yeah, you," Bel shouted. "I need you to do something for me."

"Um, Mr. McMaster," the young man said. "I was just..."

Bel grabbed the young man by the scruff of the neck. "Kid, you're coming with me."

* * *

Bel paced nervously in the lab. The young plant geneticist had been working for hours and conferred periodically with HALLIE, their murmurs blending in with the plumber's clanking from the winery. Eventually, Maureen was going to notice the young man's absence and come barreling into the wine lab.

"Hey, kid," he said. "What's taking so long?"

"I'm sorry, Mr. McMaster. The first samples were cloudy. I had to make sure the DNA in question had the right purity before I ran it through the sequencer." The young man tapped the machine. "And this ABI 3730 is ancient, bro." The geneticist reached for a pipette and bottle of ethanol and then walked toward a small refrigerator.

Bel sighed and bent over, trying to will away the clenching in his gut. There was a secret buried in that Kavali DNA. He could feel it. The secret to vines that grew huge, amazingly fast, with little light and in any climate. He had to know.

"OK, well can you speed it along?" Bel looked nervously out into the winery. The plumber was still up on top of a tank, working on a fitting. If Maureen were to come in now and see the geneticist and the plumber, there would be hell to pay.

Bel's phone buzzed and he glanced at the screen. His mother. *I'll be at the estate early tomorrow morning with my lawyers. I suggest you join me.*

Jesus Christ, his mother and his wife. At the same time. With their lawyers fighting for control of McMaster Vineyards. His stomach clenched. He didn't respond, but of course he would be there. It was his future after all.

His phone buzzed again. It was Gabby. A slow smile spread across his face as he read the text. *I need to see you. Tonight?*

His stomach was still clenched, but a warmth spread through his body and he felt that familiar firmness between his legs. He answered immediately. *Absolutely.*

He paced and looked out the window to the vineyards. The sun was beginning to set. God, they'd been in here all day. The geneticist was hunched over, deep in conversation with HALLIE. His brow was furrowed as if he were puzzled.

His phone rang. He sighed and glanced at the screen again. Nadine. She'd left a half a dozen messages. He couldn't keep avoiding his own daughter. He stepped to the side of the lab and answered, the clenching in the pit of his stomach now fully gnawing at him.

He cleared his throat. "Hi Deeny," he said, his voice cracking.

"Don't Deeny me," Nadine said tensely. "Did you do it, Dad?"

"Do what?"

"No fucking games, Dad. I need you to tell me, right now, if you stole Daisy's UAD from her bag last night at my apartment. Because if you did, you are the world's biggest shit."

Bel could hear the fury in his daughter's voice. He turned in a slow circle in the corner of the lab. All he wanted was to restore the honor of McMaster Vineyards. How was he going to explain that to Nadine now? "Nadine, honey, I know it's hard to understand but..."

"No!" Nadine screamed through the phone. "Do not patronize me! After everything we've been through, you blaming me for Ned's death, and now this!"

Bel lowered his head. There was something even more important that Nadine needed to hear. Something crazy that occurred to him after he'd seen the photo on Daisy's phone. He hoped he was wrong, but he had to tell her. "Nadine, there's something you should know about Daisy's previous girlfriend. She was a security guard at Kavali, and I think maybe..."

"Mom says you might have been helping me with my investigation just so you could break into Kavali all along." Nadine interrupted. Her voice dropped to a whisper, almost as if she couldn't believe it. "Dad, is that true?"

Fuck Maureen. Always driving a wedge between him and his daughter. Would she never stop?

"Dad, I can't believe you...you betrayed me," Nadine continued, her voice catching. "And for what, a stupid contest?"

"It's a competition, Deeny," Bel muttered.

"Go to hell, Dad!"

The phone clicked off. Bel rubbed his temples. His daughter had every right to be upset, obviously. He exhaled. His daughter was right. He was an absolute shit.

"Mr. McMaster?" The young geneticist interrupted his thoughts. "Hello, Mr. McMaster?"

Bel sighed, shoved his phone in his pocket. The geneticist's brow was still furrowed.

"Where did you say you obtained this sample?" The geneticist looked at him curiously.

Bel cleared his throat. "I didn't. So, what did you find out?"

"Whatever you found, it's self-mutating genetic material that appears to have the ability to disguise itself. The nucleotide pairs can't be sequenced once they mutate. However," Bel thought he heard a tremor in the young man's voice. "I initiated apoptosis in a small group of cells *before* they mutated and asked HALLIE to simulate whole-genome sequencing and epigenomic analysis so that we could infer cell type."

Bel shook his head slowly, barely understanding what the young man had said. "And?"

The young man paused and cleared his throat. "I found nurse cells. They're used to help neural cells make synaptic connections." The young man looked at him, eyes unblinking as if watching his reaction.

Bel struggled to remember his college cellular biology. "Um," he stammered, "but aren't neural cells..." He couldn't bring himself to finish the thought.

The young man nodded slowly. "Part of the central nervous system."

Bel licked his lips. "But plants don't have a central nervous system."

"That's right," the young geneticist spoke as if addressing a toddler. "Which means the DNA in that sample didn't come from a normal plant."

Bel sucked in his breath. "You're saying that vine," he pointed to the Kavali vine that lay chopped up on the table, "contains DNA from an animal?"

"Not just DNA, actual tissue," the geneticist's face reddened. "And not just any animal." He paused.

Bel leaned forward. "What animal?"

"That sample," the young man swallowed hard and looked away from him and at the Kavali vine, "is human."

26. MARIA

Maria darted up the narrow path to the ridge top vineyard, dodging rocks and roots along the way. The sun drifted down toward the horizon and the evening sky was gray instead of its usual gold. A gust kicked up, strong enough that she bowed her head. It was as if the wind was trying to prevent her from ascending the cliff to see Bel.

She had agonized over when to see him. Every few hours she powered up her phone against Belinda's advice just to see if there were texts from Bel. Her heart skipped as she read his words. It was the one time during the day when she found herself smiling.

She hadn't ventured beyond the redwoods that circled Belinda's home for days. Her son, oblivious to her anguish, was in heaven. A goofy dog, the forest playground, Belinda's bohemian ways. Alarico followed Belinda into the garden every afternoon to help with the fall harvest. Belinda had tapped into springs on the property for irrigation and Alarico was fascinated by the water bubbling from the ground into plastic tubing. "He'll be a farmer someday," Belinda said.

Belinda told her it was madness to venture out from the cozy home in Cazadero with both Mohan Mallick and Cadejo searching for her. Maria knew it of course, but she wanted—no, she needed to see Bel. She'd told the inn manager about her feelings for the winemaker, cracking her knuckles nervously as if confessing a sin, but Belinda hugged her and said that love knew no bounds or reason. She hadn't told Belinda of her plan to plant the strange orange card with the Kavali logo where Bel could find it and then try to get word to Mohan Mallick about the card's whereabouts. That seemed too much to confess. Regardless, Belinda's eyes clouded with concern when Maria got behind the wheel of Juan's Toyota.

Maria climbed the final stretch of path and paused to gaze across the ocean. The wind gusted from behind her, hot and dry, and whipped across the ridge and over the ocean which churned with choppy waves that melded into the distant sky. She looked far below at the Jenner Inn, clinging to the cliff by the side of Highway 1. She hadn't been there since Mohan Mallick and ICE discovered her. And tonight, she'd driven by the inn three times slowly before hiding Juan's Toyota behind the Quick Mart, petrified that Belinda's fears would come true and she'd be tracked.

Her mind spun as she gazed across the ocean. She had so desperately wanted to keep Alarico from Cadejo that she'd given up everything to flee Guate to California. But she'd failed. Her husband was dead, her best friend imprisoned, her cousin in danger and she hadn't even fully escaped the man who tormented her. Even worse, she was selfish. Her heart beat faster when she thought of Bel McMaster. She screwed her eyes shut, crossed her chest, and called out to Milagroso Señor de Esquipulas with a promise. If the saint would see her through, she would stop seeing Bel McMaster.

"Gabby!"

Maria turned. Despite her promise, her heart stopped for a beat and she knew it was a promise she wouldn't keep. Bel stood up by the small shed, his face bathed in the dim light of the setting sun. His emerald eyes flickered and he smiled. She wiped away tears with the back of her hand and wondered what he felt as he watched her walk.

"I've been worried," Bel said, embracing her. He seemed a little different tonight, distracted, maybe a little sad. "I haven't heard from you in days."

"I know. I am sorry. It's just…" She choked and paused. She didn't want the winemaker to see any tears. "My friend, Juan," she exhaled slowly, "he was taken by ICE and I can't find him."

Bel's brow furrowed. "Juan, why?" The winemaker still seemed distant. But she needed to talk to him.

"I don't know," Maria lied. "No one will tell me. I am afraid for him."

Bel grabbed her hand. "That doesn't make sense," he said, his face crossed with confusion. "But I know someone who can help. Virna in my office, she can make some calls."

Maria nodded. Shame overwhelmed her. She had asked a favor of this man, knowing that her husband killed his son. The saint would not look kindly on that. She choked again, determined not to cry, but tonight, her determination wasn't enough and the tears slid down her face.

"Gabby, what is it?" Bel lifted her chin. "We'll find him. I promise."

Maria's shoulders shook from guilt, shame, and yes, relief. She let Bel wrap his arms around her and suddenly she was weeping. Weeping for her family, for Juan, and for herself. The saint would allow that.

"It's OK," Bel said quietly. He held her and gently stroked her hair and then she looked up at him, her face streaked with tears. "It's OK," Bel whispered again. He leaned his face toward hers until their foreheads touched. They stood there for what seemed an eternity. She turned her face up and her heart thumped. She'd thought about this moment from the time he had come to the lobby of the inn with a flimsy story about car insurance. She'd wondered what his lips would taste like and how they would feel. She let him put his hands on her cheeks and they stared. She knew that once they kissed, there was no going back. The flirtations would stop being innocent, the hellos would be charged, the goodbyes aching.

Bel leaned down and kissed her. Her heart raced as the winemaker pulled her close. They kissed more deeply, her mouth exploring his and sending wild sensations through her body. He tasted different than she'd expected, sweeter somehow.

The wind outside rumbled and the roof above trembled. The last of the sun's rays folded beneath the horizon. Maria gripped him tightly, kissing the winemaker with a passion that surprised her, and as she did, she could feel Bel open. She knew that in all of her life, she'd never kissed with such intensity. For a moment, every nerve in her body was on fire.

From outside the shed there was a crack of light. The horizon was briefly lit as if with millions of candles. A moment later a boom of thunder reverberated and the tiny shed shook.

"Dry lightning," Bel muttered and glanced up, his brow creased. "Deadly without rain." The sky lit again with white hot fury and the tiny shed shook as the thunder rumbled across the gray sky.

Maria put her hands on his chest. "Are we okay up here in the lightning?" she asked. Her cheeks were flushed and her lips parted.

Bel pulled her close and stroked her hair. "The rise behind us leading to the state park is higher and the lightning will hit there first," he whispered. "We're safe here."

Maria pushed from her mind any thoughts of Juan, her son, or the Guatemalan gangster. Right now, she thought only of Bel. She unbuttoned the top of his shirt and placed her ear against his chest. His heart thudded like hers. She gazed at him, unbuttoned the rest of his shirt and pushed it to the ground.

"Are you sure?" Bel asked.

Maria nodded.

Bel spread a flannel blanket on the ground and lowered Maria, kissing her neck and running his fingers through her hair. She gazed up, wanting to imprint the memory of what he looked like at this moment. The unkempt reddish mop of hair, the scruffy gray cheeks, his bare chest, the piercing green eyes. At that moment, Maria knew she hadn't just come to leave the real card where Bel would find it or to ask for his help with ICE. Bel kissed her navel and worked his way down her thighs with his tongue. Dry lightning streaked across the sky and the thunder rumbled but Maria didn't notice.

* * *

Maria woke, momentarily confused, and sat up. The shed shook as thunder rumbled in the distance. Of course. She was with Bel on the ridge. The sky outside was inky and the dry lightning had moved out across the ocean. Bel moaned and seemed to call out, his sleeping face contorted. She frowned at his bad dreams and placed her hand on his bare shoulder. He quieted.

She reached for her dress, slipped it over her head and padded outside to the edge of the cliff and sat. Despite the crackling lightning in the distance, the wind had died for the first time in days and the ridge was clear and peaceful. Millions of stars winked above. Her eyes teared as she wondered where Juan might be. She could hardly bear to think about it. Was he held in a cage or, even worse, being beaten? She held her crucifix and murmured a prayer. She gritted her teeth and felt something well up. It wasn't an ache for Juan, or even the new longing that she felt for Bel. This feeling was different. She felt strength. Maybe it was the classes with Gabby. She looked to the heavens, balled her fists and felt a surge of power. At that moment, she knew she would do anything to protect her family, especially her little Alarico. She would deceive, shield him from danger. Kill if she had to. She gasped at the thought then looked back at the shed where Bel slept. Yes, she would even lie to the man that she was falling in love with. She gazed again at the night sky. A star streaked across and she followed it, wondering if it was a saint, agreeing with her resolve.

She exhaled and slipped back into the shed, then lowered herself on the blanket next to Bel. She reached into her pocket and pulled out two small cards, both a brilliant orange color and pitted on one side. Each card was a little bigger than a payment card. She examined them both and then took the heavier of the two—the one that her husband had stolen from Kavali Technology—and placed it under the wooden table where Bel would be sure to find it in the morning. She slipped the other card, the replica that she'd lifted from Bel back into her pocket. Then she lay down, pulled Bel's arm across her chest and closed her eyes. The shed trembled as the distant thunder rumbled but for the first time in weeks, she slept soundly.

27. BEL

Bel sat uncomfortably in his truck at the entrance to McMaster Vineyards and watched the sun rise above the horizon. He stretched, trying to relax, and felt something poke in his pocket. The orange card that Nadine fabricated. He'd found it under the table when he woke in the shed on the ridge. He held the card up in the sunlight. Strange. It felt like it quivered in the light.

His stomach churned as he considered what the young geneticist had said. Human DNA. What the hell was Mohan Mallick doing? Were those even plants in Kavali Tower? He grimaced and shoved the fake orange card into his pocket. Whatever the truth was, he'd still need the card tonight at Kavali Tower if he had any hope of making a trade for fermenting wine.

Even though making love with Gabby last night had been beyond anything he'd dreamed, he'd had nightmares. Vines coming to life with human appendages that snapped off when he grabbed at them. Repulsive. But he'd heard Gabby's voice in the background, soothing him. And then, when he awoke in the early morning, he had slipped out of the shed quietly, leaving her asleep. God she was burned in his brain. Those thick auburn tresses spread out on the flannel blanket. The way her amber eyes closed to half-mast when she moaned. Her lips, plump beyond belief. Last night, he'd worked his way down the inside of her curvaceous thighs with his mouth, desperately trying to take in every inch of her skin. It was as if he needed to drink the very essence of her, to feel her at his core. Then, when he moved inside her, he'd willed himself to prolong the moment as long as he could, until finally he'd exploded, gripping her so tightly that he'd left marks.

He put his head back against the truck seat and closed his eyes. He wanted more. Not just to take his mind off Mohan Mallick's revolting experiments or his deteriorating relationship with his daughter. No, he really *wanted* Gabby. All of her. He let the edges of his imagination blur to a fantasy where Gabby roamed the estate. There she was in the vineyard, laughing with JC. She dropped by the tasting room. The staff loved her. She slipped into his office, her hair down, wearing a flowing dress that fell off so easily. He felt something grow firm between his legs.

There was a rap at the truck window. Bel's eyes flew open. It was his mother. "How long have you been here?" she snapped when he rolled down the window, his cheeks red. Three cars were parked behind Bel's truck. Odette and her lawyers. Bel hadn't heard them arrive. "We need to be up at the estate now." She drummed her fingers on the truck door. "Let the lawyers do the talking," she instructed. "This doesn't need to devolve into a shouting match."

Bel nodded sheepishly and drove up the driveway, following his mother and her lawyers. He looked to the side of the driveway and his stomach dropped. Maureen's new, enormous grow houses stretched on and on. As soon as he was back in charge, he would have work crews rip down the despicable grow houses and uproot the cannabis. But god knows, he couldn't plant the vine he'd stolen from Kavali Tower. It was an abomination.

The vehicles ground to a stop in front of the Queen Anne and the lawyers spilled out of the cars. The door of the house swung open and Maureen stepped onto the porch. She wore a taupe-colored dress that fluttered in the early morning breeze. Bel saw disgust on Maureen's face as she looked down at him. The porch door opened again. Nadine. Bel's heart dropped. "Nadine," he called out shakily and walked toward the porch.

"Stay away from her," Maureen said, her jaw tight. His wife moved to stand in between him and his daughter.

"I need to talk to her," Bel reached the bottom of the porch stairs. He looked past his wife. Nadine refused to meet his gaze. "Nadine, regardless of what you think of me, you need to check out Daisy's previous girlfriend. She was a security guard..."

"Dad, stop!" Nadine cried. "Can you hear yourself? You sound like a crazy person. And besides, Daisy is basically forbidden to leave Kavali Tower after you fucking robbed her."

Bel started to say more but more crunching sounded on the driveway. He turned to see a large SUV. Two men and two women emerged. It took but a split second for Bel to recognize them. Cedric Tari and the Paris Wine Ministers. Here on the estate. They had come early. "What the holy fuck," he whispered under his breath. He spun to face Maureen. "What the hell are they doing here," he hissed, pointing at the Wine Ministers. His finger shook. Blood raced to his head, wondering how he would manage all this.

"Ah, Mr. and Mrs. McMaster," Cedric Tari called out. The man walked toward the group, clearly unaware of the high emotions. "It is such a beautiful morning at McMaster Vineyards."

"Monsieur Tari," Bel responded. He hoped his voice was steady. He wanted to scream at his wife. Cedric approached his mother first as if they were old friends. Odette air-kissed Cedric but glowered at his wife. The other ministers gathered around.

"We weren't expecting you today," Bel stammered. He shot daggers at Maureen. It was all he could do to keep from racing onto the porch to smack her.

"Yes, but of course, your lovely wife encouraged us to come sooner," Monsieur Tari said. He waved at Maureen. She waved back with a flat smile, her eyes narrow. "I am, however, a bit concerned that the grow houses have been erected," Cedric said and motioned toward the front drive. "I thought we discussed..."

"They'll be gone tomorrow," Bel interrupted, trying to control his fury.

"But I am more concerned about something else," Cedric continued, his brow knitted. He cleared his throat as if he had something distasteful to bring up. "Your wife invited us to taste the wine in your fermenting tanks last evening," he said. He adjusted his blazer as he said it, almost like a cartoon character delivering bad news. "It was, shall we say, a disappointment. I can hardly believe it came from the same vineyards as the pinot you were so kind to share with me. I wonder, perhaps, if there has been a mistake?"

Bel gritted his teeth and looked with outrage at his wife. How dare she undercut the one chance he had to restore the reputation of McMaster Vineyards. She was so desperate to wrest control away from him that she'd do anything, even jeopardizing the chance to win the Paris Wine Competition.

"I think there has been a big misunderstanding," Bel said. He tried to smile and stretched out his arms as if corralling the Paris Wine Ministers.

Before he could say more, sirens wailed at the end of the driveway. Vehicles sped up to the house. The Wine Ministers looked at Bel with alarm as vans and an SUV skidded to a stop in a show of flying gravel. Strobe lights flashed. His mother scowled at him, as if he knew what was happening. The emblem on the van doors was clear. It was ICE.

"What in god's green hell is this?" Odette glared at Maureen.

"Don't look at me," Maureen shrugged. "ICE is not my problem."

Agents swarmed from the vehicles and cocked their weapons. One of the agents was enormous, his uniform barely fit over bulging arms and strained around his thick, tattooed neck.

A boot emerged from an SUV and a man stood. He was immaculately dressed in all white with meticulously groomed beard stubble. Bel stared, his face screwed with confusion. What the fuck was Mohan Mallick doing here?

Bel strode toward Mohan. "You have some nerve coming here. Your sick experiments," he hissed angrily. "You told me to be at Kavali Tower tonight. We can talk then."

The ICE agents circled Bel. One dropped to his knees and unholstered a weapon. The click of the safety flicking off echoed through the parking lot.

Nadine was suddenly at his side. She looked at him incredulously. "Did you just say you'll be at Kavali Tower tonight? What the hell is going on?"

"Ah, Mr. McMaster," Mohan rumbled, the fury evident in his voice. "I took you for a liar in the Tower. I did not think you could find Maria Garcia when I could not. But of course, I was curious, so I let you go." Mohan gritted his teeth and stepped forward, his face nearly in Bel's. "But it turns out you're actually *not* a lying sack of shit. You really do know Maria Garcia. You left trails of her DNA everywhere." Mohan's eyes narrowed. "I want Maria Garcia. Right now."

Bel's head spun. Maria Garcia's DNA?

"What the hell, Dad?" Nadine looked at him, her emerald eyes screwed with confusion. "You know Maria Garcia?"

Mohan snorted and turned to Nadine. "Your father is covered in Mrs. Garcia's DNA."

"You are what?" Nadine spluttered, looking at him with astonishment.

"I have no idea what he's talking about," Bel said and took a step backward. Guns cocked and an agent poked him in the back. He flinched. A flush crept up his neck. Nadine's face hung blank and she stared at him, unspeaking.

"And besides, he's the one you should be looking at," Bel said desperately, pointing a finger at Mohan. "The plants in Kavali, they're not really plants..."

"Covered in her DNA," Mohan repeated, interrupting Bel. "I want to tell everyone what it means to be covered in someone else's DNA," Mohan turned away from him to face his family and the French Wine Ministers. "Belmond McMaster is supposedly grieving the loss of his son," Mohan's voice rose to a shout. "But, this pillar of Sonoma County has been fucking the widow of the very man who killed his son. That is how you become covered in someone else's DNA." He turned to Bel. "You sick, demented son of a bitch."

Bel gasped. "No," he mumbled, shaking his head vehemently. "That's not true." He spun. His mother, wife and daughter stared at him, eyes wide. Maureen crossed her arms. Nadine's jaw was slack, his mother's eyes were slits. He couldn't look at them.

"No," he repeated in disbelief. "I, I..."

"This woman," Mohan held up his phone with a picture on the screen, "is Maria Garcia. The widow of the murderer, Carlos Garcia. And you," he pointed a finger at Bel, "have been fucking her."

Bel looked at the picture. His blood ran cold. How did Mohan have a photo of Gabby? What was the tech titan saying? "No," Bel protested weakly. He turned to face his wife, mother, and daughter. "Her name is Gabby. She's a maid...."

"She's a maid at Jenner Inn," Mohan interrupted. "Or at least, she was before she disappeared with something that belongs to me. And her name is not Gabby. It's Maria Garcia."

He heard Nadine gasp. "Dad, you knew her all along?" His daughter stepped back from him, her eyes wide. She brought her hands to cover her mouth.

"Now where is she?" Mohan screamed in his face. "I want Maria Garcia. Right. Now."

"In my pocket," Bel stammered, unable to look at his family. Mohan must be lying. Gabby was Maria? It couldn't be. But maybe the fake card would appease him. "In my ... "

Mohan swatted him across the face. "Liar," he screamed. "Where the fuck is Maria Garcia?"

Bel recoiled from the blow and fell to one knee. "I, I don't know." Bel tried to stand but the burly ICE agent put a meaty hand on his shoulder and shoved him down.

"Stop lying to me!" The veins in Mohan's neck pulsed furiously, his face turned a dark shade of purple. He spun. "Take him," he screamed at the agent.

Bel looked up, stunned. "What?" he said incredulously. "I'm not going any-where!" He grabbed the ICE agent's hand and tried to pull it off his shoulder but the agent was too strong. The huge man was reaching to his side. Bel fell to all fours and tried to scramble backward. The gravel cut into his palms and knees. The ICE agent had unholstered a weapon. A taser. He aimed at Bel and pulled the trigger. A dart pierced Bel's neck. He convulsed. Just before he lost consciousness, he looked up to see his mother, wife, and daughter staring at him. Their jaws hanging in disbelief.

28. MARIA

Maria gazed across the churning gray Pacific. The morning had started bright and clear, but a heavy fog rolled in, covering the hilltop vineyards with thick, white mist. She shuddered and rubbed her arms, trying to warm herself.

When she'd woken, Bel was already gone. She sighed and stretched. The night had been perfect. He'd been exactly the sort of lover she'd hoped. Their bodies had entwined in unencumbered rapture, the kind she'd rarely known. When he'd been inside her, there were moments when she couldn't move, paralyzed by pleasure. But it wasn't just pleasure. She smiled guiltily and absently stroked the crucifix around her neck. No, with Bel it was something more than just pleasure. Her heart thudded at the thought.

She looked down at the Jenner Inn and gritted her teeth. ICE vehicles had been at the inn when she'd awoken. ICE agents swarmed the building and the grounds of the inn, the crackle of their radios wafting up on the foggy morning air.

She turned and walked back to the tiny shed and sat on the flannel blanket. She'd have to stay here until the ICE agents were gone. There was no possible way she could descend the path from the ridge and retrieve Juan's car from behind the Quick Mart without being noticed. It was too risky. She glanced under the table. At least Bel had found the real orange card and taken it.

Maria wandered from the shed and looked away from the ocean and up the slope, considering her options to escape unseen. She and Bel had only walked up there together once. He had pointed to the east and said that his property abutted a state park and she knew that Cazadero was just northeast beyond the park. If the ICE agents stayed much longer, surrounding Jenner Inn, she'd consider walking. But the thought of getting lost in the coastal redwoods caused her to shudder. No, she'd stay on the ridge for now and wait.

29. BEL

Bel had to urinate. The urge was unrelenting. But the urinal was on the opposite side of the holding cage and to get there he had to fight his way through the crush of detainees. Earlier, he'd tried to stick close to the urinal, but the mass of men in the cage was constantly shifting as more and more were jammed inside and so now, he stood on the opposite wall. He was thirsty, too. Of course, the only source of drinking water was a tiny aluminum sink next to the urinal so he shrugged and tried to work a kink out of his neck.

He'd been in the ICE detention center all day, or at least, he thought it was only one day. It was hard to tell. His brain was scrambled after being tased. He'd flagged down a detention guard hours ago and said there had been a mistake. Clearly, he didn't belong in an immigration detention center. "Sure amigo," the guard snorted, "none of you belongs here."

The holding cages were chain link enclosures, not even high enough for Bel to stand upright. He seemed to recall the media outrage when the cages had been wedged inside the cells of the abandoned concrete sheriff's office on the northern edge of Healdsburg. He never thought he'd end up in one of them.

His neck stung. He probed, feeling a bump that itched like hell, the place where the dart had pierced his skin. As he massaged his neck, he thought about her. There was no reason for Mohan Mallick to lie to him, so she must be Maria

Garcia. But it didn't make sense. Why would she do it, deceive him the way she had? He wanted to bang his head on the cinder block wall. To think that he'd been on the verge of falling in love with her.

The questions were endless and spun through his brain faster than he could process. Had she orchestrated an encounter with him? What could she hope to gain by meeting the father of the young man her husband killed? Was she faking when she held him, kissed him? He closed his eyes. God, he wanted it all to be a coincidence. That his truck just happened to run into Juan's car. That the things she whispered to him in the dark, the way she reacted to his body, that those things were real.

"Bel McMaster!" a voice shouted gruffly into the cage. He opened his eyes as the chain link door swung open and a guard, taser drawn, lumbered in. He looked directly at Bel. "This way," he commanded and flicked his weapon in the direction of a narrow passage between the detention cages.

Few of the men bothered to look up as Bel picked his way between them. His heart thudded. He followed the guard down the passageway between the cages packed with brown bodies. Most just stared vacantly as he limped by. A middle-aged, red-headed white man covered in blood and filth. At the end of the passageway, a light scanned the guard's eyes and a heavy metal door swung open revealing a tiny, dark room.

"Get in." The guard shoved him into the room and the door clanged shut. He was alone. The room was lit by a single dim overhead light and contained a beat-up table and a metal stool. Bel dropped onto the stool and exhaled. It felt good to sit. He'd lost track of the time he'd been stuffed in the overflowing immigrant detention cage. No visitors. No lawyers. No explanation.

He wanted out of this place, out of this nightmare. The overcrowded cages, the biting odor of urine, and his aching legs. God, even sitting was a luxury. He put his head in his hands and tried to push thoughts of Gabby—no, she was Maria, of that he was pretty certain—from his head. And the scene at McMaster

Vineyards replayed again and again. Mohan Mallick shouting to his family and the French Wine Ministers that he'd fucked the wife of the man who killed his son. His stomach clenched. God, what had he done? At best, he'd betrayed the memory of Ned. The son he'd loved more than anyone in the world. At worst...he didn't even want to think about it. How he'd lied to his daughter. Tried to deceive the French Wine Ministers. His stomach clenched so hard he doubled over in pain. The metal door banged and opened. Bel opened his eyes and looked up. Light spilled in, obscuring the person in the doorway. The man was huge. It was the ICE agent who had tackled him at the estate.

"What do you want?" Bel's throat croaked. He wanted to bang on the grimy table and demand to be let go but he was too exhausted. And maybe he did belong here. Maybe the universe wanted him to pay some debt for his actions.

The man pulled a small disk from his pocket and set it on the table. "Mohan Mallick wants to speak with you."

A beam of light shot up from the disk and a hologram flickered and took shape. Mohan towered above the table, his hologram looming large in the tiny, dim room. Bel reflexively pushed his stool backward.

"Mr. McMaster," Mohan rumbled. "I grow tired of asking the same question, but I'm giving you one last chance." Mohan was, as always, impeccably dressed. He wore a white collarless shirt and tan blazer. "Where is Maria Garcia?"

"I...I don't know," Bel stammered. He rubbed his temples viciously as if trying to erase the sepia toned images of Maria on the ridge, Maria sipping wine, Maria's lips ripe with desire. She'd lied to him. Led him along for weeks. Let him fall in love.

Mohan's face hardened and the hologram grew larger. Bel recoiled. "You are in a precarious situation," Mohan growled. "And you have a choice to make. Tell me the whereabouts of Maria Garcia and go free. Or..."

Bel lifted his head. "Or what?" he said with as much force as he could muster. He gritted his teeth and swallowed. He wasn't the only one with secrets. "I know what you're doing in Kavali Tower. I know what Synthetica is." His voice shook. He stood shakily, pushing the tiny stool backward. "Those plants," he stammered. "They're more human than plant. I can tell the world."

Mohan's chortle made Bel's skin crawl and he backed against the cold wall. "The Chinese have been using human growth hormone with plants for nearly two decades," Mohan said, seemingly amused.

"Not growth hormone," Bel gulped. "Human DNA. Those aren't really plants, they're..."

"The world agricultural system is on the verge of collapse," Mohan interrupted. "The only species that can adapt to climate change in real time is human. Do you really think that starving people are going to give a fuck about what they're eating?" Mohan's hologram grew until it nearly filled the tiny room.

Bel's heart thudded. He'd pushed himself as hard as he could against the cold wall. The giant ICE agent continued to block the door. Bel closed his eyes. He felt like he was going to suffocate. The idea of Mohan Mallick growing human flesh disguised as plants. It was repulsive. He needed to vomit. "I...I have proof," he stammered and opened his eyes.

Mohan chortled again, but this time his eyes were narrow. "We have already done you the favor of cleaning your filthy lab," Mohan said, his voice bordering on rage. "And you are testing my patience."

Bel's heart dropped. They'd raided his lab.

"And the bright young man who used to work for your wife is now a Kavali employee," Mohan rumbled as if reading his thoughts. The tech titan's face was red with fury. "So, that brings us back to where we started. Maria Garcia. Last time I'll ask. Where the fuck is she?"

Bel exhaled and leaned his head back on the wall. Tears filled his eyes and he tried to rip the memories out of his brain. Maria's lips. The perfect pinot grapes. Nadine's look of betrayal. He could barely think. He looked at Mohan with blurry eyes. He was exhausted. Beaten. "There's a small shed on the ridge above Jenner Inn," he whispered. "She'll be there."

Mohan's smile sickened Bel. Or maybe he sickened himself. He fell onto the stool, dropped his head in his hands and sat there, unseeing. He didn't know what was next and he wasn't sure if he cared. There wasn't anyone in his life that he hadn't betrayed. Massively. His stomach was killing him and he rocked back and forth in agony. When he raised his head, the burly man and the hologram of Mohan were gone. The door to the tiny room was open. No guard challenged him as he stumbled between the cages and from the building. Outside the wind on his face was hot and bone dry. Diablo wind.

30. MARIA

Maria clutched the crucifix around her neck and paced in front of the tiny shed on the ridge. She'd been stuck up here all day, waiting for the ICE agents to leave the Jenner Inn, but they stayed. Their vans and SUVs were parked at odd angles, agents continually combing the property.

She hadn't heard from Bel. She bit her lip and powered up her phone. She knew better than to leave it on and risk detection, but she needed to know if Bel had texted. The phone flickered on, barely. Still no texts from Bel. Just one from Belinda expressing alarm about her whereabouts.

She walked to the edge of the cliff to watch the sun sink toward the horizon. The wind picked up as the light faded. The Diablo gusts were from the east. She shuddered and wished she'd never heard about the power of the devil wind. Her thoughts were a jumble, her emotions on edge. Maybe it was the wind playing games with her.

She jammed her hands in her pockets and brushed up against something. The note from Carlos. The last thing he'd written. She held it in her hands, closed her eyes and tried to remember her husband's face. It was harder now, the happy memories had faded and been replaced by his lifeless body in the morgue, but if she really tried, she could conjure up the way his smile caused only his left cheek to dimple. She opened her eyes and exhaled. Yes, her heart raced when she was around Bel McMaster, but her husband would always be her first love.

The sky was darkening but she couldn't yet see stars except for one. It grew brighter as if it were approaching. The sound of blades whirred. A helicopter. Her heart skipped a beat. It was moving toward her. She darted closer to the edge of the cliff and squinted to see. The agents below had disappeared from the inn's property. Where were they? She looked toward the path that led up to the ridge. Lights bobbed, barely visible in the twilight. Her blood ran cold. The agents were on their way up. There was no mistaking. They were coming for her.

A searchlight from the helicopter. It was directly above her. She heard her name echo from the helicopter and her blood went cold. She had one choice. Run up the ridge and into the state park. It was her only chance.

She spun and raced past the three-sided shed through a row of pinot vines. The leaves pulled at her face, the vines tried to trip her. The searchlight from the helicopter probed the vineyard. Her breathing quickened. Her heart was in her throat. She wanted to scream but there was no time. The rows of vines sloped upward. She ran faster, gasping for air as she raced toward the top of the hill behind the vineyard.

Sirens howled below. The agents swarmed the ridge behind her. The searchlight from above swept back and forth. She zigged and zagged through the grape vines, frantically trying to stay out of the light. It caught her. She looked up, her eyes wide and blinded by the light. She couldn't yell. She just ran faster. Breathless. The hilltop was in front of her. If she could reach the crest she could melt into the forest of the state park.

Her side was splitting. Her throat dry. She was so close. A voice echoed down from the helicopter. Again, she heard her name but couldn't understand the rest of the words. They were garbled. She ran faster. Almost to the top. She felt like she was going to explode. And then, she was there. The top of the hillside. She didn't slow down and ran directly in the waiting arms of a man. She thudded to a stop.

"No!" she shrieked. It was the giant ICE agent. The man who had been with Mohan Mallick at the Windsor Holiday Inn. The man who had beaten down the door at the Jenner Inn and probably taken Juan. He had his arms around her in a bear hug.

"I've got her," he yelled. A voice crackled in the agent's headset.

"No!" Maria screamed again. She drove her elbow into the giant man's gut with barely any reaction. The searchlight from the helicopter above now focused on her and the giant. Maria cried out to the saints.

ICE agents pounded up the hillside. Maria gasped and looked around frantically. The giant ICE agent was squeezing her, she couldn't breathe. He frisked her roughly and reached inside her pocket and pulled out the orange card. She clawed at him, scratched his face. Red lines appeared and blood drizzled. The ICE agent was unfazed.

She heard a hum, different from the chopping helicopter. A tiny orange spherical drone dropped from the sky and hovered.

"Do you have it?" A voice emanated from the drone. Maria's heart sank. She had heard the voice before and she knew it immediately. Mohan Mallick.

The ICE agent pushed Maria into the arms of another ICE agent who'd crested the hill. "I got it, boss!" the giant yelled with strange glee. Maria stared in disbelief as he held the card up in front of the drone. For a moment, nothing seemed to move. The helicopter hung above. The drone was suspended in front of her. The ICE agent held the card up triumphantly. Maria's heart dropped.

She felt the bite of zip ties on her wrists. She was being yanked away, back down the hill and toward the waiting ICE vehicles. Her mind raced, dreading where they were taking her. She bit back the tears. She didn't have to wonder, she knew. ICE detention. She prayed that Belinda would care for her son. She had let him down in the worst way a mother could.

She looked over her shoulder at the spectacle on the hill top. It was small consolation, but she couldn't help but wonder what would happen when Mohan Mallick realized that the card he'd just taken from her was a fake.

31. BEL

Bel stumbled in the semi darkness of the old barn. Few workers from McMaster Vineyards came to this part of the estate. The barn was too far from the winery and most of the equipment here was rusted and old. Pale light from the setting sun filtered in through a dusty window and made blotchy patterns on the floor and the building's aging roof rattled in the hot gusts of the Diablo wind. Bel leaned against a splintered wooden post and brought a wine bottle to his lips. He drained what was left and then tossed the bottle aside. It clattered to the floor. He hiccupped and wished he'd brought more.

He'd spent the afternoon trying to forget the escalating events, drinking glass after glass of wine at his mother's hotel bar. By now, Gabby—no, her name was Maria—had probably been caught by Mohan. The tech titan would have what he wanted. Bel hung his head in shame. He couldn't have stopped it even if he tried. And besides, Maria lied to him. After a few glasses of wine, he'd had to get out of the hotel and away from his mother's judgmental stare, so when Odette excused herself to check on the kitchen, he stumbled out the back of the hotel and clamored into his truck.

It had been easy to get onto the McMaster Vineyards estate unnoticed. Even if his wife didn't want him here, she couldn't stop him. The Diablo wind, whipping from the east, disguised any noise he made. And no one could turn the security system back on because he was the super user. Hell, Maureen might not have even noticed it was off, she was so busy with the lawyers. HALLIE didn't seem to care that the estate had no alarm system or fire suppression. Fucking computer system wasn't that smart after all.

Bel came to this old barn and moved noisily across the dusty floor, banging into a wooden box of tools. He clutched his shin. He looked around in the half light, his sight blurry from the wine and wondered if he'd ended up in the wrong place. And then, he saw it, over in the corner and covered with a grimy sheet. He stumbled, grabbed the sheet and pulled it back. Ned's motorcycle—an old gas-powered dirt bike that his son rode like a maniac. Bel ran his hands over the handlebars. The kid had been an absolute daredevil. Ned and Nadine set up ramps in the yard to stage their jumps, and as they'd gotten older they'd torn up the hills and ravines of the estate.

Bel wheeled the dirt bike to the middle of the floor. The fading light glinted off the frame and the front headlight. As Bel moved the bike, he heard a gurgling. Fuel. He glanced at the dying light outside the window. It was enough for a quick ride. He would be back before the sun sank below the horizon. He pushed the bike outside to the dirt lane that ran into the vineyard.

He mounted the bike and turned on the choke and thrust his weight down on the kick-starter. The bike spluttered and coughed. Puffs of black smoke blew from the pipe but the engine didn't turn over. Water in the line. Bel drove his heel into the lever but the dirt bike only coughed smoke. It wasn't meant to be. He looked up at the sky and closed his eyes. He put all of his weight on the kick-starter and jammed it down. This time the bike spluttered. Bel smiled and nursed the throttle until the engine was roaring with life. He looked at the field where Ned used to ride, fast and carefree. He put the bike into gear and bumped into the field.

He rode slowly at first, navigating the ruts in the dirt road, but accelerated as his body remembered how to lean. The Diablo wind was fierce and pushed at him as he sped through the vines. He thought of all of the times he'd cautioned Ned about the wind—be careful with the bike, don't throw off sparks. Tonight though, the wind made the ride more thrilling. Bel pushed the bike harder, thumping through the field on the rutted dirt road until he came to a sharp rise.

The road turned and snaked up the steep hillside to a ridge—his son's favorite spot. If he rode fast, he could be at the top of the ridge just as the sun dipped below the horizon. He gunned the engine and the bike lurched forward and up the hill. It was exhilarating. His heart thudded with joy, forgetting the events of the past weeks. He leaned into the sharp curves, spraying gravel at every turn. He rode faster, climbing the curved road with daredevil speed in the dying light. On the straightaways, Bel opened the throttle full, tearing up the dirt road. And then he slid into the turns, barely controlling the bike as it fought for traction on the slippery gravel.

Bel couldn't stop thinking of how Ned loved this ride. He brushed away a tear and the bike trembled. He gunned the bike. It sped even faster. Now close to the summit, he made no effort to slow down. The wind was fierce as he approached the top. It pushed at his face and whipped his sandy hair. His shirt flattened against his chest and tears streamed from his eyes. He opened the throttle all the way. Chills ran down his spine. He was free, just like his son. And then suddenly, he was flying. The ground had disappeared and the bike was airborne. He crested the ridge and flew into the air.

Bel grabbed helplessly at the handlebars. He arced through the air and then slammed down. The bike spun forward as he flew off. His body crashed to the ground. Something cracked. A rib? Pain shot through his side. The bike slid crazily toward the edge of the steep cliff at the bottom of which was the small electric substation. Bel lost track of the motorcycle as he rolled uncontrollably. He clawed at the dirt, desperately trying to stop.

His body bashed into a large tree by the side of the cliff. He screamed in pain while the bike tumbled across the ridge and down the hillside. He sat up and cried out as lightning bolts of hot pain shot through his body. His eyesight was dim. He put his hand to his forehead and it was wet. Blood poured down his face. He leaned against the tree, gasping for air. His stomach convulsed and he felt like he was going to vomit.

The pain was shocking and he slipped out of consciousness. He woke, unsure of the time. It was lighter, but the light came from below not above. Bel groaned and pushed himself to the edge of the cliff and looked down the steep ravine below. He sucked in his breath. So that was the source of the light. Fire. Flames chewed up the grasses and trees in the long ravine below, biting into night air and racing up to an adjoining valley. Fingers of smoke uncurled and drifted upward, carrying burning embers that floated up aimlessly. The power station at the bottom of the valley was ablaze—the fire thumped and pounded and had already burned through the electric wires and transformers.

Bel watched in horror as the small substation in the deep ravine popped and crackled. He vomited and felt like he was going to lose consciousness again. He looked at the center of the fire. There it was—the charred husk of Ned's dirt bike lying where it had landed on top of a transformer. The transformer hummed and exploded. Unfettered electric wires burst free and arced crazily, throwing sparks into the air. Bel passed out. He lay there, unconscious as the flames roiled and raced beneath him and the wind whipped crazily up the ravine. Finally, the Diablo wind had more than just ions and emotions to play with. Tonight, the Diablo wind had fire.

Part III

32. MARIA

Maria pushed herself up from the cold cement floor of the holding cage where she'd been sitting. Her legs were numb and she shook them trying to get the blood to circulate. The cage was packed and women milled about aimlessly. When Maria arrived, she was able to rest on one of the cage's two wooden benches, but more women were shoved in and sitting was a luxury. She walked in a tiny circle massaging her shoulders and trying to stretch her aching back. The wind whipped outside, and even in the confines of the concrete immigrant detention center she could hear it pulsing, running circles around the building. She looked up as a blast of wind shook the building. The lights shuddered and flickered. Dust fell from the dirty ceiling and floated lazily down.

As the gust died, Maria leaned against the cinder block wall. She absently held the crucifix around her neck. She couldn't bring herself to pray right now. She had been so stupid. To be with Bel McMaster, drink wine with him, make love to him. And her biggest sin, to trust him. He must have reported her to ICE, it was the only thing that made sense. She bowed her head and her eyes watered. Someone must have told Bel her true identity. He then felt betrayed, furious probably. And called ICE. She opened her eyes and looked up at the ceiling. She remembered an old, unmarried aunt in the family. The aunt used to shake her finger at Maria, tell her that she didn't need a man. Maria had argued back, said that she didn't *need* a man, but she wanted one. "Men," her aunt would reply, "they will kill you." Maria wiped away a tear. It seemed her aunt was right. And to think that she'd been terrified of what Cadejo would do if he found her. It was actually Bel McMaster she should have been afraid of.

The gate to the cage opened and another group of women flowed in interrupting her thoughts. Maria overheard snatches of conversation—ICE facilities in the northern part of the county were being evacuated. There was a wildfire, she thought she heard.

"Maria? Maria it is you!"

Maria spun as arms wrapped around her. It was her cousin. Maria's jaw dropped. She burst into tears. She threw her arms around Gabby and gripped her tightly. She couldn't speak, unable to believe that Gabby was in the cage. "You're here," Maria whispered, finally able to speak. She held her cousin's hand tightly, afraid to let go as if Gabby might disappear. "They came for you."

Gabby nodded slowly. "And you, too," she said, sadly. Her teary smile turned into a grimace. "Alarico, where is he?"

"He is safe," Maria replied. She looked around the ever more-crowded cell. She hadn't talked with any of the women much. She didn't know who she could trust. Sure, they were all in this together, but given the chance, any of them would make some kind of deal. She probably would, too. "He is staying with a friend," she said. "And Ana?"

"Also with a friend," Gabby said quietly. She looked like she wanted to say more but she changed the topic. "It is bad out there," Gabby said.

"Bad?"

"The fires. They are burning much of the county. We were evacuated from the Geyserville Detention Center. The fire started up north and the wind is fierce. Diablo wind. They say they have never seen a fire move so fast." Gabby shivered. "The ICE center in Geyserville burned. Our van barely made it out." She hugged herself.

The building shuddered in a tremendous gust. Something banged loudly outside—a piece of metal unmoored perhaps—and crashed into the concrete wall. Maria moved to the tiny, barred window in the cell. The trees on the other side of the parking lot, illuminated in the harsh glow of the street lights, bowed and twisted. In the distance, the sky pulsed a sickly red. Maria sucked in her breath and turned to her cousin.

"What direction is the fire heading?" she asked, her voice shaking. If the fires spread west toward Cazadero, they would reach her son's hiding place.

Gabby shook her head. There had been little information on the frantic ride from Geyserville. The metal gate to the cell clanged open again and guards herded in more women. She saw outside of the cell, down a tiny hallway and inside the family visiting room. Maria choked. Cadejo was looking down the hallway directly at the cell.

33. BEL

Bel opened his eyes. He breathed in deeply and gagged. Smoke. Thick and putrid. He sat up panicked, gasping for air, trying to remember where he was. He looked around. He was on the ridge. It came back to him. Ned's motorcycle. The exploding electrical substation.

He stood shakily and winced. The pain in his side was excruciating. He shook his head, trying to get the roar to stop and then realized it wasn't in his head. It was fire. He coughed again, gagging for air, pulled his shirt up around his mouth and breathed in. He limped to the edge of the ridge and looked north. His jaw dropped.

The world in front of him burned. Fire had exploded in the valley below. The Diablo wind whipped the flames into a frenzy, pushing them from the valley northward, where they spilled over the ridges, consuming everything in their path. As he stood in shock, the Diablo wind howled around him. He couldn't move. The inferno had rocketed across the distant ridge and down the hillside. The unceasing gale turned the fire into a raging beast that roared over the dry forest and pounded across fields. The ground in the distance pulsed with a fierce orange glow as the fire obliterated everything in its path.

He looked up. The sky above was blood red and choked with embers spiraling through the smoky haze and exploding where they landed, on grasses as dry as kindling or shriveled evergreens. The roar of the fire was deafening, like the sound of a thousand jet airplanes.

He spun and ran to the other side of the ridge, ignoring the throbbing pain in his ribs. He tripped, winced, and pulled himself back up. At the edge, he looked down and almost wept with relief. The McMaster Vineyards estate, laid out below, was intact. Lights shimmered in the Queen Anne, but the other buildings, strangely, were dark. He turned and looked at the fire behind him. The wind was switching. Hot winds blew toward him. In a matter of minutes, the fire would race toward him and down the slopes to the estate.

As he looked at the estate, his heart stopped. HALLIE. He'd disabled everything—fire suppression, emergency backup, all security. He'd been so stupid. He bent over as the realization hit him and gritted his teeth. He was the only one who could turn the security system back on. He straightened and frantically pulled his phone out of his pocket. The screen was shattered. He pounded at it anyway.

"HALLIE," he screamed at it over the roar of the fire. "HALLIE, wake the fuck up!" The screen was dark. The phone worthless.

He heard a popping and spun. The eucalyptus trees right behind him exploded. The fire raced across the clearing toward Bel, pushed by massive gusts. The blaze was coming for McMaster Vineyards. His family was down there. He had to save them. His only hope was getting to the estate and reenabling HAL-LIE.

He ran toward the dirt road that wound down to the house, trying to ignore the throbbing in his side. His boots thudded on the dirt road, each reverberation sending shockwaves of pain through his body. As he rounded the first curve and dropped below the ridge, the roar from above dimmed but the wind gusted, hot and dry. Something stung his arm. An ember. He looked up and his blood ran cold. Embers rocketed from the ridge above and landed on the vines which danced crazily in the unrelenting gusts.

Bel panted around another curve in the dirt road and looked behind him. The blaze had reached the edge of the ridge. The powerful gusts would push it across the vineyards and to the house below. But maybe the vines would burn slowly. He wiped the blood from his brow and pounded down the road, the road he'd ridden up just hours below.

Sweat poured down his back and he gritted his teeth, trying to block the pain as he thudded on the dirt road, the very road he'd raced the twins on their dirt bikes hundreds of times over the years. He grimaced as a recurring thought burned his brain. He blamed Nadine for Ned's death. He blamed her because she was the older twin. Because she was supposed to watch out for her younger brother.

Something crashed above. He stopped and turned. A massive fir tree that used to cling to the edge of the ridge had fallen, its death echoing down the slope. The air around him turned putrid as wave after wave of soot crested over the ridge. A chill ran down his spine and he spun and continued running. He blamed her because it was true and she always knew it, he had loved Ned more. His stomach clenched at the thought. How could he have denied his own daughter the love she deserved? No wonder she despised him as much as her mother. He was to blame.

Bel stumbled. He tripped and fell to his knees on the dirt road. The roar of the blaze filled his ears. He gasped for air and took in a lungful of sooty air. He choked and looked up at the ridge. His dreams of restoring McMaster Vineyards were dying in the fire that was about to sweep across the vineyard. He screamed in pain and struggled to stand. And then the realization hit. The death of his dreams. Every time he looked at his daughter he saw not just the death of Ned, but the death of his dreams. It wasn't fair, he knew it. She didn't deserve his fury. The fire roared above as it inched over the ridge on its way to the estate.

And yet, there'd been a time when things were different. When the nurse handed him a newborn, the first twin, Nadine, the nurse turned to deliver the second twin and for a moment there was no one else in the world except Maureen and Nadine, that tiny infant in his arms. Just them. Beautiful Nadine. He'd cradled her, his firstborn, for what seemed like hours.

He cried out, cursing the injustice of Ned's death. He hung his head. No, there was no justice, but that didn't absolve him. He clenched his jaw and ignoring the pain in his side, he stood unsteadily and brushed the dirt from his knees. He exhaled jaggedly and looked at the ridge above him, now bright orange with flames that tore at the sky. He ran like hell around the final curve in the road.

He pounded through the vineyards that led to the main house. Down here, the air was clearer, the roar of the fire less intense. But the wind at his back was ominous—blistering and dry and carrying the stench of a world on fire.

He jerked open the front door of the Queen Anne. A blast of scorching air thrust him into the foyer and he limped down the wainscoted hallway and into the dining room. He blinked hard. The room was alive with activity. Large video screens had been dragged in from the den and set on the sideboard broadcasting aerial views of the estate.

"Daddy!" Nadine was the first to see him. Her jaw dropped. He could only imagine what he looked like. Blood running down his forehead. Covered in soot and grime. He staggered toward her and threw his arms around her. He dropped his heavy head on her shoulder and the tears came. Waves of sorrow and shame overflowed. The mountains of grief and guilt that he'd boxed inside for weeks, months, even years escaped in gasps. She put her arms around him gently and he winced at the pain. They stood there for what seemed like hours as he wept on his daughter's shoulder.

Finally, he raised his head. "I'm so sorry," he said, the words caught in his parched throat. "I..." he couldn't find the words.

"There will be time for that later, Daddy," Nadine whispered. "We have other things to talk about first." She put her arm around Bel and lowered him onto a dining chair. Bel sucked in his breath as he sat. The pain in his side was unceasing. Nadine handed him a glass of water.

Maureen strode over, her arms crossed, followed by JC, the look of fear evident on his face.

"So, you're alive," Maureen said, her jaw tight.

Bel cleared his throat and tried to speak but his mouth was dry and caked. He took a drink of water and then looked at his wife. "HALLIE," he croaked. "I have to turn HALLIE back on."

Maureen glared at him. Outside, the wind howled. The French doors in the dining room rattled and the chandelier above the dining table swayed back and forth as the house shifted.

"We've tried everything we can think of," Maureen said. Her eyes were dull but Bel could feel her anger. "That little stunt of yours…" She gritted her teeth.

"HALLIE can't be restarted," JC interrupted. "All systems remain offline. Fire suppression, emergency power. We don't even have the ability to turn on batteries. It's all controlled by HALLIE." He rubbed his stubbled jaw. His eyes were deep set and ringed with black circles. He seemed exhausted. "We have a technician here working on it but we aren't making progress. You were a superuser Bel, and when you took HALLIE offline, it prevented anyone from reactivating her."

"I can talk to HALLIE," Bel said, not waiting for JC to finish. He licked his dry lips. "I can bring her back online." He saw a hologram in the corner. He started to stand.

"Sit down," Maureen commanded. "It won't be that simple." She unfolded her arms. "What JC was trying to say is that when the estate substation exploded, the electrical surge knocked out HALLIE. Her brain was fried. We have a technician here, but it's going to take hours to bring her back online."

Bel's stomach turned. He glanced at the video screens where red, fiery blobs pounded the ridge. The gusts of wind would drive the fire down the hillside.

Without HALLIE, there was nothing to stop the fire.

"There will be time for recrimination later," Maureen continued flatly. "Right now, we have work to do." She pointed to the screen. "The fire is advancing fast because of the winds," she said. She pointed to the north boundary of the estate where a blob glowed menacingly. "The wind pushed the blaze toward Geyserville. The entire town has been evacuated. And now, these walls of flame are moving toward the estate."

Bel sucked in his breath and looked at his wife. She'd drawn a line directly to them.

"Here?" he asked.

"Yes," Maureen nodded. "These fire lines are advancing directly toward the house. At the current speed, we have about three hours."

"But the vineyards, they won't burn that fast."

"They will tonight," Maureen shook her head. "The winds are producing gale force gusts. The fire is moving through the air. The vineyards will be vaporized."

The lights dimmed momentarily and in the distance something groaned. Bel heard a door thrashing in the buffeting gusts. Maureen moved to the large French windows in the dining room and pulled back the drapes. Bel sucked in his breath. In the few minutes since he'd entered the house, the glow from the ridge had grown in intensity, spreading across the entire northern reaches of the estate. The fire that Bel escaped now chewed through the trees and grasses, greedily devouring everything in its path.

"There's only one way to stop the fire from reaching the house," Maureen said.

"A fire break," Bel muttered. He took a drink of water.

Maureen nodded. "But a fire break takes people to dig. And we don't have staff here."

"Then call the fire chief," Bel said almost trancelike as he stared at the blaze pulsing on the ridge above. "We'll need a fire crew."

"I've talked with the fire chief. There are no fire fighters. They've all been deployed to the eastern part of the county to save the towns. Even the prisoners are already out on the lines. They've started sending out immigrants from Healdsburg ICE Detention Center to fight the fire."

"Then ask the chief for…"

"I've talked with the fire chief." Maureen smacked her hand on the dining table. "McMaster Vineyards is not a priority. They'll let it burn unless someone steps in. Someone with connections." She held out her phone. "Call her!"

Bel stared at his wife for a moment and then it clicked. Of course. He knew why Maureen couldn't make a call. He reached for the phone and dialed. They needed immigrant detainees to dig the fire break. They needed them now. There was one person with enough power in Healdsburg to make that happen. The phone connected.

"Mother," Bel said. "I need your help to save McMaster Vineyards."

34. MARIA

The heavy metal gate of the cage swung open and ICE guards swarmed in. The cage rustled to life as the guards yelled, shouting out orders. "Up, up, get up!" The guards kicked at Maria and the women detainees.

"What's going on?" Maria rose groggily from the bench. She pulled her cousin with her. "Are we being evacuated?"

The smell of smoke was now unmistakable and hung heavy in the women's cage. A sickly orange glow filtered in through the window. The women had taken turns through the evening, watching from the tiny barred window as the fire pounded its way closer and closer, murmuring to each other about the approaching blaze.

"No," a guard yelled. "You're going to dig a firebreak."

Maria stared at the guard incredulously. "A firebreak?" she protested.

The guard shoved past Gabby and grabbed Maria roughly by the arm. "This isn't a debate, get your fucking ass moving," she screamed. The guards shoved the women into the flickering light of the hallway.

Maria reached for Gabby's hand and the two women shuffled, wide-eyed, with the other detainees down the hallway and toward the parking lot with a waiting bus and van. Maria glanced nervously at the visiting room where she'd seen Cadejo, but the room was empty.

The guards pushed the women out of the detention center's exit. A scorching blast of wind raked across Maria's face. She gasped and held up her hands, coughing from the acrid smoke. The air was thick with soot that swirled in the pounding gusts. She clung to her cousin and the two women bowed their heads against the beating wind. The line of detainees moved slowly to the waiting van.

"Look," Gabby screamed over the shriek of the wind. She pointed at a line of men—more detainees being loaded onto a bus, their bodies leaning into the gale force winds. Maria squinted, trying to see through the haze. It couldn't be. She shouted out a prayer of joy, dropped Gabby's hand and bolted over to a man, grabbing his shoulders and spinning him around.

"Juan!" she screamed above the roaring winds. She yelled his name again and again in disbelief and held him tight. He was alive. It was the one small piece of solace she'd had in days. She looked at his face. It was bruised. He'd been beaten. He hugged her back and the two of them stood in the parking lot, buffeted and thrashed by the unrelenting winds.

"I thought I'd lost you," Maria cried out, trying to keep her voice from breaking.

"I'm here," Juan said. "I am okay." He pulled her back into a hug.

The guard screamed at Maria, but her voice was muffled by the howling gale. The guard strode against the gusts to the couple. "Let's go," she commanded above the howl of the wind. She grabbed Maria by the arm. "Break it up."

"No, he..."

"Let's go, now!" The guard screamed.

"But, he..."

The guard shoved Maria. "This is your boyfriend?" The guard yelled with acid dripping from her voice. "Then how about we make you two comfortable."

The guard pulled a pair of handcuffs from her belt, slapped one cuff on Maria's wrist and the other cuff around Juan's wrist. Maria spluttered. Before she could say anything, the guard yanked them to the van, shoved them in with the other detainees and slammed the doors.

Maria looked at Juan and Gabby, open mouthed. She tugged at the handcuff around her wrist, the cuff that attached her to Juan. At least the three of them were together in the van. She couldn't stop looking at Juan. The bruises on his face. She wanted to ask what had happened, where he'd been taken. But the wind howled and they had to yell to be heard. For now, it was enough to know that he was safe. She pushed herself closer to him.

Maria looked out of the van's soot-streaked windows. She sucked in her breath. The fire was huge, much bigger than it looked from the tiny barred window in the detention cage. It was no longer a hazy orange glow in the sky. Now, the flames, massive in size, thundered across the night sky. Like lightning in reverse, the fire bolted up from the ground and illuminated the heavens. The entire northern horizon pulsed in red and orange and the air was heavy with smoke. Ash and cinders rained down. The guard flicked on the wipers and maneuvered the van across the parking lot, following the larger bus carrying male detainees. The bus and van joined a line of traffic streaming to the freeway.

"Where are you taking us?" Maria asked.

"You'll be on fire duty," the guard said, steering the van slowly through the streets packed with traffic fleeing Healdsburg.

"Yes, but where?" Gabby yelled.

"Listen up," the guard said firmly as she inched the van forward. "Don't try anything stupid. Right now, we're following the men's bus and you will be working alongside them. You'll be digging fire breaks at a winery." She paused. "And we guards will be armed."

"Which winery?" Maria pressed.

The guard looked at the detainees in the rear-view mirror and then she shifted her eyes forward. "You will have the privilege of saving the most famous winery in the county," she said. "McMaster Vineyards."

Maria stared at Gabby and Juan, her mouth agape but said nothing as the van lurched forward and then stopped. The roads were clogged with traffic.

The guard's headset crackled. The words were garbled and Maria couldn't decipher them. The guard jerked the steering wheel and pivoted the van clumsily. Maria saw that the detainee bus in front of them had done the same. She gasped as she realized that they were turning around to head northward, directly into the path of the inferno.

"Hey," she called out to the guard, alarmed. "You're driving toward the fire." She looked from Gabby to Juan. Their eyes were wide.

"Not that it's your business," the guard shouted back. "But we have to get out of this traffic. We're heading up to Lytton Springs and then turning west to the winery. Don't worry, we'll outrun the fire."

The guard tugged on the steering wheel and drove the van across the highway median. The van rocked and then jolted onto the northbound lane, landing with the thud. Maria squeezed Gabby's hand and looked at Juan. He smiled at her weakly.

The van banged forward faster now. The northbound lanes were clear of traffic and the bus in front of them accelerated, racing forward to the next highway exit. The air outside the van was choked with smoke and soot. Maria looked out of the window, struggling to find landmarks in the thickening air.

The van rocketed up an exit from the highway and then ground to a halt. Maria jolted forward, nearly smashing into the seat back. The bus in front of them had stopped next to a flashing patrol car. She pressed her face against the window, watching through the sooty haze as a patrolman, stooped against the blasting winds, approached the bus. The driver of the bus and the patrolman seemed to confer and then the bus lurched forward.

The guard driving their van lowered her window as the patrolman approached. Wind howled in through the open window, driving soot and ashes around the detainees. Maria pulled her shirt above her nose, choking on the acrid air that filled the van.

"I'll tell you what I told the bus driver," the patrolman shouted above the roar of the wind. "Yoakim bridge is out. Burned. Do not take that fork in the road, do you understand?"

The guard nodded, raised the window and nosed the van forward, following the dim taillights of the bus. The bus in front of them lurched onto Lytton Spring Road and then accelerated into the murky haze. The guard driving the van accelerated, trying to catch the speeding bus. The van trembled, pounded by the fury of the wind. Maria's heart raced. She and the other detainees banged back and forth in their seats as the van bumped against the gusts.

Maria watched the guard with increasing dread as the guard fought with the steering wheel, desperately trying to keep the van on the road and follow the bus in front of them. Suddenly, there was an ear-splitting crack and the windshield splintered. Maria shrieked. The guard yanked the van. It shuddered and bumped onto the shoulder of the road and ground to an abrupt halt.

"Are you all right," Maria looked from Juan to Gabby. Juan gave a thumbs up and Gabby nodded nervously.

"It's okay," the guard called out, her voice quavered. "Just a mailbox, liberated from its post by the wind. Nothing to be concerned about." The guard reached forward and poked the windshield which was splintered with a spider web of cracks.

"You should stop," Juan called out. "This isn't safe."

"We can't stay here," the guard grunted as she guided the van back onto the road. "We'd burn up."

The guard stepped on the accelerator and roared forward.

"She lost them," Juan whispered to Maria and Gabby.

"Lost what?" Gabby asked, her voice cracking with nervousness.

"The men's bus," Juan said, his eyes scanning out of the sooty windows.

Maria's heart dropped. They were supposed to follow the bus. Did the guard driving the van know where to go? Maria looked out of the shattered windshield. The guard was driving too fast. It was impossible to see in front of the van.

"You should slow down," Maria shouted nervously at the guard. The van shuddered as the wind pounded it, but continued to rocket forward through the soupy haze. "I said, you should slow down," Maria yelled.

"Shut your fucking mouth," the guard screamed. She accelerated and the van shook viciously.

Maria grabbed for Juan. With her other hand she squeezed Gabby's arm. Her heart raced. The van was shuddering, pounded by the wind. The smoke outside was nearly impenetrable—a solid wall of soot. She glanced fearfully out of the window. They were moving too fast through the murky air. She saw something out of the window, a road sign. It took a second for the words on the sign to register. A shiver ran down her spine. "No," she whispered. Then she screamed. "Stop! You have to stop!"

"I told you to shut the fuck up," the guard yelled over her shoulder.

"Yoakim bridge!" Maria yelled at the top of her lungs. "The sign said Yoakim bridge!"

Maria saw the guard's eyes in the rear-view mirror, wide with horror. The guard slammed on the brakes and the van screeched but continued to rocket forward. The bumping stopped abruptly. Maria gasped. The van was airborne. She stared in disbelief out of the window. The van left the road and shot across a chasm where the bridge once stood. There was no time to scream. She barely had time to look at Gabby in shock. The van smashed down, the front of it crumpling like a tin can. The van's windows exploded, shattering and blasting glass splinters through the air that rained down on Maria, Gabby, and Juan. The van slid backward into the dry creek bed. Maria jerked violently. Her head smacked onto the side of the van. She clutched it and cried out. The van tumbled and then came to rest upside down in the bottom of the creek bed. Maria fell to the van's ceiling and smacked her head. She struggled to keep her eyes open. She exhaled slowly, dizzy and disoriented. The last thing she remembered before she lost consciousness was Gabby's head twisted at an unnatural angle, blood oozing from her mouth.

35. BEL

Bel paced in the dining room feeling useless. The shooting pain in his side caused him to momentarily double over, but it was less intense since he'd taken a pill. He stood upright and stared at the video screens. He wiped the sweat from his brow. The wall of fire was pounding toward them faster than Maureen predicted. But he didn't need the video feeds to tell him. He could see the advancing inferno out of the dining room windows. The house rattled as another series of gusts blasted.

News feeds scrolled across the screen. Bel sucked in his breath. A mandatory evacuation for Healdsburg. He turned to look at his wife and daughter. "Who else is left on the estate?" he asked.

"You, me, Nadine. JC, the technician," Maureen said tensely, her eyes nervously flicking to the screen.

"Everyone goes," Bel said. "I'll wait for the immigrants."

"Absolutely not," Maureen said and crossed her arms. "You forget that I am the bank-appointed operator. And this mess is of your making. Once again, I am cleaning up after you."

"Oh Jesus," Bel muttered. He rubbed his temples and winced at the stabbing pain of what was most likely a broken rib.

"I'm not going anywhere," Nadine announced. "And you need me. I'm connected to Nigel back in the city who can hack into anything." She held up her phone defiantly.

"Except HALLIE, apparently," Bel rolled his eyes. He turned to JC. "Take the technician and get to safety."

JC started to protest and Bel held up his hand.

"I said take the technician and get to safety now!" Bel glared at JC. He needed at least one person on the estate to listen and not treat him like garbage. JC looked at him, Maureen, and Nadine and seemed like he wanted to say something. But the old winemaker simply gulped and nodded. JC grabbed the technician by the elbow and together they walked down the hallway. Bel heard the front door slam and the putrid smells of the blaze wafted in.

Bel ignored the groaning house and looked at his watch. The immigrant detainees should have been here by now. He limped to the window and stared. He could barely make out anything. The wind had whipped the soot into a frenzy and mixed it with choking smoke. He strained to see the end of the driveway. But there, two tiny pinpoints of light. He exhaled and waited. The lights got bigger. "They're here!"

He jogged down the hall, gritting his teeth at the throbbing in his side. He threw open the front door and a scalding blast of ash raced in. He heard his wife and daughter gasp. They were right behind him. He limped across the driveway and banged on the side of the detainee bus. The door opened. Bel climbed in. Rows of nervous, brown faces looked at him.

"You'll go up this fire road," Bel turned to the guard driving the bus. "As you approach the ridge, that's where you'll dig. The trench needs to be wide. The winds are powerful and will drive the flames across anything that's too narrow."

The guard nodded nervously.

"The second bus?" Bel asked, looking out of the sooty windows. "Where are they?"

"Don't know, man," the guard replied. "Lost radio contact at Lytton Springs. Called it in, haven't heard."

"Shit," Bel muttered. His mother had been clear with the sheriff that they needed at least two bus loads. "You don't have much time," Bel said. What had Maureen said, three hours? That was over an hour ago. Bel left that unsaid. He turned to the men in the bus. Row after row of detainees, here to save McMaster Vineyards, and not by their choosing. A lump formed in his throat. "Thank you," he stammered. It was the best he could do. He hopped from the bus and watched as it lumbered toward the fire road that led up to the ridge.

He limped back to the house, bent over in the howling wind. He pulled his shirt over his mouth, gasping for air as ash rained around him. The gusts pushed him across the porch and into the house where his wife and daughter waited.

"Only one bus arrived," he said. His mind spun. How would they find a missing bus in the middle of a raging wildfire?

"Nigel," Nadine said.

"What?"

"I told you, he can hack into anything. I'll tell him to hack ICE."

Bel shook his head. "The guard said he'd lost contact..."

"He'll find the vehicle GPS," Nadine said, punching at her phone. She looked up at him sharply. "He's that good, Dad."

Bel followed Maureen and Nadine into the foyer. An ear-splitting crack pierced the air. He looked up with alarm. The massive chandelier above groaned as the house shifted in the gale-force winds and thousands of pear-shaped crystals clattered violently. Bel shuddered and walked down the hall.

The dining room was strangely quiet with just the three of them. Maureen moved to the far side of the room, to get away from him, he supposed, and talked urgently on her phone. He lowered himself onto a chair and moaned softly. Nadine sat next to him.

"He's on it," she said grimly. "If anyone can find that bus, it's Nigel."

Bel nodded and grabbed for his side as another wave of pain wracked his body.

"Jesus, Dad, we need to get you to a hospital."

Bel shook his head vehemently. "I'm not going anywhere." And then he said quietly, "But thank you."

Nadine looked away from him. Yet another massive gust blasted the house and the windows rattled loudly. Bel glanced outside. The glow from the ridge intensified as the fire drew near, casting an eerie light into the dining room.

"We don't have much time," he exhaled.

Nadine stayed next to him and kept her gaze out of the window. "Dad, this isn't a great time but I have to say it," she said, an edge to her voice. "When you stole Daisy's UAD to break into Kavali Tower..."

"Nadine, I..."

"No," she held up her hand and looked at him. He felt her gaze boring into him like a drill. "You need to listen. I already know you thought Maria Garcia was some other woman named Gabby." She gritted her teeth. "I figured out that Maria lied to you. But when you stole from Daisy—my girlfriend—you betrayed *me*. I don't know if I've ever felt so violated and alone. My own father, using me like some..." Her voice caught and she wiped away a tear. She twisted a piercing in her ear and looked away.

"Nadine, please," Bel said. He bowed his head and exhaled. He spoke and hoped that she would listen. "Just now, I was running down that hillside back to the house," Bel stammered, "And the only thing I could think about was holding you in my arms when you were first born. You were so tiny. So perfect. I would have given my life for you." Bel looked up at his daughter. "And I still would." He reached out to grab her hands and she recoiled. "I know I did everything to make you *not* believe that, but you, Nadine, matter more than anything. Someday, I hope I can prove that."

Nadine continued to twist the piercing in her ear and was silent. The roar of the fire pounded outside the house, whipped by the unceasing gusts. The lights in the dining room flickered. Bel saw her swallow. "I did take your advice," she said finally. "I talked with Daisy about her ex." She grimaced and managed a wry smile. "Believe it or not, I heard you shouting at me even when ICE was tasing you."

"I don't think that was ICE," Bel muttered.

"Not entirely," Nadine agreed. "Regardless, Daisy and I were able to put the pieces together." Nadine twisted her piercings even more fiercely.

Bel's stomach clenched at the memory of rummaging through Daisy's purse. "So, she's still talking to you?" he asked, barely able to look at his daughter.

Nadine snorted. "We bonded over the fact that we both have insane fathers."

"Fair," Bel said.

"Daisy was dating a security guard at Kavali, you were right about that," Nadine continued. "It wasn't going well when Daisy found out that her girlfriend was a secret member of WACO."

"WACO?"

"World Anti-Cloning Organization. They're a guerrilla group fighting against the unregulated creation of synthetic organisms. They've been a thorn in Mohan's side for years. They've infiltrated Kavali, gotten jobs there in security, research, that sort of thing." Nadine paused. "Brie, that's Daisy's ex-girlfriend, had worked her way up for years inside Kavali, got top security clearance and then with the help of WACO, managed to hack the Kavali genetics database and download the genome Synthetica to a removable media card." Nadine exhaled and pulled at one of her piercings. "But weirdly, as part of her investigation, Brie also discovered that undocumented immigrants were being bused to the tower."

"Yes, I saw them," Bel nodded absently, recalling the bus that had disgorged a stream of people just before he broke into the tower.

"But Brie couldn't find any record of immigrants leaving the tower," Nadine continued. "She was freaked out, maybe thought immigrants were being used for genetic testing. No one knows what the genome does, after all."

"Did Daisy ask Brie how Carlos got the media card?"

Nadine's eyes clouded. "Brie disappeared," Nadine said softly. "After she told Daisy she'd stolen the genome and shared her suspicions, they had a fight. Daisy felt betrayed. No one knows where Brie went."

Bel scratched his chin. "That still doesn't explain how Carlos Garcia got the card with the stolen genome."

Nadine exhaled. "I was able to track Carlos Garcia. He crossed illegally into Texas and was captured by ICE, then held at a detention camp in Dilley, Texas. He was eventually bused to San Francisco as part of Kavali's DIGSA contract with DHS. The day he arrived at Kavali Tower..."

"Was the very day Brie disappeared," Bel finished quietly.

Nadine nodded. "Brie and Carlos must have crossed paths in the tower. Somehow, Carlos Garcia left Kavali Tower with the card and gun. Almost certainly with Brie's help. Daisy didn't even suspect the gun used to kill Ned was from Kavali until I..." Nadine choked back a sob.

Bel pulled his daughter close and this time she didn't push back. She rested her head on his shoulder. The house rumbled and from upstairs he heard something shatter. God, maybe the windows were breaking in the heat and wind. His heart thudded. Finally, they knew. He closed his eyes. He felt Nadine sobbing as he held her. He stroked her hair and exhaled. The gun that killed his son did, in fact, belong to Kavali Corporation. But there was another mystery, one that Nadine didn't yet know. The true nature of Synthetica.

"There's something you need to know about the plants in Kavali Tower," Bel licked his dry lips as he considered how to tell Nadine what he suspected. "I took a sample of the pinot vines. And, Nadine, they're not just plant DNA, they're..."

A buzzing sound interrupted them. Nadine looked at her screen. "It's Nigel," she said. She flipped on her phone and stared at him as she listened to her assistant, her eyes narrowing. She flicked off her phone.

"He found them," she said. Her forehead was creased with concern. "And..." She paused.

"And what?"

"It's a van, not a bus, and it appears to have crashed. The GPS is active and broadcasting from Yoakim Creek near the old bridge."

Bel frowned. "Is ICE on their way to rescue?"

Nadine shook her head. "No one is available tonight."

"But..."

"Dad, there's more." Nadine cleared her throat. "One of the detainees in the van is Maria Garcia."

Bel's jaw dropped. He felt like someone had just punched him in the gut. Maria. He stared at his daughter, barely able to comprehend what he'd heard. "That's impossible," he whispered.

"It's true. Nigel saw the manifest."

His mind spun and he wanted to vomit. She'd lied to him from the very first moment they met, he was certain. The look of recognition in her eyes when he introduced himself in the Quick Mart parking lot. Maybe she had planned it. God, there were no answers. And in spite of everything, his heart still raced when he thought about her. He wanted to bang his head on the dining room table.

"Dad, are you okay?"

He stood and winced. He should ignore Maria Garcia, let her burn with the others. He grimaced and looked out the window. The flames pulsed on the ridge, turning the sky a red that seemed to ooze down like blood. If the detainees up there couldn't dig fast enough, the fire would be here soon. None of this would matter. Bel closed his eyes and tried to wipe the memories of her away. Her lips, the curve of her hips, the way she looked up at him. He wanted to ignore it, the realness of their love, but he couldn't. He opened his eyes and exhaled shakily.

"I have to save Maria," he whispered.

Nadine's eyes were wide. "Are you fucking joking? After she lied to you?"

He looked at his daughter, his jaw firm and limped toward the door. His truck was at the end of the driveway. He could be there in fifteen minutes, unless the roads were out.

"Dad, stop!" Nadine called out. He looked back at his daughter and saw her exhale and shake her head. "You can't go alone," she said firmly. "I'm the better driver."

36. MARIA

Maria opened her eyes and struggled to make sense of where she was. She lay on her side, groggy. Pain shot through her arm and she tried to move it but couldn't. The air around her was thick—putrid and black. She coughed. She was still inside the ICE van, but the vehicle was not moving—it was crushed and resting on its roof.

She shifted her arm, this time it moved and the handcuff bit into her wrist. She winced.

"Juan?" she called out. Her voice shook and was drowned out by the roar of the wind.

There was no answer. With her free arm, she pushed herself up. Her forehead throbbed. Juan lay crumpled beside her, unmoving. She pulled again on the handcuffs that bound them together. He moaned softly but didn't wake.

Beyond Juan, her cousin Gabby lay still. Maria squinted to see through the sooty air and shifted toward her cousin. Gabby's face was streaked with grime and a tiny rivulet of blood oozed from her mouth.

"Gabby?" Maria called. There was no answer. "Gabby!" Maria screamed and pulled the handcuff. Juan moaned again as Maria desperately tried to move closer to her cousin. Something was wrong with Gabby. She was too still.

The van shuddered and Maria looked out of a shattered window. They were at the bottom of the creek bed filled with dry brambles and withered bushes. Maria squinted, trying to see through the smoke, and then she sucked in her breath. The blaze was in the creek bed, roaring toward the van. A hot blast of air shook the vehicle and Maria's eyes widened. The wind was pushing the fire right at her. Flames chewed through the dried vegetation and grasses with brutal speed and efficiency. She gasped. They only had minutes.

She grabbed Juan's wrist with both hands and dragged him toward Gabby, digging her heels into the metal roof of the overturned van. He mumbled but didn't wake. At her cousin's side, she reached out and squeezed Gabby's shoulder. Her cousin didn't move. Her eyes were open, unblinking.

"No," Maria whispered.

The van rumbled as the wind outside howled. Smoke oozed in through the broken windows and Maria gagged, frantically trying to breathe. She squeezed Gabby again, calling her name, but Gabby just lay there, lifeless. Maria shook her head in disbelief and grabbed for Gabby's wrist. Nothing. No pulse. It wasn't possible. She screamed out, crying Gabby's name again and again. She kicked at the roof of the van in anger. No one in the van moved. Other bodies lay about, lifeless. The backdoor of the van was partially ajar. Some of the detainees must have escaped up the dry river bed.

Maria raised her head and cried out. Then, she crossed herself with her free hand and screwed her eyes shut in prayer. How dare the saints take Gabby, the one who had guided her, been her savior again and again? No, she couldn't believe the saints would be this cruel. "Please," she whispered. "Please señor, do not take my cousin. Please, I beg of you." But it was too late. The life had left Gabby. Maria covered her face and sobbed, tears of shame running down her face.

"Oh, my beautiful one, why are you crying?" A man's voice said behind her. An oily, dripping voice.

Maria snapped her head up. It couldn't be. Her blood ran cold. She recognized the man immediately. His black hair, slicked back. The perpetual sneer. Cadejo had found her. Somehow. She screamed and pushed herself forward in the van, grabbing at Juan's wrist to pull him after her.

Cadejo's laugh filled the smokey van and made her skin crawl. "Oh Maria," he said and ducked under a seat hanging from the floor above, moving toward her. "You should give me a nicer welcome. I'm here to help you."

"No!" Maria screamed. She yanked on Juan's arm, desperately trying to wake him, but Juan only mumbled. "Stay away from me," she yelled at Cadejo. She tried to slide on the ceiling of the overturned van, pushing hard with her heels, but Juan was heavy and unmoving. Her heart thudded. She was trapped. Cadejo came closer.

"The mother of my little Alarico," Cadejo snarled.

Maria's heart sank. Her worst fear confirmed. Cadejo knew about Alarico. A boom sounded and rocked the van. She looked out of the window, panicked. A huge tree had fallen, just missing them. Clouds of ash rose up from the dry creek bed and spun in the sooty air, darkening the air even more. Her heart thudded. Cadejo was now right in front of her. He crouched down, his face inches from hers. Despite the smoke, she could smell his rancid breath. She wanted to wretch.

"Still cuffed to this man," Cadejo smirked. He grabbed Juan's face and turned it side to side. "You have such pathetic friends, Maria." Cadejo looked at her, his dark eyes narrow. "I don't suppose you have the key?" He laughed again. "And to think, I always wanted to get you in a pair of handcuffs. Somebody did it for me."

Maria grimaced and turned away from the gangster.

He slapped her across the face. "Don't look away from me, Maria."

Maria inhaled and choked on the foul air. She summoned up enough energy to spit at Cadejo. "You'll never have Alarico!" she yelled.

"As if you can stop me," Cadejo sneered. "There's no one here but us. First," he held up a finger, "we need to get you out of these cuffs." He looked behind her shoulder. "And if I had to guess, the key is in her pocket." He pointed at the lifeless guard hanging upside down from the driver seat. A chain link divider separated the front of the van from the back. Cadejo reached above Maria and yanked on the divider. It rattled but didn't move. "Well," Cadejo said, "it seems I have to go outside." He slapped Maria again on the face. "Don't go anywhere." He ducked under the hanging seats and moved to the rear of the van, his boots crunching on the broken glass. He jumped out of the van. She exhaled. She had to act now.

"Juan," she hissed. "Juan, wake up." She rattled the handcuff. Juan moaned and his eyelids fluttered. "Yes!" Maria exclaimed, "Please get up. We have to go." She slid across the van roof, ignoring the shards of glass that tore at her hands and knees. She glanced out of the broken window and sucked in her breath. The fire had advanced to the front of the van. She saw Cadejo stride through the smoking brush, bent over against the howling wind. She had only seconds. Her mind raced. The only way out was through the rear doors. If she could drag Juan outside, then what would she do? She shook her head. It didn't matter, getting out of the back of the van was her only option.

She grabbed both of Juan's wrists and pulled him. Her body tensed as she dragged him slowly across the ceiling. There was a rattling at the front of the van. Maria looked up. Cadejo was trying to open the driver's door from outside. She held her breath. The upside-down door was jammed. She struggled to hear over the roar of the blaze. More pounding and the van rocked as Cadejo kicked at the jammed door.

She had to move faster. Digging her heels into the ceiling, she ignored the glass shards that had worked their way into her back and elbows and she pulled Juan's body. They inched forward. The van rocked again and she looked up. More pounding, this time the very front of the van. She gasped. Cadejo was beating on the front windshield. It sagged. She sucked in her breath. There was a long groan and the remainder of the front windshield collapsed. Cadejo's face appeared where the windshield had once been, streaked with soot. With the cracked window gone, Maria could see the dry creek bed and a chill ran down her spine. The wall of flame was directly behind him. The blaze churned and roiled, pulverizing everything in its path as it pounded its way to the van. Waves of soot rolled into the van and Maria choked.

Through the haze, she saw Cadejo pull himself through the broken windshield and into the front of the van. But she couldn't watch, she had to get them out. She pulled on Juan, desperately dragging him. Inch by inch she pulled him toward the back of the van. Her back popped and she cried out. She stood and banged her head on the seats that hung from above. Bending over, she rubbed her head and then glanced nervously forward. It was hard to see the front of the van now, smoke poured in through all the broken windows. But she could make out Cadejo rummaging through the guard's pockets. She had only seconds. She whispered a prayer to the saints and strained, pulling harder on Juan's wrists. They were nearly to the rear of the van. The haze in the vehicle was like soup and the roar of the blaze filled her ears. She heard a pop and looked up. Her heart dropped. The front of the van was burning. A tire melted and exploded. She squinted to see through the soot that now filled the van. Where was Cadejo? It was impossible to see through the swirling haze.

They reached the back of the van. Maria took a deep breath and choked on the ash. The back doors swung wildly in the gusts and banged ferociously against the side of the van, each bang made her jump. She poked her head out. The wind drove soot and ash into her eyes and nose and she could barely see through the pounding wind. She looked down at Juan. His eyelids continued to flutter but he wouldn't wake. She bent and wrapped her arms around his shoulders. "Let's go," she whispered in his ear. She'd have to roll him out of the back of the van.

A hand clamped down on her shoulder. Maria screamed and spun.

"What in the fuck to you think you're doing?" Cadejo loomed over her, covered in ash and grime. He leered and his white teeth glistened against his filthy skin like the fangs of a coyote. "You weren't thinking of leaving me again?"

Maria scrambled back into the van, desperately pulling Juan behind her. They thumped toward the front of the van. She could feel the heat of the fire that chewed through the van. Pungent odors of melting rubber and burning plastic gagged her. Still, she had no choice but to get back in. She ducked under a seat hanging from above and kicked her feet uselessly at Cadejo as he dropped to his hands and knees and crawled toward her.

"And besides," Cadejo said. "You're going to need this." He sat back on his haunches and held up his hand. From it dangled a key on a chain. The key to the handcuffs that bound her to Juan.

Maria inhaled just as the front of the van sparked and hissed. An ear-splitting bang rocked the van as a second tire melted and exploded. She covered her face to protect herself from the soot and glass that rocketed through the van. The front of the van was now fully ablaze and flames chewed through the lifeless guard, her uniform fizzling and her skin melting away. Maria gagged at the smell.

"But first," Cadejo growled, "I want to know where my son is."

"Never," Maria screamed. She pulled desperately at Juan's arm. She couldn't go any further forward into the van. The fire was advancing too fast. Her back bristled at the waves of heat from the burning front of the van.

"I think you need some motivation," Cadejo growled, his eyes narrow. He pulled a small, blunt knife from his waistband and before Maria could comprehend what he was about to do, drove the knife into Juan's gut.

Juan screamed out and his body arced and then collapsed onto the roof of the van. He mumbled out words that were incomprehensible.

"No!" Maria yelled horrified, her eyes wide. "Please, leave him!" She clawed for Cadejo's hand but he pushed himself backward away from her reach.

"I see," he sneered. "Still loyal." He held up the knife again above Juan. A drop of blood ran slowly down the blade and quivered. "I will ask again, where is my son?"

Maria shook her head and gulped. "No, please," she begged. "Leave Juan alone."

"Once again, bargaining for the life of the faggot," he taunted. Cadejo drove the blade down into Juan's stomach again. Juan screamed out and his head rolled toward Maria, his eyes fluttering.

She couldn't breathe. The walls of the van were closing in around her. Smoke filled her mouth and nose and she gagged. Cadejo would kill Juan if she didn't tell him where Alarico was. Her mind was a whirlwind of images: little Alarico playing with his cousin Ana in the backyard. Her husband Carlos, dead and laid out under the harsh lights in the morgue. Juan looking at her from the balcony as she ran from ICE. Bel's emerald eyes in the dying light of the shed as he lowered himself to kiss her. Maria's eyes teared and she wiped her hand across her soot-streaked face. She had no choice but to save Juan.

She muttered trancelike. "Cazadero. Alarico is hiding in Cazadero."

Cadejo tucked the knife back in his belt and leaned to her. He brushed a bloody hand against her cheek. "Oh, Maria," he said, his voice guttural. "You're so naive. You don't think I came all this way for a son, do you?"

Maria shuddered and pushed herself backward, her eyes wide. What did he mean? Cadejo hovered over her, his face inches from hers.

"Every whore I've fucked shoved out a kid." Cadejo spat the words. "I have three sons. I don't need another fighting over my legacy." He grabbed a strand of her hair and fondled it, rubbing it slowly between his fingers. "No, Maria. I didn't come here for a child. I came here for you. The most beautiful woman I've ever known. You should have never tried to leave me." He cupped her face in his hands and his sneer changed into something more menacing. "Now Maria, you need to learn a lesson. We're going to Cazadero. You're going to watch me kill your son and then you're coming back to Guatemala with me. Just us. The way it is supposed to be. And this time, I'll make sure you can't run off to California." He drew out the syllables of the final word one by one, punctuated by the crazed laugh of a maniac.

Maria gasped. She was suffocating. She clutched at her throat. No. She had fled Guatemala to escape Cadejo. To raise her son here, somewhere away from him. Her self-defense training told her she needed to flee her attacker. But now she saw there was no escaping him. He wanted her for his own. She felt her blood start to boil. Cadejo was right, she had been naive.

The flames burst from the front of the van and licked at the seats above. The van rocked as the gusts pushed at its burning shell. She glanced out of the broken window. The creek bed around them was ablaze. She had no time left. She made the sign of the cross and raised her eyes to the burning seat above her. It seemed to pulse with orange life, as if inhabited by a hellish spirit. The van was moments away from exploding. The air was fowl, thick with acrid soot, but for the first time in weeks, Maria could see clearly. "Oh, saints above," she murmured, "I need your strength now more than ever. Bless my son, keep him safe in your light. And protect me and forgive me for what I am about to do."

Maria could see the rivulets of sweat making tiny tracks across Cadejo's grimy face. It was a face that had tormented her for years. But no more. Her spine stiffened and her eyes narrowed. "Rot in hell!" she hissed. With her free hand, she lunged for the blunt knife in his belt, seized it, and drove it toward his chest.

Cadejo was faster. He grabbed her wrist and twisted it. She cried out and the knife clattered to the roof of the van. "You have the passion of a jilted lover, no?" He lowered himself toward her. "Is this what you want?" The gangster's mouth curled into a sneer and he smacked Maria across the face. "You want to play with me, Maria?" He smacked her again.

Her face stung from the hits. Cadejo held tight to Maria's free wrist and she tried desperately to wiggle away but there was nowhere to go. The seats above flamed and began to drip molten plastic. She screamed as the liquid drizzled onto her bare arms.

Cadejo yelled as the scalding liquid ran onto his back. He released her wrist and batted madly at his back. She heard something clatter on the floor. The key to the handcuffs.

Maria balled up her fist and punched at his face but he dodged. She swung again but the gangster anticipated and moved. Of course, he was a veteran street brawler. There was no way she could fight with one hand. He leaned down toward her and she head-butted him, connecting her forehead with his nose.

He yelped in surprise and reached for his face. Ruby red blood ran from his nose and dripped down on Maria.

"You bitch," he yelled. He smacked her across the face. "Is that what you want? Huh, Maria, you want to play?" He rolled on top of her. His eyes were wide and reptilian—they flickered with a satisfied rage that Maria had seen once before. She screamed as Cadejo raised his arm and smacked her again.

"No one leaves me," he yelled." No one!"

Her head shook and she couldn't breathe. Cadejo smacked her again and again and shouted words, but she couldn't understand their meaning. Now, his hands were around her throat. She pushed at the gangster, madly trying to get him off of her. She tried to breathe. She was choking. The gangster tightened his hold on her. Her throat gurgled as she desperately tried to inhale. She clawed at Cadejo, dragging the nails of her free hand uselessly across his face. His sneer burned and she writhed beneath him, frantically attempting to wriggle away. She was weakening. She threw her arms behind her and raked them across the roof of the van, searching for something—anything that she could use. There was nothing. With her free hand she banged on the side of Cadejo's head. Her blows glanced harmlessly. He grimaced and spat on her.

"Weak, Maria!" He shouted above the roar of the fire. "You've always been weak."

Maria turned and looked at Juan lying next to her. His eyes were half-closed and she could see tiny bubbles of spittle forming on his lips. He seemed to be whispering but she couldn't hear.

She struggled to see. The air in the van turned black. It could have been the smoke and soot or maybe the gangster's hands around her neck, but it didn't matter. She was taking her last breaths.

"Pathetic," she heard Cadejo say. "All the way to California to die like a weak little girl. I hope your son puts up more of a fight."

Her son. She tried to grit her teeth but the life was leaving her. She could not let Alarico grow up to be like his father. No, he could not grow up to be a murderer or a gangster. Her vision clouded and she saw Carlos standing there, impossibly, in the van. His forehead was clear, there were no gang symbols. Carlos smiled and reached out his hand. Maria sighed as she remembered his warm caress. "Maria," Carlos said, his voice echoing in her head. "You are the bravest of women." She gazed up and thought of her last memory of him alive and on the bank of the Suchiate, standing resolutely as she drifted away to a better life. "You," he whispered, "are an amazing mother to two sons."

Maria gulped and struggled to breath. "One son," she stammered.

Carlos shook his head and put his finger gently on her lips. "No," he said quietly. "Two. You must save them both. Remember what I gave you."

Maria's eyes teared. She dragged in a gasping breath and nodded. The fire was scorching her face. She looked up at Cadejo and narrowed her eyes. "He won't need to fight you," Maria whispered, her voice choking. "Because you'll be dead."

With her free hand, she reached for the crucifix that hung from her neck. She jerked it hard. The chain cut into the back of her neck but didn't break. She tore it mightily, crying out a yell from the bottom of her gut. The chain burst apart. She swung the crucifix with all her might and plunged its dagger-like bottom into Cadejo's neck. She screamed and sliced the crucifix down the side of his throat, slashing bone deep. The crucifix cut coarsely across his veins as she sawed viciously. Blood spurted from Cadejo's neck, spraying through the air and drenching Maria's face.

The gangster's eyes bugged. He released Maria and clutched his throat then stared in shock at his blood-soaked hands. He fell backward, his eyes wide with confusion and disbelief. He tried to stand but thumped down against the side of the burning van, frantically clawed at the gaping wound in his neck, futilely struggling to staunch the flow of blood. The color drained from his face. His arms dropped uselessly. He fell with a thud and lay shaking as blood pooled around his head and sopped his jet-black hair. Maria gasped for breath as the gangster's life ebbed away. She exhaled unevenly.

The van groaned as the fire consumed it. Maria trembled and screamed out to the saints. She had to move.

"Juan!" She shook the handcuffs that bound them. Juan was unresponsive. She put her finger on his neck. His heart still beat. She looked frantically across the roof of the overturned van for the key to the handcuffs. She moved on hands and knees searching. The van was overheating, the roof was becoming too hot to touch. The key to the handcuffs was nowhere to be seen. She pushed Cadejo's body aside. Still no key. She had to leave now.

She grabbed Juan's arms and again pulled him to the back of the van, ducking under the seats above. Smoke poured into the van. The fire completely encircled them. She kicked at the back doors and they flopped open, wildly flapping in the gusts. She jumped to the ground and gasped. The entire van was ablaze. She tugged at Juan. "Come on," she screamed. Something was caught. His body wasn't sliding forward. The heat was unrelenting and sweat drenched her face. She reached under his body. A belt loop, caught on the door frame.

She ripped it free and pulled Juan with all of her might, screaming out to the saints. His body slid forward and tumbled to the ground on top of her.

She stood and dragged him across the smoldering grasses and away from the van. Flames were all around, everything in the arid creek bed flamed with intensity. She looked backward and fire now consumed the van. The vehicle heaved and exploded. Maria screamed as the blast knocked her to the ground. The fire rocketed down the creek bed and surrounded them. Burning trees flayed and sparked as they were eaten by the thrashing blaze.

She looked around frantically. They were surrounded. Walls of fire. But there, just in front, a tiny dirt path led up the embankment. It was her only hope. But there was no way she could drag Juan that far.

Maria crouched down and gently touched Juan's forehead. She bowed her head. "Milagroso Señor de Esquipulas," she said forcefully. "I am brave enough to ask for your help. I no longer beg. I need the saints now. Look down on us with favor."

Behind her was a massive crack as a redwood splintered at its base. She gazed up. The tree thundered down in a fiery hail of sparks and soot. The ground rumbled. Maria threw herself over Juan to shield him from the rocketing embers.

"Maria," he whispered.

She looked down at him as his eyes fluttered open. "Juan," she said urgently. "You have to stand. Now." She pulled him up. He winced as she put his free arm around her shoulders. "You must walk fast," she commanded. "There," she yelled out above the roar of the wind pointing to the tiny path. Grasses on both sides of the path burst into flame. She pulled Juan forward, squinting to see through the sooty, burning air.

They reached the path. She pushed a flaming bush out of the way and clawed her way up the steep embankment with him at her side. Juan stumbled. Maria grabbed him and held him upright.

Around them, the creek's banks were fully aflame, fire chewing through grasses and shrubs and pounding at the trees. Maria yelled above the deafening roar. "We have to go through it." She pointed at the burning grasses on the creek bank. Juan nodded. Together, they struggled up the slope, holding each other tightly.

Maria looked down, feeling a biting at her ankles. The fire ignited her pants. She swatted at the flames. Juan's pants were smoldering. She reached down and patted out the flames. Her hands burned and she shook them frantically but there was nowhere to cool them. The top of the creek bank was just in sight. The fire was in front of them now. She gasped.

"We won't make it," Juan yelled at her side.

"Yes, we will," Maria responded. She put her arm around Juan's waist and pulled. Together they scrambled up the embankment on hands and knees. The fire licked at her legs and arms. It was burning, scalding her skin. She couldn't even scream out. How her shoes were melting. Then, suddenly, they rolled through the flames and onto a narrow dirt road.

Maria lay there next to Juan, gasping for air. The fire raged around them, chewing the creek bank. And above, towering trees were ablaze, crackling and teetering. The fire was everywhere. Even the air crackled with heat and energy, almost unbreathable. In moments, the entire area would explode in a fireball, the trees would erupt in flames and the undergrowth would blow up as if detonated by a bomb.

She looked desperately up and down the narrow dirt road, lined with dry trees that swayed in the fiery winds. There was no way they could run fast enough to stay ahead of the fire. Across the tiny road was a black sedan. Cadejo's car. She made the sign of the cross and limped to the car, Juan's arm across her shoulder, the handcuff biting into her wrist. She reached for the door handle. Locked. "No!" she hollered and banged on the roof of the car. She inhaled and choked. They were out of options. She leaned against the car. Juan put his head on her shoulder and together they stood there, the ash and soot blasting around them. This is how they would die, suffocating on a tiny dirt road in Sonoma County. Maria bowed her head. Together they stood, listening to the roar of the fire consume the forest around them. But then, a sound that was not the roar of the fire. It was, an engine? A chill ran down her spine. She looked down the road again. In the distance, tiny lights grew.

"There," she whispered to Juan and pushed herself from the car.

Juan looked up, his face dripping with blood and grime.

The lights were clearer now. Headlights. Racing toward them through the sooty haze.

"Here!" screamed Maria. She waved her free arm frantically. "Here!"

The vehicle barreled toward them and squealed to a stop. It was a tattered pickup truck streaked with soot. Maria gasped in recognition. Bel McMaster. The door flew open and he dashed toward her.

"Maria," he breathed. He threw his arms around her in a tight embrace.

"How did you..." But she couldn't finish the sentence. His lips were on hers, kissing with relief. With passion. She let herself be held in his arms and kissed him back, unable to believe he'd found her. Unable to believe he still wanted her.

"Hey," a woman's voice called from the truck and she tapped on the horn. "This little reunion can wait. We need to go, now!"

Maria pushed herself away from Bel, and together they lifted Juan to the cab.

"I'm Nadine," the driver of the pickup truck yelled. "Hang on!"

The truck rocketed forward. Maria jerked her head, looking through the grimy rear window and into the dry creek bed, now roiling with flames. Tears slid down her cheeks as she said a silent prayer, this time to a new saint, her cousin Gabby.

37. BEL

The pickup truck hurtled forward, every jolt causing Bel to wince at the throbbing in his side. Still, it was nothing compared to Maria's friend, Juan. Blood gushed from the young man's abdomen. Bel ripped shreds of cloth from his shirt.

"Here," he yelled to Maria over the roar of the fire. He braced himself against the dashboard of the jostling vehicle and together he and Maria applied the strips of cloth, trying to staunch the flow of blood, pressing hard against Juan's stomach until the man cried out.

"We have to get him to a hospital, now," Bel shouted. "Nadine, up here. Left turn. It connects with Jochison. We can get to Santa Rosa Hospital."

Nadine nodded and pushed the accelerator. The pickup truck barreled forward on the dirt road, battered by the raging wind and scalding gusts. Bel glanced out of the smeared window and gasped. The blaze raced next to the truck, crackling through the dry trees and grasses that lined the road. He looked up to the sky in awe. The fire seemed to defy gravity and physics, exploding through the air, pushed by the relentless Diablo gusts. Cinders rocketed above them and erupted, fueling the blaze's roaring race with the truck.

"Faster, Nadine," Bel shouted. His heart thudded. The fire was closing around them. "You have to drive faster."

He looked at his phone. There'd been no service since they left the main estate. He grimaced and reached for the old two-way radio. He'd used it when they left the estate, but Maureen had stopped responding just before they'd reached Maria. He shook his head, something wasn't right.

"Base, come in," he tried again. "Maureen?" No answer. Just old-fashioned static. They had no phone service and now no radio. He shuddered. They were cut off.

Nadine straightened the truck as it skidded across loose gravel and bounced. Bel glanced at Maria. Her face was covered in soot and ash, her hands were covered in blood. The handcuffs that bound Maria and Juan suggested something horrible had happened. He tore another strip of cloth from the bottom of his shirt and wiped her face. Even streaked in soot and blood she made his heart race. She looked up at him and stroked his face and for a moment the roar of the fire disappeared, the ash lifted from the air. Despite everything, he wanted to kiss her right now.

The truck lurched. Nadine slammed on the brakes. They skidded, bouncing viciously and Bel thrust out his arm to prevent Maria and Juan from crashing into the dashboard. The truck jerked to a halt. An enormous Monterrey pine burst into flames and thundered to the ground in front of them, igniting the vegetation on the creek bank. There was no way to get by the fallen tree. The fastest route to the hospital was now blocked.

"Fuck!" Nadine shouted and pounded on the steering wheel. She looked at Bel, eyes wide. "Now what?"

Bel held his forehead. His side was throbbing and made it hard to think. "The Chemise Fire Road," he shouted at his daughter. "We passed it a half mile back. It leads to the north ridge of the estate."

"You've got to be kidding, Dad," Nadine looked at her father in disbelief. "I know the fire roads of the estate, too." She was right; she and Ned had raced along all of the fire roads as teens. "That takes us right through the heart of the fire. There's no way!"

"The fire has been burning for hours," Bel said grimly with as much authority as he could muster. "It might be burned out on the ridge." He looked around the truck. The fire was approaching on all sides and in seconds the air in the cab would be scalding. They wouldn't be able to breathe. They'd choke in the putrid heat. "It's our only choice," he yelled.

The downed tree in front of them crackled and exploded, throwing off cinders that spiraled toward the truck. Nadine looked at him, the nervousness obvious in her eyes. She threw the truck into reverse. The tires skidded and tore at the gravel. Bel steadied himself on the dashboard as his daughter raced the truck down the narrow dirt road.

The truck thumped in a rut and Juan gasped in pain on the seat next to him. Maria pressed the bloodied rags into the young man's abdomen and looked up at Bel, her eyes wide with fear. They weren't going to make it. Juan would bleed out. Bel reached for the radio again. Maureen could ready some bandages, anything that could prolong Juan's life. But there was no answer. He banged his fist against the truck door.

Outside, the scalding air screamed by. Every living thing out there was ablaze or melting. The fire roared up the trees, pulverizing them like matchsticks. The grasses and bushes gasped for life as the flames consumed them. The air grew darker, choked by waves of soot and grime that seeped in through the windows.

"Faster," he muttered. "We're running out of time."

"Here it is," Nadine yelled. They reached the entrance to the fire road. The rutted dirt road angled up sharply into a dark and burning forest. His daughter yanked the truck up the road. It hit a deep gully in the old road. Juan screamed in pain and doubled over. He was gasping for air.

Maria looked up at Bel, petrified. There was nothing he could do but squeeze her hand. "Come on, Nadine," he yelled above the roar of the fire. "You know these roads!"

"I do," his daughter said, jaw tight. She kept her eyes forward. "And it's going to get even bumpier." She threw the truck into low gear and it groaned, spinning on the slippery, soot-covered dirt.

Bel put his arm around Maria and pulled her tight, bracing himself against the door as the truck banged on the rutted road. Outside, the forest floor around the truck glowed a deadly orange. The fire raced through the base of the woods around them, climbed the trees and crackled above. Some trees were already charred spindles, cracking and tumbling in the unrelenting, powerful gusts.

The truck lurched as Nadine yanked it around a hairpin turn in the crumbling fire road. Maria thudded against him as the truck skidded. He heard Juan moan, softer now. Bel clenched his jaw. The young man's life was slipping away. He looked outside, agitated. They'd be approaching the ridge soon. He closed his eyes and prayed that the fire break was holding. That the estate house was protected.

The forest outside the truck looked eerily familiar. They'd entered the northeast boundary of the estate. Clouds of ash and soot hung low over the pulsing forest floor and fire smoldered in patches of glowing orange. Here the fire didn't rage. His spirits lifted. Maybe the worst of it was done in this section of the estate. Maybe the fire had torn across the north ridge and then, blocked by the fire break, burned itself out.

The truck rounded another corner as they approached the top of the ridge. Bel held his breath as Nadine accelerated the truck across the top of the rise and toward the road that led down to the estate. She brought the truck to an abrupt halt.

Bel's heart stopped. The hillside below them was a massive ocean of flame. The blaze was enormous—a wall of fire that pounded down the slope, chewing and grinding everything in its path. The groves of eucalyptus and pine that ringed the vineyards were ablaze, the grasses and fences burned with ferociousness, and even the air crackled and exploded as the sooty, scalding gusts whipped across the vineyards, lighting up the vines which smoked and popped.

Eyes wide, Bel opened the truck door and limped woodenly to the edge of the ridge. He stared down at the McMaster Vineyards estate below.

"Dad," Nadine called. He could barely hear her over the rushing wind. "What are you doing?"

Massive cinders rained down and burned his face and arms but he didn't flinch. Just below where he stood were the remnants of the fire break, like an ancient dig in a faraway land abandoned during a disaster. The immigrants must have thrown their shovels aside and raced away as the blaze bore down. The fire break had failed.

As he stared at the churning blaze, he realized the nightmare was about to come true. He doubled over in agony. McMaster Vineyards was going to burn to the ground.

38. MARIA

Maria gasped in disbelief. She clutched the bloody crucifix, now in her pocket, and said a prayer. The fire below them roared. They'd traveled through the eye of hell and for what? To be separated from their escape by a wall of flame. She looked out of the filthy windshield at Bel on the edge of the ridge, doubled over in the blasting wind. She wanted to run to him, but she was chained to Juan. And the blaze was all around them, it wasn't safe out there.

Juan rested his head in her lap. His breathing was labored now, every breath gurgled as he fought for air. The strips of cloth that she'd pressed into his belly were soaked through with blood. She placed her free hand on his forehead. "Stay with me, little brother," she whispered into his ear.

Juan's eyes fluttered and he looked up at her. He coughed and a trickle of blood ran down his cheek. He reached toward her face. "Saint Maria," he smiled. "You have always been the one to save me."

Maria's eyes watered and she gritted her teeth. She would not cry in front of Juan. But it was true. "That's what a big sister does," she said quietly. Her breath shook as she exhaled. She couldn't imagine a world without Juan. A world without her best friend.

The truck door opened and Bel got in followed by a churning blast of soot and ash. He put his head in his hands. "Oh god," he muttered. His eyes were vacant. The truck rocked back and forth in the gusts.

Maria looked from Bel to his daughter. Nadine's face was caked with grime and tear tracks ran down her cheeks. Maria closed her eyes and whispered her prayers. She had come close to death too many times today. The saints had been with her, of that she was certain. Would they stay with her? There was only one way to find out.

"You must drive," she said forcefully.

"No," Nadine protested and pointed to the wall of flames in front of them. "Driving through that is suicide."

"Juan will die if you do not drive," Maria said. "And I will not let that happen. Now drive. Please." She looked at Bel, her jaw set.

Bel looked down at Maria. "I have to get closer to Nadine," he said. He climbed over her and Juan in the cab and slid in next to his daughter. Then, he leaned to Maria and put his hand on the back of her head. His lips met hers and they stayed there for what seemed like hours. "For luck," he murmured.

Maria grabbed his hand. Her heart thudded. She leaned over Juan. "We need to hold on," she whispered into his ear.

Bel turned to his daughter and spoke loudly. "You need to drive through that fire."

Maria thought she heard a tremble in his voice.

"Dad, no!"

"You said you were the better driver!" Bel shouted above the roar of the wind. Maria felt Bel's body move next to hers. She watched as he grabbed the shift away from his daughter and threw the truck into gear. Bel kicked his daughter's foot aside and slammed his foot down on the accelerator. The truck roared to life and lurched forward, screaming down the hillside.

"Dad!" Nadine shrieked and grabbed the steering wheel. Nadine pulled the wheel hard as the truck rocketed into the first turn of the serpentine road. The truck slid madly, the rear end threatening to skid out of control.

Maria bent over Juan, holding him tightly as the truck bounced. She looked up at Nadine. The young woman's eyes were wide and she seemed to barely control the careening truck. Maria cried out as she and Juan banged into the side door. She gasped and pulled Juan closer.

The truck straightened its wheels grinding on the dirt road. Maria could feel the vehicle gain speed. Bel was jamming his foot down even harder on the accelerator. Her heart raced. The truck rocketed forward.

Maria raised her head and peeked out of the soot-stained windshield and sucked in her breath. Even through the grime, she could see flames shooting up around them. The heat was intense. A hairpin curve was approaching. She looked with horror at Nadine. Bel didn't let up on the accelerator. Maria held her breath as Nadine pulled on the steering wheel. The truck listed sideways and skidded into the turn, barely slowing. The rear of the truck swung out, the tires spinning madly on the dirt road and flinging gravel into the air.

Maria crossed herself. The truck shuddered and banged and then straightened.

"Dad, you have to let up!" Nadine shouted, but Bel kept his foot firmly braced. The truck skidded through another turn. Maria smacked against the side of the cab as the truck jolted and slammed its way through the curve. She clutched Juan. His eyes were wide and his mouth moved but no words came out.

"Hurry," Maria screamed, pulling Juan close.

The truck blasted around another curve. Maria gasped. The wall of flame was directly in front of them. Bel pushed his foot down harder. Maria held the bloody crucifix and pleaded with the saints. The truck bolted toward the blazing wall that reached all the way to the heavens. The gusts roared around them. And suddenly, they were inside the blaze. Flames engulfed them. The entire world was on fire and they were at its center. Even the air burned. Brilliant oranges, yellows, and reds blazed on all sides of the road. Maria craned her neck forward and looked up through the crusty windshield. The sky had turned into a pulsing orange. Alive. Beating. She sucked in her breath and spoke to the saints, asking them if this was hell. Or maybe this was heaven but the priests had been wrong. The fire was its own being. Of that, she was sure.

The truck rocked violently as if it were trying to shake the life from them. Maria looked at Nadine who held onto the steering wheel with a death grip. The air in the cab was foul as smoke and putrid fumes oozed in—melting rubber, disintegrating tubes, leaking fluids. Maria choked. Beside her, Bel pointed and yelled, bellowing directions at his daughter as they raced through the roaring inferno. The road turned sharply right. Nadine pulled the steering wheel and the battered truck slid and banged through another turn.

Maria put her hand on Juan's forehead. He was burning up. Fever was setting in, and the truck's cab was blazingly hot. The inside was a spark away from exploding. Maria jumped as dribbles of liquid spattered across the windshield. "What is that?" she yelled at Bel.

Bel grimaced and shook his head. "It's paint," he shouted. "It's melting off the truck." The truck slammed into a rut and Maria jerked backward and banged her head on the rear window of the cab. The truck lurched forward and out of the rut and banged down the dirt road. Juan moaned.

Maria leaned over him. "We're almost there," she whispered.

It was impossible to see out of the front windshield. The smoke was thick and the blaze surrounded the truck. Flaming embers torpedoed through the air, propelled by gusts that shook the truck so hard it seemed the vehicle could be blown from the winding dirt road. Still, they rocketed forward with paint and fluids streaming. Another curve loomed in front of them, a tight curve that dropped steeply. Maria wiped the soot from her eyes and squinted. She looked out the window. Impossibly the sky seemed to be lightning. She grabbed Bel's shoulder. He looked at her and nodded. She let herself think that they might make it.

She watched as Nadine pulled the steering wheel hard and she lurched to the right. In front of them, the smoke lessened. Maria held her breath and squeezed Juan's hand. He barely squeezed back.

The truck rocketed forward and burst out of the blaze. They were clear of the flames, if only for seconds. She felt Bel's arm around her and she cried out with relief.

Bel's daughter accelerated and the charred pickup truck raced toward a large estate house. Maria crossed herself and begged the saints to give them time to get to the hospital.

The truck jerked to a stop in front of the house. Maria looked out and her heart stopped. The fire had already jumped from the vineyards. Flames licked at the rear of the house and raced toward its roof. It would only be minutes before the house was ablaze. She exhaled and closed her eyes and whispered, "Oh Señor, please save us from this valley of death."

She spun to Bel. "Do you have anything to cut this?" She held up her hand-cuffed wrist.

Bel looked at her and then glanced over her shoulder at the large house. She realized he might still have family there. But he nodded.

"Nadine," he shouted. "Go find your mother. I have to get the bolt cutter." He turned to her. Maria felt her heart thud as he caressed her cheek. And then, he was gone. Disappeared into the murky, scalding haze.

His daughter Nadine slid from the truck and darted toward the house. Maria was left in the cab with Juan. She could feel bloody dampness on her leg oozing from his wound. She wiped his brow.

"Juan," she said. "We're almost there."

He didn't respond.

She put her finger on his neck and waited. Her eyes watered when she felt nothing. But then, there it was. The faintest of heartbeats.

The door jerked open and the roar of the blaze filled the cab. "Hold up your hand," Bel commanded. He struggled with the tool and grunted until Maria heard a loud clunk. The chain broke. The cuff was still around her wrist but she could move. She jumped from the cab and nearly fell over in the blasts of scalding wind.

"You need to go now, get him to the hospital," Bel yelled over the deafening gusts. "I have to stay here with my family."

Maria nodded. She was almost out of time. Juan's breathing foretold a death knell. She pulled Bel toward her and put her head against his chest. The wind around them rose to an unquenchable fury, screaming in anger and driving scalding embers around them in a maddening cyclone. Bel rested his chin on her head and for one brief moment Maria listened to the thumping of his heart pounding with fear, life, and love. She pressed her ear harder against his chest and at that moment, she was one with Bel, they were two halves of the same being. She pulled him tighter, desperately.

Then she pushed him away, climbed behind the wheel of the truck.

"Take Westside Road to Santa Rosa General Hospital," Bel shouted into the cab. "You'll be safe from the fire."

Maria nodded and threw the truck into gear. It shuddered and moved forward, buffeted by the scalding gusts. She inched toward the main gates of McMaster Vineyards, struggling to see through the sooty wind. Oleander and pines that once lined the graceful driveway now burned viciously. She looked down at Juan. His eyes were open and unmoving. Maria exhaled and crossed herself. His life was in the saints' hands now. They would decide his fate.

She looked in the rearview mirror. Bel stood there, growing smaller and smaller until he was finally eclipsed by the billowing smoke. She wiped tears from her grime-streaked face and accelerated. The battered pickup lurched through the gates of McMaster Vineyards, rumbling out of the fiery hellscape and toward Westside Road. Maria stopped looking in the rearview mirror and focused on the road ahead.

39. BEL

Bel stood in the blasting gusts, squinting to see the pickup truck through the choking clouds of soot. The truck's brake lights flashed at the end of the driveway. His heart leapt at the thought that Maria might turn around but the truck lurched through the main gates and disappeared into the swirling haze. He exhaled, wiped his grimy face and turned to the Queen Anne. He gasped. Flaming cinders, pushed through the air by the pounding wind, rained down on the roof of the old house and exploded like bombs. The fire was already chewing through the roof. Chills ran down his spine, he could swear he heard the old house crying out as the fire ate mercilessly through its wooden bones.

He raced toward the house, holding his throbbing side and shielding his face against the scalding gusts. From the corner of his eye, something glinted and he stopped. An SUV, parked nearly out of sight by the garage. He frowned. It didn't belong to McMaster Vineyards. He moved closer and sucked in a breath, nearly choking on the soot. The logo on the side was unmistakable. It was Kavali.

He spun and stared at the house. Maureen hadn't answered the radio. Nadine hadn't returned. His heart dropped. It couldn't be. He ran, ignoring the pain in his side. He took the porch stairs two at a time and skidded through the door into the main foyer. The air inside the house was hazy—foul-smelling but not yet scorching like the gusts outside. The massive chandelier hanging three stories above him groaned, its thousands of crystals clattering madly as the house shook, battered by the ever-increasing intensity of the blaze.

"Maureen? Nadine?" Their names echoed in the vast foyer and were swallowed by the roar of the blaze. There was a crackle in front of him and he gasped. Flames spurted from the wainscoted hallway. The fire ws already in the house and had sped through the kitchen. The flames cast an ominous orange glow and smoke poured out, thickening with air with putrid fumes.

"Maureen, Nadine, where are you?" He called again and stood still, listening intently.

"Dad." Nadine's voice was thin. He could hear the fear. "We're up here."

Her voice came from the landing above the foyer, up the curved staircase. He bolted for the stairs. The smoke from the fire in the kitchen was already drifting to the second floor. He nearly choked as he reached the landing. His jaw dropped and he skidded to a stop. Maureen and Nadine stood by the long ornate banister at the edge of the landing overlooking the foyer below. They didn't move. There was a gun pointed directly at his wife's head.

"Oh god, no," Bel whispered to himself. Mohan Mallick stood rigidly by his wife and daughter. Even through the soot that thickened the air, he could see the fury on Mohan's face.

"Mr. McMaster," Mohan shouted above the deafening roar of the fire. "You have lied to me for the last time."

Bel stepped slowly toward his family.

"Stay where you are!" Mohan screamed. "You fucking moron, did you think I would be fooled by this?" Bel only then saw in Mohan's other hand an orange card a little bigger than a payment card, pitted on one side. He gulped.

"It's a fake!" Mohan yelled. He threw the card at Bel. It bounced on the floor and came to rest near Bel's feet where it cracked in half. It was the plastic version that Nadine and Nigel had fabricated in Nadine's studio.

"I...I," Bel stammered and his mind raced. How had Mohan gotten the fake? Why didn't the tech titan have the real one, the one he'd surely retrieved from Maria? Bel's mind raced. He had misplaced the fake in the shed but then found it days later and...suddenly it clicked. Bel sucked in his breath. She'd switched the cards. Maria had given him the real card without his knowledge and taken the fake one. That was the only possibility. Why, he didn't know, but she had. That's why the card felt so different in his hands and vibrated in the sun when he held it in the cab of his truck. And that meant the real card was...in his pocket.

He reached into his pocket and paused. If he gave it to Mohan now, there was no guarantee that any of them would leave this house alive.

"Stop stalling!" Mohan screamed. "Tell me where it is or I start killing your family!" The tech titan's face turned red. He pulled back his fist and let it explode in Maureen's face. She shrieked and tottered backward against the banister. Blood spurted from her nose and Mohan grabbed her by the hair and yanked her up.

"No," Bel screamed. "Please, no."

Bel watched in horror as Mohan shoved the barrel of the small gun back against his wife's head. Above, an earsplitting crack boomed above the roar of the blaze. Bel looked up and his eyes widened. The ceiling was burning. The blaze had spread through the house like cancer. It would only be minutes before the flames chewed through the rafters. Then, the massive chandelier would come crashing down. The foyer would collapse.

"I have it," Bel shouted.

"No!" Nadine screamed out. "No," she repeated forcefully. "I have it. I have the real card." She shook her head wildly at Bel. He looked at her with eyes wide. What was she doing?

Brittle explosions boomed ominously from the bedrooms. Windows shattering in the heat. New gusts of soot blasted across the landing. Bel choked and covered his mouth. Above him the burning ceiling screeched. Cinders rocketed down and flamed out on the granite floor.

Through the soot and haze, Bel could see Mohan's eyes blaze with fury as the man looked from Bel to his daughter. "What kind of fucking game are you two playing?" He pushed the gun harder against Maureen's head. "Give me that media card right fucking now or I blow her brains across the floor!" The veins in Mohan's neck popped with anger.

A wave of soot blazed across the landing with sounds of more mini explosions as windows shattered in the heat and pounding wind. Bel fought for breath as a gust roared through the smoke-filled landing, churning up cyclones of soot and ash spun that crazily through the air. Something landed on his head and he yelped. A chunk of flaming ember rocketed down. He looked up and gulped. The ceiling sixty feet above throbbed with orange flames. It was ready to collapse. And below, the fire had burst from the main hallway and climbed the walls of the foyer.

"I said now!" Mohan shouted. The tech titan pushed his wife and daughter against the landing's banister. Bel gasped. The banister bowed out over the foyer below, dangerously weakened by the raging fire. In just seconds, it would disintegrate.

Another squeal ricocheted through the foyer, drowning out the howl of the wind. The massive chandelier high above jerked downward several feet before jolting to a stop. Bel sucked in his breath. It was about to come crashing down. Mohan, Nadine, and Maureen stood right below it.

Bel gritted his teeth and felt the card in his pocket. He had no choice. He would have to give it up. But before he could pull it out, Nadine jumped forward.

"OK, you want it?" his daughter screamed at Mohan. "Go get it." She whipped something from her pocket. Bel squinted. He could barely see through the sooty haze. She held something orange and rectangular in her hand. She moved so quickly her barely had time to see. She tossed the object toward the banister. Bel sucked in his breath. The object spun through the murky air, spinning rapidly and reflecting the brutal orange of the churning blaze. He watched as it sailed over the banister and toward the yawning openness of the burning foyer.

Mohan's eyes were wide. "NO!" he screamed. He released Maureen, his hands grasping for the flying object.

Above, an earsplitting shriek. Bel looked up. The fire had chewed through the chandelier's mooring. The massive fixture broke free and plummeted down, rocketing directly toward Mohan and his family. Crystals hurtled from the chandelier and shattered on the landing and the granite floor. There was no time to think. Bel sprang forward. His body slammed into Mohan and they crashed into the sagging banister. It splintered and they burst through it. Bel barely had time to gasp. They were spiraling out over the smokey abyss. The foyer's granite floor twenty feet below.

The plummeting chandelier jerked to a stop, its chain caught on a rafter. It swung crazily, just off the edge of the landing.

Bel and Mohan slammed on top of the wildly swinging chandelier. It broke their free fall. Bel on top of Mohan. Barely balanced on a crossbar of the massive fixture.

Bel scrambled to get his balance. His side screamed in pain. Mohan still held the gun. Bel reached for it and banged Mohan's wrist against the crossbar of the jerking chandelier. Mohan yelled and clawed at him. Bel brought Mohan's wrist to his mouth and bit. Mohan screamed. The gun fell from his grip. It spiraled away and clattered to the floor far below.

The chandelier shuddered and fell a few feet before jolting to a stop. Heart thudding, Bel teetered and reached out but there was nothing to grab. He tumbled onto a lower crossbar of the chandelier, smacking his side. He cried out. Mohan leapt on top of him, eyes like slits of rage. The man's hands were around his neck. Bel clawed at Mohan. He couldn't breathe.

"Where the fuck is my card?" Mohan screamed, his hot spittle flying on Bel's face.

Bel frantically tried to suck in a breath. He was pinned. His back on the chandelier crossbar. Mohan's hands wound around his throat. He desperately pried at Mohan's fingers. "Get off me, you son of a bitch," Bel gurgled. The chandelier careened wildly, its chain screeching as it slipped from the rafter. In seconds, it would plummet to the granite floor.

Bel's mind spun. The card. In his pocket. If he could just reach it and distract Mohan. He desperately reached and there it was, the pitted metal card. Cool to the touch.

The chandelier screeched and jolted down a few inches. He had only seconds. He yanked the card from his pocket, gasping for air.

Bel's eyes widened as Mohan drew his fist back and slammed it into Bel's nose. Bel's hand fell to his side, still clutching the metal card. His mind was going dark. He could barely see, blinded by the sooty air and Mohan's pummeling.

Something vibrated in his palm. The card. Behind Mohan, through his swollen eyes, he saw an orange beam shoot up through the sooty darkness from the card. And then another and another. The orange beams of light intersected to form a helix that pierced the dark clouds of ash. The helix grew and began to spin, illuminating the room with an orange glow even more intense than the fiery blaze. The spinning helix sucked in the air around it, cyclone-like, and roared like a thousand freight trains.

Mohan looked up frantically at the helix, his eyes wide. "What have you done?" he screamed. The tech titan scrambled from Bel and tried to stand on the spinning chandelier. "It's activated by natural light, you stupid fuck!" He swatted at Bel, reaching for the card and the ever-growing helix. "Keep it away from me!"

The chandelier jerked and Mohan tripped, falling backward. Bel looked up.

The ceiling pulsed in orange and red, huge chunks of flaming plaster rocketing down. It would collapse in seconds.

Below the ceiling, the spinning helix spun faster, seeming to suck energy from the fire. The card in Bel's palm vibrated mightily and heated his hand, but he held it steady. The helix was now screaming, a wild, piercing, human scream. It had become a tornado, sucking in ash, pieces of plaster, crystals from the chandelier.

Mohan seemed frantic. He pushed himself away from Bel, clumsily on the chandelier, desperately ducking as the helix grew in size. "You don't know what it does, you goddamn moron!" the tech titan screamed.

"Daddy," he heard his daughter yell just above him. He looked up. Through the haze, he saw Maureen and Nadine, perched on the edge of the landing, their arms urgently stretching toward him. "Jump here, we'll grab you!" His daughter's face was pinched with fear.

The chandelier jerked again and Bel stumbled. As he flailed, the spinning helix sliced through the haze and caught Mohan in its interwoven beams. Mohan jerked, his eyes filled with terror. "Get it away from me!" he cried out and tried desperately to back up on the cross beam. But he'd come to the end of the chandelier. Behind the tech titan was a yawning, soot-filled abyss.

As the spinning helix engulfed him, Mohan's skin began to bubble and change color, turning a putrid shade of gray that Bel could barely see through the swirling ash. Mohan's screams rose above the roaring of the fire and the brutal hum of the spinning helix that now consumed the billionaire.

"No!" Mohan screamed, his face filled with terror.

Bel tried to move the helix, but it seemed to have a mind of its own. It had a lock on Mohan. Nothing Bel could do would shift the helix from grinding at Mohan.

Mohan shrieked. It was the cry of the dying. Except he wasn't dying. Bel watched in fascinated horror as Mohan transformed. The tech titan's face drooped, sagging unnaturally. Mohan pawed frantically at his cheeks. His eyes widened in terror. The tech titan's skin turned a sickly green. Strands of green goo slide from his face. His body was altering, turning into something completely different. His arms thickened and from the tips of his fingers tiny buds appeared.

"Stop," Mohan screamed again but his voice was weaker. Gurgling.

"Daddy, you have to come here, now!" Nadine shouted at him. But Bel couldn't pull his eyes away from Mohan. He sucked in his breath and choked on the bitter ash. It was impossible. He could barely wrap his head around it, but Mohan was turning in a plant. The man's body stiffened, his legs forming a rigid stalk, his arms morphing into branches.

As Bel watched, barely balanced on the rocking chandelier as flaming embers rained down, the awful realization hit. His stomach clenched. Mohan hadn't just created a new genome. He had created a way to turn people into plants. A further realization struck him and he wanted to vomit. The busloads of immigrants who filed into Kavali Tower but never came out. They were being turned into plants—grown for food on the enormous panels hanging in Kavali Tower.

"Daddy," he heard Nadine yell through the roaring blaze. "NOW!"

Bel tore his eyes from Mohan. The chandelier jerked again and the orange card flew from his hand, bouncing on the chandelier's cross beams. It came to rest on a strand of crystals several feet below, the massive churning helix still rotating around the tech titan.

The ceiling above groaned. Bel had to go. Now. He stumbled unsteadily on the chandelier crossbar toward Nadine and Maureen's outstretched arms. The ceiling above screamed. He had no time. The chandelier plunged. He jumped from the chandelier crossbar and threw up his arms. His fingers brushed Maureen. He missed. He was going to plummet to the granite floor below.

A hand wrapped around his wrist. Nadine. He looked up. Her face was tight.

"Hang on," she screamed.

The chandelier plunged to the granite floor taking what was left of Mohan with it. The fixture exploded in a cacophony of splintering crystals and shattering glass. Soot and ash clouds billowed and burning pieces of the ceiling rained down.

Bel swung, suspended by his daughter. Nadine grunted and Maureen reached down, grabbed his collar and gritted her teeth. His heart thudded. His wife and daughter strained, dragging him over the lip of the landing. He rolled and the three of them lay there, gasping for breath. But there was no time. Bel looked up, eyes wide. The ceiling was coming down.

He stood, ignoring the shooting pain in his side. He reached for Maureen and Nadine and together they bolted down the burning staircase and clamored to the foyer. Bel choked and held up his arm, futilely trying to shield his face from the heat and soot. Ash rained down and fiery chunks of plaster spiraled from the buckling ceiling, whistling past them like missiles that exploded on the granite floor. The blaze screamed, the ceiling roared and buckled. The house was about to collapse.

"Run, now!" Bel screamed. The ceiling pounded down, massive burning beams and flaming plaster tumbling around them. Bel clamored over the wrecked chandelier. There was no sign of Mohan. The churning helix had disappeared. Maureen stumbled over a crossbar and fell to the floor.

"Get up," he yelled and yanked his wife to her feet. Nadine was at the front door. She kicked it open, eyes wide. Bel dragged his wife. They burst onto the porch as the ceiling collapsed and the foyer exploded. Flames shot from the front of the house and clouds of ash billowed after them.

They fell down the porch stairs and tumbled onto the fiery lawn. Bel turned to look at the blazing house. The roof roared as section after section disintegrated and collapsed downward. The walls vaporized and crumbled away, leaving a flaming skeleton exposed. The Queen Anne screamed out, announcing to the world that she was dying. The house collapsed in a final explosion of fire and soot, shooting bitter orange flames a hundred feet into the early morning sky. The only home Bel had ever known was gone.

* * *

Bel stood up shakily. Nadine and Maureen rose, eyes wide. Everything around them was burning, even the lawn. Bel choked. He could barely breathe. Nadine doubled over, frantically trying to draw in air. They had to get inside somewhere, away from the blaze. He squinted and tried to see through the thick soot.

"Dad, look," Nadine coughed and pointed toward the garage. Flames chewed at the building. Every vehicle inside was burning. "We have no way out," she shouted.

Nadine was right. Even Mohan's SUV was a charred hulk. To his left was a deafening crack. The old redwood that stood for centuries cried out as its trunk gave way. Bel watched with wide eyes as the massive tree, now a pillar of flame, tottered. In a whoosh of ancient whispers, the tree thundered to the ground and blocked the entire driveway. Bel stood in stunned silence, the reverberation of the felled tree still shaking the ground. The fire ringed them on all sides. The slopes to the north burned ferociously and the Diablo wind had pushed the blaze to the east and west. The wind had even whipped the fire to the south. Now, the driveway was cut off. There was no way to leave the estate. They were trapped. And the air was nearly unbreathable. He couldn't stand to watch his wife and daughter struggle for every breath.

But there was a place. Bel snapped his head up. A building built into the south slope and tucked away behind the tasting room. The gusting blaze might not have reached it. Bel spun. "The winery!" he shouted over the roar of the fire. "We have to get to the winery."

"But, how do you know..." Maureen protested.

"NOW!" Bel screamed. Maureen looked at her husband, bleary and beaten.

She grabbed Nadine's hand and together they thumped across the lawn. They rounded the corner of the fiery tasting room and there it was, the only building of McMaster Vineyards not yet destroyed. The winery stood, ringed by fire but protected by the small slope. Even so, the brutal winds pushed the fire which raced toward the building. They had little time.

"Hurry," Bel coughed, and they scraped forward. Bel strained to slide the door to the winery open and they stumbled in. He breathed in deeply. The air inside was still cool but smoke hung thick. The fire would follow.

"This will burn just like all of the other buildings," Maureen protested. "There's still no way to turn on the fire suppression."

Bel shook his head. There was a way, maybe. He looked nervously at the ceiling and the pipes that the plumber had worked on. He'd connected the fire suppression system to the fermenting tanks. The plumber had said it was idiotic. But maybe, just maybe, he could reverse the flow of the wine from the tanks if the pressure of the fermenting wine pushed the liquid up into the pipes. It was the only hope they had.

The fire was already racing across the roof of the winery. He had little time. He ran to the nearest fermentation tank and hoisted himself to the top, wincing at the pain in his side. He scrambled to the valve at the top and pulled hard to the left. The valve squeaked open. He held his breath. At first, nothing. But then, liquid started moving up and into the pipes. The fermenting contents rumbled upwards into the pipes above. Bel exhaled. It might work.

"Bel," Maureen cried, "There's nothing you can do!"

"It could work," Bel shouted. He slid down from the tank and crashed to the floor. He screamed out as pain throbbed through his side. He sucked in a breath and stood shakily and then limped to the next tank. He pulled himself up the ladder on the side of the tank and then opened the valve, listening for the fermenting wine as it shot up into the pipes.

He looked across the winery. There were more tanks to go. He clutched his side. The throbbing threatened to double him over. He felt something burning on his shoulder. He flicked it away but it was replaced by a hot sensation. He looked up and gasped. Enormous cinders floated down from the burning ceiling and started tiny fires where they landed. The ceiling had caught fire fast. It was already starting to sag. It would collapse in moments.

Bel looked down from the top of the tank at Maureen crouched by their daughter. The air in the winey was thickening. Bel struggled to see. Maureen positioned herself above Nadine to shield their daughter from the spiraling cinders which flew down furiously. Bel's heart twinged. He looked up and gulped. The ceiling was fully ablaze. The orange flames licked at it greedily, chewing through the rafters. He had to keep going. He tried to ignore the pain in his side and clamored down from the tank and limped to the next. His head screamed *faster* but he could barely move. The pain in his side was nearly crippling. Still, he pulled himself up to the top of another tank and desperately turned the valve. The pipes above were filling with fermented wine.

He looked up. The ceiling was going to collapse. There was barely time to open the remaining tanks, and still there was one more set of levers close to the ceiling that controlled the sprinklers. He climbed down to the winery floor, wincing furiously. He limped across the winery floor to a ladder that led to a catwalk high above, screaming in pain as he held his side. He put his hands on the ladder and looked up. The ladder ascended into clouds of soot and ash. He exhaled jaggedly and grabbed a rung of the ladder. He pulled himself up, his face scrunched in agony. Rung after painful rung, he pulled himself up the ladder. The soot was thicker up here and he gasped for breath. At the end of the catwalk were pipes that ran from the vats to the sprinklers. He needed to throw open the levers to activate them.

Bel limped down the length of the catwalk. He choked. The air was scalding. He couldn't breathe. He struggled and fell to his knees, frantically trying to draw in a breath. Desperately he crawled forward, trying to suck in air. He panicked.

The levers were right there, at the end of the catwalk. He was so close. But the smoke. He was suffocating. He collapsed.

As he lay there, he heard the ceiling above him screech. It would only be seconds now before the winery collapsed on him, his wife and daughter. The fire would win. He'd managed to stay a step ahead of the blaze all night, but his luck had run out. His thoughts drifted and he heard a voice, an unmistakable voice he hadn't heard in ages.

"Bel, you have to get up."

"I can't," Bel mumbled. His brain was addled. He couldn't move. He just wanted to go to sleep. Somehow, death by suffocation up here on the catwalk, suspended above his family didn't seem so bad. It was warm and comfortable. He would close his eyes and go to sleep. Sleep would feel so good and he could stop fighting, stop feeling inadequate. It would all be over. He hoped his family's deaths would be equally painless.

"Bel," the voice said, "you don't have a choice. You have to save them. Your wife and children need you."

Bel opened his eyes. In the haze of flames and ash, he thought he saw a figure. "I made such a mess," Bel mumbled.

"No," the voice said. "You made hard choices. Now get up. Your family needs you."

Bel was delirious from the lack of oxygen. He grabbed the rail of the catwalk and strained. There was no one there. He stumbled toward the levers, clinging to the railing and sucking in scalding breaths. He reached the wall and panted in the thick and noxious air. Flames licked through the ceiling. The walls around him pulsed in reds and oranges. His eyes drooped but he forced them open, reached out and grabbed a lever and yanked it with all of his might. The pipe bubbled and shook, and then rattled as the fermenting wine raced through the sprinklers. He reached out and yanked open a second lever and a third. The liquid shot through the pipes to the sprinklers which gurgled to life, spraying wine into the sooty air and drenching the building and its roof.

The walls hissed and the ceiling steamed. As rapidly as they'd spread across the roof and walls, the flames retreated, pushed back by the wine which gushed from the sprinklers.

Bel fell to his knees on the catwalk and gasped as the air cleared. He tilted his face heavenward, closed his eyes, and let the wine bathe him from above.

Part IV

40. MARIA

Maria pulled open the glass door and leaned forward, into the dairy cooler, sighing as the chilled air brushed her swollen legs and skimmed the top of her feet, exposed in her worn sandals. They were the only shoes she could squeeze into these days. She breathed in deeply, pulling in the cool air, holding it, as if to take it with her back out into the sweaty night. The biting lights of the convenience mart flickered and buzzed, casting a purple glow that, strangely, only seemed to make Maria appear more serene. She reached forward and took a bottle of milk, hoping it would soothe her indigestion. It will make your baby taller, her grandmother used to say, drink milk when you're with child. Maria smiled, rubbed her swollen belly. "You're going to be tall," she whispered. "Just like your father."

She turned and lumbered to the front of the store, ignoring the periodic spasms of lightning that rocketed through her body. The clerk glanced up, smiled, and pushed aside her e-tablet. "When are you due?" she asked, kindly. Maria smiled. It seemed to be the only question she'd been asked for months.

"Past due," Maria sighed. "Two weeks."

The clerk nodded, scanned the bottle of milk and reached for a small bag. "My roommate is studying to be a midwife," she said. "If it's your first baby, I think that's normal to be late."

"My second," Maria smiled and reached for the bag. It was funny how people behaved as her stomach swelled. The questions, the glances, the suggestions, as if her body was no longer hers. Was she something more than she'd been before? Maybe she was a link, a physical connection between the past and the future and that gave people hope. But there were also sneers about her baby's nationality. She brushed those aside and turned away.

"Your husband, does he like to fix things?" the clerk asked, pointing to Juan, squatting on the ground next to their tattered pickup truck, filling a worn tire with air. Alarico sat by his side, playing with a wrench.

Maria glanced at the parking lot, nearly empty at this hour, where Bel's old pickup truck, now spray-painted a dark, unremarkable slate gray, was parked. Better to avoid attention, Juan had said when they'd slipped out of the Bay Area. Maria smiled softly. Juan's recovery had been a miracle. When they'd arrived in Santa Rosa during the madness of the wildfire, a doctor was frantically triaging the injured in the emergency room just as the hospital was being evacuated. "Sorry, he won't make it," the doctor had said gruffly after taking Juan's pulse. But Juan had been loaded into an ambulance anyway and raced to San Francisco General. Maria and Juan were nervous about being discovered, so as soon as Juan could stand, they'd left the hospital and followed the field work, drifting south in the winter to pick greens and lettuces near Salinas, then east, into the Central Valley, for the pepper and tomato season, and then turned further south in the spring to catch the early harvest of asparagus. They'd picked strawberries, too, which were the most back breaking. Bending, snipping, picking ever faster under the eyes of the field foremen while Alarico played at the side of the fields with the other children. Maria enjoyed the work, the predictability of the days and the expanse of the brilliant blue sky above.

Juan went with her to the free family clinics in the small dusty farm towns, practiced breathing with her, and listened to the earnest young doctors. They never went to the same clinic twice.

"He does like to fix things," replied Maria with a smile, rubbing her distended belly. "He's good at it." She collected her milk and moved slowly through the door, pausing to gaze at the sun dipping below the horizon, dragging with it the last strands of light. In the distance, the lights of San Diego flickered, humming with the laid-back vibe of the beach city.

Maria inhaled sharply. A sharp pain cut deep and was as brutal as it was sudden. She yelled out, grabbed her stomach and doubled over. "Juan!" she screamed.

She fell to her knees, the milk crashed to the asphalt and the bottle's lid flew. Milk lapped at the hem of Maria's dress. Juan threw down the wrench and sprinted to her side. She huffed, her chest rising and falling, breathing into the searing pain. "It's now," she said.

"We'll go to the open clinic, like we planned," Juan replied, lifting Maria to her feet.

Another wave of pain, this one even more ferocious, wrapped her body, impossibly tight, smothering her and daring her to breathe. Maria looked down. A river, warm and fast, gushed down her legs, pooling around her feet and mixing with the milk.

"No," she grunted, shuddering in pain. "It's happening now." She'd been through this before. She knew, and she cried out again, arched her head back and screamed at the sky.

The clerk dashed to the open door. "I called my roommate," she breathed, nervously, excitedly. "She's right down the street at the fabric store. She'll be here in just a sec."

Juan nodded, barely hearing. "We need something," he said. "Something soft to lay her on." Bright colors fluttered by the entrance to the parking lot and he put Maria's arm behind his neck and lifted her gently. "Over there," he shouted and pointed just below the store's road-side sign, blinking atop a tall metal column. At its base, two women, weathered and wrinkled, were busily taking apart their roadside stands—small booths where they bargained and sold turquoise jewelry, braided leather bracelets, and small wallets from their nearby reservation. "Blankets," said Juan. "They will have blankets."

Juan shouted out to the women, and supporting Maria, loped toward them, stopping with her every contraction, every spasm of searing pain. The women looked up, wide-eyed and one dashed toward Juan and Maria while the other reached down toward a cardboard box and yanked out a brilliantly colored blanket which she smoothed to the ground.

"Here," Juan said as he gently lowered Maria. She reclined, propped up on her elbows, her face twisted by the throbs. "Remember what we learned, breathe together," Juan commanded softly.

Maria laid back into the lap of one of the women whose brightly beaded braids swung just above Maria's forehead. Maria screamed again, cursing. The other woman positioned herself at Maria's legs and pulled back Maria's skirt, rinsing her hands with a small bottle of antibiotic gel. She nodded to Juan and smiled, her worn, brown face crinkled.

Suddenly, there was another woman, through the daze of her pain, Maria barely noticed. She was young, like the store clerk, with a scarf around her head. "I'm Dariya," she said and knelt in between Maria's ankles next to the braided woman. "I'm a midwife," she announced. "Well, almost." She smiled, looked carefully at Maria and glanced up at Juan. "The baby is moving quickly," Dariya said. "This could be fast, it's already crowning."

Maria was numb from the incessant waves of pain. She squeezed Juan's hand, gripped him tightly. The woman above bathed her forehead, murmured in a language that Maria couldn't understand, or maybe she could but any meaning was rendered incomprehensible by the contractions, the pulsing waves of pain.

A voice, perhaps Dariya or maybe Juan, commanded her. "Push, Maria, you have to push."

Juan gazed down from above, his face now in sharp focus then blurred, suspended above her. "It's time," he said and squeezed her hand.

Maria threw her head back and screamed like she'd never screamed before. White lights of pain danced above her and obliterated her vision. The baby came forward and entered its new life. Maria clenched, gripped Juan and seized the arm of the woman next to her. At that moment she knew, she understood. She was not alone. She was not only Maria. She was mother. She was one. One with Juan, one with Dariya and the store clerk, one with the old women whose names she didn't know. She was one with Carlos. She was one with Bel. She was past. She was future.

The sky exploded above her, the heavens opened and were ablaze. Radiant reds, exploding oranges. For a moment Maria thought she was hallucinating, that the pain was causing her to see illusions or relive the past.

"It's fireworks," said one of the old women, tilting her head back to the sky's cacophony of light and explosion. "Fireworks."

41. BEL

Bel took off his helmet and hung it from the handlebar of the motorcycle. He ran his fingers through his sandy red hair. He couldn't remember the last time his hair had been this long. Years perhaps. He hadn't had a haircut since he'd left McMaster Vineyards. The wind whipped and threw dust in his face. Santa Ana wind, they called it here in Southern California. And just like the Diablo wind in the north, the Santa Anas were blamed for crazy behaviors. An old man at a convenience store weeks ago told Bel that the Santa Anas charged the ions in the air, made people do stupid things. Bel had just smiled and started his motorcycle. People don't need the wind to do stupid things, he'd said to the old man.

The wind gusted again and he shuddered. The gusts made him nervous, even months later. Sometimes he could feel the scorching heat on his face and hear the howl of the blaze as McMaster Vineyards collapsed.

Despite the destruction of the estate, only one person had died on the property during the fire. Michael Mohan Mallick—who turned out to be born to a donut shop owner in New Jersey and eventually became the world's richest man. Mohan Mallick's death was discussed nonstop by the media and in conspiracy forums. For months after the fire, podcasters and conspiracy wing nuts scoured the ashen grounds of McMaster Vineyards, searching for clues to Mohan's death. Bel and Maureen finally hired private security to clear the property of the nut jobs.

Bel stood on the edge of a field. He wasn't even sure what was planted in this one. The fields had started to look the same weeks ago. As he'd traveled further from McMaster Vineyards, he'd initially been fascinated by the differences in the fields—some with bushy rows of asparagus, others with tidy lines of lettuces. But eventually, they were the same, and always at the side of the field a long row of beat-up cars belonging to the day workers. Nearby would be a portable toilet and a folding table with water jugs. Bel felt like he'd seen almost every field in central and southern California. And, he'd met countless men and women named Juan and Maria.

Bel shaded his eyes and walked over to the foreman and did what he'd done a hundred times before, he flashed Maria's picture on his phone. He steeled himself for the inevitable head shake and shrug of shoulders. But the foreman squinted at the picture and leaned forward for a closer look.

"Maria, did you say?" The foreman looked up at Bel. "She's a looker, that one. And a hard worker. Just had a baby and got herself back out in the field." Bel looked up sharply from his phone, not sure he'd heard correctly. The foreman picked at his teeth with a long toothpick and looked toward the field. "I think she's over there," he said, waving carelessly in the general direction of a group of pickers, their shapes indistinct in the blur of the late afternoon sun.

Bel starred in the direction that the foreman had pointed. After so many dead ends, he didn't know how to respond. And she'd just had a baby? He stood completely still, the Santa Ana wind whirling around him as the realization hit. It had been just over nine months since he'd seen Maria. Bel's spine tingled. He pushed past the foreman and jogged in the direction of the field workers and broke into a run. He began shouting as he drew closer, calling out her name at the top of his lungs. She was here, in this very field. Maria Garcia, the woman he'd been searching for. And now, improbably, maybe he was a father, again.

The pickers looked up as he approached, a crazed, middle-aged man with unkempt, stringy red hair and emerald eyes flashing in the late afternoon sun. They pointed at him with amusement but he didn't care. As he drew closer, one man looked up, astonished. The man had jet black hair and a square jaw. His mouth gaped open as he straightened up. It was Juan.

"Maria," Bel shouted at Juan. He darted to the young man. "Maria," he shouted again and grabbed Juan by the shoulders and shook him. "Where is she? Where is Maria?"

Juan stared at him, not seeming to comprehend that Bel McMaster was standing in front of him in a desolate field hundreds of miles from Sonoma County. Bel could barely contain himself, his heart thumped in his chest and his breathing was shallow. Where was she? She must be here in this field if Juan was here. Bel glanced around frantically at the shapeless field workers. They all seemed alike in their loose-fitting clothing and baseball caps.

"Bel?" A voice behind him spoke. It was a woman's voice.

Bel spun. A gust of wind blew and kicked up a dust cloud which rose from the ground and surrounded the woman. She took a step forward and emerged from the swirling dirt. She wore the baggy clothing of a field worker. Her face was heart shaped and her auburn hair was pulled back in a braid beneath a large hat which shaded her features, but even so, there was no mistaking the color of her eyes—amber and flecked with gold. It was Maria.

Bel's heart skipped as she approached. He was speechless as the wind whipped and dust rocketed through the air. She stopped in front of him and grabbed his hands and they stood there, still and unspeaking. At that moment, Bel knew in his heart that the future would not be easy. But maybe, just maybe, it would be filled with love.

ABOUT THE AUTHOR

Hunter Spicer has written about technology and business for over twenty years. BLOOD OF THE VINE is his first novel. He lives in San Francisco with his husband and two dogs.

ACKNOWLEDGEMENTS

I'd like to thank Eric Mann for reading, rereading and for constant support. I'd like to thank Holly Payne for doing all of the things a great editor does. I'd like to extend my appreciation to Adrian Ting, Amy Spicer, Bruce Rogers, Dave Jacobson, Jan Rogers, Lenny Brown, Lois Jacobson, Lucky Garcia, Matt Sanchez, and Tim Lynn for their support and encouragement.

www.ingramcontent.com/pod-product-compliance
Lightning Source LLC
Chambersburg PA
CBHW032150190626
46814CB00005BA/1928